LET THE CIRCLE BE UNBROKEN

"Miss Taylor conveys the textures of life among black as well as white and writes not with rancor or bitterness over indignities but with pride, strength, and respect for humanity."

—The New York Times

"A vivid, complex, carefully crafted, moving novel."

—Children's Book Review Service

"This is fine writing, and readers will be moved by the intense drama of individual scenes and by their historical significance."

—School Library Journal

"The fear, cruelty, and the bewildering injustice of a hopelessly racist society are transcended by a family's strength, self-respect, and determination. The characters, both young and old, in all their variety and individuality come alive with penetrating humanness, while the effect of the storytelling is intensified by a lean, understated style and made more poignant by touches of lyrical sensitivity."

—The Horn Book

Mildred D. Taylor

Let the Circle Be Unbroken

Sequel to
Roll of Thunder, Hear My Cry

PUFFIN BOOKS

From the author—
I gratefully thank Mr. James E. Taylor, Mr. Eugene Taylor,
Mr. Norman Early, Mr. David E. Conrad, Mr. Peter Ramig,
Mrs. Lorraine Ramig, and the many others
who advised me on this book.

PUFFIN BOOKS
Published by the Penguin Group
Viking Penguin, a division of Penguin Books USA Inc.,
375 Hudson Street, New York, New York 10014, U.S.A.
Penguin Books Ltd, 27 Wrights Lane, London W8 5TZ, England
Penguin Books Australia Ltd, Ringwood, Victoria, Australia
Penguin Books Canada Ltd, 10 Alcorn Avenue, Toronto, Ontario, Canada M4V 3B2
Penguin Books (N.Z.) Ltd, 182-190 Wairau Road, Auckland 10, New Zealand

Penguin Books Ltd, Registered Offices: Harmondsworth, Middlesex, England

First published in the United States of America by Dial Books, 1981
Published in Puffin Books, 1991

60 59 58 57

Copyright © Mildred Taylor, 1981
All rights reserved
Library of Congress Catalog Card Number: 91-53030
ISBN 0-14-034892-1

Printed in the United States of America
Set in Caslon Old Face

I will continue the Logans' story with the same life guides that have always been mine, for it is my hope that these books, one of the first chronicles to mirror a black child's hopes and fears from childhood innocence to awareness to bitterness and disillusionment, will one day be instrumental in teaching children of all colors the tremendous influence that Cassie's generation—my father's generation—had in bringing about the great Civil Rights Movement of the fifties and sixties. Without understanding that generation and what it and the generations before it endured, children of today and of the future cannot understand or cherish the precious rights of equality which they now possess, both in the North and in the South. If they can identify with the Logans, who are representative not only of my family but of the many black families who faced adversity and survived, and understand the principles by which they lived, then perhaps they can better understand and respect themselves and others.

Mildred D. Taylor
*from her Newbery Award
acceptance speech, 1977*

1

"Ain't that Wordell?"

Papa and the boys peered out into the deepening shadows as a slight figure slipped from the dense forest on our right and across the defile to the hardness of the red road and vanished into the trees on the other side. My eldest brother, Stacey, sat beside Papa on the wagon seat; Christopher-John and Little Man were in the back of the wagon with me.

"Could've been, Cassie," Papa said, slapping the reins lightly across the mule's back, urging him on, for the November light was slowly failing and we had one more stop to make before we went home. Already we had passed the Morgan place, or at least what used to be the Morgan place but which was now government land like so many other farms taken for taxes by the state of Mississippi in the four years since 1930. We had passed as well the Great Faith school and church grounds with its semicircle of five fragile looking, weather-beaten buildings on skinny brick feet. Now we were approaching the Granger plantation, which sprawled southward, northward, and westward for some 6,000 acres, almost ten square miles. Up ahead the Silas Lanier house, standing unpainted and gray in the midst of the drying cotton stalks, marked the beginning of it. Past the Laniers were the Mason Shorters, and across from them, tucked behind a growth of untrimmed bushes and second-growth trees, were the Page Ellises and their aunt, Mrs. Lee Annie Lees.

At the rutted, narrow trail leading to the Ellises Papa pulled up short on Jack's reins, turning the wagon inward. Going up the trail, we entered a clearing where two tenant shacks, one belonging to the Ellises and the other to Mrs. Lee Annie and her grandson, Wordell, stood catercorner to each other. Sitting barefoot on the porch of the Ellis house were two of the Ellis boys, Son-Boy and Don Lee. With them were Little Willie Wiggins, one of Stacey's best friends and a fellow eighth grader, and his brother Maynard.

"How y'all young folks doing?" Papa asked as we stepped down from the wagon. Papa was a tall, pecan-brown-skinned man with both a reputation and a bearing that commanded respect; all four boys stood to greet him.

"Jus' fine, Mr. Logan," they answered. "How you?"

"Doin' right well." Papa shook hands with each of the boys as if they were men and looked around. "Where's everybody?"

Son-Boy nodded toward the backyard. "Mama and Papa, they's 'round back. Aunt Lee Annie too. They tendin' to that ole mule of ours. Down with the colic again."

"They's 'fraid he ain't gon' make it this time," put in Don Lee, the younger of the two.

"That's a shame," said Papa. "Guess I'll just go on back and see if there's anything I can do."

"Yes, sir."

We watched Papa go between the two houses toward the barn, then settled on the porch. "How long y'all been here?" Stacey asked of Little Willie, beside him on the steps. "We jus' stopped by y'all's house and your mama said you and Maynard and Clarice had done gone up to the Averys."

Little Willie nodded. "Mama had some milk and preserves and stuff she wanted 'em to have. We was on our way back home, but Clarice claimed she jus' had to stop by here a minute and see Thelma."

"Shoot! The way ole Thelma talk," said Son-Boy of his older sister, "y'all be lucky to get 'way from here 'fore nightfall."

"I tell ya, Stacey, women!" sighed Little Willie. "Talkin' 'bout a minute and here it been a good half hour already."

"Ain't that the way," Stacey said, like he knew what the way was.

"Aw, man, you don't know nothin' yet. Jus' wait till Cassie there get older."

"Now jus' how my name get into this?" I demanded from the porch rail. "I'm jus' sitting here minding my own business, ain't done nothin'!"

Little Willie slid a sly glance my way. "But you will."

I scowled down at him. "And jus' what I'm gonna do?"

"Jus' wait. You'll find out."

"Boy——"

"How was everybody at the Averys?" said Stacey, cutting me off, an irritating habit he had recently picked up.

Little Willie leaned back on the steps, his elbows supporting him, and shrugged. "'Bout the same. Ain't none of 'em looking too perky."

"You had a brother down in jail, I don't much 'spect you'd be looking too perky either," I pointed out.

He glanced back at me and grinned in agreement. "You sho' 'nough right 'bout that, Cassie. Don't 'spect I would."

"They had any news?" asked Stacey. "'Bout a trial, I mean."

"Well, to tell the truth, they ain't said nothin' and I ain't asked . . . ain't thought I oughta."

Stacey let out a labored sigh. "Lord, I hate this. Who'd've thought jus' a year ago . . . who'd've thought . . ."

All of us pondered his words in the late afternoon silence. Then Son-Boy shouted, "Hey, Dubé! Dubé Cross!"

We looked out past the wagon to the trail, where a tall, muscular boy had just entered the yard. Sixteen years old, Dubé Cross looked more like a man than a boy; yet despite his size, he was just in the fifth grade. Barefooted, he crossed the yard in a rudely patched pair of pants that were too short and a mended shirt that was too small and greeted us in the stutter that was natural to him. Then he turned to Stacey. "I-I-I was j-j-jus' on my way dddd-down to y'all's place when I s-s-seen y'all turn in. Mama need m-milk for the younguns and I was j-j-jus' won-d-d-derin' if y'all had w-work."

"Dubé," I said, "Big Ma say y'all can jus' have that milk—"

Stacey cut me off. Again. "Well, ain't got no work we don't 'tend to ourselves, but ya wanna come milk in the morning, I'd 'spect Papa'd consider that payment enough."

"But that's our job," spoke up Little Man, who took everything he considered his quite seriously. Christopher-

John, a round boy with a bit more tact, gave Little Man a sharp nudge in the ribs and he grew silent.

"W-w-well, w-we'd be obliged to y'all."

"Y'all's welcome to the milk, ya know that," Stacey assured him. "Fact to business, y'all be doin' us a favor y'all take it. With times like they are, it don't hardly pay to take it into town. Can't get nothin' much for it. Jus' have to give it to the hogs to keep it from goin' to waste."

Dubé nodded, accepting Stacey's words somewhat awkwardly. He was a proud boy, and despite our willingness for his and other families who had no milking cows to have the milk we didn't need, I sometimes felt that Dubé was ashamed to ask for it. He did though, mainly because he considered himself the man of his house. Living with his mother and an assortment of younger brothers and sisters in a one-room, tar-papered shack along the row on Soldiers Road, Dubé had for years helped his mother take care of the fatherless family. But for all he did, things were still bad for the Crosses. Like others along the row, the Crosses had no land, rented or otherwise, to till. They were day laborers who picked cotton for wages, and day laborers were the least paid and the worst treated of the farming community. For them life was even harder than it was for the rest of us.

"Why don't you come on back with us?" Stacey suggested to him. "We'll be heading home directly, and there's plenty of milk fresh in the pantry from this morning y'all can have for supper."

"Th-thank ya k-k-kindly, Stacey, b-b-but I'd rather do the milkin' f-first, ya don't mind. I-I-I be on down first th-thing in the mmmm-mornin'."

Stacey nodded, understanding. "Suit yourself."

"Well," said Little Willie, getting up, "look like ole

Clarice done ⸺ in there. Clarice! Come on, girl! We gotta go!"

Clarice ⸺ good time about coming out. When she finally ⸺ nses left, going back down the trail along with ⸺ papa and Mrs. Lee Annie Lees came from the backyard.

"Well!" exclaimed Mrs. Lee Annie, stopping at the corner of her house. She put her hands on her hips and tried to look vexed. "Well, ain't y'all gonna give me no sugar?"

Although Stacey, Christopher-John, Little Man, and I agreed that all this hugging and kissing business was really quite unnecessary, we didn't mind so much when it came to Mrs. Lee Annie. Heavyset, in her mid-sixties, with bones that were fine and skin that was the color of clear honey and as soft as the down on a baby chick, she was one of the most beautiful women we had ever seen. Besides that, she was fun and we loved her.

Once Mrs. Lee Annie had gotten her hug from each of us, she ushered us toward her porch. "My boy, Russell, he gonna sho' 'nough be glad to see y'all," she said. "Sho' is."

"Russell?" I questioned.

She stopped to look at me. "Ain't Son-Boy and Don Lee done told y'all? Why, Russell, he come late this morning. He over there visitin' with Aunt Callie Jackson, but I done sent Javan for him. He'll be comin' on up here directla."

The boys and I exchanged delighted glances. We liked Russell; everybody did. The son of Mrs. Lee Annie's oldest daughter, Russell Thomas had been brought up by Mrs. Lee Annie, as had his cousin, Wordell. A little over a year ago he had gone north to live with an uncle in Indiana, and we had not seen him since.

Mrs. Lee Annie laughed happily. "Always was crazy 'bout

you, David," she said to Papa as she opened the door. "'Member how he used to tag after ya so?"

Inside we were greeted by Mr. Tom Bee, an elderly, toothless man who was a cousin of Mrs. Lee Annie's and lived farther down on the Harrison Road. "Y'all come on in and join me and these here peanuts!" he invited, beckoning us to where he was comfortably seated by the fire with a black pan on his lap.

"You lookin' mighty good there, Brother Bee," Papa said, going over and shaking his hand.

"Lookin' good and feelin' good too!" boasted Mr. Tom Bee. "Sho' is—y'all sit on down."

The one-room house smelled strongly of burning pine and roasted peanuts mixed with the unmistakable smell of mustard greens. All were good, lived-in smells, and the boys and I with handfuls of the warm peanuts to munch on had just settled back on Mrs. Lee Annie's corn-husk mattress to enjoy them when Mr. and Mrs. Page Ellis came in. A few minutes later Son-Boy and Don Lee's older brother, Javan, arrived with Russell Thomas, a dark-skinned young man of nineteen dressed in an Army uniform.

"Well, looka here," said Papa, standing to greet him. "You gone and joined the Army!"

Russell smiled widely and shook Papa's hand. "Figured that was better than starving, Mr. Logan." He greeted Stacey, Christopher-John, Little Man, and me with a fond grin, and settled in front of the fire with the rest of the adults. "Yes, sir, I figured after more'n a year away, I jus' better get myself on back home and get me some of Mama Lee's fine cooking 'fore I waste away to a little of nothin' at all."

Laughing, Mrs. Lee Annie slapped her grandson's knee with delight.

"How you come?" Papa asked him. "Hoping you gonna be with us awhile."

'Come by train far as Jackson, then took the bus on down to Strawberry. Sad thing is, only got four days. Figure to take the bus Monday morning back up to Indianola to see Mama, spend a day with her, and head on back. Ain't got hardly no time at all, but I jus' had a hankerin' to see everybody."

"Well, we all sure glad you come," said Papa.

"Amen!" agreed Mr. Tom Bee.

"Well, I done already told this boy, though," said Mr. Page Ellis, pulling a tobacco pouch from his shirt pocket, "he better be watchin' hisself goin' through to that Delta country in that soldier outfit. Them's some mean white folks up in that Delta."

Papa's face lined into a wry smile. "There's some mean white folks everywhere."

Russell laughed. "Ain't that the truth!"

"'Sides that," interjected Mrs. Ellis, "lotta Bilbo folks up there."

"That ole devil," muttered Mrs. Lee Annie.

"Anywhere there's rednecks, you got Bilbo folks," Papa said.

"Who's Bilbo?" I whispered to Stacey.

Stacey frowned. "I think he used to be governor or something. He up in Jackson or Washington somewheres."

"Oh," I said, wondering why somebody up in Jackson or off in Washington would be of any interest to Papa or Mrs. Lee Annie.

Mrs. Lee Annie leaned over in her seat to stoke the fire. "You know, I heard him once when I was workin' for them white folks up in Jackson 'bout twenty years back. Him and that no-good Governor Vardaman, too. Them two musta figured colored folks wasn't no more'n animals. Figured God meant for the white folks to rule." She looked around, a mischievous glint in her eyes. "I'd've ever gotten a-hold of either one of them devils, I'd've shown 'em a little black folks' rule."

All the adults but Mrs. Ellis laughed. "Well, what I say is Russell still better be careful." She looked directly at him. "You oughta take that uniform off."

"Ah, Cousin Leora, they ain't gonna bother me none." Russell winked at the others. "I represents the United States government."

Mrs. Ellis sniffed. "United States government, my foot! What they care 'bout any United States government? They soon's kill you as look at you up there, you give 'em any sass. They bullwhipped three colored boys in that Delta not so long ago and they was representing your United States government too."

Russell nodded soberly, conceding the point. Then he said, "Talkin' 'bout your mean white folks, I understand y'all had a bit of trouble down in here y'allselves this summer."

Both Stacey and I looked to Papa, who was calmly placing his empty pipe between his lips.

"It was more'n a bit of trouble——" volunteered Mrs. Ellis.

"——and it ain't hardly over yet," added Mr. Tom Bee.

"Joe Avery's boy, T.J., went and got hisself into trouble," Mr. Ellis explained. "Messin' 'round with two of them no-count Simms boys——"

"Them white boys?" questioned Russell incredulously.

Mr. Page Ellis nodded. "The three of them upped and robbed Mr. Jim Lee Barnett's store in Strawberry——"

"You 'member that place, don'tcha, son?" asked Mrs. Ellis.

"Sure do. That ole redneck owns it too."

I began to fidget, not wanting to hear.

"Well, he got killed," said Mrs. Ellis.

"Ya don't say!"

"They said the Avery boy and two other colored boys done it," continued Mr. Ellis. "Wouldn't believe it was them Simmses. And then them men come out over to the Averys and would've done lynched the boy, that fire hadn't've come up on Brother Logan's place—"

"The hand of God," interjected Mrs. Lee Annie, shaking her head. "The mighty hand of God."

"Burnt a good quarter of your crop too, didn't it, David?"

Papa pulled on the pipe, his eyes meeting Mr. Ellis's, and nodded without expression.

Russell digested all that had been said in the silence that followed. "Well," he said finally, looking around. "What come of the boy?"

Mrs. Lee Annie nodded in the direction of Strawberry. "He still in jail down there in town."

"Don't know what they doin'," observed Mr. Tom Bee with a shake of his head. "I seen the time they woulda done took care of him long 'fore now."

"You 'spect they gonna give him a trial?" Russell asked.

Mr. Ellis shrugged. "They ain't gon' hardly waste no time on no trial for no colored boy. They know what they gon' do to him anyways."

"Well, he do get one, it'll be 'cause of Mr. Jamison," put in Mrs. Ellis. "He been tryin' mighty hard to get him one."

Mr. Tom Bee's displeasure showed on his face. "Don't see how come he wanna bother. They gonna hang T.J. anyways. Ain't no doubt 'bout that thing . . . 'cause they sho' is. . . ."

His statement was final and undisputed; I longed to go.

As if Son-Boy had sensed my discomfort, he jumped off the bed and motioned the boys and me to come with him. Relieved, Little Man, Christopher-John, and I followed with Don Lee. Stacey came too, though he lagged behind, and once we were outside on the porch, stood apart from us staring out toward the woods. The rest of us tromped to the end of the porch, where Son-Boy wheeled around and announced: "I got something to show y'all."

"Well, what?" Christopher-John, Little Man, and I demanded.

Son-Boy grinned widely and delved deeply into his worn pants. "Look here, see what Russell brung us." He pulled a clenched fist from his right pocket and opened it slowly. Don Lee did the same. "Ahhhh!" Christopher-John, Little Man, and I exclaimed in unison.

In their palms lay ten marbles apiece, each a different color.

"And that ain't all," said Don Lee. "Show 'em the real beauty."

Even slower than he had brought forth the other marbles, Son-Boy dug into his other pocket and, with his face plastered in a prideful smile, produced his treasure. And it was a beauty, a penetrating blue swirling through an island of misty emerald green. Son-Boy held it up toward the pale November sun and then brought it close so that each of us could peer through it.

Little Man and Christopher-John "ahhhed" in appreciation, and even Stacey admitted that it was "nice," but I was totally fascinated by it. I could feel my eyes growing big as I stared at it, and without thinking, I reached out to take it from Son-Boy so I could inspect it more closely. Son-Boy firmly closed his fist around it.

"Ain't nobody touchin' this baby but me," he said.

"And me," reminded Don Lee.

Son-Boy made no comment, but I had a feeling that Don Lee wasn't coming any closer to that marble than any of the rest of us.

"Ah, shuckies, boy!" I exclaimed. "Ain't nobody wanting your ole marble. I just wanted to get a good look at it, that's all. Come on and open your hand."

Son-Boy turned deaf ears to my request as he pocketed his treasure, patting it through the thin cloth of his pants to make sure it was secure. Then, as if somewhat remorseful about his selfishness, he again opened his right fist. "Wanna play?" he asked.

I dug out the marbles I had won from Curtis Henderson a few days ago. Son-Boy frowned disdainfully. "That all you got?"

"That's all I need," I said, confident that after three quick shots, three of his marbles would be mine.

"I got one too," proclaimed Little Man, adding a fourth marble to my pile. "I get a shot," he added.

"We better get down here," said Son-Boy, hopping from the porch with its wide spaces between the porch slats.

Don Lee, Christopher-John, Little Man, and I jumped down too, but Stacey remained on the porch.

"Ain't you gonna play?" I asked.

"Naw. I'm going back inside," he said, starting back down the porch.

I stared irritably after him. A year ago he would have been right down here playing too, but now at thirteen he had changed so much that he seldom deigned to play with us at all anymore. Mama said that was because Stacey was becoming a man, that it was natural for him to change, and that I would change too. Maybe that was so, but I didn't like his changing and I didn't like the thought of my changing either. Maybe it was the way of life to change, but if I had my way I would put an iron padlock on time so nothing would ever have to change again.

"Stacey's taking it bad, ain't he?" observed Son-Boy, who knew, as everyone else did, how close Stacey had once been to T.J. Avery. For years Stacey had been T.J.'s best and just about only friend. Although a lot of people, including myself, had never been exactly crazy about T.J., Stacey had remained his friend until he had caused Mama to lose her teaching job at Great Faith last spring. But even with all that T.J. had done, Stacey had not deserted him. On the night Jim Lee Barnett was killed, T.J. had turned to Stacey and Stacey had helped him.

"Ya s'pose they really gonna put ole T.J. to death like folks say?" Son-Boy wondered, absently shaking the marbles in his hand, the impending game for the moment forgotten.

I faced him with an icy gaze. I didn't want to think about T.J. or what had happened or what could happen. "Thought you wanted to play," I said.

Son-Boy's eyes met mine and he shrugged. "All right then, let's play."

Picking up a stick, he outlined the outer and inner circles for the game. He placed Little Man's and my marbles, alternating them with his, around the inner circle, then took the last of my marbles, a red, and one of his, a yellow, and shook them up in his hands. Don Lee, his eyes covered by Christopher-John's pudgy hands, made the draw from his brother's hand, picking the red. I got the first shot.

"Cassie, let me shoot," demanded Little Man, neatly avoiding any dirt as he, like I, sat on his haunches. "One of 'em's mine, ya know."

I started to object to Little Man's shooting at all, but decided against it since I needed his marble and did not want him to snatch it from the circle. "Jus' let me shoot down one of their men first," I said, "then you take your turn."

Little Man frowned and conceded. He was a very rational boy and accepted the fact that I was a better and more experienced shot than he.

The object of the game was to knock the opponent's marbles out of the circle. Any such marbles then became the property of the person who knocked them out. I did very well, but on this particular day neither Son-Boy, who was usually an excellent shot, nor Don Lee was having much luck. Little Man and I handily took four of their men in a row. Even Christopher-John took a roll and scored. In fact, we were on our way to wiping Son-Boy and Don Lee out when Papa said: "What y'all doin' here?"

I looked up, my shooting marble still in hand. We had been so engrossed in the game we hadn't heard him come out. "Playing marbles," I answered.

"And we whippin' the pants off 'em too, Papa," boasted Little Man.

"That a fact?"

"Yes, sir!" grinned Christopher-John, still jubilant over having claimed one of Son-Boy's marbles for his own.

"Well, I think y'all best give Son-Boy and Don Lee's marbles back to them."

"But, Papa," I protested, "we won 'em fair!"

Papa motioned toward the marbles. "Son-Boy, you and Don Lee take your marbles."

Christopher-John, Little Man, and I regarded Papa with dismay as Son-Boy and Don Lee joyfully scooped up the marbles which rightfully belonged to us.

"What 'bout them?" Papa asked concerning the three remaining marbles on the ground.

"They're ours," I answered.

"Then give 'em here."

I gathered up the marbles and gave all of them, including the one in my hand, to Papa, who deposited them in his coat pocket. "All right, go get in the wagon. We going now."

Once we had said good-bye to Mrs. Lee Annie and the Ellises and had started home again, Papa said, "I don't want y'all playing marbles no more."

Little Man, Christopher-John, and I stared aghast at Papa. Stacey, however, showed no concern. Since he now considered himself above such childish games as marble playing, he no doubt felt the edict didn't affect him one way or the other.

"I seen it lead too many times to gambling, and that gambling's like a sickness, a terrible thing. Can destroy a person. Anytime you take possession of somebody else's things through a game, there's usually gonna be hard feelings. Now, that marble shooting might go on perfectly all right for a while, then one day somebody'll get mad 'bout losing, or cheating, or something, and there'll be trouble. Then again somebody'll decide winning marbles ain't enough, and they'll start betting money and you into gambling."

"But, Papa," I protested, "we wasn't doin' nothin' wrong."

"Not now, Cassie girl, and I don't want you to either. That's why I want y'all to leave this marble playing alone. There's plenty of other games to play."

"But Papa—"

"There ain't no changing my mind about it, so you just might as well make up yours to the fact you've played your last game of marbles. You decide otherwise, you know what I'm gonna have to do, don't you?"

"Yessir," all three of us murmured with a noticeable lack of enthusiasm. Although I knew perfectly well that Papa would whip us good if he found out we'd been shooting marbles again, the whole thing made no sense to me. We hadn't been gambling and I for one had no intention of doing so. There was nothing I loved more than a good game of marbles. And I was good at playing them too, better than most anybody, including Son-Boy. I hated the thought of giving up the game, but I knew as well as Christopher-John and Little Man did that Papa had meant what he'd indicated about the whipping. There were no if's, and's, or but's about that.

It was Son-Boy who started it all. There I was sitting in Sunday school with my Bible verse firmly planted upon my lips when he pulled out the emerald-blue marble and started flashing it to all the boys and girls securely hidden by the first row of students. Rolling it between his thumb and forefinger, he had every marble addict present drooling over his prize. But true to his word, he allowed no one to touch it but himself. Finally, unable to stand it any longer, I whispered to Little Man beside me, "I'm gonna get that thing."

Christopher-John, sitting on the other side of Little Man, turned toward me horrified. "C-Cassie, you can't! You know what Papa said!"

"I gotta have it."

"I betcha you gonna have a whippin' too," predicted Little Man.

"Maybe so, Papa find out, but I gotta figure out a way for Son-Boy to let go of that marble. Maybe——"

"Cassie?"

It was Mrs. Lettie Love, the elementary Sunday school teacher.

I stood quickly. "Yes'm?"

"You learn your Bible verse for the week?"

"Yes'm. 'Thou shalt not covet thy neighbor's house or anything that is thy neighbor's,' " I said dutifully without a moment's guilt.

Mrs. Love smiled, happy that one of her students had learned her verse so well. I sat down smiling too as I stared down the row at Son-Boy. He might as well get in his last few minutes of glory with that marble, because I planned for it to be mine within the hour.

Immediately after Sunday school Little Man and I found Maynard Wiggins and Henry Johnson, who had kept marbles jiggling in their pockets since school had begun, and put a proposition to them. If they would put up their marbles against Son-Boy's ten, I would do the shooting with the promise that if I began to miss, Maynard or Henry could take over to recoup their losses. If I won, they would each be richer by the number of marbles they'd put up. If I lost, then that was just the chance we took. All I wanted from the deal was Son-Boy's emerald-blue.

As we were making our plans, Joe McCalister wandered over carrying Son-Boy's sister's baby. Joe was a short, bandy-legged man with a face that could have been twenty or forty. There was just no telling what age he was by looking at him. Big Ma said that was because he didn't have any worries to speak of, and folks with no worries didn't show their age much.

"What y'all younguns up to?" he asked.

"Nothin', Joe," I said. Everybody called him Joe.

"Y'all see this child here," he said, indicating Doris Anne, who was almost two years old. "She sho' like ole Joe."

"That's nice," I said, just wanting him to go so we could get on with the business at hand.

"Her mama always askin' me to look out for her. Her papa too. They know ole Joe take good care of her."

"Yeah . . . well . . . ain't that her mama callin' for her now?" asked Henry.

Joe stood still, cocking his head toward the church. "Didn't hear nothin'," he said.

"Thought I did," said Henry.

"I better go check."

"Yeah, maybe you better."

Joe walked off a little way, then stopped. "Gots to ring that bell come church time. They 'pends on me for that, ya know."

"Yeah, that's nice, Joe," I said.

"Now," said Maynard as soon as Joe had gone on his way, "Son-Boy ain't gonna hardly put up that emerald-blue."

"Yes he will," I said with confidence.

"How you know?" questioned Henry. "And how you know he gonna wanna play anyhow?"

"'Cause he greedy, that's why! Look, y'all gonna give me your marbles or not? We only got half an hour to church time."

Maynard and Henry went off for a short conference, then came back agreed that they would risk their fortunes on me. We decided that it would be best for them to make the arrangements with Son-Boy. As they hurried off, I hollered after them, "Tell him he's gotta play all ten. It won't be no good 'less he play all of 'em . . . and don't say nothin' 'bout playing that emerald-blue. You do, he probably won't play."

Christopher-John, who had stood disapprovingly apart from these troubling proceedings, hurried over and tried to make me see the folly of my ways. "Cassie, Papa gonna skin you alive sure, he find out—ya know that? What's the matter with you, anyway? You gone crazy?"

He certainly had a point; but not even the thought of Papa's belt could turn me from the course I had set for myself. That emerald-blue had a nasty hold on me, and if I could just get my hands on it, I promised myself and God that I'd never shoot marbles again. And perhaps, if luck was with me, Papa would never even have to know I'd disobeyed him.

Soon Maynard and Henry returned. The deal was set. We would meet Son-Boy down by the fallen tree about five minutes deep into the woods.

"What!" exclaimed Little Man, not too pleased about the chosen site. To reach the fallen tree we had to scurry through some pretty heavy growth, and chances of a stain were great. Little Man was a most particular boy when it came to his clothes, his school materials, his anything. He frowned down at his immaculate jacket, pants and shoes, then at Henry and Maynard, and demanded, "Couldn't y'all find no place better'n that?"

"Can't play no closer to the church," replied Maynard. "Y'all goin' or not?"

"Yeah, we goin'," I said, hurrying toward the middle-grades class building. The path leading into the woods was behind it.

Little Man, deciding that too much was at stake to remain behind, followed with Maynard and Henry. Christopher-John pulled up the rear shouting warnings that not only was Papa going to get us but God too.

"Why don't you jus' go on back and stop bothering me?" I told him when we reached the fallen tree where Son-Boy and Don Lee, along with Curtis Henderson, were already gathered.

"Y'all come too!"

"Not till I get that emerald-blue," I whispered.

Pushing my coat out of the way, I dug into my dress pocket, the only useful feature in an uncomfortable garment, and pulled out the marbles Maynard and Henry had placed in my keeping. Then I settled down on my haunches trying to keep my dress from dragging in the dirt.

The battle began.

Luck was with Son-Boy. He got first shot, then immediately captured three of our men. Nervously, I made my shot and missed.

"Cassie!" cried Maynard, as he and Henry scowled down at their rapidly dwindling marbles. Their faith in me was quickly ebbing.

Son-Boy laughed. "Didn't y'all know couldn't no girl be good as me?" He shot again, but this time his shot marble hit nothing.

"Serve ya right," judged Little Man.

I went for my turn feeling the perspiration trickling down my arms despite the chilliness of the day. But before I could shoot, Maynard grabbed my arm. "Better let me shoot," he decided.

I snatched my arm from his grasp and, before he or Henry could object, shot and connected. After that, the game was mine. I sent the last of Son-Boy's marbles hurtling into our hands, then sat back on my ankles and stared across at Son-Boy, who looked as if he did not quite realize he had just been wiped out. Meanwhile, Little Man, Maynard, Henry, and yes, Christopher-John, too, were whooping it up at our victory.

"Would y'all shut up!" I demanded. It was almost time for the bell to ring and there was still the matter of the emerald-blue. Immediately, everyone hushed.

"Look here, Son-Boy," I said, "to tell you the truth, I hate to see you wiped out like this. I mean, seeing Russell just give you them marbles."

I grew thoughtfully quiet as Son-Boy's face began to show signs of hope at my sympathetic attitude.

"I tell you what," I said when I felt he was appropriately hopeful enough to hear my next statement. "If you want, we'll give you a chance to win all your marbles back, plus ours, with one shot—"

"Now hold on just a minute there, Cassie!" cried Maynard with Henry backing him up. Already they were dividing the marbles and had forgotten that I still did not have what I had come after.

I cut my eyes at them, copying the look Papa gave people when he was angry or deadly serious. Both Maynard and Henry grew silent.

"But—but I ain't got nothin' to shoot 'gainst," said Son-Boy.

"You got your emerald-blue."

Son-Boy's lower jaw dropped.

"You win," I propositioned, "you get to keep it. Not only that, but you'll have twenty other marbles jiggling in your pocket. What we'll do is both shoot for the emerald-blue. First one knocks it beyond the outer circle gets it." I inhaled deeply as I made my final ploy. "I'll even let you go first."

Little Man and Christopher-John looked at me in pure disbelief; Henry and Maynard just looked sick.

Son-Boy considered.

All was quiet.

He pulled the emerald-blue from his pocket and whirled it around in his palm.

The emerald-blue was almost mine, yet I couldn't help but feel sorry for Son-Boy. In a few minutes he had lost almost all of his treasure, and if he was the boy I thought he was, he would risk the rest of it to try and get it back.

But if he'd just use his head, he could keep the most precious part; the rest of the marbles were nothing compared to what he held in his hand. I decided that if Son-Boy played the emerald-blue, he was a fool.

"Okay," he said, placing the marble on the line of the inner circle.

Papa had been right. If gambling was anything like shooting marbles, then it was a sickness. But then, I hadn't totally used good sense either—risking one of Papa's no-nonsense whippings for a piece of glass. Maybe I was as big a fool as Son-Boy.

"Go on," I said. "Shoot."

Son-Boy nervously licked his lips and shot.

He missed.

I didn't.

"Ya done it, Cassie! Ya done it!" cried Little Man and Christopher-John, slapping me on my shoulders as I reached out to claim my prize.

Tenderly caressing the emerald-blue between my fingers, I held it toward the sun. It was a beautiful thing.

"We'd better get back," Christopher-John reminded us. "That bell's gonna start ringing."

We all jumped up, dusting each other off. Only Little Man had no need to dust; he'd seen to that.

Son-Boy, his face long, glanced at me and the emerald-blue with sad, vacant eyes and hurried on with Don Lee. I hadn't liked the feeling of that look. Son-Boy was my friend. Nevertheless, with the marble cradled possessively in my hand, I didn't have time to think about Son-Boy now. I couldn't help it if he was a fool. I hurried with Little Man and Christopher-John after Henry and Maynard, and we emerged from the forest happily assessing our victory.

It was then that our luck ran out. Standing near the middle-grades class building was Papa.

I looked at Christopher-John and Little Man. They looked at me. Then all of us looked at Papa.

"Come on over," he said.

Papa's eyes searched us slowly once we were standing before him, then he nodded toward my fist tightly clenching the marble. "You got there what I think you got?"

I swallowed hard, twice, trying to wet my throat. Papa's eyes were steadfast. "Y-yes, sir." There was no use denying it. I only wondered how he had known.

"Uh-huh," said Papa. "Well, then, I s'pose you'd best be giving it back to whoever you got it from, don't you?"

"Yes, sir, Papa."

"Now, let's get on back to church. Service's 'bout ready to start."

Papa didn't mention anything about a whipping, but then again he didn't need to. What Papa promised, Papa gave. And one other thing was certain too: Our marble playing days were now over.

As we marched back toward the church with Papa behind us, our stomachs churning into acid pits of nausea, Son-Boy's sister Lou Ella Hicks headed our way.

"Mr. Logan, you seen Joe?" she asked. "I let him hold Doris Anne a while back and I ain't seen him nowheres."

"He must be near here," Papa said.

"I done looked in the church. They ain't there. I thought maybe he walked on down to the school with her."

The big iron church bell clanged loudly. It was time for church to begin. Papa looked up toward the belfry and, instinctively, so did Lou Ella. She let out a faint gasp and Papa touched her arm. Riding the rope that pulled the bell was Doris Anne, giggling with unbridled delight. No one else could be seen.

"Don't call her," Papa cautioned. "She might let go."

He left us then, running toward the far side of the church to the side entrance which led up to the belfry. Mr. Page Ellis saw him and asked Lou Ella what was wrong, then dashed off after him, followed by Lou Ella and us.

By the time we all reached the side door, Papa was standing on the ladder that led through a small hole to the belfry. Above him on the landing was Wordell Lees holding Doris Anne. A slightly built, handsome, brown-sugar boy of fifteen with haunting sandy-colored eyes that were now fixed on Papa, Wordell was considered peculiar by just about everyone. He seldom spoke, though it was said he could speak, and he never smiled, though he was supposed to be able to do that too.

"Boy, what you doin' with that baby up there!" Mr. Ellis cried up to him. "You ain't got the brains of a two-year-old! Don't you know that child could fall?"

Papa seemed about to speak, but then his eyes caught the slight shake of Wordell's head. Wordell stared at Papa for a long, long moment, then looked at Mr. Ellis. Doris Anne was secure in his arms, but he made no move to come down.

"Give me the baby, son," Papa said softly.

Wordell hesitated, his eyes searching Papa's; then, seemingly reassured, he handed over Doris Anne. Papa came down the ladder and gave the child to her mother.

"Get on down here," hollered Mr. Ellis. Slowly, Wordell descended, his feet bare, revealing the absence of a little toe on each foot. Before he reached bottom, Mr. Ellis jerked him off the ladder. "Boy, you done lost what little mind you got?" he asked. "I oughta whip you right here and now 'bout taking that child up there."

Wordell's gaze settled on Mr. Ellis; there was no change in the blank expression on his face.

"Open your mouth, boy, and talk! What you doin' with that baby up there?" Mr. Ellis demanded, angered even more by Wordell's silence.

Papa put a restraining hand on Mr. Ellis's shoulder. "Let the boy go on into church, Page. No harm's done."

Mr. Ellis relaxed his grip on Wordell and immediately Wordell escaped him, slipping down the steps and through the crowd which had gathered. He ran off toward the woods.

"You don't understand how that boy is, David," Mr. Ellis said. "He ain't like most younguns—he ain't right in the head. You gotta teach him hard 'bout right and wrong. He jus' don't know no better."

"He wasn't gonna hurt the baby," Papa said. "I think he just went up there to get her down."

"You tellin' me she got up there by herself then?"

"No. . . ." Papa hesitated. "No, I ain't saying that. Only I wouldn't be hard on the boy. I got a feeling he was just trying to help."

Mr. Ellis only looked at Papa, then came on down the steps. Everyone turned and went around to the front of the church. When we reached the church door, I looked back out to the woods where Wordell had fled. Suddenly from nowhere Joe appeared and ran into the woods also. I glanced up at Papa, wondering if he'd seen. Then a thought occurred to me: Where had Joe been all that time when Doris Anne had been up in the belfry? He was the one who was supposed to ring the bell. Before I could ask Papa about it, he ushered me inside the church, where we were greeted by the congregation's singing of "Look Out, Sinner! Judgment Day's A-Comin'!" which reminded me of my own impending punishment and that I had more than Joe to worry about.

2

Clarence Hopkins brought the news. He dashed across the school lawn just minutes before the afternoon bell was to ring, crying out to Stacey, who was standing with Little Willie Wiggins, Moe Turner, and several other eighth-grade boys beside the tree which shaded the well. He caused such a ruckus with his yelling that all the students still lingering outside were alerted that something important was up. Immediately Son-Boy, Maynard, and I left the steps of the middle-grades building to join the growing circle as Little Man and Christopher-John came running from the far corner of the toolshed, where they had been throwing horseshoes.

By the time we had pushed our way into the group, Clarence was already into his story. He had gone home for lunch and had gotten the news from his mother, who had gotten it from Mr. Silas Lanier, who had just come back from Strawberry: T.J. Avery was to go on trial next month.

"You sure?" questioned Stacey. "They gonna really let him have a trial?"

"That's . . . what . . . Mr. Lanier . . . said," Clarence replied between gasps to recover his breath. He had run all the way from home. "He said it's all over town. That's all the white folks talkin' 'bout." Clarence breathed in deeply before he continued. "They say there ain't no need of no trial, but Mr. Jamison, he been worryin' all this time to get one . . . and he sho' 'nough got it—"

"My daddy said a trial ain't gonna do no good," remarked Moe, a quiet, gentle boy who usually had little to say in a crowd, but whose opinion was always respected.

"Maybe not," agreed Little Willie, "but leastways he got one. That's better'n nothin', I 'spect."

Stacey frowned. "Don't know 'bout that. They ain't gonna believe what T.J.'s gotta say no way so what's the use of a trial?" His words were bitter and no one attempted to answer him as silence settled over the group. Then Stacey asked if anyone had seen T.J.

"Nobody I know 'bout," said Clarence, "'ceptin' maybe his folks and Mr. Jamison." He was silent a moment, then added, "I'd sure like to go to that trial."

At first no one commented, then Little Willie scratched his head. "You s'pose they gon' let colored folks in?"

Clarence looked surprised. "I don't see why not! We got a right—"

"What day is it?" Stacey asked, brusquely ignoring Clarence's summation of what rights he thought we had.

"The tenth," answered Clarence, unruffled. "December tenth."

Moe turned to Stacey. "You gonna try to go? You go, I'll go."

I looked at Stacey, curious as to what he would say, but he didn't answer. The afternoon bell began to ring and he left the circle. The rest of us watched him go; then we were forced by the bell to disperse. Christopher-John in the third grade and Little Man in the second slowly wandered off to the primary-grades building. Son-Boy, Maynard, and I crossed in silence to the middle-grades building, where we went into our fifth-grade classroom and wordlessly slipped into our seats. Class began and I opened my book, with T.J. Avery on my mind.

On a dry day the walk home took about an hour. On wet days, what with the slipperiness of the mud road and having to scramble onto the forest bank to avoid any passing vehicle, the journey took some fifteen minutes longer. Today the weather was fine and we arrived at the second crossroads in good time. With the long shadowing arms of the Granger forest trees stretching over us, we walked the last half mile toward home. Finally, towering alone and beaconlike, the old oak which marked the boundary of our four hundred acres came into view. On the right side of the road the forest continued. On the left it ended, leaving in its stead the massive oak and the open richness of red Mississippi farmland.

Beyond the oak lay the east pasture, and beyond it the cotton field, left dead-looking by the August fire which had started there and swept across the rows of green and purple stalks, taking fine puffs of cotton ready for picking and bolls of flowered richness still blooming. The fire had destroyed a quarter of the year's crop and damaged much of the rest with its smoke and heat. The pasture, which before the fire had boasted a soft greenness, was scorched brown, and the oak had been singed by the heat of the fire, a fire Papa himself had started to stop the lynching of T.J. But no one except the family and Mr. Wade Jamison knew Papa had set the fire; it was too dangerous for anyone else to know.

The fire had not extended beyond the pasture. Men who had come to hang T.J. had ended up fighting the fire instead, in order to stop its encroachment eastward to the Granger forest. None of Mr. Harlan Granger's 6,000 acres had been touched.

The cotton field ran to within a hundred feet of the house and was bordered with a barbwire fence which continued to the back of the house and the garden gate. Past the fields was the lawn, long and sloping upward to the house. On its western edge a dusty driveway cut from the road to the barn. Beyond the lawn and the drive lay the west fields where hay, corn, soybeans, and sugarcane were planted each spring. The fire hadn't burned them, but it wouldn't have mattered as much if it had. Mostly, the hay and the soybeans and the sugarcane were not cash crops; it was the cotton we depended upon for our income. Perhaps too much.

Going up the drive, we followed the path of giant rocks leading to the back porch and entered the house through the kitchen. There we found Big Ma at her usual place by the cast-iron stove stirring a pot smelling strongly of collard greens. One look at her and it was evident where Papa had gotten his looks. Tall and strongly built, her coloring was the same pecan-brown and she carried no fat. She turned as we came in, with a smile that started vanishing when she saw our faces. The years had taught her to discern whenever something was wrong, and before we could say anything she demanded to know what was the matter. When Stacey told her, she shook her head muttering, "Lord, Lord," and absently continued to stir the collards.

Stacey watched her a moment, then went through the curtained doorway which separated the closetlike kitchen from the dining room, and into the room he shared with Christopher-John and Little Man to the right of it. Christopher-John and Little Man followed him, but I stayed behind to ask Big Ma about Mama, Papa, and Mr. Morrison. Once I had found out where they were, I left as well, going through the dining room and Mama and Papa's room to the room Big Ma and I shared. There I finally shed the school dress and slipped into the comfort of well-worn pants. My first impulse was to toss the dress on a chair, but knowing the fussing that was sure to come, I was about to hang it up when I heard a wagon turning into the drive, and deciding on first things first, tossed it anyway and ran outside.

The wagon rolled to a stop and Mr. L.T. Morrison stepped down. An awesome figure, Mr. Morrison was over seven feet tall with skin that was black, hair that was gray, and bulging muscles of an ironlike hardness despite his sixty-three years. He smiled down at me in his gentle way and spoke in a voice that rolled low and deep.

"Hello, Mr. Morrison," I said quietly.

He walked to the back of the wagon where a hay loader was sitting and lifted it out, a task that should have taken two men. I followed him as he took the hay loader into the barn, then out again and helped him clear the rest of the wagon. After a while he looked down at me curiously. "You mighty quiet there, Cassie."

"Yes, sir."

"Anything the matter?"

I looked up at him. "T.J. got himself a trial . . . next month."

He appeared just a bit surprised, then softly touched my head with his giant hand. "That's better'n nothin', Cassie."

"Yes, sir," I said, continuing the unloading. But he and I both knew it wasn't much better.

When the boys came out, they spoke to Mr. Morrison, who watched us all with worried eyes; then the four of us crossed the road to the forest. Hearing the thudding echo of an axe beating out a dull rhythm, we followed the trail that wound through pines and oaks and sweet gums to a vast clearing where standing trees gave way to those that had fallen more than a year ago when lumbermen had come and chopped them down.

Mama stood alone near the pond chopping one of the fallen trees for firewood. A tall, thin woman with fragile beauty in a strong-jawed face, she hardly looked to have the strength needed to swing the axe in such a hefty fashion, but her looks were deceiving. She had been born in the Delta, a sharecropper's daughter, and she knew hard work. At nineteen she had come to Spokane County to teach; a year later she had married Papa. Since then she had worked as hard as he to keep the farm going, and when Papa had gone to work on the railroad in Louisiana, Mama had not only run the farm but had continued to teach as well. That is, she had taught until Harlan Granger had decided it was too dangerous to have her teaching and she had been fired, supposedly for destroying school property. But everyone knew what the real reason was: Mama had organized a boycott against the Wallaces, white brothers who ran the store on the Granger plantation, and Harlan Granger hadn't liked that, not one little bit. And when Harlan Granger didn't like something he always did something about it.

She stopped chopping as we entered the clearing and smiled at us. Sinking the axe into a log, she took off the raw leather gloves she wore and the scarf which revealed long hair neatly pulled into a chignon at the nape of her neck. "How was school?" she asked.

"All right," said Stacey, looking around. "Where's Papa?"

Mama wiped the back of her hand across her forehead and went over to the water pail. "He's down farther."

"Mama, y'all hear?"

"Hear what, honey?" She uncovered the pail and dipped out some water with a ladle.

"'Bout T.J." Mama looked at Stacey, the ladle at her lips. "Come next month, he gonna get a trial."

Mama lowered the ladle without drinking. "Where'd you hear that?"

"At school. Clarence found out when he gone home for dinner. Mr. Lanier was there and he'd just come back from Strawberry. Said that's all folks talking 'bout."

"I can imagine."

"What this mean, Mama?" Christopher-John asked. "This mean T.J. gonna come home now?"

Mama poured the water, untouched, back into the pail. Suddenly, she looked weary. "No, that's not what it means."

"Well, what it mean?"

"Means they can do it legally now."

"What's that, Mama?"

There had been a bitter edge to Mama's voice as she spoke. Now she turned from the wagon to look directly at Christopher-John, his round face showing bewilderment at this latest news about T.J., and her words were softer. "A trial means that T.J. can tell his story and there'll be people there who'll decide whether he's telling the truth or not."

"Then that means he'll be comin' on home then." Christopher-John smiled happily at this conclusion.

"No. . . ." Her eyes went slowly over each of us. "No.

The people who'll hear T.J. and make the decision will be white. There'll be somebody else who'll be saying that what T.J. says is not the truth. He'll be white too. There'll be a judge there and he'll be white. All white, do you understand?" She paused. "T.J. won't be coming home." She looked down at Christopher-John, who was still very much disturbed. "What is it?"

It took him a moment to speak. When he did, the fear had welled in his voice. "Mama . . . Mama, you think they'll ever come get us like they done T.J.?"

"Us?" She looked surprised at his asking. "They've got no reason to come after us."

"But they come after T.J.!"

"I know."

"Well, it ain't fair!" he objected. "T.J., he ain't done nothin', and now folks say they gonna hang him."

"Now wait just a minute. You call breaking into that store nothing? That was wrong and there's no way around it. It was wrong too for T.J. to be running around with those white boys in the first place. He knew that, but he was too hardheaded to listen to anybody, and this trouble he's in is what came of it." Her voice had risen angrily as she spoke, for it deeply bothered her that she had seen T.J.'s downfall coming and had been unable to prevent it. She calmed herself and went on. "You know, there's nothing I'd like better in this world than to make what happened this summer not to have happened. But it did, and not your papa or Big Ma or Mr. Morrison or me or anybody can make it go away. We teach you what we do to keep you safe. The way things are down here, what happened to T.J. was bound to come. I don't like it and your papa doesn't like it, and most decent folks don't like it, but right now all we can do is try to keep it from happening again."

"But what 'bout T.J., Mama?" Christopher-John persisted. "He gonna die?"

Mama put a slender arm around him. "On that, baby, we'll just have to wait and see."

For a moment we stood in silence, only the forest sounds cracking the stillness. Then Stacey muttered something about finding Papa and, rounding the pond, headed northward. As he left, Mr. Morrison drove up in the wagon and we began to load the firewood. When Stacey returned with Papa a short time later, Mama looked at Papa and said: "Stacey tell you?"

Papa nodded and, swooping Little Man up, set him onto the back of the wagon and gave him a stick of wood to stack. Little Man quickly placed the stick at the wagon's head, then ran back for more.

"Y'all got quite a bit of chopping done down in here," Mr. Morrison said as he brought an armload of wood to the wagon.

Papa looked around the clearing. "It'll be a while yet 'fore it's all cleared out. Them lumbermen did a lotta damage . . . a lotta damage. . . . Got another load stacked farther down. We finish this, then in the morning I figure we'll go get that other."

"Papa—"

Papa turned to Stacey. For a moment, Stacey faltered; then he said: "Papa, I wanna go to that trial."

Mama, walking toward the wagon with an armload of wood, stopped so suddenly, several sticks fell off. "Now that's the last thing you're going to do," she said.

"Mama, I gotta go! T.J. gonna need me. Maybe there's something I can say. Maybe tell 'em 'bout him comin' here that night—"

"You think these people are going to believe anything you have to say? T.J.'s going to trial before an all-white jury and a white judge in a town and a state and a country ruled by white folks. For you to get up there and say anything will just make it worse."

Stacey's look was defiant. "I seen him that night . . . 'fore them men come. Could tell 'em what T.J. said. Tell how beat up he was."

"Now just calm down here a minute," Papa said. "You've done a lotta learning and a lotta growing the last few years, and I figure you know by now things ain't fair in this life for hardly nobody, and for a black person there ain't hardly no such thing. Now we done all we could for T.J. the night of the fire, but I tell you, son, there ain't nothing else we can do. He's in the hands of the law now and that law like jus' 'bout everything else in this country is made for the white folks. You get up there talking 'bout being with T.J. that night, maybe them white folks in town might just get to thinkin' you was one of them boys broke in that store with T.J."

Stacey looked uneasy. "T.J., he'll—he'll tell 'em it wasn't me—that it was them Simmses."

Papa waited a moment, his eyes hard on Stacey. "And you think the jury's gonna believe that?"

Stacey was silent. He glanced at the pond, then back at Papa and Mama. His eyes changed. The realization had hit him.

It had hit me too. I felt a surging feeling of panic at the thought of Stacey's facing the same ordeal as T.J. After all, Stacey had been with T.J. the night Jim Lee Barnett had been killed, and he had helped him. We all had.

He didn't say anything else. Turning away, he gathered several more sticks of firewood and, in silence, put them on the wagon.

After supper we sat before the fire in Mama and Papa's room as we did each evening, attending to our evening tasks: the boys and I at our table by the window, attempting to study; Big Ma sewing; Mama reading; Papa mending the sole of Christopher-John's shoe; and Mr. Morrison carving a piece of wood which had not yet taken on a shape of its own. Sounds of the fire popping and of Mr. Morrison's knife scraping against the wood blended with Big Ma's soft humming, lending a quiet peace.

As the evening wore on, we heard a car on the road and we all looked up. Mr. Morrison, sitting near the front window, stood and pushed the curtain back. The boys and I peered out into the darkness with him, watching as a faint light coming from the east illuminated the road, growing brighter as it neared. Finally, the car slowed and turned up the drive. Mr. Morrison waited a moment until the driver stepped out, then said, "It's Wade Jamison."

For longer than was necessary and with his car headlights still on, Mr. Jamison poked around his front seat as if arranging his briefcase, a procedure he always followed whenever he came at night so that we could see who it was. When Papa called out to him, he turned out his lights and came up the rock path to the porch, leaving the briefcase behind. He shook Papa's hand and, taking off his hat, greeted the rest of us.

Since the night of the fire, we had not seen Mr. Jamison very much; we had heard he had had troubles of his own. His defense of T.J. that night had caused his unpopularity in the white community to grow even further, and the week following the lynching attempt his office had been burned, then his dog poisoned. It was said, too, that threats had been made against both him and his wife. But Mr. Jamison himself had never mentioned the threats to us. What he had said, however, was that his family was old-line Mississippi and not even Beelzebub himself was going to run him out or change his way of thinking. I believed him, too.

Mama offered him one of the rockers and he sat down tentatively, as was his custom, crossing one long leg over the other. In his fifties, with graying hair and sad gray eyes, Mr. Jamison was one of the few adult white people that I truly liked.

"I'm only going to be here a minute," he explained as Mama took his hat and laid it on the bed. "I was just down to the Averys and thought I'd stop by before I went back to town to see if you'd heard about the trial."

As usual, Mr. Jamison came straight to the point. He understood as well as we did that the friendship and good will we shared with him was different from that which we shared with our neighbors in the black community or that which he shared with his friends in the white community. There was a mutual respect and, because the years had proven it justified, a mutual trust; but there was no socialization other than the amenities. Neither he nor we would have felt comfortable in such a situation, for the unwritten laws of the society frowned upon such fraternization, and the trust and respect were valued and needed more than the socializing.

"We got the news this afternoon," Papa replied. "The children heard 'bout it at school."

Mr. Jamison glanced over at the boys and me, then back to Papa. "Judge Havershack'll be presiding. I tried for Judge Forestor, who's quite a bit more free thinking, but he was tied up in something else up at Tree Hill. Hadley Macabee from Vicksburg'll be prosecuting."

Papa was silent a moment before he observed, "I don't s'pose it really matters that much who the judge or the prosecutor is, does it? It's the jury's gotta decide, and I figure it made up its mind long before that boy broke into that store."

Mr. Jamison sighed and ran his fingers through his hair. "A different kind of judge, though, maybe could make a difference . . . a big difference."

Papa shrugged. "You naturally got more faith in the law than I do."

Mr. Jamison took Papa's comment in silence. Papa had no illusions about the trial and Mr. Jamison knew it. He glanced around the room before he spoke again. "David, there's been something that's been on my mind quite a little while, and now that we've got the trial coming up, I think it best we talk about it."

I stopped breathing and glanced at Stacey; his eyes did not move from Mr. Jamison.

"It's about your children."

Relief was on Stacey's face. I began to breathe again. Mr. Jamison was not going to talk about the fire.

"Now I've spoken to T.J. and he's told me all his actions on the night Jim Lee was killed. I know that he came by here first and that your children helped him get back home."

Christopher-John and Little Man shot a nervous glance at Stacey, their eyes revealing their worry that we might be in trouble all over again.

"Mr. Macabee is aware of this as well, but he and I both agree that there's no point in taking T.J.'s testimony beyond the time he says he got a ride back from Strawberry. If we go beyond that time, we'll have to get into the whole business of the lynching attempt and Macabee doesn't want that. And I don't want your children involved . . . in any way."

Papa nodded and Mama said, "We appreciate that, Mr. Jamison. More than you know."

Mr. Jamison appeared to be somewhat embarrassed by Mama's words. He looked at her, allowing a slight nod.

"Excuse me, Mr. Jamison," said Stacey, "but there any chance of colored folks getting to be on that jury?"

I expected Mama and Papa to reproach Stacey for butting into so serious a conversation. Neither did.

Mr. Jamison's gray eyes met Stacey's and his answer came as straightforward as always. "Selection of jurors is made from people registered to vote, Stacey. Seeing that there are no colored voters in Spokane County, there won't be any colored voters to draw from. And even if there were and a colored person was called to duty, there'd be so much pressure on him, he probably wouldn't serve anyway."

"Well, ain't there nothin' can be done for T.J.?"

Mr. Jamison studied the floor for a moment, then looked back at Stacey. "Son, I'll promise you this. I'll be doing all I can. What I'm planning to do is put T.J. on the stand. That means, of course, that he'll have to admit to the burglary. But if he can testify, I'm hoping that I can convince the jury that he was not the one who killed Jim Lee Barnett. If I don't put him on the stand, we don't have anything. After all, there's that farmer who picked him up right outside of Strawberry, and R.W. and Melvin Simms will be testifying that they saw him running from the Mercantile. And then there was that pearl-handled gun found in T.J.'s mattress. I can perhaps punch some holes in the prosecutor's case, but not enough. He'll *have* to take the stand."

"And . . . and if they don't believe him?"

"Then we'll try to get an appeal, another trial."

Stacey nodded and said no more.

Mr. Jamison waited as if expecting more questions. I kept hoping that one of the grown-ups would ask the questions I would have liked to ask about the proceedings, but none of them did. It was as if the verdict was already in.

With no more questions asked, Mr. Jamison said, "David,

there was something else. I was wondering if any of you are planning on going to the trial?"

Papa took his pipe from his pocket and hit it hard against his palm as if he expected ashes to come out, but since there had been no tobacco for several months, the action was more out of habit than expectation. "Don't know yet. The Averys are close friends."

"I know that," said Mr. Jamison, his words slow and spaced and full of meaning. "They know it too. They know also how folks in town feel about you. That feeling, it's still there, and if you or Mr. Morrison or any of your family go into town, it could make things worse for the boy. Folks haven't forgotten about that boycott, and they blame you for it." He paused, then added, "And then, there's still the coincidence of that fire. . . ."

My heart began to race wildly.

Papa put the pipe in his mouth. He never said anything where any white people were concerned, not even Mr. Jamison, without having carefully thought it through first. There was no rushing him. Withdrawing the pipe, he smiled faintly. "I ain't hardly forgotten that. You think I would?"

Mr. Jamison returned his smile, showing he understood. "No, David, didn't think you had." He stood up. "Well, I guess I'd best be getting on back toward town. My wife's probably been looking for me this past hour. Mrs. Logan, I'd thank you for my hat."

When Mr. Jamison had left with both Papa and Mr. Morrison walking out with him, Big Ma commented: "It sho' gotta be hard on that man tryin' to help T.J. like he is."

"Probably more than we even know," Mama said.

We heard the car leave, and after a few minutes when

Papa and Mr. Morrison did not return, Little Man went to the front door and opened it.

"Clayton Chester, don't you go out there!" Mama said, forbidding his leaving with his given name, so seldom used.

Little Man glanced back at Mama, not daring to disobey, but there was fear in his eyes, for since the fire he had been afraid that Papa or Mr. Morrison or Stacey would leave at night and never return.

"But Papa—"

"He's all right. Mr. Morrison too. Now close the door."

Little Man obeyed but didn't move from the door, and as soon as he heard footsteps on the steps swung it open.

Papa's eyes met Mama's as he entered and saw Little Man. "Well, thank you, son," he said. Little Man trembled and Papa took his hand. "Looks like ole man winter's gone and got you cold. I 'spect you best get your book and come sit over here closer to me and this fire and get yourself warm."

Little Man hurried to do his bidding. Retrieving his book, he dashed back to Papa's side, and taking the chair which Papa had pulled close to his own, he opened his book, then looked up at Papa. Papa winked and Little Man smiled. He remained at Papa's side the rest of the evening.

The days before the trial were long and filled with few thoughts other than what would happen to T.J. At school older students talked of little else. At home Mama and Papa tried to make the boys and me see that, most likely, the trial would change nothing. They did not want us to get our hopes up. Still, though I knew they believed what they told us, I couldn't help but wish that a miracle would happen and T.J. would go free. After all, the Bible was always talking about miracles. I figured that if Daniel could get out of the lion's den alive and Jonah could come up unharmed from the belly of a whale, then surely ole T.J. could get out of going to prison.

T.J. consumed my mind. Each night I prayed long and hard asking God to save him, and once I was asleep, my dreams swept me back to the heat of the August night when T.J. had come pounding on our door and Stacey, Christopher-John, Little Man, and I had sneaked out into the thundering night to walk him home, only to deliver him into the hands of a mob ready to lynch him. Sometimes in those dreams I became T.J. and I awoke with a scream, shaking and unable to dispel the memory of the coarse rope binding my neck. Big Ma would hold me to her and Mama and Papa would come in from the next room, but I would not talk about the dreams. They were too real.

I knew that Mama and Papa were worried about the boys and me. Sometimes I found them, and Big Ma and Mr. Morrison as well, watching us as if trying to read our thoughts. When they talked to us about what we could expect of the trial, about what could happen to T.J., we listened but said very little, for it seemed that everything had already been said. Of all of us, I believed that they worried most about Stacey. He was silent and moody and was always going off alone to the pond or the fields or the pasture. More than once I saw Papa or Mama staring after him when he went, but they said nothing to him. Once Mama had started to follow, but Papa held her back.

"Ain't nothin' more we can say to him, sugar. What he gotta do is work it out in his own head how things are. He need us, he'll come on back and talk."

Mama had conceded somewhat doubtfully to Papa and had not followed; but I had. I was worried about Stacey too. I knew that he was upset not only because of what was happening to T.J., but because Mama and Papa were not allowing him to go to the trial. When I caught up with him, I tried to talk to him about it.

"Boy, how come you mopin' 'round like you are? Don't it make sense to you how come Papa decided not to go to that trial?"

Stacey didn't answer.

"And how come they ain't gonna let you go either?"

Stacey looked at me and turned away. There had been an old man's sorrow in his eyes, and a deepening frown across his forehead which now seemed always to be there.

"You know," I said, "what happened to T.J., it ain't your fault."

"Ah, I know that. It's just that . . ."

"What?"

"I just keep thinking that . . . that maybe I should've tried more to talk some sense into him—"

"Couldn't nobody talk any sense into T.J. and you know it!" I exclaimed, not liking to see him this way. "T.J. was a fool, and if the truth was known most likely still is."

Stacey cast me a disapproving glance as if T.J.'s impending fate made it disrespectful to talk of him this way. But I didn't care. It was the truth.

Stacey shook his head at my outspokenness, then, dismissed it, and confided: "Little Willie's talking 'bout going to the trial."

"Is?"

Stacey nodded. "Clarence too."

I grew scared. "You—you ain't thinkin' 'bout disobeying Papa and trying to go?"

He looked at me, his eyes searching mine to see if he could trust me. I tried to hide my fear, but it showed through.

"Ah, Little Willie and Clarence, they just talking," he scoffed with a hurried laugh.

I stared at him suspiciously. "You sure?"

"Don't worry. Ain't none of us goin' nowhere."

But I did worry, and on the morning of the trial I found that all my fears had been justified. As Stacey, Christopher-John, Little Man, and I approached the second crossroads on the way to school, Moe and Clarence were waiting.

"We got us a way in," Clarence announced as soon as we were within earshot.

Immediately I pounced on him. "A way into where?"

Clarence, looking somewhat uneasy, hooked his arm into Stacey's and stepped with him and Moe to the side of the road. Christopher-John, Little Man, and I stepped right behind them.

"Aunt Callie Jackson's sending Joe into Strawberry for somethin' or 'nother."

Stacey looked up the road. "You ask him 'bout taking us?"

"Yeah. He said okay."

"You tell him how come we wanna go?"

Clarence shook his head. "Said we had some errands— we'll tell him later. He waiting, so we'd better go."

"We'd!" I exclaimed. "Stacey ain't goin' nowheres!"

Stacey ignored me. "Moe, you going?"

Moe shrugged. "Like I said, you go, I'll go."

"Stacey, you know you can't go! Papa gonna wear you out, you go—"

"Go where?" Little Man inquired.

"Cassie, I don't go, I most likely ain't never gonna see T.J. again."

"Go where?" Little Man repeated.

"Well, that ain't no great loss!" I cried, too afraid for Stacey's safety at the moment to concern myself with T.J.'s future. "You gettin' into trouble ain't gonna help him none."

"Look, Stacey, we gonna have to go, 'cause Joe ain't likely to wait too long," urged Clarence.

"Where's he waiting?"

"Down past the school."

Stacey glanced down toward Great Faith. "What 'bout Little Willie? What's he gonna do?"

"Haven't seen him yet," admitted Clarence. "But he was talkin' like he'd go if we found a way to get into town."

"It's near eight o'clock already," said Stacey. "We ain't likely to get there now 'fore noon, and even if the trial's still goin' on, we ain't gonna get back till after school's out."

Moe nodded, acknowledging the precarious timetable. Stacey and Clarence looked at him and at each other, each aware of the fate which would be awaiting them upon their return. It was Stacey who made the decision. "All right, let's get Little Willie."

"Where y'all going?" Little Man demanded once more.

"They think they going to Strawberry," I told him.

Christopher-John's eyes widened. "Strawberry! Stacey, you can't go do that! Papa said——"

"I know what Papa said, but this here is somethin' I gotta do. I'll get my whippin' when I come back, but I'm gonna have to go—done made up my mind to that."

"Well, you just better unmake it," I advised.

Stacey glared at me, but with no time to argue the point started down the road toward school between Moe and Clarence. As Christopher-John, Little Man, and I ran along behind them, I pleaded with Stacey, cajoled him, and threatened him with every dire consequence I could think of, but none of my talk changed his mind. When we reached Great Faith, he stopped.

"Now, y'all gonna have to let me do this my way. When

school's out, y'all go on home and tell Papa what I done—"

"What!"

"Tell him what I done so's y'all won't get into trouble. I'll be all right." And with that, he walked up the lawn with Moe and Clarence in search of Little Willie. Christopher-John, Little Man, and I watched him go.

"Cassie, Stacey, he gonna be all right?" worried Christopher-John. "I don't like him goin' all the way to that place by hisself."

"Me neither," admitted Little Man.

I made no comment as I watched Stacey, already nearing the middle-grades building. In a few minutes he would be back again and on his way to Strawberry. I figured if I lit out running for home, Papa riding our mare, Lady, could overtake Stacey before he got there. But only part of me wanted to do that. The other part wanted to jump on that wagon and go with him, not only to make sure he remained safe, but to see firsthand what was to become of T.J. I knew that Stacey would never allow me to go, but if he went, I knew good and well that I was going too. After all, a whipping could last for only so long, and a day like this perhaps would never come again.

I made up my mind. "I'm gonna go with him," I said. "Y'all go on up to school."

"Unh-unh," defied Little Man. "Y'all goin', I'm goin'."

"All y'all crazy!" Christopher-John declared. "Y'all know we can't be goin' all the way to Strawberry by ourselves!"

"Look, y'all just stay here. I gotta get on that wagon 'fore Stacey comes."

I ran down the road. Little Man was right behind me and Christopher-John, coming at a slower, pudgier pace, behind him. For a moment I faltered, wondering if I should turn back because of them, then ran on telling myself that they would be all right. When the wagon came into view, I stopped. I didn't see Joe, but sitting on the front seat turned sideways so that he saw us coming was Wordell Lees. Little Man, Christopher-John, and I glanced at each other, apprehensive about our proposed adventure and about approaching a figure as mysterious as Wordell. But there was no time to think about Wordell's peculiarities now. There was a tarpaulin on the wagon. If we were going anywhere, we had to get under it before the others came.

"What you gonna say to him?" whispered Little Man.

I shrugged, not knowing, and went on. Little Man and Christopher-John came slowly behind. At the rear of the wagon I nodded at Wordell. He did not nod back. Deciding that there was no time to say anything but the truth, I blurted out: "You mind if we get under this here thing so's we can ride into town with y'all? Stacey, he's goin' too, but he don't want us to go, but we gotta go if he go, but he can't know 'bout it till we get on down the road toward town so's he can't send us back. That be all right with you?"

Wordell stared at us, his sandy eyes unreadable; then he looked away into the woods as if it were no business of his. If the gesture was not one of permission, it was not denial either, and wasting no more time, I hurried into the wagon and under the tarpaulin. Little Man quickly followed my lead, but Christopher-John stood unmoving, staring up at us as if this time we really had gone mad.

"Ain't y'all even thought 'bout what Papa gonna do when he find out? And Mama and Big Ma, they's gonna be so worried—"

"We'll be back by the time we usually get home. Now shut up and get up here if you going. You ain't going, then get on back to school 'fore Stacey sees you."

Christopher-John glowered angrily up at me, his face an anguish of indecision. I knew that he did not want to go, but I also knew that if the rest of us were committed to going, he would not be left behind.

"Well?" I demanded. "What you gonna do?"

Grumbling, he got into the wagon.

"How far is it, Cassie?" Little Man asked, filled with curiosity about this town he'd never seen.

"Twenty-two miles or so."

"We gonna have to ride all the way there under this thing?"

"No—jus' far 'nough so's they can't send us back. Now y'all both be quiet and don't move and don't say nothing till I tell ya."

"We gonna sho' 'nough get a whippin'. . . ."

The road to Strawberry was rough and the wagon bed hard. As far as I could figure, we endured almost an hour under the tarpaulin before being discovered. At first I was afraid that Little Man or Christopher-John—especially Christopher-John—would give us away during the first minutes. When neither of them did, I began to wonder how two little boys who were usually so restless could remain so still. Eventually I found out as the sound of soft snoring disrupted the quiet which had settled over the wagon. Immediately, the tarpaulin was thrown back and we faced the shock and then the wrath of the four older boys.

"Y'all know what kinda trouble I'm in now!" Stacey fumed. "Me going to Strawberry by myself, Papa would've whipped me, but he'd've understood. But y'all comin' along, he ain't gonna understand that! Don't y'all know I'm responsible for y'all?"

"Then you should've stayed at school," I responded, feeling stiff from having had to lie so still and not at all like soothing his disturbed conscience.

He stared at me with fierce hostility, then turned gloomily back to the road. Everyone waited for him to say something. "Joe!" he called at last. "You gonna hafta go back."

"Ah, Stacey, what they gonna get into?" questioned Little Willie. "Look, you gonna get a whipping anyways you look at it, so why don't we go on in like we planned so's we can be with T.J. and come on back 'fore your folks get a chance to be worried. We'll all watch out for 'em."

Stacey looked away, trying to make up his mind. I started to say something, but decided I'd better not.

"Things go for T.J. the way folks say," Moe said softly, "we probably feel a lot worse than a whippin', we don't go."

Moe's statement settled it and we remained in the wagon.

By noon we were rolling down the main street of Strawberry. Christopher-John and Little Man stared out at it with bright, curious eyes, but the rest of us, having been there before, glanced around dully in a hurry to get on to the trial. Nothing much about Strawberry had changed since I'd first seen it a year ago. The verandas still sagged and the buildings still stared grayly out at the three-block asphalt road which, along with the spindly row of electrical poles lining it, brought the only touches of modernity to the place. The street, however, was strangely deserted. When I had come the one time before, it had been market day and the streets had been filled with country people and townspeople alike, sauntering along the sidewalks and in and out of the shops. Now the doors to the shops were closed, and the few people whom we did see seemed to be in a hurry to get someplace else.

We passed the Mercantile which had belonged to Jim Lee Barnett. I pointed it out to Little Man and Christopher-John. The shades were drawn as if it were closed, though I had heard that Mrs. Barnett with the aid of her brother had kept the store open after her husband's death. A farm wagon loaded down with a white family and household furniture was parked in front of the store. We glanced at them, then quickly looked away before they saw us. We guessed they had lost their farm. These days dispossessed farmers were not an uncommon sight. Another block down was where Mr. Jamison's office had stood and where rebuilding was already underway. Across from his office was the courthouse square, but before we reached the square, Joe pulled up on the reins and stopped the wagon.

"What you stopping here for?" demanded Clarence. "The courthouse is down thataway."

Joe's eyes followed the direction of Clarence's finger pointed northward, up Main, then looked back at Clarence. "This here's far as I'm gon' go thisaway."

"Ah, Joe, go on down to the courthouse," wheedled Little Willie. "It ain't gonna take you but a minute."

Joe shook his head with great animation. "Not me! No sirreeee! One time I gone farther'n this, up McGiver Street there, and Mr. Deputy Haynes seen me and he asked me what I was doin' goin' down that street on the white folks' side of town and I told him I ain't even knowed that there was the white folks' side and he sez to me, he sez, ya knows it now. Then he sez he better not never catch me down there no more less'n I got business, and he ain't gonna neither! Now y'all get on out and walk if ya goin' and don't be takin' no long time comin' back here 'cause I'se gon' be ready to go back home 'fore that sun get past them trees yonder."

"Ah, Joe, come on——" started Clarence.

"It ain't but a block," Stacey said, jumping down. "We jus' wasting time here."

As soon as we were off the wagon, Joe, without a backward glance, let out a "ged on up, ole mule" and rolled away. For a moment, we stood watching the wagon and feeling just a bit deserted, then with Stacey leading the way walked the block down Main to McGiver Street and turned up the dusty street to the courthouse.

The courthouse was a wooden building in need of a coat of paint. It faced a wide yard and a colorful flower garden which gave the area a festive air. Standing around the yard and on the steps were clusters of farm people, faded-looking men in faded overalls and faded-looking women in dresses cut from brightly patterned cotton flour sacks; townspeople stood apart from them, looking a bit smarter in their serge suits and store-bought fashions.

"Is it over?" I said.

No one knew so no one answered. Not daring to ask any of the people gathered on the lawn, we made our way through the crowd to the other end of the building, where we saw an elderly Negro gentleman sitting under a gnarled pine. Stacey approached him and asked if the trial was over. He was told that the jury had only been selected. The trial was to start after lunch.

The day was warm and the courtroom windows had been raised. We went over to the building and, climbing onto the concrete ledge which ran along its base, peeked in. Only a few people remained inside. A group of men stood talking at the front, where two sizable tables and a towering desk set upon a platform dominated the room. Two women in dark, sober-looking hats and print dresses sat on a bench midway back, and at the very rear of the room, in the left-hand corner, sat Mr. and Mrs. Avery and three of their eight children. With them were Mr. Silas Lanier and the Reverend Gabson, a few other members of Great Faith, and three people I didn't know. T.J. was not in the room.

We returned to the old man and asked him if he thought we could sit inside. He laughed. "Y'all younguns see that speck of space the colored folks squattin' in? Ain't none of 'em gon' move 'cause they's 'fraid they lose they space."

"You mean that's all the room there is for the colored?" said Stacey.

"What y'all see is all they is. White folks thinkin' they's doin' good to 'lows that much."

We thanked the man for his information, then settled beside him to wait for the trial to resume. We decided that since we could not get into the courtroom, we could station ourselves close enough to the windows to at least see T.J.

As we waited, Mr. John Farnsworth, the county extension agent walked past. Mr. Farnsworth was a pleasant-looking man whose job originally had been to visit all the farms in the area to give agricultural advice. But since last year—1933—it had also included administering the government's crop-control program, which meant keeping a close eye on each farmer's cotton production. Mama and Papa said that this additional responsibility had made him less than popular. Now as he walked through the crowd, he was greeted with cold stares and angry grumblings.

"Hey, Farnsworth!" called a white farmer nearby. "Too bad it's near winter, ain't it? Ain't got no cotton for ya to go plowin' up!"

Mr. Farnsworth ignored the taunt and went up the steps into the courthouse.

The farmer stared malevolently after him, then spat on the ground. "Like to plow him up."

"Don't start," said a man with him, his voice stringently testy.

I glanced over at the group and recognized the man as Mr. Tate Sutton, a white tenant on the Granger plantation.

The first man turned angrily. "I'll doggone start if I wanna. Got a right to say many times as I feels like it what that Farnsworth done. Here I done planted them ten acres in cotton a year ago this past spring and him and Mr. Granger come along and says I gotta plow three of 'em up! Lordy! All that seed and fertilizer and sweat gone to waste and what I got to show for it? Huh? John Farnsworth tells me the government gonna pay Mr. Granger and Mr. Granger gonna pay me, but more'n a year done gone by and I ain't seen a cent. Not a blasted cent!"

"And you think the rest of us have?" demanded Mr. Sutton. "You talkin' like you the only one it happened to."

The first man looked away.

A third man cleared his throat and spoke. "Hear tell there's some folks talkin' union."

"Union?" said Mr. Sutton. The first man turned back.

"That's right. Say that maybe that's the only way we get our money."

"You mean that union business with niggers?" said the first man.

"Mos' likely."

"Well, far's I'm concerned, hell's gonna hafta freeze over 'fore I go joinin' anything with a stinkin' nigger."

"Same here," hastily agreed the man who had brought up the union talk. "Things may be bad, but ain't nothin' that bad. . . . Lordy! Nothin'!"

The clusters of people began to break up and drift back into the court building. As they did, a thin boy with corn-blond hair wove his way toward us. He was Jeremy Simms, the younger brother of R.W. and Melvin Simms.

"Hey, Stacey. Moe. All y'all," he said.

Stacey and Moe stood to greet him.

"Hey, Jeremy," we replied.

"When'd y'all get here? Didn't see ya inside."

"Few minutes ago," Stacey answered without going into why we had not come earlier. "What's happening in there?"

"They picked the twelve men for the jury, that's all."

"Yeah, we know. It take all mornin' jus' for that?"

Jeremy shrugged. "Folks say it shouldn't've, but Mr. Jamison, he was asking a lotta questions of every man up for jury duty—"

"Like what?"

Jeremy looked uneasy. "Like . . . like did they respect the law and would they ever take the law in their own hands? . . ."

His voice trailed off, but we knew what Mr. Jamison had been trying to do. Everyone, black and white, knew of the attempted lynching. "No wonder it took so long," I muttered. "I'm right surprised they even got their twelve."

Stacey glanced at me with harsh disapproval, warning me not to be so open about how I felt in front of Jeremy. The look was justified. It was just so hard to remember that I could not say in Jeremy's presence what I could when Moe or Little Willie or Clarence were around, for Jeremy was a friend despite being a Simms. More than once he had proven that friendship and we all knew it. But he was still white, and that was what separated us and we all knew that too. Resigning myself to say nothing else, I got up and walked back over to the courthouse. Christopher-John and Little Man went with me.

"He there?" Christopher-John asked as I climbed to the cement ledge and peered in. The benches were quickly filling, but the area in front was still empty.

"Nope."

"I gotta go," Little Man said. "Where's the outhouse?"

I surveyed the area. "Maybe it's 'round back." I jumped down and we went to see. There was nothing.

"I *gotta* go!"

"Well, go on over there in them bushes then," I suggested. "Won't nobody see."

Little Man was outraged. "I ain't neither! There's folks all 'round here!"

I shrugged, ready to dismiss the problem and let Little Man work it out for himself, when I remembered what Uncle Hammer had said about some people in town having plumbing. "Maybe it's inside," I told him.

Little Man looked doubtful. "Inside? What'd it be doin' inside?"

"Come on, we'll see," I said. We found a side door and we all went in. Following a narrow hallway, we came to double doors which opened to the main corridor. A man and woman, walking briskly as if they were afraid they might miss something, hurried toward us and turned into a room midway down the hall. Two more people did the same. The rest of the corridor was empty.

Christopher-John nodded toward the open doors where the people had entered. "You s'pose that's where they got T.J.?"

"Most likely that's the courtroom," I said.

"Where's the outhouse?"

I sighed irritably. At the moment Little Man's mind was on only one thing. Leaving the protective cover of the doors, we ventured down the corridor looking from side to side, not really sure what kind of structure we were looking for.

"Look there," said Christopher-John with a nod toward a man in the last stages of buttoning his pants coming through a door marked "Gentlemen." Without a word, Little Man dashed down the corridor and through the door. Christopher-

John followed him. The man took no notice of either of them as he too headed for the courtroom.

For several moments I waited outside the men's room, then, drawn by the open doors, went down to the courtroom entrance where I tried to peek between the spaces not filled by people, several deep, lining the back wall. I thought about squeezing in and working my way around to where Reverend Gabson and the Averys were, but before I could make up my mind to do so, a man stepped to the doors and closed them. It hadn't been such a great idea anyway.

With nothing further to see, I turned and headed back down the corridor. As I did, a young woman came from an office and bent over a water fountain. I watched her drink, the water arching toward her like a colorless rainbow. When she stepped away from the fountain, she saw me watching her. She glanced at me somewhat oddly, then crossed the hall, her high heels clicking noisily against the wood floor, and went back into the room. As soon as the door closed behind her, I hurried over to the fountain and twisted the knob. The water shot up, slapping me coldly across the face. I jerked back, startled, then tried again.

"Cassie!"

I looked around. Jeremy Simms stood at the main entrance of the courthouse staring down at me.

"What's the matter?" I said.

Walking, then running, Jeremy came toward me, his arms waving frantically. "Cassie! Get away!" he hissed in a whispery cry which filled the empty corridor.

"Boy, jus' what's the matter with you?" As Jeremy reached me, I could see that his face was flushed. "You sick or somethin'?"

Jeremy didn't answer as he looked nervously around him.

"C-Cassie, you can't—you can't drink from there. Ya best get 'way 'fore somebody sees ya."

"You crazy? You ain't Stacey. You can't be tellin' me what to do—"

Before I could finish, Jeremy grabbed my arm and pulled me several feet from the fountain. I jerked loose, furious. "Boy, you jus' wait till we get outside—"

"Cassie, Cassie," he murmured hoarsely, waving his hand to silence me. There was an urgency in his manner as he turned away and stared down the corridor. I followed his gaze. Three farmers had just entered. They plodded heavily to the courtroom, opened the door, and disappeared inside. With his eyes still on the door, Jeremy asked where Christopher-John and Little Man were.

"Jus' don't you worry 'bout where they are, 'cause boy, you done torn your britches with me."

Jeremy looked at me now. "Where, Cassie?"

Again, there was that urgency.

"They in there," I said, pointing to the men's room.

Without another word, Jeremy rushed over to the door and swung it open. Before the spring had pulled it to again, he was at the entrance with Little Man and Christopher-John in tow. With his right arm outspread, keeping Little Man and Christopher-John securely behind him, he searched the corridor. Finding no one there but me, he pushed them out and toward the side entrance. He didn't say a word to me. I followed them, as he no doubt knew I would. Once outside I lit into him again.

"Jeremy, how come ya done that, huh? How come ya went and pulled me like ya done?"

Jeremy stopped and looked at me. "You—you jus' shouldn't've been drinking in there, Cassie."

"Whaddaya mean I shouldn't've been drinking there? I was thirsty!"

"I—I know, but—"

"Other folks was drinking there—"

"Yeah, but—"

"Aw, you jus' make me sick. I wasn't even finished."

"I'm jus' real sorry, Cassie, but—"

"—You ole peckerwood!"

Jeremy's face paled as he stared at me through eyes that were a faded blue. Before he looked away, I saw the pain there.

"Jeremy—"

"Stacey," he said, pointing up ahead and not letting me finish. "Here he come."

I looked around. Stacey was coming with Moe beside him. That he was furious was obvious.

"Lord-a-mercy, Cassie, where'd y'all go off to?" he demanded, anger and relief both mixed in his face. "We been looking all over the place for y'all. Little Willie and Clarence even gone back up to the main road and here the trial is gettin' started. Now where y'all been?"

Jeremy answered for us. "They was in the courthouse, Stacey. Cassie, she . . . she was drinking the water and Christopher-John and Little Man, they was using the toilet."

Stacey's face changed. He glanced anxiously from Jeremy to Christopher-John, Little Man, and me, then back to Jeremy. "Anybody see 'em?"

Jeremy shook his head. "Don't think so. I—I better be gettin' back." He turned to go, but as he did so, he looked at me. That awful pain was still there. Then he hurried up the courthouse steps, bouncing on the balls of his feet as he walked. I had hurt him and I knew it. No matter how angry I was at him, I should never have called him what I had.

Still, he had wronged me badly, pulling on me like he had, and I wasn't about to forget it.

"Stacey, you know what that doggone Jeremy done? He grabbed my arm like this here," I said, replaying the scene by taking hold of Stacey's upper arm, "and jus' come jerking me 'way from that water and I wasn't even finished——"

Stacey pulled his arm from my grasp. "Jus' hush up, Cassie. Hush up!" he snapped. "That water in there and them toilets, they belong to the white folks, and the white folks don't want no colored folks using neither one. Somebody'd caught y'all, we'd be in a real mess of trouble. Papa say folks done got killed for less. Doggonit, I was afraid of this! Papa gonna wear us all out as it is. You think I want him worrying 'bout somethin' a whole lot worse?"

"But——"

"Don't wanna hear no buts! Y'all just stay next to me from now on, ya hear?" Little Man and Christopher-John stared up at Stacey in bewilderment. Moe looked on, his face sympathetic, his manner backing Stacey. "Ya hear?" Stacey repeated, demanding an answer.

Little Man and Christopher-John gave him one, but I was too puzzled to answer. There was so much to learn, too much of it bad. Water was water, a toilet a toilet. Were the people crazy?

Stacey seemed to read the question in my eyes for he nodded, the scowl of anger etching deeper into his face. "Let's get on back," he said and directed us toward the tree where the old man still sat. "T.J.'s in the courtroom."

3

From our perches in the trees which overlooked the court-room, we could see T.J. sitting beside Mr. Jamison. He looked even skinnier than he had been when I had last seen him four months ago, and he seemed nervous, biting at his lower lip and jumping visibly at the sounds around him. As the proceedings began, he glanced back at his parents, then turned stiffly to face the prosecutor, Mr. Hadley Macabee.

The first witness called was Mrs. Jim Lee Barnett. Her story was that she and her husband had gone to their second-floor living quarters above the Mercantile shortly after six, as was their custom, had supper, and retired about eight o'clock. They were awakened about an hour later by noises from below. With Mr. Barnett leading the way, they went downstairs to investigate and found three Negroes standing there and the store's safe open. Mr. Barnett, trying to stop the burglary, had attacked one of the Negroes, but a second Negro holding an axe had hit him on the back of his head with the blunt of the axe. Once Mrs. Barnett saw her husband down, she had attacked the men herself, but was swiftly knocked out by one of them. When she came to, she found her husband still unconscious and bleeding badly from the head wound. The men were gone. At this point she started screaming and ran outside for help.

When Mr. Macabee asked Mrs. Barnett who were the first to come to her aid, she replied that at the time she was quite dazed and couldn't remember everyone, but she did remember Mr. Courtney Jones, proprietor of the pool hall, and R.W. and Melvin Simms.

Mrs. Barnett's testimony was liberally laced with tears and emotion, and it was clear that most of the court spectators greatly sympathized with her. The jury members sat with their backs to us, so we could not see their faces, but I had no doubt that they too were sympathetic. Even I, as much as I disliked the woman and felt no loss at all for her bigoted husband, felt pity for her.

But not for long.

Once Mr. Macabee had finished with Mrs. Barnett, Mr. Jamison, speaking loudly enough to be heard by everyone, yet evoking a calm quiet that seemed almost a whisper, began to question her. He was very gentle, apologizing that he had to ask her to relive that night again, but that he needed to know exactly what she and her husband had done upon hearing the noises in the store. Mrs. Barnett seemed leery of Mr. Jamison at first, but recounted that night's events as she had been asked.

She repeated that they got up.

"Yes," said Mr. Jamison.

And went to their bedroom door.

"Yes."

And through the living room—

"Yes."

And to the hall and down the stairs—

"Just a minute, Mrs. Barnett," Mr. Jamison gently interrupted. "Did you turn on the light first? As I recall, there is a light switch at the top of the stairs leading down to the store."

Mrs. Barnett frowned in thought, trying to remember, then she said: "No sir, we didn't turn it on 'cause it hadn't been working for more'n a month. The one downstairs worked, but not that one. Jim Lee—bless his heart—had been intending to fix it, but never got 'round to it. It still ain't fixed."

Mr. Jamison bowed his head slightly as if in respect for the kind intentions of the departed, then probing just as gently asked if the light was on downstairs in the store.

Again Mrs. Barnett was thoughtful. No, she conceded, as if to a friend, the light was not on. She and Mr. Barnett always turned it off before retiring and the thieves had not turned it on.

"Then, Mrs. Barnett, how did you see?"

"Oh, we had a flashlight," she answered matter-of-factly. "We always kept one by the bed. An oil lamp too. Never could tell when the electricity might go out."

"I see. You had a flashlight. . . . You didn't tell me." Mr. Jamison's tone was not one of accusation but of feelings hurt by her neglecting to confide that bit of information to him.

"I'm sorry," apologized Mrs. Jim Lee Barnett.

"What about your glasses, Mrs. Barnett? Did you have time to put them on? I notice that most times when I've seen you, you have them on . . . like now."

"Yessir, I always wear them. Had to since I was a young girl. Nearsighted, you know——"

"And did you wear them that night?"

There was silence as Mrs. Barnett pondered the question. "You know, I don't believe I did. No, I didn't, 'cause the flashlight was on Jim Lee's side of the bed and I didn't have no light. I remember reaching for my specs, trying to feel them on the nightstand with my hand, but I was so nervous and Jim Lee was already at the door going into the living room, and I was 'fraid he was goin' downstairs by hisself."

"So you didn't have on your glasses—which you say you need—and you did have a flashlight, and you started down the stairs——"

"That's right."

"And did you and your husband go straight down the stairs and into the store——"

"Yes——"

"——or did you stop on the stairs, just for a moment or two?"

"Come to think of it, you know we did stop. That's when we saw them."

"Saw whom?"

"The nigras."

"I see. About how far would you say you were from the intruders? Could you tell us in relationship to the courtroom?"

Mrs. Barnett frowned again. "'Bout as far back as them middle benches there, I'd reckon."

Mr. Jamison nodded. "About twenty feet then."

"Yes," she agreed.

"And just where were the intruders standing when you first saw them?"

"Well, one of them was at the gun counter and them other two was by the safe."

"You stated previously that one of the intruders struggled with Mr. Barnett and another one hit him from behind with the axe. Now which two men were involved in this? The ones at the safe, or did the one from the counter join in?"

"It was them two by the safe, but I figure that other one would've joined in if he'd've gotten a chance."

"Just answer the question, Clara," Judge Havershack said from his bench. "Wade didn't ask you about what that fella *would've* done."

Mrs. Barnett heaved an exasperated sigh.

"It was the two by the safe," Mr. Jamison repeated. "Did that third person—the one by the gun counter—strike Mr. Barnett at all or attempt to harm him physically in any way?"

Mrs. Barnett conceded that he had not.

"Now, Mrs. Barnett, when your husband went down the steps, did he still have the flashlight?"

"He did. Used it to defend hisself 'gainst them murderers. Dropped it when he fell. Light stayed on though, so's I was able to see."

"Mrs. Barnett, you said that you saw three Negroes. I understand from Dr. Crandon that for many people with uncorrected myopic vision—nearsightedness—everything is blurred from a distance of twenty feet and that they would not be able to define any facial features. Were you able to distinguish the facial features of the intruders?"

"I know a nigra when I see one!" she snapped.

"Yes, ma'am, no doubt, but could you describe these particular Negroes to us?"

"They was black, that's all I know."

"But you did not see their features?"

"No, I didn't."

"What about other features, such as height? Could you distinguish the height of the intruders at the distance of twenty feet?"

Mrs. Barnett seemed uncertain.

"Mrs. Barnett, I wonder if you'd take off your glasses so that we can try a little experiment?"

Mrs. Barnett turned toward Judge Havershack, a surging rebellion on her face, and Mr. Macabee stood to object.

"What's this leading up to, Wade?" asked Judge Havershack.

"Mrs. Barnett has told us she didn't have on her glasses. I think that we all need to know just how much she could see."

The judge considered. "All right," he decided. "Take off your glasses please, Clara."

Mrs. Barnett let out another sigh and took them off. Mr. Jamison then went down the aisle and spoke to several men seated on a bench near the center of the courtroom. The men stood and came into the aisle; R.W. and Melvin Simms were among them. Mr. Jamison asked Mrs. Barnett if she recognized any of the men. Mrs. Barnett squinted fiercely, but finally admitted she couldn't see who they were. He then asked if any of the men were the same height as the intruders. She was not to worry, he said, that the men standing were white; they were simply helping out the court. With no hesitation, Mrs. Barnett dismissed three of the men as being either too tall or too short. She said the remaining two were the right height. The two were R.W. and Melvin.

"And how can you be so certain about the height?" Mr. Jamison asked her.

"'Cause Jim Lee and them two he was fighting with were

near to the same height. Jim Lee was five ten. Them two gentlemen standing next to you look to be near the same height as you from here, and Jim Lee and you was the same."

"How tall was the man behind the counter?"

"Well, I didn't much pay attention to him. He never got close to Jim Lee."

Mr. Jamison turned to Melvin and R.W. and asked them their heights. They blanched, looking uneasy. "It's just to get a fix on the height of the intruders, gentlemen," Mr. Jamison assured them. "Nothing personal." The Simmses glared at him suspiciously, but gave their heights: five feet nine inches and five feet ten and a half inches.

Mr. Jamison then asked that T.J. be brought down the aisle. Slowly T.J. stood and I saw that his hands, which he had kept under the table, were cuffed; his legs were free. Led by Deputy Haynes, he walked toward Mr. Jamison and stood beside R.W. and Melvin Simms. The courtroom was silent as everyone noted the difference in size. T.J. was much shorter and smaller.

"Mrs. Barnett, look at T.J. carefully now," Mr. Jamison directed. "Having just identified men of five ten and a half, and five nine of being the approximate height of the men who fought and struck your husband, can you say that T.J. was one of these men?"

Mrs. Barnett bit into her lip. There could be only one answer. But Mrs. Barnett said, "I don't know . . . it was dark. . . ."

"Not that dark. You yourself said that throughout there was light from the flashlight. That you could see. Now, was T.J. one of the men?"

Mrs. Barnett put on her glasses and replied crisply, "I can't be certain." Mr. Jamison gazed at her with great patience. "Well . . . maybe he wasn't. . . . I can't be sure. . . ."

"Can't you?" Mr. Jamison's voice was suddenly stern. "You just told this court that the two men who—"

Mr. Macabee jumped up and objected. He said that Mrs. Barnett had already given her answer and that should satisfy the court. Judge Havershack agreed. He ordered R.W. and Melvin to sit down and for Deputy Haynes to bring T.J. back to the defender's table.

Mr. Jamison turned again to Mrs. Barnett. Softly, he said, "Mrs. Barnett, I know you want—as does most everyone in this room including myself—the murderer of your husband to pay for his terrible crime. Now, with that in mind, I want you to think very carefully about this next question." He paused as if trying to put the question right in his mind before saying it. But to my surprise, he asked no question right then. Instead, he walked over to the court table and opened a thin box and lifted out its contents. Walking back to Mrs. Barnett, he displayed what was in the box: two black stockings.

"Mrs. Barnett, these as you know are ladies' stockings. They were found in the trash outside your door the day after your husband was murdered. Such items are, of course, usually worn in times of grief." He nodded at Mrs. Barnett, who crimsoned just a bit and tucked her own blackened legs farther inward to her chair. "Or sometimes just to give an aura of blackness. Now, ma'am, please forgive the personal question, but outside your time of mourning as now, have you worn stockings of this coloring?"

Mrs. Barnett said she hadn't, and to Mr. Jamison's question as to whether or not she had been in mourning at any time during the past year and had perhaps just thrown away such stockings, she again said she had not.

"Now, Mrs. Barnett, please look at my hand." Mr. Jamison held up his hand for her to see, then slipped it inside one of the stockings. "What color does my hand appear to be?"

Mrs. Barnett looked from Mr. Jamison's hand to his face, then back to his hand again. "Well . . . black."

"Mrs. Barnett, since you yourself said that you saw no features of the men, but that they were definitely black, do you think that it was possible that the men could have been wearing stockings? Black stockings?"

A murmur rose in the courtroom.

"That perhaps the men who fought with your husband, who killed him, might not have been black at all, but white men wearing black stockings so that you would think that they *were* black?"

A wave of disbelief rose and crescendoed as Judge Haveshack wildly pounded his gavel and threatened repercussions until all was quiet again. Then he glowered down at Mr. Jamison. "Now, Wade, you know all that's supposition. You got no right to ask this witness to testify to what was in the minds of her attackers."

Mr. Jamison nodded. "Then Mrs. Barnett, tell me this. Without having seen any of their features—noses, mouths, eyes, hair—only the blackness of their faces, can you swear that the men who killed your husband were Negroes? Before God Almighty, can you swear that?"

Mrs. Barnett stared at Mr. Jamison. Doubt had set in. She stared at the stocking still covering Mr. Jamison's hand, then up at Mr. Jamison. She puckered her lips, wet them, and answered: "No, I can't say that I can. I surely can't. . . ."

R. W. Simms and Melvin Simms followed Mrs. Barnett on the witness stand. Both testified that they had seen T.J. and two other Negroes running from the back of the Barnett Mercantile when they had come into town to shoot pool at Courtney Jones' place. When asked by Mr. Macabee why they hadn't become suspicious and stopped them, they told the court that they had recognized T.J., whom they had once befriended, and T.J. had told them that he and the other Negroes had just come from Ike Foster's shed, where they had been playing cards and had been accused of cheating. They claimed, according to R.W. and Melvin, that they were fleeing with their winnings.

R.W. laughed. "At the time, I thought it was nigger business. Let them take care of it. . . ."

To our surprise, Mr. Jamison did not question R.W. or Melvin, but passed over them with what he called the right to recall.

Mr. Macabee then called the white farmer who had given T.J. a ride back from Strawberry in his wagon on the night of the break-in. He testified that he had picked T.J. up shortly after nine o'clock on Soldiers Road, and that T.J. had told him he was coming from Strawberry. Mr. Jamison asked the farmer if he had noticed whether or not T.J. had been hurt. The farmer said that T.J. had been hurt and that he had said two men had beaten him, but had not said who. Following the farmer, Sheriff Hank Dobbs testified that the gun Mrs. Barnett had earlier identified as having come from her store had been found by Clyde Persons, a citizen of the town deputized to apprehend the thieves.

"Deputy, my foot!" I grumbled. "Ole Clyde Persons was one of them lynchmen."

"Hush, Cassie," Stacey ordered. I hushed.

Clyde Persons was called, and testified that he had indeed found the pearl-handled pistol in T.J.'s corn-husk mattress. Next Dr. Crandon told of Jim Lee Barnett's and Mrs. Barnett's conditions when he arrived on the scene. He described Mr. Barnett's head injury, what treatment he had administered, and told the time of death.

With his testimony the prosecution rested its case, and Mr. Jamison stood up. "I'd like to call T.J. Avery to the stand," he said.

All the fidgeting that had gone on during the last testimonies ceased, and all grew quiet. The faces of the boys around me were tense, anxious, waiting. I stopped breathing as T.J. stood. He looked around the courtroom, bewildered, as if too afraid to move. Mr. Jamison nodded to him; T.J. moved mechanically to the witness stand. He was sworn in, then sat down.

Mr. Jamison started his questioning of T.J. by asking him to tell all that had happened that evening. T.J. began with the revival meeting when R.W. and Melvin had brought him up to Great Faith in their pickup. T.J.'s words were halting and unsure, all the cockiness gone.

"And just how did you come to be with R.W. and Melvin Simms that evening? Was that unusual?"

T.J. looked out over the courtroom, then quickly down at the floor. Throughout most of his testimony, he kept his eyes there. "N-no, sir. I'd been with 'em mos' of the time for the last four or five months. They even give me stuff, too, cap and tie. I . . ." His last words were mumbled.

"Speak up, T.J.," Mr. Jamison admonished kindly, "so the court can hear."

"I—I said I thought they was my friends."

A knot formed in my throat.

"Did you stay for the revival service?" Mr. Jamison asked.

"No, sir. R.W. and Mel—" T.J. stopped and looked around, realizing his mistake. R.W. and Melvin had told him he could address them using only their given names, but like everything else they had said, that too meant nothing. T.J. lowered his eyes again. "I mean Mr. R.W. and Mr. Melvin, they said to come on and we gone right to Strawberry and—"

R.W. jumped up. "That's a downright lie!"

Judge Havershack pounded his gavel and ordered R.W. to sit down and be quiet. Sullenly, R.W. looked around the courtroom, then back at the judge, and sat.

Mr. Jamison resumed his questioning. "T.J., what was your purpose for going into Strawberry?"

"Mr. R.W. and Mr. Melvin, they said they was gonna get me that pearl-handled pistol at the Barnett store. Said they'd take me up to church like I wanted, but then we was gonna go on into town to get that pistol."

"When you got into town, was the store open or closed?"

"It was closed. Mr. R.W. and Mr. Melvin said there was no sense in comin' back for the pistol after we'd come all the way into town jus' to get it. Said we'd jus' go in and get it, and if Mr. Barnett or Miz Barnett come down, we'd jus' tell 'em we was plannin' on payin' for it come Monday."

"Did you go directly into the store?"

"No, sir. We waited 'bout an hour first till the lights upstairs gone out and we figured the Barnetts was gone to sleep."

"How did you enter the store?"

"Through the back. There was a window there, real small, and I got through it and opened the door for Mr. Melvin and Mr. R.W."

"Was the window big enough for a person the size of Melvin or R.W. Simms to get through?"

T.J. shook his head. "It was tight jus' for me."

"When you opened the door, was there anything different about the Simmses?"

T.J. nodded. "They was wearing black stockings over their heads and they had on gloves. I got scared then, 'fraid they was gonna do more'n take the gun, and I wanted to leave, but they told me to stay. Then they broke the lock on the gun case and they give me my pistol."

"And just what happened then?" Mr. Jamison asked.

T.J. answered, but the boys and I couldn't hear what he said; for coming across the courthouse lawn, fussing at the top of his voice, was Joe McCalister.

"Ah, Lord, no," sighed Little Willie. We had lost all track of the time.

Stacey looked from Joe to T.J. and started down. "Well, we better go try and shut him up 'fore we get in more trouble than we already in."

Little Willie, Clarence, and Moe followed him down. Christopher-John, Little Man, and I stayed behind in the tree.

"It's way past time to go!" Joe cried. "I told y'all young-uns on the way down here my Aunt Callie get after me I ain't home 'fore dark and I jus' been a-waitin'. Y'all knows I don't like to be down here in the white folks' street!"

I was afraid that the people inside the courthouse would hear Joe's hollering, but no one seemed to notice.

When the boys reached him, they turned him back toward the wagon. But Joe stopped halfway there, waving his arms angrily in the air. After a minute or so, Stacey left the group and went over to the wagon, where Wordell was haunched by one of the wheels staring silently out at the scene. Stacey haunched beside him, then stood again, waiting. Wordell looked up at him, got up, and walked over to Joe. There were several more long moments of hefty yelling by Joe before finally he turned with Wordell and went back to the wagon. Stacey, Clarence, Little Willie, and Moe came back to the tree.

"What happened?" I asked Stacey as he settled onto his branch.

"Joe wanted to go right now, but Wordell got him to stay. What's happening down there?"

"He did? He actually talked?" I asked, my fascination for Wordell momentarily forcing out more important matters.

"Course he talked," Stacey snapped. "Now be quiet."

I turned my attention back to the trial.

"—and you say it was R.W. Simms with a black stocking covering his face who hit Jim Lee Barnett with the axe, and that it was R.W. who shoved Mrs. Barnett, rendering—leaving—her unconscious." Mr. Jamison leveled his gaze at T.J. "Is that correct?"

"Y-yes, sir." T.J. went on to explain what had occurred after both the Barnetts had been knocked out. He told of his trying to run, his threat to tell of what had happened, and the Simmses beating him.

Mr. Jamison turned so that the spectators could see his face. His look was thoughtful, concerned. "T.J., you've said that R.W. and Melvin Simms told you they were going to get the pearl-handled gun for you. And you've said that you reached the store after closing and that R.W. and Melvin Simms said that you would just go in and take the gun." Mr. Jamison turned back toward T.J. and lowered his voice so that it was softer, confidential, but could still be heard.

"Now, T.J., I want you to be very truthful, both with yourself and with the court. Did you realize you were doing wrong?"

T.J. looked at Mr. Jamison. He bit into his lip, then looked back at his cuffed hands. "Yes, sir."

"Then why did you do what you did? Why did you break into that store?"

T.J. looked up, his eyes wide, as if he was sure everyone had already understood. He hesitated a moment, then said meekly, "They told me to. . . ."

"At any time, T.J., for any moment, did you do physical harm against either Mr. Barnett or Mrs. Barnett?"

"No sir, I didn't! I never did! I ain't never lifted a hand 'gainst neither of 'em and I wish—I wish to God I ain't never gone in there. . . ."

Mr. Jamison sat down; Mr. Macabee stood up. For an interminable time he gazed at T.J. and T.J. cowered under that gaze. Then Mr. Macabee approached the witness stand.

"You've done a lot of talking, boy . . . about the Simmses and yourself," said Mr. Macabee. "About what-all they done for you and about what they told you to do. In fact, you've done so much talking, a body would just about suspect that you didn't have much to do at all with the murder of Jim Lee Barnett . . . that you are simply a victim of circumstances. But what I want to know is why you have chosen to malign two hardworking young men who only did good by you?"

"I—"

"You say R.W. and Melvin Simms gave you things—a cap, a tie—and this is how you repay them? By trying to put the blame on them when it was actually two of your own kind who killed Mr. Barnett?"

"No sir, it was—"

"I say it's so. That you're protecting the two other nigras who took that money—"

Tears began to roll down T.J.'s face.

"—and killed Jim Lee Barnett—"

Mr. Jamison stood swiftly. "Your honor—"

"—and I also say that you knew exactly what you were doing when you entered that store, and that you are guilty of murder—"

"I object, your honor!" interceded Mr. Jamison.

"—because whether or not you actually was the nigra who dealt the death blow, the blood on your black hands is just as red and it won't wash off—"

T.J. was sobbing hysterically.

"Judge Havershack!"

"All right, Hadley, that's enough now," Judge Havershack reprimanded him without enthusiasm. But it seemed to me that Mr. Macabee couldn't have cared less about the reprimand. He had said what he had set out to say. He continued to question T.J. in a less dramatic fashion, contending that the beating T.J. had incurred was indeed the result of a falling-out among thieves: black thieves. The money had never been found; neither had the two other murderers. T.J. had just been unlucky enough to be caught, and he contended that T.J., no matter what he said, was guilty of murder. When T.J. was led sobbing back to his seat by Mr. Jamison, I noticed that the faces of the spectators had hardened, and I had the sinking feeling that it was all over.

Reverend Gabson was then called to the stand. Mr. Jamison asked him if he had seen T.J. on the night of the burglary. Reverend Gabson said that he had seen T.J. at the Great Faith revival meeting with the Simms brothers, but that none of them had stayed; all had left together. He added that most of the congregation had seen them, for they had come just before the service, which began at seven o'clock. Mr. Jamison asked if he had overheard anything that had been said between the Simmses and T.J.

"Yes, sir," replied Reverend Gabson. "Mr. R.W. and Mr. Melvin said something 'bout come on, you still want that pearl-handled pistol. They said something 'bout all of 'em going into Strawberry."

"What was T.J.'s physical condition at that time? Had he been beaten?"

"No, sir. He was fine at the church."

Reverend Gabson stepped down and Mr. Jamison called R.W. back to the stand. "Mr. Simms," said Mr. Jamison after taking several long moments to look unhurriedly through his notes on the table, "Reverend Gabson has just testified that he and a number of people at Great Faith church saw you and your brother Melvin with T.J. Avery on the evening of August twenty-fifth. Do you concur in this?"

R.W. looked sullenly at Mr. Jamison. "We was with him, if that's what ya mean. We seen him walking on the way to church and we give him a ride. That's what we done for him . . . had pity on the nigger, and look here see how we gets repaid. See these here filthy lies he been tellin'. You give a nigger an inch and he take a mile, so I guess what could we expect?" He looked past Mr. Jamison, directing the question to the people in the court. Several of the men nodded, showing they agreed.

"Did you also bring him into town?"

"Naw, we ain't done that. Him and a few of the nigra younguns had a falling-out down at the church, so he decided not to stay and we brought him on back toward his house—down far as our own place—and let him off."

"While you were at the church, did you or Melvin say anything about going into Strawberry?"

"We ain't."

"Did you say anything about getting a pearl-handled pistol for him?"

"We ain't."

"I see. All those people at the church misheard you then." There was a hint of sarcasm in his tone, but Mr. Jamison gave R.W. no time to reply. "When you left the church, you said you dropped T.J. off in front of your place. Did you then go directly to town?"

"Naw, we gone into the house first."

"How long were you home?"

"Oh, I don't know—'bout an hour, I reckon."

"And then you went?"

"That's right."

"Directly?"

"Yeah."

"In your truck?"

"Yeah."

"You and your brother Melvin?"

R.W. sighed. "Yeah, ain't I said that?"

Mr. Jamison nodded and walked from R.W., talking to him as he crossed to his table. "And why did you decide to go into Strawberry at that hour—it was quite late, was it not?"

"Wasn't so late. Me and Melvin jus' had an itch to play some pool, that's all, and Mr. Jones' is usually open late Saturdays. There ain't nothin' wrong with that."

"No," agreed Mr. Jamison, "nothing wrong with that at all." He turned to face R.W. "Just what time did you get into town?"

"How'm I s'pose to know that? Ain't got no watch. I'm just a dirt farmer, not no fancy nigger lawyer."

Mr. Jamison ignored the remark. "Well, perhaps I can

help you out. Reverend Gabson testified that church services at Great Faith began at seven o'clock and that you arrived with the Avery boy just a few minutes before that and that you left shortly after. So would you say that it was about seven o'clock when you were at the church?"

R.W. stared somewhat dubiously at Mr. Jamison. "I reckon," he said.

"And you said you then went home, dropping T.J. Avery off at that point. Now about how long would that take?"

R.W. shrugged. "Five minutes or so."

"Um," murmured Mr. Jamison rubbing his chin. "Now you stayed what you say was about an hour at home, then went into town. How long does it take for you to make that trip into Strawberry in your pickup?"

R.W. looked annoyed by the question. "'Bout forty minutes—forty-five—fifty—somewheres in there."

"So that would make it—let me see—starting from seven o'clock with ten minutes to go home, an hour at home, and some forty-five minutes to come into town—about nine o'clock when you got here. Is that correct?"

R.W. hesitated.

"Is that correct?" Mr. Jamison's voice was sharp.

"Yeah . . . Yeah, I guess so."

Mr. Jamison nodded. "Can you describe your truck to us?"

"What's that got to do with anything?"

"Just describe the truck please."

"It looks 'bout like any other 'round here."

"But if it were parked with fifty others, you'd know it?"

"Course I'd know it."

"How?"

R.W. fidgeted just a bit in his chair, glanced at the people watching him, and answered. "It's a old Model T—don't know the year. It's black mostly and kinda beat up, with a right blue fender."

"A right blue fender?" questioned Mr. Jamison.

R.W. smiled. "Yeah, me and Melvin started to paint it one time and we run outa paint."

The spectators laughed. Mr. Jamison smiled as well. "A very distinctive truck then," he said. "One most likely not to be confused with any other, wouldn't you say?"

The grin left R.W.'s face. "Reckon not."

Mr. Jamison again turned his back to R.W. and lowered his head as if in deep thought, then faced him again. "What would you say if I told you that I have a man here who says he saw that distinctive truck of yours with its blue fender parked near the Barnett Mercantile on the night of August twenty-fifth, a few minutes after eight o'clock, an *hour* before you said you and your brother were in town. Just what would you say to that?"

Talking swelled in the courtroom as people discussed this new possibility. Judge Havershack's gavel brought silence once more. The judge looked down at R.W., who had lost all coloring, then pointed an accusing finger at Mr. Jamison. "There you go with that suppositioning again, Wade. Now you got such a witness?"

There was a pause before Mr. Jamison answered.

"I have," he said.

"Some lying nigger, no doubt," accused R.W., his eyes flashing angrily.

"No," said Mr. Jamison calmly, then nodded to the center of the courtroom. "Mr. Justice Overton."

All eyes in the courtroom turned to a slight, bald man dressed in a dark suit and looking quite respectable amidst his peers.

For a moment all was quiet.

Then R.W. stood up, hat in hand, the color returning to his face in an angry red, and pointed accusingly at Mr. Jamison. "I knows what you tryin' to do, Wade Jamison! I knows it and everybody else here knows it! You're a nigger in white skin, that's what you are. Fact, you worse than a nigger—"

Judge Havershack beat his gavel against the table, but R.W. paid no attention.

"You went 'gainst your own kind supportin' them niggers in their wagoning up to Vicksburg last spring, and here you supportin' 'em now. All you wants is to get your niggers off! You don't care what lies you spread 'bout decent white folks—"

"Now, R.W., I'm not going to have this," threatened Judge Havershack. "You remember where you are."

"I remembers all right and I jus' wanna say this." He turned to the jury. "What kinda country is this when a white man's gotta defend hisself 'gainst a nigger? Huh? I jus' wants to know that? Well, I ain't sayin' no more. I done said the truth, and if a white man can't believe that over what that lyin' nigger said, then . . ." Once again his eyes fell upon Mr. Jamison. "He jus' might as well be a nigger his own self."

Mr. Justice Overton was called, and Melvin Simms recalled. Then Mr. Jamison made his summation, pleading to the jury to be merciful and reminding them that a verdict of guilty with no recommendation for clemency would result in the death penalty. "You have heard the testimonies of all the witnesses involved," he said. "You have heard Mrs. Barnett admit her doubt that T.J. was the one person who struck her husband, thereby killing him. You have heard T.J.'s account of what happened. You have heard him tell you that his accomplices that night were not black, as Mr. Macabee contends, but R.W. and Melvin Simms. You have heard as well, from both R.W. and Melvin Simms, that they had spent considerable time with T.J. and that they *were* with him that night. You have heard from Reverend Gabson that he heard the Simmses tell T.J. to come into Strawberry with them the night of the murder to get the pearl-handled gun. And you have heard the testimony of Mr. Justice Overton that he saw the Simmses' truck parked in back of the Mercantile an hour before R.W. and Melvin Simms said they were in town."

Mr. Jamison walked the length of the jury box looking at each juror in turn.

"T.J. Avery has confessed to what he has done. But I ask each of you, what really is his crime? He followed two white men blindly. They told him to break into the Mercantile and he did as he was told. Now whose fault is that? Haven't we always demanded that Negroes do as they are told? Haven't we always demanded their obedience?" He waited as if for an answer before going on. "If we teach them to follow us in what we deem is good, isn't it logical that they should follow our lead into what is not good? We demand they follow us docilely, and if they should dare to disobey, we punish them for their disobedience, as Melvin and R.W. punished T.J. by beating him. T.J. murdered no one. His guilt lies more in his gullibility, in his belief that two white men cared about him, than in anything else.

"If you are asking yourselves, did the Simmses actually play a part in all of this, ask yourselves, Why would T.J. lie about it? He is a black boy. The men of this jury are white. The man who was killed was white. Why would T.J. accuse white men of being part of the break-in that night, of being the actual murderers, when this very accusation could turn you against him? Why? Because, gentlemen, it is the truth." He searched their faces and repeated, "It is the truth. . . ."

Mr. Macabee's plea to the jury demanded that they remember that the murder of a fine, upstanding citizen had been committed and that that, above all else, had to be the deciding factor, not the age of the defendant, the color of his skin, or the color of the man murdered. He said all that and the jury heard all that, but I didn't believe for one minute that he believed it or the jury did. But they nodded and left to cast their votes.

The spectators stood and stretched. Some left the courtroom and came outside; most stayed, waiting. The boys and I joined the people on the ground and stood near the old man still sitting at the foot of the tree. None of us said anything as we avoided looking at each other, afraid our fear would be seen, until Christopher-John adamantly declared: "But T.J. ain't killed nobody! He ain't!" Stacey put his hand on Christopher-John's neck and brought him near, but said nothing. There was nothing to say now.

"Well, what you think of that nigger's story in there?"

We looked around. A group of white farmers stood nearby dividing a chaw of tobacco.

"Aw, it's just nigger talk," scoffed one of them. "Like R.W. said, the nigger was lyin'."

"Yeah . . . well, most likely," said another. "But I knows Justice Overton to be a fine and upright man, and he wouldn't be lyin' on nobody deliberate."

"Yeah. Yeah, know that. But he was mos' likely jus' mistaken this time . . . jus' thought he seen that truck."

"Yeah . . . mos' likely . . . I reckon. . . ."

Stacey moved us away.

"Stacey, what you think, huh?" I whispered. "What you think?"

Stacey looked up at the courthouse. "It's bad, Cassie. That's all I know."

"Stacey Logan! Is that you?"

We turned and found Mrs. Wade Jamison standing before us. She was a plump woman in her fifties and was dressed soberly in a dark-blue suit and hat. Although we saw her seldom, we had no trouble recognizing her, for she had one gray eye and one brown one, and a smile that seemed always to be tugging at her lips.

"Wade told me your papa said he wasn't coming in for the trial. Where is he?"

Christopher-John, Little Man, and I looked to Stacey to answer, but he didn't. He was staring at Mrs. Jamison, resentment in his face. Moe, Clarence, and Little Willie stood to the side saying nothing; Mrs. Jamison had not addressed them.

"I said where is he?" she repeated. When she still received no answer, she gazed down at us, suspicion in her double-colored eyes. "Don't tell me he's not here?"

We neither confirmed nor denied this.

Her expression hardened. "Stacey, how'd you come?"

Stacey waited, the resentment still there, then said: "Wagon."

"Whose wagon?"

"Friend's."

"Your folks know you here?"

Stacey glared at her, showing her he felt it was no business of hers. "We had to see T.J. was all."

"And your folks think y'all at school? Lord, Lord! They must be plumb out of their minds with worry 'bout you all

. . . or leastways they will be before long. How you getting home?"

"Same way we come."

"By wagon? It'll be way past this little one's bedtime by then." She put out her hand to touch Little Man's face. He stepped back, away from her. Mrs. Jamison sighed deeply, looking at all of us, and went back into the courthouse. A few seconds later Mr. Jamison appeared in a courtroom window and stuck out his head.

"Stacey!" he summoned.

Stacey looked up and walked over.

"After the verdict's in, all of you wait for me. I'll take you home."

"We got a way home."

"Not a way that'll get you there before your folks start getting worried."

"There's seven of us and we got a ride with folks waiting on us."

Mr. Jamison glanced past Stacey to Moe, Little Willie, and Clarence. He had been around their families enough to know who they were. He nodded. "You can all squeeze in. Tell your friends in the wagon to go on."

"What 'bout the Averys? Won't they need a ride back?"

"They're staying in town tonight. They want to be near T.J." He started to turn away from the window. Stacey stopped him.

"Mr. Jamison, how much longer?"

Mr. Jamison looked out at the sun, low on the horizon. "The longer it takes, the better. Let's hope . . ." He did not finish. "Now, you all wait," he said, and left the window.

We did not have to wait long. In less than thirty minutes the jury returned. The vote poll was taken. Twelve men on the jury. Twelve votes of guilty. There was to be no mercy.

T.J. received the death penalty.

Mrs. Avery screamed. The courtroom erupted in sporadic clapping. Judge Havershack ordered immediate silence, then thanked the jury members for their fine service and dismissed them. T.J. he remanded to the hands of Sheriff Dobbs to be taken at the first opportunity to the state penitentiary at Parchman. Then he stood, adjourning the court, and left. The white courtgoers spilled from the building. Mr. and Mrs. Avery, Reverend Gabson, Mr. Silas Lanier, and the others stayed seated in their tiny corner until beckoned by Mr. Jamison to come forward.

T.J. still sat in the courtroom. He showed no emotion at all, not crying, not talking. When he had stood for the verdict, he had looked as if he had not heard it and, since he had sat again, had not moved. Now as his mother reached him, throwing her arms around him and crying as she had done the night he had been almost lynched, it must have hit him that he had been found guilty, for he let out a mournful yelp like a wounded animal, hunted, captured, and now about to die.

We 'n't watch anymore.

"Little Man, Christopher-John, Cassie, go on down," Stacey said. We obeyed him and he followed with Moe, Little Willie, and Clarence.

"Yeah, jus' like I figured," said the old man who had sat under the tree throughout the ordeal. "Trial or lynching, it always be's the same. Sho' is. Always the same. . . ."

Mr. Jamison came out from the courthouse and over to where we were. His face was drawn and his eyes bloodshot. "We can go now," he said.

"Mr. Jamison," said Stacey, his voice sounding hoarse,

"we—we wanna see T.J. 'fore we go." He paused as Mr. Jamison studied him. "We gotta do that."

Mr. Jamison nodded toward the corner of the courthouse. "They'll be bringing him out that side door to take him back to jail."

We went—Stacey, Christopher-John, Little Man, Moe Turner, Clarence Hopkins, Little Willie Wiggins, and I— to the door to wait. Others waited there too, curious to see the prisoner. Shortly the door opened and Sheriff Dobbs and Deputy Sheriff Haynes came out. T.J. was between them. There were irons on his ankles now, making him shuffle when he walked, and his hands had been cuffed behind him, making him look even more like the prisoner he was.

Stacey cleared his throat. "Hey, T.J.," he said.

At first there was no response from T.J. His head was lowered; his eyes saw no one.

"T.J. It's Stacey. We all come. . . ."

Slowly, T.J. raised his head. The dark eyes brightened in recognition, and for a moment the smile that had once come so easily flashed across his face, making me forget how much I had disliked this frail, frightened boy. Before any more could be said, Deputy Sheriff Haynes shoved his way through the crowd, taking T.J. with him. Looking back over his shoulder at us, T.J. smiled one last time, then the smile and he were gone as he bowed his head and walked on. Tears stung my eyes and he blurred before me.

We were never to see T.J. again.

4

Winter came in days that were gray and still. They were the kind of days in which people locked in their animals and then themselves and nothing seemed to stir but the smoke curling upward from clay chimneys and an occasional red-winged blackbird which refused to be grounded. And it was cold. Not the windy cold like Uncle Hammer said swept the northern winter, but a frosty, idle cold that seeped across a hot land ever looking toward the days of green and ripening fields, a cold that lay uneasy during its short stay as it crept through the cracks of poorly constructed wooden houses and forced the people inside huddled around ever-burning fires to wish it gone.

Through these days the boys and I continued to trudge to school and, once there, to scramble for one of the two pot-bellied stoves which warmed each building. After putting in our eight hours, we trudged home again. Uncle Hammer, Papa's older brother, came Christmas Eve, but the day after Christmas he was gone again, unable to stay longer. Papa and Mr. Morrison filled their days with winter chores—mending tools and making new ones, and on milder days stringing fences and chopping wood—and talked of spring and the fields. Big Ma, who enjoyed every season, settled down to her winter quilting, spreading out the pieces of her pattern by the fire as soon as breakfast and the morning chores were finished, to sew and talk with other women of the community until it was time to put supper on. As for Mama, she had her students to keep her busy.

Since the school year had begun in the fall, Little Willie and Clarence had been stopping by afternoons to ask Mama's help; now the number of students who came by daily after school had grown, and Mama practically ran a school after school. And she loved it. While the weather was still good, she often sat right on the front lawn, her legs folded beneath her, her students gathered around. Now in winter they filled the sitting area in the hour or two they could snatch before attending to their evening chores as Mama patiently explained what they did not understand. On Saturdays she actually taught lessons of her own in addition to reviewing the lessons of other teachers and, frankly, I was somewhat amazed by how many students sacrificed a morning free of school to come.

As January became February and February mellowed toward March, the boys and I looked forward to the last day of school, which would come at mid-March. School usually ended at this time so that students could return to the fields for spring planting. Had the school year extended any longer, classrooms would have been empty, for cotton sustained life, and no matter how greatly learning was respected, the cotton had to be planted, chopped, weeded, and picked if the family was to survive. Few parents expected their children to do any work other than what they and their parents had done, and education was usually sacrificed if a choice had to be made between it and the fields. Students knew this and understood it, and because they knew nothing else, for the most part did not resent it. But there were some boys and girls, like Moe Turner, who, though they did not know what else they could do outside of farming, knew that they did not want to spend their lives sharecropping, and each year they planned their escape from it.

"We gonna make it this year all right," Moe said for the third year in a row as we walked from school. "I mean it this time. Papa and me, we figurin' on planting ten acres in cotton. Crop come good, we can get off ole man Montier's place."

My comment to that ridiculous statement was: "Boy, you know good and well y'all ain't hardly gonna—"

"Cassie, wouldja hush!"

I cut my eyes at Stacey and grew silent, not out of any resignation to his so-called authority but because I figured if he wanted to let Moe continue to delude himself about this sharecropping business, then that was up to him. Yet he knew as well as I did that there was little chance of Moe's family going anywhere at the end of cotton picking. The Turners had sharecropped on the Montier plantation since the 1880's and it was less than likely that one good crop would free them from doing the same for another year.

As sharecroppers they were tied to the land for as long as Mr. Montier wanted them there. Mr. Montier provided everything for them—their land, their mule, their plow, their seed—in return for a portion of their cotton. When they needed food or other supplies, they bought on credit at a store approved by Mr. Montier where high interest rates upped the price tremendously on everything they bought. At year's end, when all the cotton had been sold and the accounts were figured by Mr. Montier, the Turners were usually in more debt than they had been at the beginning of the year. And as long as they were in debt, they could not just up and leave the land on their own, not unless they wanted the sheriff after them. And here Moe was talking about earning enough to quit sharecropping. It was pure foolishness, and if I knew it, Stacey had to know it too.

Nevertheless, a quiet rebuke of me welled from not only Stacey but Christopher-John and Little Man as well for having said anything. Moe, however, continued his trek seemingly unaffected by my words. In deep thought he walked mechanically along the road, taking no notice of me. Then, when I was beginning to think that Moe's sharecropping hallucinations had been completely dispelled by my remark, he said, "I know y'all think we can't do it . . ."

"Now, Moe, I ain't said that," objected Stacey, "and you can't pay no 'tention to Cassie here."

I shot a hostile glance Stacey's way.

"Anyways, I know it's hard," continued Moe. "Times being like they is and all. But I figure times been hard all my life. Now don't seem so much worse'n any other. Like I told my daddy, we got us as much chance of makin' it this year as any other I seen."

"You ain't seen but fourteen," I pointed out.

"What your daddy say?" Stacey asked.

Moe waited a moment before he answered. "Said he give

up tryin' to make it. Said he give up long time ago. All he care 'bout now is seeing us younguns growed and off that place."

Stacey stooped to avoid the low-hanging branch of a sweet gum tree and, breaking off a twig, stripped it down and chewed on it a moment before turning again to Moe. "I ain't saying you can't do it, Moe. Papa say you can do jus' 'bout anything you set your mind to do, you work hard enough. But you can't never tell 'bout cotton prices. 'Fore the government program we weren't getting more'n six cents a pound for good long-staple cotton. And even with the government stepping in and we getting some twelve cents a pound last year, you can't never tell 'bout what'll happen 'tween planting time and picking. Then, too, you know with the government restrictions you can't plant much as you wanna."

Moe's gentle features settled into firm lines of determination. "Gotta get out," he whispered hoarsely. "Gotta."

Stacey and I both stared at Moe. Usually such a level-headed boy, he was totally illogical when it came to the subject of sharecropping.

"Yeah," Stacey sympathized. "I know."

"No, you don't," Moe said quietly. "Y'all got y'all's own land." There was no bitterness in his voice; he was only stating the truth.

Stacey nodded, still chewing on his stick. Then he said: "Look here, Moe, you thought 'bout what if you don't? I mean, 'sides the low price of cotton, there's all the deducts to figure, and I understand you can't never tell 'bout them."

Moe sighed heavily as he considered the reality of the "deducts," the credit charges made by a sharecropper during the year which could wipe out all the money earned before the cotton seed had even hit the ground. "Don't care 'bout no deducts," he said impassively. "We gonna get out anyway. I'll get me some WPA work if I hafta. Maybe even the CCC."

"WPA?" I questioned, looking from Moe to Stacey. "What's WPA?"

"Don't know if you get any money on the CCC," Stacey said.

"I said what's WPA?" I knew what the CCC was. Civilian Conservation Corps. Stacey and other boys in the area had certainly talked about it enough. Another one of Mr. Roosevelt's programs, it trained boys in agricultural and forestry methods, and several boys from the community had gone to join it. Stacey had even wanted to go, but he was too young, and besides, Mama and Papa wouldn't have let him go anyway. But I didn't know about this WPA. "Well, what is it?"

Stacey sighed at my persistence. "Mama say they're projects or something President Roosevelt's setting up to give a lot of folks jobs. Works Progress Administration, I think she said. That hospital they're talkin' 'bout building on the old Huntington place, that's one of 'em." He turned from me and asked of Moe, "You'd leave this place and go off alone? You do that, then what your daddy gonna do?"

"Leave it?" Moe repeated incredulously. "Leave it? You doggone right I'd leave it! Leave it and ole man Montier and that nothin' son of his too." A mean scowl burnt across Moe's usually pleasant face. "You know what that ole man done the other day? Told me I oughta quit being so selfish and leave school and stay home and help my daddy. Said he thought I'd gotten just 'bout all the schooling I needed to be a farmer . . . like I care what he thought."

Moe frowned deeply. He had it in his mind that whatever he was going to turn out to be, it wasn't going to be a farmer. For the last four years, since he had finished the fourth-grade school near Smellings Creek, he, along with a few other boys and girls, had walked the three-and-a-half-hour distance to school each day, leaving their homes before dawn and not returning until after dusk. Most boys and girls who attempted the trek gave it up after a year, but not Moe. Moe was determined to finish twelfth grade and get his high school diploma, and if Mr. Bastion Montier didn't understand that, then that was just too bad.

"You tell your papa what Mr. Montier said?" asked Stacey.

Moe shook his head. "I just told Mr. Montier I wasn't planning on being no farmer and I needed my schooling."

Stacey eyed Moe. "You best watch what you say."

Moe gestured wildly. "Ah, I ain't said nothin' but the truth. I ain't gonna go talkin' outa turn or nothin'—you think I wanna get us all killed? But I tell you this one thing. I'm gonna get us some money and get us off his place any way I hafta. I'm tired of them Montiers and I ain't 'bout to let these folks down here do me the way they done T.J.—"

Moe stopped abruptly and glanced around self-consciously. Christopher-John, Stacey, and I avoided his eyes, but Little Man stared directly at Moe in silent accusation before looking away into the forest. Since Mr. Jamison had come a few weeks ago and told us his appeal for a new trial had been rejected, we had spoken very little of T.J. It was too painful.

Moe, having said too much and knowing it, continued along the road in silence. As we neared the crossroads where he would leave us, he started to speak again, but stopped as a car appeared in the crossing, coming from the north. The driver saw us, waved, and stopped the car.

"Speak of the devil," sighed Moe. "Lord, what he want?"

Driving the car was Joe Billy Montier. His sister, Selma,

sat beside him. Joe Billy rolled down his window as we approached. "Hey, Moe," he said, then nodded toward the rest of us. "How y'all doing?"

We said we were fine.

"You on your way home?" Joe Billy asked of Moe.

"Yessir," answered Moe, as he was expected to do.

"I just picked Miz Selma up at Jefferson Davis and we going on home now. You want, you can get in."

"Miz" Selma was no more than fourteen. Joe Billy looked to be eighteen or so.

Moe looked directly at Joe Billy. "I gotta stop somewheres else 'fore I go home, but thank ya kindly anyways."

I knew Moe didn't have anywhere to go but home. I think Joe Billy knew it too, but he only nodded and rolled up his window. Gassing the Ford, he sped away.

"Least he offered you a ride," I said.

"Oh, Joe Billy's all right most of the time, I guess," Moe conceded. "It's mostly his daddy I can't stand."

We said good-bye to Moe, who would follow the Granger Road as far north as Soldiers Road and from there turn westward toward his home, which was just this side of Smellings Creek. It would be dark by the time he got there.

When the boys and I arrived home, we found the county extension agent, Mr. John Farnsworth, talking to Papa in the driveway. Both Papa and Mr. Farnsworth nodded as we came up, then continued their conversation.

"Now, David," said Mr. Farnsworth, "I know how things were for y'all in thirty-three when you all signed up, but it was a new program then and a lotta things went wrong. I figured the government should've waited until thirty-four to begin their crop-reduction program 'stead of plowing up cotton ready for picking in the middle of thirty-three and leaving it to rot in the fields. Now I ain't liked that any more than anybody else."

The boys and I stopped at the well to get some water, an excuse to listen further.

"But I ain't had nothing to do with that. That decision came from Washington." Mr. Farnsworth sighed and glanced out to the west field, already planted in corn. "And, David, I ain't had nothing to do with that check business either."

Papa only looked at Mr. Farnsworth and said nothing. The boys and I waited, knowing too well how put out Papa was with the government's crop-reduction program. Although I found the government's program confusing and understood very little about it, one thing I did understand was that the government had asked us, along with all the other farmers, to plow up nearly half of our cotton two years ago, cotton already planted and blooming in the fields, and they were supposed to pay us for it. Well, they had paid us all right, with a government check. The only problem was that Harlan Granger's name had been on it.

Mr. Granger had claimed that he held a first mortgage on our cotton crop, and as Mr. Farnsworth explained it later, the government's policy was to list first mortgage holders as co-payees on the checks so that they would be sure to receive any money owed to them. Of course Mr. Granger had never held a mortgage on our crop, but since it was his word against ours, it seemed useless to fight him. As for the check, there was no way for us to cash it without Mr. Granger's signature, and if Mr. Granger signed, part of the money would go to him. So Papa, Mama, and Big Ma had decided not to sign the check at all and Harlan Granger hadn't pressed them to sign; after all, it wasn't the money he wanted. He just didn't want us to have it.

"Now I know what you thinking," said Mr. Farnsworth. "I'm the one brought you the check to endorse and I'm the one representing the Agricultural Adjustment Administration. Well, that's both so. But the truth of the matter is, all the people that signed for the program had to list everybody had a lien on their cotton. You remember that?"

"I remember," Papa said. "I remember too I ain't put Harlan Granger's name on that contract."

"Well . . . he come after you signed and said he had a lien. . . . I had to put his name down."

Papa was silent.

Again Mr. Farnsworth glanced away. "Thing is, I had no idea the government was gonna issue the checks like they done, made out to the signer and to anybody had a first mortgage on the signer's crops. It was my understanding the check was supposed to go to the farmers to give them some relief."

"Well," said Papa, "that ain't what happened."

Mr. Farnsworth nodded before going on. "Now last year you all didn't join the program and you planted as much cotton as you wanted, but what'd it get you? You lost over a quarter of your crop anyway. If you'd've been part of the program, then you would've at least had the money the government would've paid you for not planting all your cotton acres.

"I don't see it that way."

"Well, I told you I would've made sure Mr. Granger's name wasn't on the check this time, even if he made the claim again. Anyway, it's done with now and nothing we can do 'bout it. Last year's contract was for thirty-four and thirty-five, so unless you want to sign for this year now, you won't have to worry 'bout a contract . . . but you are gonna have to worry 'bout the new cotton tax."

I glanced over at Stacey; he kept his eyes on Papa and Mr. Farnsworth.

"The government's gonna have its way on this thing, David, and there ain't nothing you or me or anybody else much can do about it." He turned back to his car. "You've got the tax exemption forms there so you can put in for your bale tags. You'll need them to show how much you're allowed to grow when you take your cotton to market."

At the car he hesitated and looked again at Papa. "You know, David, I don't like these restrictions any more'n you or most anybody else. Wish the government had just hired agents of their own to do this restricting business, and let us extension agents do what we was hired to do—help you farmers with your crops. Most folks don't seem to understand that. They blame me for everything's gone wrong. . . ." He looked at Papa as if wanting his understanding, then got into the car. "See you next week," he said and backed out of the drive.

As Mr. Farnsworth headed east on the road, Mr. Granger's sleek silver Packard came from the other direction and the two cars stopped. Papa watched them a moment, then crossed to the well. "Can I get a little of that too?" he said.

"Sure thing, Papa," said Little Man. He filled the dipper with fresh water and handed it to him.

"Papa, this here cotton tax," I said. "What that mean?"

Before Papa could answer, Stacey laid a hand on his shoulder and nodded toward the road. "Look like Mr. Granger's coming up here." We all stared at the Packard, keeping our eyes on it.

Of the four major landowners in the area—the others were the Montiers, the Harrisons, and the Walkers—Harlan Granger had the largest holdings and was the most powerful. He was accustomed to getting what he wanted, when he wanted it, and one thing he had long wanted but had not gotten was our land.

The Packard sped up the road and slowed at the driveway. Mr. Granger honked his horn, summoning Papa. Papa stared at the car, then finished his water and gave the dipper back to Little Man before going down. The boys and I waited until he was halfway to the road before following him as far as the mulberry bush.

"David."

"Mr. Granger."

"Just seen Mr. Farnsworth on the road. Said he'd just been here to see y'all."

"That's right."

"He told me he spoke to you 'bout the government's tax."

"He did."

"You know why the government had to do that, don't you? To keep folks not under contract from planting as much cotton as they feel like and making more money'n folks done joined the program." He stared pointedly at Papa. "This tax is an understandable thing when you look at it right. After all, how're we gonna keep prices up if folks keep glutting the market? You and me both know prices'll fall to six, maybe five cents again."

Mr. Granger waited as if expecting Papa to say something. When Papa didn't, he added, "It's for the good of everybody."

"So I understand," Papa said.

"Good. . . . You know, David, I like you. You run foolish sometimes, but far as I can see, you got a streak of sense in you and I admire that. What I'd like to do is help y'all out. Now we done had our differences and I gotta admit you done riled me good several times—both you and Mary, and your mama too—but y'all done a good thing for me last summer keeping that fire from spreading 'cross to my place, and I ain't forgot. Now I know y'all need money, so I'd like to help y'all out if I can—maybe pay your taxes and y'all can pay me back when y'all can."

Papa tilted his head slightly at the offer, but he said: "Well, Mr. Granger, I thank you kindly for your offer, but we always take care of our taxes ourselves."

"Well, I'd be glad to. Wouldn't've offered otherwise."

"Like I said, I thank you."

Mr. Granger's eyes met Papa's; he smiled again. "All right, David, but you change your mind, you let me know."

"Don't 'spect I'll be changing it."

"Well, you never know. . . ." Mr. Granger shifted gears and Papa stepped back from the car. "By the way, you hear tell of a union man talkin' to anybody down in here?"

"Can't say that I have."

"Heard there was some socialist up organizing 'round Vicksburg." He shook his head. "Hope that rottenness don't come down in here. That's a nasty business, that union, and no good'll come of it." He pulled into the drive and turned around. "One other thing, David. You find you don't need all your bale tags, I'll be glad to take them off your hands. Pay you a good price for 'em. Don't forget my offer now 'bout your taxes. Be glad to help. Anytime."

The boys and I went over to Papa, standing motionless watching the rolls of dust as the car sped back up the road. "Papa, how come Mr. Granger being so nice?" I asked.

"Nice?"

"Yes, sir. Offering to pay our taxes and all."

Papa laughed. I shot him a puzzled look.

"Listen, sugar," he said, putting his arm around me. "You boys, too, and remember. Any time that man offer something, you jus' look to see how he gonna gain from it."

"But, Papa, how could he?" asked Stacey. "He'd be putting out money."

"'Cause, Stacey, he pay our taxes and his name'll get on our tax record, and then one day he could put in his claim against our land. Could take it to court and the land maybe could become his."

Stacey and I looked at each other.

Papa nodded. "That's a fact. Most likely figured I didn't know." He put his other arm around Christopher-John's shoulders and we headed back up the drive. "Something else to remember too. Gotta always stay one step ahead of folks like Harlan Granger . . . two if you can."

At the entrance to the backyard, the boys and I turned toward the house. Christopher-John and Little Man ran noisily down the porch and into the kitchen, but Stacey lingered a moment by the entrance then ran after Papa, who was headed toward the barn. Curious, I followed.

"Papa, 'bout this tax Mr. Farnsworth mentioned, what was he talking 'bout?"

Papa looked at Stacey, and took a moment before he answered. "Bad news, son, that's what it is. The government's gonna charge us a fifty-percent tax on all the cotton we grow 'bove what they figure we oughta be growin'."

"But we ain't got no contract! We don't hafta grow what they tell us!"

"Looks like we do now, son. Like Harlan Granger said, this here's to keep everybody following the government's program whether they got a contract or not."

"But a fifty-percent tax! Papa at twelve cents a pound, that'd mean we'd only be getting six cents a pound. That ain't hardly worth the trouble of planting!"

A wry smile edged Papa's lips. "That's what the government figures."

I came closer. "Papa, I don't rightly understand all this tax and contract business."

Papa looked my way. "What don't you understand, sugar?"

I frowned. "Well, the whole business . . . the government program and the contracts and now this here new tax."

"Well, it ain't exactly a new tax. Government put it on last year, after we'd already planted, but we didn't feel it 'cause we'd lost so much of our cotton to the fire. . . . But I know it's confusing all right." He glanced out toward the walnut tree standing at the edge of the backyard near the garden. "Come on and let me see if I can clear it up for you." The three of us walked over to the tree and sat on the bench under it. "Now you know we into what folks are calling a depression?"

I nodded. I knew that well enough. I had been hearing about it most of my life. "Well, with this here Depression, prices fell way low on a lotta things—corn and potatoes and hogs . . . fell on cotton too. Fell to five and six cents a pound."

"And that's way low?"

"That's way low." Papa shook his head and smiled. "Back in 1919—that was the year I met your mama—prices for cotton got up to thirty-five cents a pound."

"Did?"

Papa nodded. "But right after that prices started falling, so come this here Depression, cotton prices were already low, and they just hit bottom with this five and six cents a pound."

"And that's when President Roosevelt come in," said Stacey.

I shot him an irritated glance. "Papa's telling this."

"He's right," Papa said. "Back in thirty-three when Mr. Roosevelt become president, this here Agricultural Adjustment Administration—"

"The AAA?" I said.

"That's right. It come into being. And the folks on this AAA figured that the way to get prices up again was to cut back on the amount of cotton grown and put on the market. Reasoning was that when something's scarce and more people want what's left, then folks'll pay more for it—"

"And prices'll rise?"

Papa smiled at me. "Exactly. Well, the government figured that they had to get their program started right away, so they come around in the summer of that same year—thirty-three—and they asked all the cotton farmers to plow up part of their crop—"

"And it was already blooming. I remember that."

"It was blooming all right. Looked to be a good crop. But the government figured it couldn't wait, so to get folks to plow up their cotton, they said they'd pay everybody for the acres they plowed up."

"And that was in the contracts," Stacey interrupted again. This time I didn't say anything to him and Papa went on.

"Anyways, the contracts sounded pretty good, but then you know we signed like jus' 'bout everybody else and you know what happened—Harlan Granger's name was on our check."

I nodded, remembering.

"The next year—thirty-four—the government come out with a new contract. Said they'd pay folks *not* to plant. Said if folks didn't plant some thirty-five to forty-five percent of their acres they were used to planting in cotton, then they'd pay 'em so much per acre. For thirty-five, they wanted folks not to plant some twenty-five percent of their cotton acres; said though they could plant crops to improve the soil or crops for use just on the farm. It all sounded good, but we decided we'd better not sign up again cause of that check business."

"Yes, sir." I was thoughtful a moment. "Moe said their government check go straight to Mr. Montier and he take all of the money."

Papa shook his head at the injustice. "Folks 'croppin' like the Turners and Miz Lee Annie and the Ellises, things are even harder for 'em now than they were before the government stepped in. They're hard on us too—don't get me wrong—but on 'croppin' folks, well, it's really bad. Lotta that money that was s'pose to go to them been ending up in the pockets of the landlords. Landlords claim the government money belongs to them 'cause of the credit they give to folks 'croppin' their land. Claim all the people 'croppin' on their places owe them money and some of 'em I guess are telling the truth on that. Still there're some of these landlords that are making a nice tidy sum from the government and the AAA when they oughtn't be."

"No wonder Mr. Granger can afford a new Packard," I surmised.

Papa laughed. So did Stacey.

"That's a fact," Papa said. Then he stopped laughing. "Thing is, though, while Harlan Granger and the like are getting this government money, folks that're s'pose to be getting part of it too are having hard times. They're planting less and getting nothing in return. A lot of them are getting put off their farms 'cause the government wants to cut back so much on the number of cotton acres planted. Harlan Granger and the rest take the government money and just put a lotta folks off the land to cut back on the number of their acres planted. Ain't s'pose to, but they do anyway. Then come picking time, they use day laborers."

I looked at Papa. "And that's how come we see so many folks with all their stuff piled on their wagons. They been put off their land."

"It's a crying shame, but they got no place to go."

I heaved a heavy sigh and looked out over the land. "But that won't happen to us."

Papa's eyes followed my gaze. "Not as long as I have anything to say 'bout it, Cassie girl." I glanced around and saw Stacey nodding in silent affirmation, as if Papa's words went for him too; still, the same worried look was on both their faces.

"Know what I heard?" said Christopher-John, smiling broadly as we started off to school the next morning.

"What?" asked Little Man.

Christopher-John looked from Little Man to Stacey to me and beamed. "Papa ain't goin' back to the railroad!"

I stopped. "Ain't?"

"That's what I heard. Ain't that somethin'!"

Stacey looked at him warily. "Where'd you hear that? Papa or Mama tell ya?"

"Naw. But I heard them talkin' this morning off the back porch. Mama, she said: 'David, I don't want you going back to that railroad.' And then Papa, he said: 'Well, sugar, I don't wanna go back neither.' How 'bout that?" Christopher-John then grinned with happiness as Stacey, Little Man, and I stared at him waiting for him to go on.

"Well?" I said finally.

Christopher-John looked puzzled. "Well, what?"

"Well, what else?"

"Nothin'. They seen me and they didn't say nothin' else."

"Ah, shoot, boy!" I exclaimed. "Papa not wanting to go back don't mean he ain't gonna go back." I walked on in irritated frustration that Christopher-John's news meant nothing. For three years now, since the cotton market had gotten so bad, Papa had been going to Louisiana each spring. From there he traveled into Oklahoma, Arkansas, Missouri, and Texas repairing and laying railroad track. He had been lucky to get the job, and because he was a good, dependable worker he had kept it as well. But then last spring he had been shot and his leg broken in a run-in with the Wallace brothers. He had not been able to go back to the railroad. The money he would have earned was sorely missed, yet despite knowing how much we needed the money, I was glad Papa had stayed home and I didn't want him to go again.

"But Stacey, don't it mean he's thinkin' 'bout not goin' back?" Christopher-John asked, undaunted.

Stacey sighed. "He thinks 'bout it every year, Christopher-John—don't you be thinking he wanna go away—but there's the property taxes and seeding and farm tools to pay for; and the cotton, it just don't bring in enough to pay for everything. We need that railroad money."

For several minutes we walked in silence. Then Christopher-John, ever hopeful, said: "What 'bout if Papa got another job close to home?"

"That ain't likely. You know he looked before and ain't no work 'round here."

"Well . . . I sure wish he could stay on home and not go back on that railroad no more."

"Me too," put in Little Man.

I said nothing else and neither did Stacey as the four of us continued solemnly toward school wondering if this would finally be the year Papa would really stay.

From the second crossroads, we could see the Jefferson Davis school some distance to the north. It was there that white children attended school. Farther down, at the next crossroads, was the Wallace store, where much of T.J.'s trouble had begun. We glanced down the road; then, hearing the Great Faith warning bell, quickened our steps. Once on the school grounds, we slowed our pace, for seven hours at Great Faith was nothing to rush toward. Midway across the yard, Christopher-John and Little Man waved good-bye and headed for their class building. Stacey and I headed for the middle-grades building. That I had "caught up" with Stacey when he continuously liked to remind the world of how old he was getting certainly didn't please him, but lower grades or upper grades, they made no difference to me. I wasn't particular about any of them.

At the steps of the building, Stacey joined Clarence and Little Willie. Seeing only Mary Lou Wellever and Gracey Pearson from my own class with whom to while away the last minutes before the final bell, I went inside. As I entered the classroom, Son-Boy Ellis and Maynard Wiggins were involved in a challenge of tussle against the tarpaulin curtain which divided our class from the sixth graders next door. The two boys wrestled good-naturedly against the curtain, to the pushings of invisible fingers and audible taunts on the other side. In the back of the room, Dubé Cross and several other teen-age fifth graders glanced over, absently waiting for class to begin. I joined the students who had gathered to watch the match, but just as Son-Boy was about to force Maynard to the floor, the final bell started clanging and Mrs. Crandell walked in. The pandemonium fizzled to an end and I scooted into the third-row bench I shared with two other students. Mrs. Crandell called the roll, then opened her history book.

Another dismal school day had begun.

Although school this year was no more exciting than my previous four years, it did at least offer one thing: a classroom free of Miss Daisy Crocker. Miss Crocker had reigned over my fourth-grade class with a personality in direct contrast to my own, and a hickory stick which had more than once gotten its wear against my skin. This year, however, good fortune had smiled on me and I had Mrs. Myrtis Crandell, a rather shy but sweet lady. Despite the fact that her teaching style was no more exciting than Miss Crocker's, at least she didn't continuously repeat herself about the same boring nothing, and she tended to be more sympathetic to my lapses into inattention, so I was content. Today as she presented the rudiments of United States government to students whose major concerns were picking cotton and slopping hogs, the boredom of it all was suddenly broken by my recognition of a name she had just written on the blackboard.

"Pat Harrison and Theodore Bilbo," said Mrs. Crandell, turning to the class with a smile. "Who can tell me who these two men are?"

I raised my hand. The name "Bilbo" had stuck with me. It was such a funny little name.

"Cassie?"

I stood promptly. "I don't know who that Harrison fella is, but that other one is the governor of Mississippi."

Mrs. Crandell smiled, pleased. "Was, Cassie, was. He's our senator now, just elected last fall. And Pat Harrison is our other senator—you remember, every state has two. You know anything else about Senator Bilbo?"

I knew a lot about Bilbo now. Since I had first heard his name, Mama, Papa, and Big Ma had spoken of him several times. "Well, I don't know all he done, but I betcha I know one thing. When that little rascal was governor—"

Mrs. Crandell's face abruptly changed. No longer smiling, she reprimanded me, "Cassie, we do not refer to our senators as 'rascals.' "

I frowned, then decided to rephrase. "Well . . . that ole devil—"

"Sit down, Cassie!"

An explosion of giggles erupted.

"It's not funny and she's not funny!" Mrs. Crandell declared, though wide grins and bright eyes from her students denied this. "I want it silent this minute, and Cassie Logan, I'll see you after class."

At noon I remained seated as the other students noisily made their escape. When we were alone, Mrs. Crandell called me to her desk.

"Cassie," she said, "I didn't think that was one bit funny what you did in class today."

I stared blankly at her. I hadn't tried to be funny.

"You've got a good mind, Cassie, but sometimes you say things you shouldn't—"

"My papa said Bilbo was a devil," I blurted out, feeling that she had wronged me badly. "Him and other folks say he ain't nothin' but a devil 'cause of the way he do us and—"

"That's enough now, Cassie." Mrs. Crandell's pale yellow face seemed suddenly drained. "I don't want to hear what your papa and other folks are saying about the senator. I only care what goes on in this classroom, and I won't have any disrespect in here—you understand?" Her voice had risen sharply. "You leave your daddy's comments to yourself when you enter this room. I won't have you endangering my position with your mouth. I won't lose my job like your mother lost hers—you hear me?"

I didn't answer.

"You hear me!"

"Yes'm," I mumbled, deciding that I did not like Mrs. Crandell so much after all. "Can I go now?"

Mrs. Crandell nodded, avoiding my eyes. But as I reached the door, she stopped me. "Cassie," she called.

"Ma'am?"

She stared at me apologetically. I wasn't going to make it easy for her. "Nothing," she said finally, slumping back into her chair. "Go on."

Outside Mary Lou Wellever, Alma Scott, and Gracey Pearson were waiting to taunt me. They laughed as I came down the steps.

"You get whipped again, Cassie?" asked Mary Lou.

I made no comment, just kept on walking. But that didn't satisfy Mary Lou, who seemed to think the fact that she was the principal's daughter gave her some sort of mysterious immunity from my fists.

"My daddy said the next time Cassie get in trouble, he gonna back the teacher's whippin' with one of his own," she announced to Alma and Gracey.

I stopped and looked from Mary Lou to Mr. Wellever, who was standing near his office talking with another teacher. He was a short, bespectacled man and didn't really look like much of a threat. Besides that, I had it from Stacey that compared to Papa's swing Mr. Wellever's was absolutely nothing to fear, and if Mary Lou kept it up, I would gladly risk one of his whippings to flatten her. I looked again at Mary Lou and matched her smile with a slow, menacing one of my own. Hers quickly faded and she backed away.

"Come on, y'all," she said, and with Alma and Gracey hurried off.

I stared after them a moment, then scanned the yard trying to decide where to eat my tin-can lunch of eggs and oil sausages. I spied Henry Johnson and Maynard sitting on a stump by the road eating and watching a group of older boys playing catch on the lawn. I went over and joined them. Standing nearby were Stacey, Little Willie, and Moe. As I sat down beside Maynard, Little Willie nodded toward a black Hudson coming east along the road. "Look there," he said.

Joe Billy Montier was in the car, but it was his friend Stuart Walker who was driving. Stuart's family owned a plantation on the other side of Strawberry and was co-owner along with Mr. Granger of the local cotton mill. Another young man, Pierceson Wells, who worked for the Walkers, sat in the back. The car slowed and the three young men started talking to Alice Charles and Jacey Peters, two tenth-grade girls standing near the road.

"Jus' look at 'em," hissed Little Willie, his eyes hard on the car. "I wish them scounds would come messin' with one of my sisters. I'd beat 'em to a pulp."

Pierceson hollered something we could not hear and the girls giggled. Then Stuart leaned out the window and with a wide grin said, "Hey, come on down here a minute." Stuart was good-looking and he knew it.

Again the girls giggled.

"Come on—you, the pretty one in the plaid—I got something to tell ya."

Jacey, an attractive, perky girl known for her daring, left Alice and started toward the car. But before she reached it, Miss Daisy Crocker came hurrying across the lawn with those giant strides of hers. "You young gentlemen want something?" she called, stopping Jacey.

Stuart kept grinning but shook his head. Then, laughing, he accelerated and the car sped away, leaving a trail of dust in its wake. Miss Crocker, loudly upbraiding the two girls, led them back to the class buildings. Stacey, Moe, and Little

Willie scowled after the car, then moodily moved out onto the lawn to play. I listened to the last echoes of Miss Crocker's mouth, glad that for once it wasn't me she was chewing out, and turned to my lunch; but before I could get the can open, Son-Boy came running up from the road.

"Hey, Cassie!" he hollered. "My Aunt Lee Annie wants you."

"Me? What for?"

Son-Boy shrugged, ready to be off again. "I think she wants you to write something for her. You better go on, 'cause she said she want you to do it 'fore school start up again." Then before I could ask him anything else, he was gone, heading over to a group playing a game of marbles. Since I couldn't join in the game anyway, I hurried on to the road with my lunch can in hand.

At Mrs. Lee Annie's I ran up the plank steps and knocked on the door. It opened almost immediately, and Mrs. Lee Annie grinned down at me. "Hello, Miz Lee Annie," I said. "Son-Boy, he said you want me to write something for ya."

"Sho' do," she said, hugging me to her before walking over to a table near the stove where some paper and a book were lying. I followed her. "This here letter come from Jackson," she said, picking up a sheet of sky-blue paper, "and I gots to answer it."

"Miz Lee Annie, can't you write?"

"Oh, I does all right for an old woman, but I ain't had me much school learning, Cassie. 'Sides, this here letter is from an educated white woman." She laughed. "Now what I know 'bout writing some educated white woman?"

"Well, how come you don't get Son-Boy to write for you?"

"Ah, that youngun can't sit still long 'nough to write no letter. 'Sides, he can't hardly spell good as me." She put the letter back on the table and turned to the stove. "Now put that bucket of yours right on down and have some dinner with me. Got cracklin' bread and crowder peas."

I grinned. Mrs. Lee Annie knew I loved cracklin' bread. "Miz Lee Annie," I said as she scooped up three plates of food, "Wordell here?"

"Yeah, he back there. Ow-you, Wordell!" she called. "Come on and get your dinner, boy."

I waited, my eyes on the curtain which divided the room. Mrs. Lee Annie finished filling the plate, then brought it over to the table. "Ow, Wordell!" she called again. When he did not appear, she went over to the curtain and pulled it back, exposing a narrow bed. Wordell sat on the far side of the bed, his head turned toward the window. "Boy, didn't you hear me callin' you?" she fussed. "I just been a-callin—"

Wordell swung himself across the bed and stood up.

"Hey, Wordell," I said.

Wordell glanced at me without recognition and grabbed his jacket from a wall peg.

"Now where you goin'? Ain't you heard me tell you dinner was—"

Ignoring his grandmother, Wordell opened the back door and went outside.

Mrs. Lee Annie watched him go, then turned back to me. "Go on, child, and eat 'fore it get cold."

I picked at the crowder peas. "Miz Lee Annie, how come Wordell don't talk much?"

"Oh, he talk when he wanna," she said, sitting across from me.

"He ain't never said nothin' much to me."

"Well, he right spare with his words all right, but I tells ya one thing 'bout that child. When he open his mouth, he usually got somethin' worth sayin'. And what he care 'bout, he sho' take care of it. Person or thing, he don't let nobody hurt it, he can help it. Sho' don't." She nodded toward the bureau. "See that there?"

"That harmonica?"

"That's right. Well, Russell, he brung him that when he was here, and he can play that thing like he talkin'. Play it right good too. Ya know his mama was right musical-minded."

"I don't remember her."

"Well ya wouldn't. She died soon after Wordell was born. When she died, then that give me another grandbaby to raise. Already had Russell. My daughter Truce had done left him with me when she married her second husband."

I wanted to ask more questions about Wordell, but Mrs. Lee Annie gave me no opportunity as she picked up the blue letter again and changed the subject. "How's your penmanship, Cassie?"

"My what?"

"Yo' writing, child? You write nice like your mama?"

I shrugged. "I do all right."

"Well, you gonna have to do better'n all right, 'cause what I wants you to do is write down my letter, then take it on home and have your mama take a look at it. I wants to mail it tomorrow. You think you can do that for me?"

"Yes'm."

We finished eating and Mrs. Lee Annie gave me the letter to read. It was from the daughter of a man she used to work for telling Mrs. Lee Annie that the man had died. "Hazel, she sent me this here book," Mrs. Lee Annie explained, pushing the book toward me. I peeped over at it. Entitled *Mississippi Constitution—1890*, it was a thick, wide book. I opened it. The print was small, almost too small to read. I read a few lines aloud, then looked up, annoyed. "Miz Lee

Annie, this don't make no sense. How come she to send it?"

Mrs. Lee Annie let out a mighty laugh. "Well, ma'am, it belonged to Hazel's daddy, the judge, and I used to sneak into his office when he was gone and try'n read it. Well, the judge he caught me one time and says to me: 'Lee Annie, how come you tryin' to read what don't concern you?' And I says, 'But you said this here book had somethin' to say 'bout everybody in Mississippi and I was jus' trying to find out what it had to say 'bout me.' Then he come lookin' right sheepish. Said that book was white folks' things and I best leave it alone. Said I wanna know something, then ask him and he'd 'splain it to me."

She laughed again. "Well, I wanna know now and I figures I find out for myself. Not be askin' some ole white man who be tellin' me jus' what he wants me to know." She was thoughtful, her rough hands fingering the page. "I had any gumption, maybe I'd even go try and vote."

"Vote?"

"Body gotta take a test to vote, though. Test be's on what's in this book here. This here constitution."

I looked at her with new interest. "Miz Lee Annie, you thinkin' 'bout votin'?"

It took her a moment, but then she laughed and shook her head. "Not these old bones. Course now, my papa voted. Back in the times of the Reconstruction when the black men got the vote—women didn't have no vote. Walked right up to that votin' place and made his X. Didn't hafta take no test back then."

Mrs. Lee Annie's face lost its cheerfulness. "Then them night men took to the road. Tarring black folks goin' to vote, beatin' 'em up, lynchin' 'em. Beat my papa somethin' terrible . . . seen it myself. They dragged him on the road. . . . Lord . . . ." She shook her head again, as if to shake the memory of it. "Well, wasn't no more votin' after that, from hardly nobody. They put a stop to it good, them night men. Sho' did . . ."

She sighed and was silent for several moments. Then she fixed her eyes on me. "Cassie, child, how'd you like to help me read this here? I ain't much count at reading and you read right nice."

"Ah, Miz Lee Annie, I can't read that mess."

"Seemed like you was doin' all right a minute ago. Tell you what, you ask your mama if you can."

I frowned, not really sure if I wanted to ask Mama anything about spending my time reading boring tidbits of Mississippi law. But Mrs. Lee Annie paid no attention to my hesitation as she handed me a pencil and paper and began dictating her letter to me. She finished just as the school bell began to ring. "I gotta go, Miz Lee Annie," I said, folding the letter to take with me.

"Well, I sho' do thank you, Cassie." Mrs. Lee Annie got up from the table and walked with me to the door. "Now you be sure and have your mama take a look at that 'fore you go copyin' it in ink. I don't want no mistakes in no letter goin' up to Miz Hazel."

"Yes'm," I promised, running down the steps.

"And you be sure and ask your mama 'bout comin' to read with me, ya hear?" she hollered after me. "I gots a powerful yearning to know all that's in this here book. . . ."

That night when I asked Mama and Papa about reading with Mrs. Lee Annie, Papa drew on his pipe, as he often did when he wanted time to think, and stared into the fire longer than I thought necessary for such a simple decision. When he did speak, he surprised me by first nodding toward the boys. "You can go, but Christopher-John and Little Man'll have to go with you."

Christopher-John and Little Man looked up at their inclusion in the conversation.

"But Papa," I said, "Miz Lee Annie don't live more'n five minutes from school and I don't need nobody to go with me—"

"I don't want you walking them roads by yourself."

"But Papa, I walked farther than that by myself before and—"

"I got my reasons, Cassie girl. You go over there, Little Man and Christopher-John'll go with you."

He put his pipe back into his mouth and I knew that the discussion was ended. I didn't understand why he wanted Christopher-John and Little Man to go along, but it didn't bother me that he did. Perhaps he, like some others, thought Wordell was crazy, and that if all three of us were together, we could protect each other if Wordell went completely mad.

"Papa, you think Wordell kinda touched in the head?"

Papa looked at me, his eyes thoughtful. "Why you ask that?"

"Well, I seen him today over at Miz Lee Annie's and he acted funny—like he always do—and some folks say he is. What you think?"

"I tell you, sugar . . . I got a feeling that Wordell's mind is as good as anybody's."

"Even after him having Doris Anne up in that belfry?"

Papa's nod was slow in coming. "Even after that," he said finally.

I considered that. Papa was an excellent judge of people. "Well, then," I decided, "he sure got some mighty peculiar ways."

Papa suppressed a smile. "All of us got some peculiar ways, Cassie, and ain't nothing wrong with that long as they don't hurt nobody."

"Yessir . . . I guess not," I said, though I couldn't help thinking that anybody with that many peculiar ways ought to try and do something about them.

Some folks said he was crazy. Some folks said he was just plain ordinary stupid. But whatever folks said about Wordell Lees, most agreed on one thing: He was not like anybody else.

Folks who contended Wordell was mad swore up and down that they had once seen (or had heard about from the most reliable of sources that they had seen) Wordell roll over on the ground like a dog, with a wild look about the eyes. Others said not only that, but that he had been observed standing perfectly still in the woods, down behind Great Faith church in a trance, not moving for more than an hour. And he had been holding a bird in his hands. Nothing else. Just standing there and holding that bird!

Supporters of the opposite point of view shrugged off such tales, mainly because Wordell was often with Joe McCalister, whom everybody conceded was mentally retarded but harmless. It was a matter of being branded by association. In addition to all that, Wordell seldom spoke, which added to the stories about him. He was, in short, a confusing mystery, and the more I learned about him, the more I wondered about him. Once I had put the matter to Stacey: Was Wordell stupid or was he crazy?

"Why don'tcha ask him?" Stacey had mocked.

"Boy, you crazy! You know I can't go askin' him that!"

Stacey looked at me with extreme annoyance. "I didn't mean just ask him outright, Cassie. You so nosy 'bout finding out, what you need to do is just talk friendly like to him."

"'Bout what?" I questioned.

"'Bout . . . 'bout things."

"That time you talked to him at the courthouse, what'd you say?"

"I just told him 'bout T.J. and that we wanted to stay till the trial was over."

"And what'd he say?"

"Nothin' much. Just walked over to Joe and said, 'Let 'em stay.' "

"That all?"

"That's all. He wanna be bothered with ya, he'll answer."

I pondered Stacey's advice for several days, then gave it up as useless. If Wordell was merely retarded, I figured I'd be all right, but if he was crazy, he was likely to whop me over the head with something as soon as look at me. So I left it alone. That is, I left it alone until I started reading with Mrs. Lee Annie. Being with her and having Wordell so near stirred my curiosity again.

Once when I was reading with her, one of the older Ellis boys rushed in and told Mrs. Lee Annie that Joe had just come up from the woods babbling something about Wordell and that there had been blood on his hands. Mrs. Lee Annie immediately jumped up and, telling me to go back to school, rushed off with her nephew. I wanted to go with her, but she made it clear that she did not want me to come along. Later I learned that Wordell had hurt his head. Big Ma, who was good at medicines and was often called upon to tend to the sick instead of Dr. Crandon from Strawberry, had been summoned to Mrs. Lee Annie's and had ended up spending most of the night there. When she returned home, she commented wearily: "That boy, one day he gonna end up killin' hisself doin' the crazy things he do."

The next time I went to Mrs. Lee Annie's, Wordell was up and out again. As Mrs. Lee Annie and I read, we could hear the steady chopping of Wordell's axe in the woodpile out back.

"Wordell all right now?" I asked.

"Oh, I guess he all right. Won't stay put though. I told him he oughta stay in that bed awhile, but he don't pay no mind half the time. . . ."

When it was time to go back to school, I ran outside looking for Little Man and Christopher-John. They had been playing in the front yard when I started reading with Mrs. Lee Annie, but they weren't there now. Thinking that perhaps they had gone to watch Wordell's wood chopping, I ran to the back of the house. They were not there either. At first there appeared to be no one in the backyard at all, but then I spied Wordell, his head still bandaged, sitting on the other side of the woodpile. I thought of making a hasty escape, but it was too late; his eyes were already on me.

"Hey, Wordell," I said.

As usual, Wordell said nothing.

"I—I was looking for Christopher-John and Little Man. You seen 'em?"

When Wordell made no attempt to reply, I shrugged and turned to leave. But then it occurred to me that this was a perfect opportunity to get some of my questions about him answered. Stacey had said I should just talk to him. I glanced over at the kitchen door. Mrs. Lee Annie was right behind it. I judged the distance between where I stood and the door, then glanced over my shoulder to where Wordell was seated. Yes, I could make it, if not that far then at least over to the woodshed on the other side. With my plan of escape routed out in case Wordell went berserk, I turned to face him again. But now that I had resolved to talk to Wordell, I didn't know what to say. Then I remembered the harmonica.

"I seen your harmonica," I started. "Miz Lee Annie said Russell gave it to ya."

Wordell's eyes were unwavering.

"She—she said you can play it pretty good too. I always kinda thought I'd like to play something, but I ain't never had nothing to play on. . . ."

I stopped a moment to watch him. He was, of course, watching me, and when I stopped talking there was only silence.

"Now, Stacey," I continued, "he got a windpipe. Jeremy Simms gave it to him, but he don't play it none, and if I asked him to let me play it, he wouldn't let me."

Again I stopped. Again there was silence.

Seeing that my discourse on music was getting me nowhere, I decided to try another tack. "I—I was sorry to hear 'bout your head. Big Ma said it bled something awful. . . . I hope you're feeling a whole lot better now." I paused, knowing there would be no reply, then went on. "Miz Lee Annie said Joe was with you when you hurt yourself. Said he cried most of the night scared you was gonna die." I thought a moment. "Joe's your best friend, ain't he?"

Something, though I was not sure what, changed in Wordell's eyes. They had never been cold, but now they seemed softer somehow.

"You know, I like Joe," I said truthfully. "Now some folks make fun of him 'cause he's like he is, but Papa said that ain't right. Papa said each of us got something to do in this life, and if we do a good job at that, then we can be right proud. He said Joe's job is to keep the school and church looking nice and to ring that bell, and Joe does a good job at it too. Only one time I know of he didn't ring that bell like he was s'pose to, and that was that Sunday you—"

I stopped abruptly, realizing too late that my talk had led to a subject that could possibly set Wordell off. But when I looked directly at him, his eyes seemed to encourage me to go on, so I did.

Frowning, I thought very seriously about Wordell and Joe and Doris Anne and that bell. "You know, I never did understand that, 'cause Joe, he always rings that bell and he was the one that had Doris Anne, but then somehow Doris Anne was up there ringing that bell and you was there and Joe wasn't."

I stopped, rethinking that Sunday morning.

"But then when we was going into church, I seen Joe runnin' off to the woods after you . . . and he hadn't been with none of us down outside the church. . . ."

This time when I stopped, I did not look at Wordell; my mind was too busy trying to figure out where Joe had been. Then I remembered what Papa had told Mr. Ellis: that he thought Wordell had only gone up to the belfry to get Doris Anne down. Then it came to me, something I should have seen a long time before.

"It was Joe!" I exclaimed. "It wasn't you at all! It was Joe took Doris Anne up there, and you jus' went to get her down! And Papa knew it too, didn't he? But he didn't tell it 'cause you didn't want him to, didja? You let them folks blame you for something Joe done! How come you done that, huh? How co—"

Wordell stood up. With that one liquid movement I was immediately aware once again to whom I was talking. Wordell was no longer looking at me and I could not see his eyes. He walked over to the woodpile. The head of the axe lay embedded in one of the logs. With one yank at the handle, he pulled it out and started around the woodpile toward me, his hand nestled tightly around the handle just below the head.

I began to back away, looking over my shoulder toward the kitchen door. I wanted to holler for Mrs. Lee Annie, but I couldn't get the words out. I thought about trying to make a run for the door, but when I had planned my escape route, I hadn't figured on the axe and I was afraid to turn my back on Wordell. I kept my eyes steady on the axe, wondering what Wordell was about to do. Some ten feet from me, he stopped and raised the hand that held the axe.

Without further indecision, I turned and fled, believing that at any moment I would be cut down. Then it happened. I fell.

Terrified, I looked over my shoulder at Wordell. He was staring at me curiously, the axe still raised. For several long moments he gazed at me in total silence, then raising the axe to shoulder level with his hand still just beneath the head, he stretched out his arm and pointed the axe toward the woods.

"Your brothers," he said, "they gone down there." Then without another glance at me, he walked to the woodshed and disappeared inside.

I scrambled up, thankful to escape, and dashed down the path leading into the forest, but it wasn't until I came to the stream called the Little RosaLee, and found Little Man and Christopher-John haunched on its bank throwing pebbles in, that I realized that for the first time Wordell Lees had actually bothered to speak to me.

5

"Christopher-John, come on. Claude ain't comin'."

Christopher-John glanced back at me, then looked hopefully again up the forest trail where for two years his friend Claude Avery had come running with his brother T.J. to meet us each school morning. But this year Claude had only occasionally come down that path, and then because his mother made him. Always a shy boy overshadowed by his older brother, he had retreated into a lonely world of his own since last summer, and no one, not even Christopher-John, could enter it. When Claude did come to school, he separated himself from the other students and often could be seen sitting on a stump at the woods' edge mourning for T.J. in sobbing, hacking spasms that made everyone turn away from him, embarrassed.

"Come on, Christopher-John," Stacey said gently. "He ain't likely to come."

"Maybe he just late this morning, Stacey. He come twice last week, 'member?"

"I remember we was late too twice last week," I grumbled, not wanting to think about Claude or T.J. or any of what had happened.

Stacey looked at me reproachfully. "If he's comin', he can catch up," he told Christopher-John. "But we'd better go on now. We can't be late again." With that he walked on, with Little Man and me falling in stride. Christopher-John took one last expectant look up the trail, then followed.

At the crossroads we turned northward off the Harrison Road and began to listen for the Jefferson Davis school bus which plagued us throughout each school year. At this time of year its coming was particularly bad, since the narrow, winding road was usually soft with sloppy red mud and the wide gullies on either side of it were filled with water, making it difficult for us to hop onto the steep forest bank for refuge. Now as we heard the bus approaching, we scrambled onto the bank, where we watched in silent resentment as it passed, then jumped down again. Continuing on our way, we were soon halted by a familiar cry ringing from the forest.

"Stacey! Hey, y'all! Wait up a minute!"

Running heedlessly down the steep decline was Jeremy Simms. We had not seen him since Christmas. Already ridiculed by the students at Jefferson Davis because he had chosen to be our friend, he had since the trial become an outcast as well, for talk had begun to spread among the white community that perhaps what T.J. had said about R.W. and Melvin's having had something to do with the murder of

Jim Lee Barnett might be true. As far as I knew, no one
had ever come right out and accused either of the Simmses—
after all, it had only been T.J.'s word against theirs—but the
bad feeling and the talk had gotten so intense that both boys
had gone north to Jackson in late December and had not
come back. Shortly after, Jeremy's mother had taken Jeremy, his sister Lillian Jean, and four younger brothers and
sisters to Jackson as well.

"Hey, y'all," Jeremy said, out of breath and grinning
widely as he approached. "I . . . I was 'fraid I was gon'
. . . gonna miss y'all."

I glanced at Stacey; there was no expression on his face.
"When you get back?" he asked.

"Last night. Pa wanted us back in time for plantin'. He
picked us up in Strawberry—we come down from Jackson
on the bus. It was 'bout midnight 'fore we got back. Ernest
and Leroy, they was so sleepy they ain't even up yet, but I
. . . I wanted to see y'all." He stared at us, his happiness
genuine.

"Where's Lillian Jean?" I asked dryly. "She come back?"

"Naw," Jeremy replied. "She's in school up there in Jackson and she most likely gonna stay."

"Good!" I said. Jeremy eyed me knowingly. He was quite
aware that Lillian Jean was someone I could easily live without.

"Hey Little Man, you grown since I seen ya?"

Little Man held up his head. "I'm always growing."

Jeremy smiled. "I reckon so. . . . Christopher-John, you
all right?"

Christopher-John nodded. "You?"

"Just fine." He paused a moment, then said, "I—I sure
missed y'all."

Stacey glanced over at him, then back at the road as we

started walking again. He had never quite known what to think about this strange white boy who had offered his friendship even when we had not wanted it and had defied his family to be our friend. It was true that his brothers had helped cause T.J.'s destruction, but Jeremy had had nothing to do with that. Jeremy had simply always been just Jeremy.

Stacey put out his hand. "It's good to have you back."

Jeremy took Stacey's hand and pumped it eagerly. Relief was on his face.

"You know I—I didn't know how y'all was gonna feel," he said as we began walking again. "I mean, after what R.W. and Melvin done—I mean what some folks say they done—" He reddened at the correction, glancing over shyly to see if we had noticed. None of us said anything; after all, R.W. and Melvin were his brothers.

"That's done with now," said Stacey without emotion. "It wasn't your doing."

Jeremy nodded, his face showing the guilt he felt despite Stacey's words. Then he dug into his shirt pocket. "Look here, I brung something for ya." Pulling out a paper-thin package wrapped in tissue paper, he opened it carefully to reveal a picture of himself. Beaming proudly, he laughed. "Don't I look funny? Ma had it made up in Jackson. I ain't never had no picture made before."

I peeped over at the black-and-white photograph. In it Jeremy looked scared and uncomfortable, but the warmth and shyness which were so much a part of him showed through clearly. "I don't think it's funny," I said frankly. "I think it's nice, Jeremy."

Jeremy looked at me, surprised. He seemed touched. "You really do? Ma said I shoulda smiled."

I restudied the picture. "Nope. It's just fine like it is."

"Here, then, why don't you take one?" he said, thrusting

the picture at me in a spur-of-the-moment gesture. Then he pulled it back. "Wait a minute." He dug into his pocket. "Got a pencil here somewheres." He found the pencil and, stopping, wrote on the back of it in a slow, awkward hand, "To Cassie, From Jeremy."

"Thanks, Jeremy," I said as I took it from him.

He grinned, pleased, and pulled out a second picture. "And Stacey, this here's for you . . . I mean if you want it."

Stacey hesitated before taking the picture. "Yeah . . . thanks, Jeremy."

"I wrote something on the back."

Stacey flipped the picture over. Written simply was "To Stacey Logan, my friend for always."

Stacey, looking ill at ease as he often did when Jeremy displayed signs of affection, nodded stiffly and shoved the picture into his shirt pocket without saying anything further. Since I had no pockets, I slipped my picture into my reader.

"Well?"

We all looked over at Little Man.

"Well what?" I asked.

"Well, don't Christopher-John and me get no picture?" he demanded.

Jeremy looked surprised. "Well, I—I only had two."

Little Man scowled at him as if that were hardly an adequate excuse.

"I tell you what though. I get me a chance to get back to Jackson again, I'll go have some more made. That be all right?"

Little Man sighed in acceptance—if that was the best Jeremy could do.

"Me too?" asked Christopher-John.

Jeremy chuckled softly. "Course you too," he said, then

stuffed his hands into his pockets and talked all the way to the crossroads in spurts of enthusiasm, in that awkward way he had, about his trip to Jackson. At the crossroads he said good-bye to us, then turned back toward home.

"Ain't you going on down to Jefferson Davis?" said Stacey.

Jeremy looked down the road toward the whitewashed school and shook his head. "Don't wanna go back there no more." He lowered his head and kicked at the road. Without his saying why, we knew. "'Sides, with R.W. and Melvin in Jackson, Pa need me to help him, and he says seventh grade's more'n 'nough education, now's I can read and write and figure . . . that's more'n him. . . ."

He said good-bye again, waved, and walked on. The boys and I watched him go. Jackson hadn't changed Jeremy a bit. He was still the same old friend.

"C-C-Cassie, how y'all c-c-come to get this land?"

I glanced over at Dubé Cross sitting at the other end of the front porch looking out at the fields as his two younger sisters, Lannette and Hannah, swayed gently on the swing. It was Saturday morning and they had come for Mama's review session, but finding themselves the first to arrive, they had chosen to sit on the porch until the others came. I was keeping them company.

"Grandpa bought it."

"B-b-but how? How he mmmm-manage it?"

I was pleased by Dubé's interest and was happy to tell him. "Well, Grandpa Paul Edward bought it long time ago, in 1887. Had himself some money saved from furniture making and he bought two hundred acres from a Yankee. Then come 1918, he took himself a loan and bought them other two hundred acres from Mr. Jamison."

"M-M-Mister Jamison?"

"Don't you know? The Jamisons used to own a lotta land back in here. 'Fore then, this here was Granger land."

Dubé looked truly surprised.

I told him then about how part of the Granger plantation had been sold for taxes during the Reconstruction and how the Yankee, Mr. Hollenbeck, had bought it. I told him about Mr. Hollenbeck's selling it off again in 1887 to a number of farmers and how Mr. Jamison's father had bought a thousand acres of it and Grandpa two hundred. I told him also how Harlan Granger had started buying back the land in 1910, and how by 1918 he had managed to get it all again, all except the first two hundred Logan acres and the second two hundred Grandpa bought from Mr. Wade Jamison. The thing I didn't tell him was all Mr. Granger had done to get our land since then.

Dubé shook his head, impressed. "One of th-these here d-d-days, gonna have myself a place. Nice p-p-place like th-this of m-my own." His eyes swept the land. "Y-y-y'all some kkkk-kinda lucky."

I followed his gaze, knowing that it was true.

More students arrived and Dubé and his sisters joined them inside. Most of the students, like the Crosses, were from day-laboring or sharecropping families and, accustomed to their own one-room, tar-papered shacks, some with no more than a dirt floor, they moved shyly into our house which, with its five rooms, was larger than most and even a bit on the grand side, I suppose, with a fireplace in each bedroom, a door leading to the outside from each room, three porches, and space enough for the family to live comfortably.

Some of the boys and girls seemed intimidated by the life-size facial photographs of family members which stared down at them from the walls in Mama and Papa's room, and by the massive, sturdy furniture, built by Grandpa, which filled the house, and they touched nothing if they could help it, as if afraid they might break something. But there were others, barefooted and ragged, who when they thought no one from the family was watching ventured to run timid fingers along the frame of Mama and Papa's bed and stare in amazement at its pine headboard reaching halfway up the twelve-foot wall; to poke a finger in the feather mattress unlike their own stuffed with corn husks; to stand shyly before the full-length mirror in the chiffonier gazing at themselves; to trace the curve of Grandpa's rolltop desk, now Mama's; and to sit down gingerly before the fireplace in one of the four cushioned, wicker-backed chairs, closing their eyes as they sank deep into its comfort.

With examinations less than a week away, students soon overflowed the sitting area, but Mama, unperturbed, opened up other rooms and, dividing the students into groups, moved from one room to another reviewing lessons, answering questions, and assigning review exercises. Students worked long and hard without a grumble, and since the boys and I had to study anyway, we sat right there with everybody else. But as soon as Mama dismissed the sessions, we shot out back to find Papa and Mr. Morrison. Crossing the backyard, we ran through the garden gate and along the path that separated the cotton field from the garden, through the orchard with its apple, pear, peach, and fig trees, and into the open pasture. At the pasture's edge, just beyond the orchard, was the old one-room tenant shack where Mr. Morrison slept and just beyond that the bull's pen. Papa and Mr. Morrison were standing there as we ran up.

"Don't get too near that fence," Papa warned us.

Mr. Morrison waved languidly toward three-year-old

Dynamite, who was staring sourly out at us. "How much you s'pose he weighing now?"

"Oh, I'd say somewhere 'round a thousand pounds. His daddy's a good couple of thousand—you've seen him. Henry Harrison's twelve-year-old."

"Yeah, I seen him all right. That's a mean bull he got and this one's comin' up just like him."

Papa grinned and nodded toward Dynamite. "I don't much care how mean they get, long as they're good stock and do the job."

Mr. Morrison agreed. "You sell him now, you ain't gonna get near 'bout what he's worth."

I looked around sharply. "Papa, you ain't thinking 'bout selling Dynamite?"

Papa pulled one of my braids. "Gotta sell something, honey."

There was no argument I could make to that.

"You can hang on to him," Mr. Morrison continued, "he'd more'n pay for himself. What with him bein' able to breed now, you could develop yourself a right fine stock."

Papa stared thoughtfully at the bull, but did not reply.

Mr. Morrison glanced at Papa's somber face and added, "Course, you know all that. . . ."

"Stacey! Stacey! Y-your papa bbbb-back there?"

Stacey waved at Dubé standing in the middle of the backyard. "Yeah, he here!" But Dubé, instead of coming to join us, disappeared, going back toward the drive.

"What he want?" I wondered.

"Beats me," Stacey admitted, then stiffened as Dubé reappeared with two men. One of the men was white. "Papa, there's a white man coming."

Both Papa and Mr. Morrison turned at the warning and

waited, their eyes on the men coming through the garden.

"M-M-Mr. Logan," said Dubé as they came into the pasture, "th-th-these here gentlemen say they wanna s-s-see ya. I s-s-seen 'em outside and thought I'd b-b-bring 'em on b-back."

"Name's Morris Wheeler," the white man said, extending his hand to Papa. "This fella with me is John Moses."

John Moses also shook Papa's hand, then Mr. Morrison's.

"L.T. Morrison's the name," said Mr. Morrison.

Mr. Wheeler smiled. "Figured you had to be. Heard 'bout you already." He too shook Mr. Morrison's hand, then looked again at Papa. "Ya don't mind, I'll get right to why we come. Y'all heard of the Farm Workers' Union?"

Papa studied Morris Wheeler before he answered. "Heard some talk."

"Well, I'm one of the organizers of it. Come down from Arkansas way. Was a county extension agent when this Agricultural Adjustment Administration—AAA—came into being and I tell you, I just didn't take to what was happening. Tenants and sharecroppers getting thrown off their land. Money supposed to be coming to them getting put in the pockets of the plantation owners. John Moses here, he was a sharecropper. Lost what little he had 'cause he didn't get that government money like he was s'pose to. His landlord didn't think he owed it to him. Ain't had no place to go. Wife got the pneumonia 'long with his two younguns living out in the open. All of 'em died. That's what come of this Agricultural Adjustment business."

John Moses, his eyes blank, nodded in affirmation.

"Where I was, folks was having a sorrowful time and blaming me for it too," continued Mr. Wheeler. "Got roughed up a couple times, but I couldn't blame nobody. It's hard on folks seeing their cotton plowed up when it's just ready for picking, then not even getting a red cent for it."

Mr. Wheeler waited a moment before going on. "Now don't get me wrong. Something had to be done to try and get prices back up. I just don't figure the government's going about it the best way. One day I just got tired of seeing people going sick and hungry. Got tired of seeing a few poor souls who got up the courage to ask their landlords 'bout their money getting put off their farms 'cause of it.

"That's when me and a couple of other folks decided to do something and form the Farm Workers' Union. Got it together last summer and we planning to take it all across the South. There's other unions like ours and most figure to get tenants and sharecroppers to join together and demand some changes about these government payments. Make other conditions better too." He glanced around at Dubé standing next to John Moses. "Didn't you say you was a day laborer, boy?"

"Yes, suh."

"How much you get a day?"

"F-four bits."

"Fifty cents. Sunup to sundown," remarked Mr. Wheeler with a disgusted shake of his head. "What's top wage 'round here?"

"Ssss-seventy-five cents."

Mr. Wheeler turned back to Papa. "Now you and me both know that's a crying shame. The union wants to get them wages raised." He met Papa's eyes. "And we gonna need your help."

Papa studied him, a question in his eyes. "From what you been saying, this union's for tenants and sharecroppers."

Mr. Wheeler nodded. "Day laborers too."

"Well, I'm just wondering why you come to see me then. Figure if you know who I am, you know, too, my family owns this land."

Mr. Wheeler looked over at John Moses and the two exchanged a knowing smile. "That's a fact. But to tell the truth, we come 'cause since we've been down in here, your name's come up several times. . . . We heard 'bout the boycott."

I caught the swift glance of Stacey's eyes, and looked again at Mr. Wheeler.

"Heard you and your wife got it organized against the Wallace store 'cause the Wallaces was supposed to have set a couple of colored fellas on fire down 'round Smellings Creek. Heard too more'n two dozen families joined in with you, and you and Morrison here hauled goods from Vicksburg to keep 'em going. Seems you managed to keep it going a good three months 'fore the landlords broke it."

Papa's eyes were steady on Mr. Wheeler; he said nothing.

Again Mr. Wheeler smiled. "Now I know you're wondering why I brought that up. Well, simply put, because I was very impressed by what I heard. You got folks who was scared to death of what could happen to them to try and change things around here. You got 'em to join together and stand up for something. I figure you did it once, most likely you could do it again."

"Folks join anything," Papa said, "it's 'cause they make up their own minds to do it."

"That's a fact. But when they see somebody they respect supporting a thing, then it's easier for them to join themselves. It's a risk they'd be taking—like the boycott—but you support this union and I suspect there'll be a lot of folks thinking more 'bout joining."

"This union you got," said Mr. Morrison, "it jus' for the colored?"

Mr. Wheeler hesitated. "No . . . colored and white."

Papa and Mr. Morrison looked at each other. From their faces it was obvious that any support Mr. Wheeler might have been gaining lessened with this information. Mr. Wheeler realized what the look meant and spoke hurriedly. "It's colored and white 'cause that's the only way this thing can work. If we go one without the other, we just ain't gonna be strong enough. Now I ain't saying I'm for social changes across the board—I'm just being honest with y'all now, telling y'all the same thing I'd tell a white farmer—but we gonna win this thing, we gonna have to join together. There just ain't no way around it, and folks are just gonna have to make up their minds to what's more important: their racial feelings or keeping a roof over their heads. That's just what it comes down to. One can't do it without the other."

Dynamite snorted loudly and Papa took the time to look out at him. When he turned again to Mr. Wheeler, he said, "What you say makes sense. But I always like to think a thing through 'fore I decide."

Mr. Wheeler seemed pleased. "Heard you was that kind of man and I'm glad to see you are. I ain't rushing no decision from you. Jus' keep in mind too that as a mixed union we've been able to bring a lot of what's been going on locally to the attention of folks in Washington, like the things some of these local and county AAA committees been pulling. Ya know they the ones make a lot of the decisions concerning the way the program's carried out—how many acres can be planted and so on. And you know who's sitting on your committees here? Granger, Montier, Walker—the big landholders. Not a colored farmer, not a sharecropper or a small landholder among 'em. And believe me, they're making this thing work for 'em too."

Mr. Wheeler waited a moment as if expecting Papa to say something. Papa didn't.

"People out of Washington been investigating complaints about these landlords and how they been misusing the AAA. As a union, we can put the pressure on and keep it on."

John Moses finally opened his mouth and spoke. "I done been in colored unions befo'. Always got broke up. White folks be's in this one, it ain't gonna be so easy to go breakin' us up, 'cause some of them same ones be in our mixed union be's the ones bustin' up the colored union."

Mr. Wheeler nodded, confirming his statement.

"We gonna be meeting with folks the next few weeks through here. Planning on meeting in groups of ten at different places till we cover everybody. Don't want where we meeting and what we doing to reach the wrong set of ears. . . . One other thing." He paused, hesitant. "We'd be interested in using your barn for one of the meetings."

Papa only stared at him, and he hurriedly amended, "I know, I know. I'm a white man and you don't know nothing 'bout me, and I understand that. But I'm an honest man. What I believe in I fight for tooth and nail, and a man go 'long with me in something, I wouldn't never turn my back on him. Now that's the truth of it."

"Well, like the other thing," said Papa, "I'll have to think on it and discuss it with my family."

"Fair enough. By the way, these first meetings won't be mixed. We figure it's better to keep them separate till folks decide just what they wanna do." He put out his hand to Papa and Mr. Morrison once more. "Well, I won't keep y'all from your work no longer. Just hope y'all'll think 'bout joining us." He turned then and headed back toward the house with John Moses following. "Don't bother to walk back front with us. We'll see ourselves out."

"No bother. We was headed back that way," Papa said. He motioned toward Lady and Jack grazing near the forest on the southern side of the pasture. "Stacey, y'all go bring them in. I wanna take a look at their shoeing."

"Hey, Dubé, you wanna go with us?" Stacey said as the men walked away.

Dubé shook his head. "N-n-no . . ." His eyes were on the union men. "Th-th-think I'm g-g-gonna catch up with them union men. G-g-got me ssss-some questions." Then, waving good-bye, he ran after them.

The boys and I watched him a moment, then crossed the pasture. "Bet I can get there 'fore y'all," challenged Little Man and took off. Christopher-John and I followed, racing across the pasture, but Stacey, too old for such things on this particular day, chose to walk.

"I'm gonna ride Lady!" Little Man proclaimed when we reached the animals.

"Not me! I'm gonna ride Jack," declared Christopher-John, who for some strange reason always preferred the sturdy plod of the ornery mule to the sleek swiftness of Lady.

"Wait a minute, Christopher-John," Stacey said, knowing that Jack had a mind of his own and that after only a short while of munching the drying grass, would not feel too pleased about having an eight-year-old boy riding his back. Stacey helped Christopher-John on, then turned to help me. But I didn't need his help. In the past few months I had mastered the art of leaping onto Lady without a saddle, a stunt none of the grown-ups had seen me perform and one which Stacey had warned me about. Now I executed it with such ease that he only frowned as Little Man looked on with admiration.

"Soon's I get me another inch, I'm gonna be able to do that too," he said.

"An inch!" I declared, insulted. "Boy, you gonna need a whole lotta inches 'fore you can do anything like that. Come on."

Since Little Man objected to being lifted onto the horse, Stacey cupped his hand for Little Man's foot and Little Man climbed on behind me. Stacey climbed onto Jack in front of Christopher-John, and the four of us raced the wind across the wide pasture laughing and yelling. As always, Jack, once he recognized that Stacey was master, joined in the spirit of the race and tried to outdistance us. But he was no match for Lady. Lady was the granddaughter of a Thoroughbred. Lady was magic.

At the edge of the pasture we slowed Lady and Jack to a walk. Stacey, Little Man, and I jumped down to lead the animals along the path, but Christopher-John raised up on Jack and squinted across the unplanted cotton field toward the road. "Look there," he said. Coming toward the house was a yellow car trimmed in black. "Ain't never seen no yellow car before." We watched the car until we lost sight of it as it disappeared on the other side of the house.

"Come on," said Stacey. Christopher-John jumped down from Jack's back and we all continued along the path to the backyard. Crossing the yard to the barn, we looked again toward the road. The yellow car had slowed, as if the driver was looking at the house. For a moment we all stared at the car, then Christopher-John dropped Jack's reins and ran down the drive.

"Uncle Hammer!" he cried. "Uncle Hammer, that's you, ain't it?"

The car picked up speed and turned into the driveway. When it stopped, a tall, well-dressed man wearing a three-piece suit and felt hat, and looking very much like Papa, got out.

Christopher-John had been right: It was Uncle Hammer. Christopher-John was first in his arms. The rest of us hurried to meet him, leaving both Jack and Lady to munch the side-yard grass. Uncle Hammer laughed as he hugged us, then stood back.

"Lord, it ain't been but three months since I seen y'all, and look here, each of y'all must've grown a good several inches." He shook his head in amazement. "How's everybody?"

"Jus' fine," we replied in unison. Then Little Man noted: "Uncle Hammer, you went and got a new car."

"Well, it ain't hardly new, but it'll do."

Little Man frowned. "How come it yellow?"

"Why not?" questioned Uncle Hammer, a smile spreading across his face at Little Man's conservatism. "Truth is, I got it for a little of nothing from a man who liked bright, briiight colors. Said bright colors made him feel good. 'Specially liked yellow. Said yellow made him feel like the sun was shining all the time. Now ain't nothing wrong with that, is it?"

"Hammer! Good Lord, son, somethin' wrong?" We turned. Big Ma was standing on the back porch, her face etched in surprise. "We wasn't 'spectin' you."

"You want, Mama, I'll turn 'round and go on back to Chicago," he teased.

"You hush up, boy," Big Ma reprimanded him and

stepped down from the porch. "Come on over here and hug these old bones."

Uncle Hammer laughed and went to her. "Just got me a few days and thought I'd come home and help with the planting. Figured that was the least I could do, seeing I couldn't stay no time when I come home Christmas." He hugged Big Ma to him warmly and, letting her go, turned to find Mama, Papa, and Mr. Morrison coming down the porch, and the hugging started all over again.

"Sure is good to see y'all. Sister, how you doing?"

"I'm fine, but you taking care of yourself? You look thin—"

"Just working hard, that's all. . . . David, that leg's looking good now—"

"Feeling good too. See you got yourself a car."

"Man, had to. Mr. Morrison, how you making it? Still taking care of things?"

"Trying to, Hammer. Trying to."

Uncle Hammer put an arm around Big Ma. "Mama, now I know y'all done had breakfast a long time ago and dinner's still a good couple of hours away, but I tell you what my mouth's really watered up for, and that's some of them fine biscuits of yours, some oil sausages, and some clabber milk and some good ole cane syrup. Think I could bother you for some?"

"Boy, what you saying? I know you ain't half eatin' up North and you probably ain't ate much of nothin' on your way down here. Come on in this kitchen." In less than an hour Big Ma had not only rolled out a batch of biscuits for Uncle Hammer, but cooked a pot of grits, oil sausages, gravy, and eggs as well. She also brewed a pot of the coffee he had brought with him and when everything was ready, we all sat with him at the table, the adults sharing the coffee with him, the boys and I the food.

As we ate, the boys and I sat engrossed as Uncle Hammer talked of the North and of his trip South. Three years older than Papa, Uncle Hammer was unmarried and came whenever he could. He was the only uncle we knew, and we loved him dearly. Yet we were often spellbound when he was near, for we were in awe of him and had never quite been able to talk to him as easily as we could to Papa or Mr. Morrison. He was, as Big Ma described him, just a little wild, and was known throughout the community for his temper, something a black man in Mississippi couldn't afford to have.

"Sure am glad you brought this coffee," Papa said as he put down his cup. "We ain't had coffee since summer sometime."

"I'd've brought some Christmas if I'd've known y'all didn't have none."

Papa smiled at him. "Way you was traveling, you couldn't't've carried much more than you was."

"Ain't that the truth. But I tell you one thing. I'd rather ride the rail anytime than take them no-count buses. When you ride the rail, leastways you ain't gotta pay to sit in the back."

"Well," said Mr. Morrison, "you ain't gotta sit in the back no more, now you got yourself another car. When'd you get it?"

"End of January. It ain't much, but it gets me where I'm going. After I got rid of that Packard, I figured I oughta be able to walk awhile—I done it enough before I got it—but then when I come home last coupla times and took that bus I said I wasn't gonna take no more buses or trains down here, leastways none I had to pay for, and seeing I be coming home whenever I can, I figured I needed that old heap out there."

"I like it, Uncle Hammer," commented Christopher-John, then immediately grew quiet again.

"Glad you do, son. We'll go riding in it 'fore long— Man, pass me some more of them hot biscuits sitting right there in front of you, will you son?" Little Man, grinned, pleased to be the one called upon, and with both hands carefully passed him the plate. Uncle Hammer thanked him, took two of the fat biscuits, and smeared them with fresh butter. "By the way," he said, "coming up the road there I passed a truck with a white fella driving and two colored fellas sitting up front with him. Looked like one of 'em was Miz Rosa Cross's boy."

"Was," said Papa. "I was jus' telling Mary and Mama 'fore you come that two union men come by. They was gonna drop Dubé off near home."

"Union? Y'all mentioned something 'bout that when I was home Christmas. I didn't think it was down this way yet."

"Well, it is now."

Big Ma shook her head in puzzled disbelief. "Jus' can't believe this union talk. Maybe the union make out 'long Arkansas way, but these here white folks in Mississippi ain't never gonna stand for no union. 'Specially no mixed union."

"Just what they planning on doing down in here?" asked Uncle Hammer.

Papa told him what Mr. Wheeler and Mr. Moses had said. He also told him about the visits of both Mr. Farnsworth and Mr. Granger, and the government's fifty-percent cotton tax.

Uncle Hammer was silent when he finished. He thought a moment, then said, "What you gonna do 'bout the tax?"

"What can we do 'bout it?" questioned Papa. "They got us between a rock and a hard place. We gotta plant like everybody else, contract or not, with that tax. Won't get any government money on them acres we don't plant, but least we oughta get the same selling price on our cotton."

Uncle Hammer let out a deep sigh. He had the same worried look Papa had had after he had first heard about the tax. "Well, one good thing—they take you back on the railroad, you won't have to totally depend on them crops. That's more'n a lotta folks."

Papa rubbed his fingers on the table in a slow, thoughtful motion. "Well . . . I don't know 'bout that."

"What?"

"I don't know if I'll be going to the railroad."

"You don't think you'll be able to get back on?"

"I've asked him not to go."

Uncle Hammer looked over at Mama. "Oh?"

"David, he been lookin' for outside work 'round here," Big Ma explained.

Uncle Hammer drank the last of his clabber milk. "Any luck?"

"Not so far," said Papa.

Again Uncle Hammer glanced at Mama. "You don't get anything, David, you still planning on staying?"

"You and me both know I can't stay, that be the case." Mama's face tensed. Papa looked down the table at her; she looked away. "Course with my leg broke last spring and I ain't been back, I might not even be able to get back on the railroad, less'n I jus' happen to get there at the right time and the right man's in charge."

"Then you'll have to be deciding soon," Uncle Hammer concluded.

Papa nodded. "That's right," he agreed, his eyes still on Mama. "Soon. . . ."

Later in the day, when Papa mentioned to Uncle Hammer that he had to go over to the Wigginses to fix their grist mill, Uncle Hammer dug into his pocket and pulled out his car keys. "Why don't you drive over? It'll give you a chance to see how the car rides."

Papa grinned. "Bet it don't ride like that Packard."

Uncle Hammer grinned back. "Man, ain't nothing in this world gonna ride like that Packard."

Since no objections were voiced about our going along, the boys and I eagerly climbed into the car with Papa and Uncle Hammer. As we sped past the cotton field, Uncle Hammer said: "Every time I think 'bout that fire, it just makes me sick."

"Make me sick too," Papa admitted. "But just you wait. This year's crop's gonna be good."

"Another fire don't come up. . . ."

Papa glanced at him and half smiled. "Let's hope not."

When we were on Granger land, Uncle Hammer waved a hand toward the forest path leading up to the Averys' place. "You seen much of the Averys?"

"See them up at church but that's 'bout all. Mostly they been keeping to themselves."

Uncle Hammer shook his head. "I know it must be some kind of hard on them. It's a crying shame that— What's this up here?"

Up ahead where the Harrison and Granger roads crossed stood Jacey Peters with Joe Billy Montier and Stuart Walker. As we neared they looked up. All three appeared a bit apprehensive upon seeing the approaching car, but when Stuart saw who we were, he relaxed and continued talking to

Jacey. Joe Billy, however, moved toward his car as if ready to leave.

"Now, what she think she doing?" Uncle Hammer's voice had changed. The warmth which had been there only a moment before was gone and his body had stiffened, now on the alert.

Papa slowed the car, but before we were at a full stop, he cautioned, "Now watch it, Hammer." He rolled down the window and spoke to Jacey. "You goin' somewhere we can give you a lift?"

Jacey looked embarrassed. "No, sir, Mr. Logan. I—I'm just on my way home from the store." Jacey lived farther down the Harrison road on the Granger plantation.

Papa looked from Jacey to Stuart, who eyed him insolently. With his eyes steady on Stuart, Papa said: "Your papa give you leave to talk 'long the way?"

"N-no, sir. I just got stopped a minute ago and I was going on right now—"

"Then go on then," said Papa, "before your mama gets worried."

Jacey nodded and moved off to obey. "See you, Jacey," Stuart called after her. Jacey, clearly unsettled, glanced back at us in the car and hurried down the road.

Papa watched her until she had turned up the path leading to her house, then he put the car in gear and started backing away.

"Now how come you went and sent her away?" Stuart called with an easy insolence. "We was just getting into some good conversation."

"Come on, Stuart," said Joe Billy in an attempt to ease gracefully out of the encounter. "Let's go."

But Stuart continued. "Seems to me what's between us and Jacey is our business."

Uncle Hammer retorted: "And just what is the business?"

Stuart smiled. "What you think? What other business we'd have with a nigger bi—"

Before the word was out, before Stuart realized that he had made a terrible mistake, the car door swept open and Uncle Hammer cannoned out of the moving car. Papa, practically stripping the gears, put the car in neutral and leapt from the other side to halt Uncle Hammer before he rounded the car and reached Stuart. Stacey too jumped out, running after Papa. Little Man, Christopher-John, and I sat wide-eyed watching, afraid, for we now knew what could happen to Uncle Hammer if he touched Stuart.

"Hammer! Hammer, now hold on!" Papa cried, reaching him before he reached the retreating Stuart. "We've had enough trouble! Leave it alone!"

"That peckerwood needs his neck broke—"

"Get him outa here!" Papa shouted at Joe Billy as he pushed against Uncle Hammer. "Both of y'all go on. We don't need this kind of trouble. Go on!"

Joe Billy nodded and elbowed Stuart to get into the car, but Stuart, realizing that Papa was not going to allow Uncle Hammer to touch him, grew insolent once more. He knew that the power was in the color of his skin, and when Joe Billy put his hand on his arm to pull him toward the car, he jerked away. Eyeing us with a superior smirk, he slowly walked over to the car and got in. When they had driven away, Papa released his hold on Uncle Hammer, but Uncle Hammer was no longer fighting him. He had stopped at the sight of the white boy's insolence and had stood watching him with a coldness greater than I had ever seen in him.

"You all right?" Papa asked.

"What you think?" said Uncle Hammer and came back to the car. Papa and Stacey followed. I sat waiting for someone to say something; no one did. Uncle Hammer was too angry to talk and Papa knew it. There could be no reasoning with Uncle Hammer when he was angry.

When we reached the Wiggenses', I pulled Stacey aside. "What was Jacey doing with them boys?" I questioned.

Stacey turned away without answering. I pulled him back. "I wanna know!"

"Now how you think I know!"

"How come Uncle Hammer got so mad?"

"'Cause when a white boy's 'round a colored girl, they's up to no good, that's why. You jus' remember that."

"Well, don't get mad at me! I ain't done nothin'! Anyway, how come I gotta remember it?"

"Let go, Cassie." Stacey pulled away and headed for the barn, where Little Willie was waiting.

Christopher-John, having witnessed the encounter from the Wigginses' front porch, hurried over as Stacey walked away. "What's the matter, Cassie?" he asked.

I shook my head. I didn't know, and I certainly didn't know what Jacey Peters' talking to Stuart Walker and Joe Billy Montier had to do with me. I wasn't interested in any kind of boys.

6

On Sunday morning Uncle Hammer, neat and dapper as always in a brown serge suit, backed the car out of the barn. All the red mud which had gathered around its fender and splotched its yellow body was gone, for Uncle Hammer and the boys and I had washed it after our return from the Wigginses'. One thing Uncle Hammer couldn't abide was a dirty car. He had worked silently, his anger still bottled inside, but by suppertime his mood had softened, and this morning as we prepared for church he was once again laughing and warm. As he had done yesterday, he handed Papa the keys and told him to drive. All of us except Mr. Morrison, who was not a churchgoing man, piled into the car. Papa started the engine and we swept down the drive into the road.

At church Papa parked the Ford next to Mr. Wellever's Model A, the only other car amidst the battered farm wagons. As always, Uncle Hammer was greeted enthusiastically, for he was one of the few people who had ever ventured north from the community and, in the eyes of the people at Great Faith, had made quite a success of his move. The fact that he had arrived walking only a few months before had not dented people's conviction that he was doing well up in Chicago, for hadn't he come down in a car just like Harlan Granger's just a year ago? It didn't matter that he had had to give it up; after all, everybody had hard times. It didn't matter either that the Ford was ten years older than the Packard. It was better than anything they had ever had, and Uncle Hammer's supposed prosperity somehow reflected on them.

A small crowd had gathered when we arrived, but Big Ma soon broke it up, shooing us inside as the bell began to ring for Sunday school. An hour later, when Sunday school was over and everyone escaped for the half-hour break before service, the crowd began to form again. The boys and I squeezed in among the men, finding their gathering more interesting than our own friends this morning.

"Didn't I tell ya, Page? Didn't I tell ya?" said Mr. Tom Bee. "When ole Hammer come walkin' down that road at Big Meetin' I said he ain't gon' be walkin' long. No sir! There was some folks said once you sold that Packard most likely you wasn't gon' get another one. And here you come in this fine yellow thing!" he exclaimed with admiration, choosing to ignore in his enthusiasm the car's age. "Always did fancy yellow—"

"Yeah, it's nice all right," put in Mr. Silas Lanier; "but

y'all 'member last year when Hammer come home in that big ole fine Packard like Mr. Granger's? Now ain't nothin' gonna ever be fine as that."

"'Member it?" cried Mr. Tom Bee. "'Member it! Owwww, Looooord, have mercy, that thing sho' did do me good. Ole Harlan Granger was 'bout fit to be tied when he seed ole Hammer with that car." He chuckled with satisfaction. "Sez to me, sez: 'Tom, how you reckon Hammer come by a car like that?' And I sez, I sez: 'I sho'ly don't know, Mr. Granger . . . but ain't it fine?'" Again Mr. Tom Bee laughed heartily, exposing his toothless gums. "Ow-weee! That there thing done me so much good. Sho' did. . . ."

"Well, I likes this one," said Joe, who had been standing a little outside the circle admiring the car.

"Boy, what you know 'bout what you like and don't like?" questioned Mr. Page Ellis. "You know 'bout as much 'bout cars as I do 'bout white folks' politickin' . . . nothin'!"

"I knows what I like!" contended Joe, as all the men except Papa and Uncle Hammer laughed at his childlike defense.

Papa, who was standing nearest Joe, asked: "How come you like it, Joe?"

The laughter died as the men noted Papa's seriousness.

"I likes the color," Joe spoke up. "I likes yellow. One of these here days I'm gon' get me a car and go on up North and visit Hammer. That be all right, Hammer?"

"That'd be fine, Joe."

Mr. Page Ellis snorted his disbelief.

"Well, I is! Gon' get me one just like Hammer!"

"You like this car better than that one I had last year?" Uncle Hammer asked.

"That one with all that gray and pretty insides and looking like Mr. Granger's?" Joe spurted out excitedly.

Uncle Hammer nodded. "That's right. I didn't have it long."

"No, sir, sho' didn't," Joe agreed. Then after a moment's pause, he added, "But ya had it long 'nough."

Uncle Hammer smiled in appreciation of Joe's frankness.

"It was sho' nice all right . . . but this here, it's better 'cause that one 'minded me of it raining all the time. This here, it 'minds me of the sunshine." Joe timidly put out his hand and ran his callused fingers gingerly along the car's hood. "I sho' wish I could take me a ride——"

"Boy, get your hands off Hammer's car 'fore you get it dirty!" ordered Mr. Ellis.

"My hands ain't dirty! They clean as yours——"

Papa put a hand on Joe's shoulder, quieting him, and glanced at Uncle Hammer. "It all right with you if I take Joe for a short ride? There's time yet 'fore church."

Uncle Hammer nodded. "Go 'head."

"Ya mean it? Ya mean it?" Joe gushed. "Gon' get me a ride in Hammer's car!" Excitedly and with a triumphant look at Mr. Ellis, who had ridden in neither the Packard nor the Ford, he climbed into the front seat.

"David," said Mr. Silas Lanier, "'fore you go, there's something I wanna find out. Any union men come by your place yesterday?"

"A Morris Wheeler and a John Moses."

Mr. Lanier nodded. "Said they had. Thought I'd check. What you think?"

"'Bout the union?" Papa took a moment as the men waited. "Well . . . if I was a sharecropping man, I might consider it. What they had to say made sense. Only thing is this here business of unionizing with white folks. I don't much trust that."

"Well, I sho' don't trust it," said Mr. Wiggins, Little

Willie's father. The Wigginses, like us, owned their own place. "Don't trust nothin' white folks gonna be part of."

Mr. Lanier agreed, but said, "Thing is, though, I think he's tellin' the truth of it. We got us a better chance of gettin' something done 'round here, we all join in together."

"Well, I tell y'all," said Mr. Ellis, "I jus' don't know what we gonna do, Mr. Granger don't let up on that government money. We plantin' less and gettin' less money too."

"Ah, man, waitin' for Mr. Granger to give us that money's like waitin' for hell to freeze over," Mr. Lanier scoffed.

"Ain't that the truth," Mr. Tom Bee agreed.

Mr. Lanier rubbed his chin, then shook his head at the dismal prospects. "Well, seem like maybe the union's the best way to go then. Leastways, see what them union men got in mind to do."

All the men were silent. Then Mr. Ellis said, "We go joinin' unions 'round here, some heads gonna roll. Mr. Granger done already told me that. Said anybody joins can jus' get off his land."

And once again the men were silent.

"David, come on!" Joe called from the car. "Gonna have to ring that bell any minute now!"

"David, you think it's all right?" Mr. Ellis asked as Papa turned to the car. "'Bout the meeting?"

Papa met Mr. Ellis's eyes. "What I think ain't as important as what you think. We ain't affected the same way."

"But you goin' to the meeting?"

Papa glanced over at Uncle Hammer, then back to Mr. Ellis. "Most likely," he said and got into the car.

Little Man and Christopher-John scrambled in for the ride, but Stacey and I remained with Uncle Hammer. For several minutes the men continued to talk of the union, then of their crops, their families, and what life could hold for them in that far-off place called the North. Then Mr. Page Ellis said: "Hammer, I 'magine David done sho' 'nough started somethin' by takin' that boy Joe for a ride, 'cause that's all he gonna be talkin' 'bout from now on. Now if he'd had a chance to ride in that Packard—"

"Lord, never woulda heard the end of it," laughed Mr. Tom Bee.

"Seems to me like that Packard's all I'm hearing 'bout as it is anyways. Just how you come to sell it? Payments get too high?"

Everyone in the circle looked around searching for the man who had spoken. Our eyes settled on a heavyset, dark-skinned stranger standing a little outside the circle. The man was smiling at Uncle Hammer. The rest of us looked curiously from the man to Uncle Hammer, for no one who knew Uncle Hammer would have dared ask him such a question.

Uncle Hammer studied the man. Finally, he said, "I know you?"

"Name's Jake Willis," said the stranger with a broadening grin that revealed two gold teeth. "Come down visiting with my friend Jesse Randall here and his folks." He gestured toward a short, thin man standing behind him. I knew the man. He was the son of Mr. and Mrs. Moss Randall, who lived over near Smellings Creek. Mr. Jesse Randall looked just a bit uneasy as Jake Willis continued to talk. "Course I know who you are," he said. "Should. All I been hearin' 'bout since I got to church this morning is Hammer Logan." The grin was still on his face, but there was something in his tone which made me uncomfortable.

"You from 'round these parts?" Uncle Hammer asked, not returning his smile. "I know most folks far as Strawberry."

"No sir, as a matter of fact I just come from Jackson a couple of weeks back. Heard they was gettin' ready to set up some government jobs down here. Thought I'd be here waiting for 'em when they come."

Uncle Hammer nodded, his eyes steady on the man, and Jake Willis went on.

"I'm sure hoping I can get one too. I hear tell the government's set aside some jobs for colored so's the white folks don't take 'em all." He laughed. "Course now, I know even if I do get lucky and get me a job, I know I ain't gonna near 'bout be making no kind of money to go and buy me no Packard—"

"Jake," interrupted Mr. Randall, looking haplessly from Uncle Hammer to his friend, trying to stop him. "Jake—"

"—like some folks—"

"Jake, I think—"

"Most niggers I know can't get them no kinda car at all, let alone no Packard. White folks can't hardly buy nothin' neither. Just wondering how come you so lucky."

Stacey and I looked at each other, then back to Uncle Hammer, who after a solemn appraisal of Mr. Willis, said: "Luck, Mr. Willis, ain't had a thing to do with it."

Mr. Page Ellis cleared his throat and Mr. Tom Bee looked uneasily toward the church. "Wonder how come that boy ain't rung that bell yet," he mumbled, seeming to forget that Joe was out riding with Papa.

"Jake, we'd better join Grandpa in church," Mr. Randall said. "Bell's gonna ring any minute now."

Jake Willis waited a moment before agreeing, then, with sudden consternation, looked around the circle. "Hey . . . I sho' hope I ain't said nothin' out of place or anything. I sho' didn't mean no offense. . . ."

The Ford came onto the church grounds and the men

gratefully turned their attention to its arrival.

"Hey, Hammer, that's one fine car all right," hollered Joe, jumping out. "Sho' is! One fine car—gots to ring that bell now!" With that, he dashed for the belfry and the men began to disperse.

"Come on, Cassie, Stacey," Papa called as Uncle Hammer joined him, Christopher-John, and Little Man on the other side of the car. "We'd better get on into the church."

Stacey and I followed them, passing Mr. Jesse Randall and Jake Willis. As we passed, Mr. Randall said, "You ain't from 'round here so you don't know, but man, don't you go messin' with Hammer Logan. That nigger's crazy!"

Jake Willis glanced over at Uncle Hammer, who had by now reached the church steps. The lips pulled back over the gold teeth and he grinned widely.

"Ya don't say!" was all he said.

Reverend Gabson was in splendid form. I listened attentively for his first hour, as he recounted the birth of the baby Jesus, my favorite sermon—and his too, for it mattered not to him what time of year he preached it. But then when the wise men and the shepherds had paid their visit and Mary, Joseph, and the baby had fled into Egypt, my attention began to wane. Reverend Gabson began to expound on the theory that too many of us were like King Herod, suspicious and jealous of someone who wasn't even thinking about us, and that we should be loving our neighbors instead of sitting around worrying about what they were doing.

I knew that now he had hit on the real meat of his sermon, he would preach on for another good hour. Unfortunately, because he preached here only every other Sunday, dividing his time between Great Faith and New Hope in Strawberry, he seemed to think he would be remiss in dismissing the congregation after only one hour. At least in winter his long sermons were easier to take; in the heat and sweat of summer, the long hours in the small church were hell itself. Now as he droned on, I attempted to fight off the drowsiness which was quickly slipping over me. I pinched myself, I bit my lips, I even went so far as to dig my nails into my arms. Nothing helped. Reverend Gabson's sermons were just made for sleeping.

Big Ma woke me with a sharp nudge and, after a disapproving glance, leaned over and shook Christopher-John, sitting beside me snoring blissfully. At her touch he awoke, looked around shamefaced, then folded his plump hands and gazed with great earnestness at Reverend Gabson. Little Man, sitting between Mama and Papa, was wide awake, his hands folded in his lap, and his eyes on a spider crawling up the pew in front of us. Stacey, who never fell asleep in church, sat beside Uncle Hammer paying strict attention like the adult person he thought he was. With Big Ma's attention once again on the preacher, I looked around the church. Half the children were dozing. At the back of the church sat Jake Willis with the Randall family. He wasn't smiling now. His eyes were directed on Reverend Gabson, but there was something in his look that made me think he was paying less attention to the sermon than I.

"Girl, turn 'round," Big Ma said.

I started to obey, then noticed another stranger. He was sitting in the very last pew, two rows behind the Randalls. He wasn't from around here—I knew that—and I couldn't remember ever having seen him before, yet there was something about the square-jawed cut of his face that seemed very familiar.

"Cassie!"

I turned quickly and went back to the business of trying

to stay awake. By the time Reverend Gabson opened the doors of the church and welcomed all visitors to stand, the stranger was gone. But when we were finally dismissed and left the church, I spied him standing beside a car parked near Uncle Hammer's. He watched as the people came out, then, seeming to recognize someone, pushed his way through the crowd. He stood outside the small group which had gathered to say hello to Uncle Hammer. I thought that perhaps he knew Uncle Hammer too and was waiting to speak to him, but then he said: "Mary Louise, how'd you like to turn 'round and take a look at a genuine grown Delta boy?"

I looked from the man to Mama, who was turning in surprise. She stood for a moment, stunned, then ventured quizzically, "Buddy? Buddy, is that you?"

"Who else?" said the man, laughing.

"Bud! Oh, good Lord, Bud! I don't believe it! David!" Mama tugged excitedly at Papa, whose back was to her. "David, this here's Bud!" And with that, she threw her arms around the man and began to both laugh and cry at once.

"Who's Bud?" I whispered to Stacey.

Stacey stared at the man. "The way Mama's carrying on, I s'pose he must be some kind of kin or something."

"So this is Bud!" Papa said, shaking the man's hand when Mama let him go.

"And you're David—"

"Sure have heard enough 'bout you!" Papa laughed.

"And I bet wasn't none of it good."

"Now I wouldn't say that," Papa protested.

"Lord, just look at you," Mama said with a shake of her head, as if unable to believe that the man was actually there. "You sure are a sight for sore eyes. Mama, you remember me talking about my sister Lottie's boy?"

"Now how you think I'm gonna forget somethin' like

that?" demanded Big Ma. "Come here, boy, and give me a hug. You one of mine too."

The man laughed as he embraced Big Ma. Then Mama introduced him to Uncle Hammer and the boys and me. He was Cousin Bud Rankin. Now I knew why he had seemed so familiar. His picture hung on the wall above Mama's roll-top desk. Cousin Bud was introduced to the others standing near, then as people began to head for home and Sunday supper, Big Ma asked him how he knew where we were.

"Well, I managed to find my way to your place and there was a man there——"

"Mr. Morrison," said Big Ma.

"Yes, ma'am . . . huge fellow. Well, he told me y'all was here and I come on down."

It was decided that Mama would ride back with Cousin Bud. Little Man and Christopher-John chose to go with them as well. The rest of us climbed into Uncle Hammer's car. Papa pulled out first, followed by Cousin Bud. As I glanced back at Cousin Bud's car, I noticed Jake Willis standing off to the side staring after us. Despite what Reverend Gabson had said about being suspicious about folks, I found myself wondering about Jake Willis. I couldn't help it. I just didn't like the looks of that man.

Cousin Bud was a handsome man with a winsome smile and a pleasant way about him. He was Mama's nephew, even though he was three years older than Mama. The son of Mama's oldest sister, Cousin Bud had grown up with Mama and had been like a brother to her. Throughout dinner the two talked practically nonstop, laughing and joking, reminiscing about their childhood, and when dinner was over and we all sat in front of the fire, they began their storytelling in earnest. Soon all the adults joined in, telling stories of long ago, stories about themselves, about people the boys and I knew well, and about people whom we would never know except through stories. We laughed a lot, remembered a lot, and enjoyed the day.

Then as night came and the hour grew late, Mama asked Cousin Bud to sing. He hesitated at first, saying he hadn't sung for quite a while, but when Mama insisted, the music slipped from him like water from a well, rising in sweet, smooth sounds to our ears. He sang several festive songs I hadn't heard before, followed by several more songs in which we all joined. Then, at Big Ma's request, he sang:

> *Lord God A-Mighty,*
> *stand by me.*
> *Lord God A-Mighty,*
> *stand by me.*
>
> *There'll be a time*
> *when trouble comes;*
> *There'll be a time*
> *when I'm all alone;*
> *There'll be a time*
> *when no one's near,*
> *None of my family,*
> *no one dear.*
>
> *There'll be a time*
> *when I'm sick and frail,*
> *Treated like dirt*
> *and thrown in jail;*
> *There'll be a time*
> *when I'm in deep despair,*
> *Lost all hope,*
> *no longer care.*

> *And I ask myself,*
> *how can I go on?*
> *Lord God A-Mighty,*
> *stand by me.*

When Cousin Bud finished, no one stirred. He had sung the words with such depth, such feeling, that we were all awed to silence. Finally, Big Ma wiped her eyes and thanked him. "My Paul Edward loved that song, sho' did. I thanks ya for it."

Mama smiled proudly at Cousin Bud. "You've still got it, Bud. That voice'll charm anybody."

"Don't I wish," Cousin Bud laughed.

"It's mighty fine, all right," Papa said. "Mighty fine."

"Used to get him into a whole lot of trouble too, that voice of his," Mama said. "Once he got to courting age, every time I turned around he was busy wooing some girl, singing to her. And wouldn't just be wooing one or two, but more like five and six at a time. Then when the girls would find out about each other, they'd get mad at him and me too. They figured I knew about all the others and should've told them. Some of them even wanted to fight about the thing— me, not him!"

"But you always won," laughed Cousin Bud.

Little Man looked up, surprised. "Mama used to fight?"

"She ain't told ya?" exclaimed Cousin Bud. "Well, look right here." He pointed to a thin line running from his hairline down his forehead to his eyebrow. "That there was put on me by your mama when she was 'bout eight years old. Took the biggest stick she could lay her little hands on and hauled off and hit me with it."

Mama smiled girlishly. "Well, you made me mad."

All of us laughed.

"Sho' did do it," chuckled Cousin Bud, remembering. He fixed his eyes on the boys and me. "Let me tell y'all, there ain't nothin' in this world worse than having a sassy aunt younger than you are. When she couldn't have her way, she'd say: 'But I'm your aunt and you hafta do what I say!' Then I'd say: 'That ain't nothin'! I'm older and bigger too!' Then we'd go to it—"

"And we'd both end up with a whipping," interjected Mama. "Sister Lottie or Papa, one would wear us out."

"Sho' would," agreed Cousin Bud. Then the smile left his face. "You been home since Mama died?"

Mama shook her head. "Not since Papa passed. With him and Sister Lottie both gone, I didn't much want to go back."

Cousin Bud nodded, indicating he felt the same. "Ain't wanted to go back myself. Fact is, this my first trip back down here since Mama died."

Uncle Hammer got up and put another log on the fire. "Jus' what brings you back now, Bud?"

"Well . . . my wife. She's visiting here."

"She's here?" Mama questioned. "Well, why didn't you bring her with you?"

Suddenly Cousin Bud looked uneasy. "Well . . . she jus' wanted to come see her folks this trip. She come before me and went on down to McComb. I . . . I come to get her."

"I thought you married a Northern girl."

Cousin Bud fidgeted in his chair. "Did . . . but we didn't stay together."

"Oh, I didn't know . . . you never wrote me that."

"Things just didn't work out."

"Things happen that way sometime."

"Me and Lydia—that's my wife now—we got married a few years after I got to New York. Got us a daughter fifteen.

Name's Suzella. I told you in my letters."

"You didn't tell me much else," Mama teased. Then she smiled, pleased for him. "Well, I sure would like to meet Lydia—Suzella too. Try to get Lydia to come back this way, will you?"

Cousin Bud turned to Mama, his look strange. Then he shook his head. "Mary . . . I gotta tell you something."

Mama looked at him in silence, her head tilted, waiting.

"Course you ain't gonna wanna hear it."

"What is it, Bud?"

He rubbed his hands together nervously and stared into the fire.

Mama reached toward him. "Bud?"

He turned suddenly to face her. "She's white, Mary. Lydia, my wife . . . I married a white woman. She left me and I come to get her back. I—"

Mama's reach stopped in midair. Cousin Bud looked slowly around the room. No one spoke.

I knew that by his words, Cousin Bud had separated himself from the rest of us. From their faces I could tell that the boys knew it too, for white people were part of another world, distant strangers who ruled our lives and were better left alone. When they entered our lives, they were to be treated courteously, but with aloofness, and sent away as quickly as possible. Besides, for a black man to even look at a white woman was dangerous. A year and a half ago Mr. John Henry Berry had been burned to death, killed for supposedly flirting with a white woman, and his uncle, Mr. Samuel Berry, who tried to defend him and his brother, had lain like a charred log until he had died a few months ago. A white woman was foreign, dangerous, and here Cousin Bud had gone off and married one.

Cousin Bud shrugged and smiled somewhat lopsidedly.

"I told you, you wouldn't wanna hear it."

Again there was silence. Then Uncle Hammer slowly stood, his chair scraping noisily against the wood floor. He stared down at Cousin Bud. "You're a fool," he said.

"Hammer—" Big Ma protested.

"Coming down here running after some confounded white woman—"

"Hammer, Bud's Mary's kin," Papa said quietly. "Leave it be."

Uncle Hammer's eyes met Papa's, then glanced again at Cousin Bud, who looked away, not saying anything at all. Uncle Hammer kept his eyes on him a moment longer, his look contemptuous, then crossed to the side door and went out.

"Children, I think you'd best go to bed now," Mama said.

Mr. Morrison stood. "Guess I'd better turn in myself."

He left and the boys and I went off to our rooms. Soon after, I heard Papa go outside to join Uncle Hammer, and right after that Big Ma came in to bed. Mama was left to talk to Cousin Bud alone.

"How you s'pose he coulda done it?" I asked Stacey the next morning as we did the morning chores. "How you s'pose he could've gone off and married a white woman?"

"Maybe he loved her," suggested Christopher-John.

Stacey whirled around. "Boy, you get that outa your head right now! Can't love anybody white and don't you never try! The man's just a fool like Uncle Hammer said."

Christopher-John, startled by Stacey's attack, dropped one of the eggs he held. He looked down at the broken egg, then back up at Stacey, his eyes growing big. Christopher-John did not like to rouse anyone's anger and especially not Stacey's. Both he and Little Man idolized Stacey, and to incur his anger was a hurting thing. "I—I didn't mean nothin'," he mumbled weakly. "I jus' thought . . ." His voice trailed off.

"You'd better clean that up," I said when Stacey, without a word of consolation, only glanced at the egg and continued milking the cow, Nadine.

Obediently Christopher-John carefully put the good egg he still held into the egg basket, and taking the shovel, scooped up the broken egg and took it off to the hogs' slop. When he returned, he went quietly back to work, but Little Man said: "One thing I know. Uncle Hammer sure 'nough's mad. He so mad Papa told him to jus' hush."

I looked up. "When he tell him that?"

"On the back porch when they was washing up this morning. Papa said: 'He's Mary's kin and you gotta respect that.' "

"What Uncle Hammer say?"

"Said: 'Ain't gotta respect no fool.' "

"What'd Papa say to that?"

"Said: 'Then respect Mary.' Then Uncle Hammer, he nodded and didn't say nothing else."

I turned to Stacey. "What you think? You think there'll be trouble between Uncle Hammer and Cousin Bud?"

Stacey continued to milk. "What I think is Cousin Bud best stay outa Uncle Hammer's way or—" He reached for another bucket and didn't finish.

"Or what?"

He turned slightly to look at me. "Or leave. Now that's what he oughta do. He oughtn't've come here in the first place."

Maybe he shouldn't have come, but Cousin Bud was here now and Mama tried to make him feel welcome. At breakfast she talked with him about old times and nothing was said about last night. Papa, Big Ma, and Mr. Morrison also joined the talk, but Uncle Hammer said nothing at all; and despite the constant chatter his silence made the breakfast tense, and I for one was glad when it was over. After breakfast while Little Man and I did the dishes, Cousin Bud remained sipping one last cup of coffee and talking with Mama. Little Man and I worked quietly, listening with avid curiosity.

"You know, Mary, maybe it'd be better if I went on and left today."

"I thought you were planning on staying until Wednesday."

"Was. But you know Hammer don't like me being here."

"Don't you mind Hammer."

"I understand why he feels 'bout me like he do . . . that's why I'd better get on outa here."

Mama sighed. "It's been so long, Bud. Wait at least until tomorrow."

"All right, you think it'll be all right. . . ." He laughed softly, but the sound was sad. "I guess I'll never quite get over it, how people take the news I'm married to a white woman. Lord, I get to feeling so guilty 'bout it, like I stuck a knife in somebody or something. Lydia, she feels the same. That's why she's gone, just couldn't take it any longer. But who'd we ever hurt 'sides maybe ourselves and our little girl?"

He was silent a moment; Mama didn't speak.

"You know, Mary, it ain't all that awful being married to somebody white. I mean it's awful 'cause of what folks say and think and what some folks'll do, but when it comes right down to it, they're just folks like us."

"No, Bud, not like us."

"Mary, you've always been reasonable. Most times Lydia's

just a woman to me. She ain't got no color at all. And she's a lovely woman, a good woman. It's just that this thing's been as hard on her as it's been on me."

"Don't expect me to understand about you and this woman," Mama said testily. "Just don't expect me to understand."

"Well, what'd I do that was so wrong? Marry a woman I loved, that's all!"

It was an angry, frustrated outburst. Mama did not respond to it.

"And I did love her, Mary. Still do."

"What will you do when you find her, Bud? You don't really expect to just walk up to her on the street or march up to the front door of her family's house and tell her to come back. They'll lynch you before you've even got the words out."

"I'll . . . I'll think of a way. I just need to talk to her, that's all. I can talk to her, she'll come back."

"You said you have a daughter. What about her? Is she with Lydia?"

"No. Left her with some friends of mine." I heard him sigh. "That's one thing I wanted to talk to you about, Mary. About my girl, Suzella. She's one of the main reasons I come through this way. It ain't easy on her, being what she is. She could almost pass for white . . . naw, that ain't so. She *can* pass, and I know she does it too. She can't when she's with me, but her mama encourages her. Says it'll make life easier for her."

Cousin Bud cleared his throat and waited a moment before going on.

"What's worse is that Suzella's ashamed of me, Mary. Oh, she loves me all right—it's just that I can feel the shame. Still, I can't fault her for it. The child just don't know where she belong, and most times I think she believes she don't belong no place. She stays to herself and ain't got no friends much, 'cepting maybe at that school she go to—her mother's got her in a Catholic school outside the neighborhood. I get the feeling sometime that Suzella, she don't much want anything to do with the colored younguns . . . the colored anything."

He paused, as if waiting for Mama to say something. After a moment, she obliged him. "Well, I guess that's to be expected."

"Mary, I want her to accept being who she is. She's colored and she's gotta accept that. I may be married to a white woman, but that don't mean I'm trying to be white. Suzella's a colored girl because her daddy's a colored man, and no matter how much she might wish she ain't and I ain't, we both stuck with what we are and I don't want her wishing otherwise. I don't want her passing!" He took a moment, then said, "Mary, I gotta ask you something."

"What, Bud?"

"Well, I know it might be hard on you, but I was thinking I'd like to send Suzella down here awhile to stay with you."

Little Man and I shot surprised glances at each other.

"You'd be good for her, Mary. You and David, your whole family. You're close and she needs that. It'd give her a chance for a real family, more'n me and Lydia been able to give her."

"What about Lydia?"

Cousin Bud sighed heavily. "She loves Suzella. I don't think she'll be able to stay away from her, if I can just talk some sense into—"

"What if she doesn't want Suzella staying with us?"

"Don't matter. This is one thing I'm bound and determined to do. I mean for Suzella to have this if you're willing."

I took my hands from the dishwater and went through the curtain. Mama, looking thoughtful, was swallowing the last of her coffee. She put the cup down, her fingers lingering on the handle as if to give her more time before replying to Cousin Bud's request.

"Mama, you finished?" I asked.

She looked around. "Yes, baby, you can take it. Bud, you want some more coffee? There might be one more cup left."

Cousin Bud shook his head and drained his cup. "No, this is fine," he said, handing the cup to me.

I took both cups and saucers and returned to the kitchen. As I placed the dishes in the dishpan, Mama gave Cousin Bud her answer. "I'll have to speak to David, but if it's all right with him about Suzella, it's all right with me."

On the way to school, Little Man and I told Stacey and Christopher-John about Cousin Bud's conversation with Mama and that his daughter might be coming. Christopher-John speculated as to what this half-white cousin would be like while Stacey commented sullenly once again that Cousin Bud should never have come. Still discussing the matter, we turned off the first crossroads and followed the curve of the road past the Simmses' place. As the road straightened, we saw two cars parked up ahead. Doors to both cars stood open, but we saw no one. We kept on walking. Then Stacey halted us with an outstretched arm, waited a moment, and motioned us into the forest.

Hidden from the road, we waited anxiously as the sickening sounds of flesh pounding flesh broke the morning silence. Finally the thudding stopped and four men appeared, got into one of the cars, and left. We waited several more minutes before cautiously slipping back to the road and walking toward the remaining car. Drops of blood splattered in the dust beside the car led us farther down the road and to the defile on the left-hand side. There a man was lying, facedown. Apprehensively, we looked at each other; then Stacey turned him over. It was Mr. Farnsworth, the county agent.

"He—he dead?" asked Christopher-John, his eyes wide as he gazed at the bloody figure.

Stacey hesitated, then knelt down and placed his ear against Mr. Farnsworth's chest. "His heart's still beating."

"Well, he sure look dead," observed Little Man.

Stacey stood again and stared down at Mr. Farnsworth. We waited for him to decide what we were going to do. "Well, one thing, we can't be taking him no place," he said after a look up and down the road. "White folks see us and they be thinking colored folks beat him up like this. Be thinking maybe even Papa or Mr. Morrison did it, and he die, he can't tell no different. And we go home, it take too long . . ."

I looked from Stacey to Mr. Farnsworth. "What we gonna do then? Just leave him?"

"No!" objected Christopher-John. "He die sure then, Cassie!"

Stacey studied Mr. Farnsworth, then checked the road again. No one was coming. "Got an idea. Let's get Jeremy."

"What he gonna do?" I questioned, seeing very little sense in bringing him into it.

"Him being white, he can take him somewhere."

"Well, what 'bout Mr. Farnsworth? Shouldn't some of us stay with him?"

"Nothing we know to do for him, Cassie, and somebody white come along we better not be here. Ya'll come on with me to get Jeremy."

Running, we left Mr. Farnsworth in the defile and headed back down the road and up the steep trail that led to the Simmses' farm. At the top of the trail the land leveled out and newly plowed fields came into view. Fortunately Jeremy was working at the edge of the field near the trail busting clumps of dirt with his hoe and only his younger brothers Leroy and Ernest were with him to witness our arrival.

"What y'all niggers doin' up here?" cried Leroy, who was no bigger than a minute and younger than me.

Jeremy turned on him with a piercing reprimand, and Leroy grew silent. His hoe still in hand, Jeremy came across the field apologizing for Leroy. "Oughta be in school, both him and Ernest. But Pa made 'em stay to help with the fields."

Stacey looked around. "Where is your pa?"

"He ain't here. Said he had some stuff to do."

I looked back toward the trail. "I jus' bet he did."

Stacey let me have one of those disapproving looks of his, then said to Jeremy: "Look, here, we was thinking maybe you can help us with something." He waited a moment before going on. "Mr. Farnsworth, he laying out there in the road by his car all beat up and needing somebody to get him to where he can get some help."

Jeremy's eyes widened. "Mr. Farnsworth?"

"That's right. And we figure it'd be better you take him somewhere than us. . . ."

Jeremy thought a moment and frowned. "Ya know my pa don't much like him none."

"He don't like us neither," I reminded him, "but you don't let that seem to bother you none."

"Where you wanna take him?"

"I figure you could drive him to Mr. Granger's."

"You—you mean you want me to drive his car?"

"You can drive, can't ya?"

Jeremy shook his head. "Didn't get a chance to learn 'fore R.W. and Melvin took the truck up to Jackson."

Stacey looked back toward the trail trying to decide what we should do now. "Well, I know how," he said finally. "Uncle Hammer, he taught me." He turned again to Jeremy. "If I drive him up to Mr. Granger's, will you go get the help?"

Jeremy nodded. "Sure thing. But let's not take him to Mr. Granger's. He be asking too many questions."

"What that matter?" I said. "You don't know the answers."

Jeremy still didn't like the idea. "Let's take him over to Mr. Tate Sutton's. He ain't much caring for Mr. Farnsworth none either, but he'll help and won't be asking a whole lotta questions."

With the decision made, Jeremy ran back to speak to Leroy and Ernest, and leaving his hoe with a fussing Leroy ran down the trail with us.

"You tell 'em 'bout Mr. Farnsworth?" I asked.

"No . . . just that they better not tell nobody I was gone or I'd take care of 'em when I get back."

When we reached the defile, Mr. Farnsworth was still lying motionless. With all of us helping, we picked him up as carefully as we could and set him in the passenger's side of the front seat. Then with Stacey in the driver's seat and the rest of us in back, Stacey started the car, turned it around and headed north. At the second crossroads, he turned west, away from Great Faith, and a few minutes down the road stopped in front of the Suttons'. Stacey glanced up the drive to the house, set some distance from the road, then at Jeremy. "You ready?"

"I guess . . . but ya know, Stacey, I been thinkin'. What

if we jus' slide Mr. Farnsworth over so's it look like he come up this far by his own self?"

Stacey considered. "That oughta work just as well," he said, obviously feeling that Jeremy had as much right to look out for his own well-being as we did ours.

Gently we moved Mr. Farnsworth to the driver's side; then Stacey, Christopher-John, Little Man, and I hurried into the forest on the other side. Once we were securely hidden, Jeremy laid on the horn, blasting the morning silence. Within seconds, Mr. and Mrs. Sutton came hurrying down the trail to investigate.

Lying expertly, Jeremy said he had just come along and found Mr. Farnsworth beaten up in his car and, as Jeremy had assumed, the Suttons asked no questions. Mrs. Sutton checked Mr. Farnsworth's eyes and told her husband they had to get him to Doctor Crandon's in Strawberry. Mr. Sutton called for one of his grown sons to help him, and placing Mr. Farnsworth once more on the passenger's side of the car, he sat at the wheel while his son followed in their pickup. Mrs. Sutton and Jeremy stared after them for a moment before Mrs. Sutton turned and went back toward her house and Jeremy started down the road.

Stacey, Christopher-John, Little Man, and I walked along the forest edge until we figured we couldn't be seen from the Sutton place, then joined Jeremy and walked as far as the crossroads with him. There Jeremy turned to go back home and we went on to Great Faith. School had already begun by the time we got there.

That evening when we told of what had happened, everyone worried about any possible repercussions if Mr. Farnsworth should die, and about our part in getting him the help he needed. Long after the boys and I had been sent to study, we could hear the grown-ups talking in the kitchen, their words muffled behind the closed door. Eventually we heard the kitchen door to the porch open and then the sounds of Papa, Uncle Hammer, and Mr. Morrison talking as they headed for the barn. We expected Big Ma, Mama, and Cousin Bud to join us now, but when none of them did, we did the best we could to concentrate on our last week of lessons.

Outside it was not yet dark as the winter days gave way to the longer days of spring, and it was raining, the sound of it pelting like a melody upon the tin roof. Though the day had been warm, a chill hovered over the evening and Stacey made a fire. Little Man, not yet allowed to build a fire himself, helped him. For a while Little Man stood with one small hand placed on Stacey's shoulder as Stacey knelt before the hearth waiting for the fire to catch hold, then the two came back to the study table.

"Looks like we got some mighty studious folks here," Uncle Hammer said, coming in the side door. He smiled as he passed the study table, then stooped and picked up something from the floor. He was about to put it on the table when he noticed that it was the picture of Jeremy. He stared at it, read the words on the back and set his eyes on me. "This here got your name on it," he said.

I felt a sudden nausea.

His eyes narrowed. "Now just what you doing with a picture of a white boy?"

"I—I . . ." There was a terrible pounding in my chest. "He gave it to me."

"He gave it to you? What for?" Uncle Hammer's voice was calm, quiet, but it terrified me. I had seen him like this before and knew that a terrible anger lurked behind the calm. I had always been fearful of that anger ever being directed at me, and now I could only stare up at him, unable to speak.

"He—he just gave it to her, Uncle Hammer." I looked over at Stacey, silently thanking him for coming to my rescue. "He gave me one too . . . jus' his way of being friendly. He didn't mean nothin' by it. . . ."

"Didn't mean nothing by it?" Uncle Hammer repeated, his voice soft. He turned Jeremy's picture over in his hand and stared at it in silence. Christopher-John and Little Man looked at me, then back at him, waiting for the explosion to come. "You let a white boy give your sister his picture and then you sit there and tell me he didn't mean nothing by it?"

Stacey glanced nervously at me, then met Uncle Hammer's eyes with a steady gaze. "Well, Uncle Hammer, Jeremy, he just come home from Jackson and was glad to see us and he had some pictures of himself, that's all. He—he ain't like most of the white boys round here, and he—"

Uncle Hammer held up his right hand and Stacey stopped. I realized that in that one movement Uncle Hammer was attempting to keep his anger under control. I knew also that in defending me—and Jeremy—Stacey had now brought the brunt of Uncle Hammer's displeasure down upon himself.

For a time Uncle Hammer said nothing. We waited. When he spoke again, there was an unleashed anger in his words, anger that stemmed not from us, but from what he now told us. "Stacey, you soon gonna be fourteen. Now that ain't so very old, but it's old enough to know how things stand, and if you don't know it already, you better start learning right fast how white men think 'bout black women. You seen it just Saturday with them two white boys hanging 'round that Peters girl. If that girl had've been mine, I would've whipped her till she would've been thinking twice 'fore she went sashaying 'round white boys again, and if her

folks don't get her straight soon, it's gonna be one sorry
mess, 'cause that sorta thing don't ever come to no good.

"A white man think he can just have his way with colored
women, can have them for the taking. I've known 'em to go
to a black man's house while that man was in the field working trying to take care of his family, and that colored woman
didn't have no more respect for herself than to take up with
him. I've known too of colored women telling their hus-
bands or their daddies or their brothers 'bout white men
trying to mess with them, and I've seen their menfolks killed
for trying to protect their women. And it's the same up
North. They come riding through our neighborhoods in
broad daylight trying to pick up our womenfolk and don't
care nothin' 'bout how they use them. White men like that
ain't nothing but dogs far as I'm concerned, and I'd rather
see Cassie dead than take up with one of 'em."

The blood rushed to my head, and the silence which filled
the room pounded against my eardrums. I felt sick and
wanted to run from the room. But Uncle Hammer wasn't
finished.

"You just look 'round you and see how they treat our
women, then you take a look at how they treat their own
women. They think every man in the world wants one of
their women, and if a colored man even look sideways at one
of 'em, they start talking 'bout lynching. A colored man
caught carrying 'round a picture of a white girl like Cassie
got of this white boy wouldn't be long for this world. Fact to
business, when I was 'bout fourteen, there was a boy your
papa and me knew who lived over by Smellings Creek that
was messin' with a white girl, and a bunch of men come out
to his place one night and cut off his privates—that's just
how bad it is."

He looked at each of us. "Now I know it's hard, but there

ain't no easy or pretty way to say it, and the sooner you learn how these things are down here, the easier it's gonna be on you. Cassie, you gotta always respect yourself and your family and your menfolks, and you boys, you gotta always respect your own women and take care of your sister. Y'all understand what I'm saying to ya?"

We were too stunned to answer.

"What'd you say?"

"Yes, sir," Stacey responded, and the rest of us immediately did likewise, though Christopher-John and Little Man looked to have understood very little but his anger.

Uncle Hammer nodded and started across the room. As he did, Mama came in from the kitchen with Cousin Bud behind her. "Hammer, I thought I heard you in here," she said. "You know I've been meaning to ask you——" She stopped as her glance fell on the boys and me. "What is it?"

Uncle Hammer waved a hand at Cousin Bud. "And, Lord, whatever y'all do, don't be no fool and go crying after some white woman——"

"Hammer!"

"It's—it's all right, Mary," said Cousin Bud. "I . . ." He faltered. "Lord, he's right. Don't you think I know he's right?" Then, like a man beaten, he met Uncle Hammer's unrelenting gaze and went back into the kitchen.

"You shouldn't have done that, Hammer," Mama said, her voice flat, angry. "Bud's family."

Uncle Hammer glanced toward the dining room door. "He may be family, Mary, but that don't keep him from being a fool." Then, turning from her, he crossed to the fireplace and without hesitation threw Jeremy's picture into it.

The boys and I watched it burn.

7

"Looks like the rain's letting up."

I turned as Papa climbed the porch steps and came over to the swing. He sat down beside me making the chains supporting the swing creak wearily. "Yes, sir."

For a while he said nothing as he stared out at the field, then he looked around at me. "I hear you and your Uncle Hammer had words."

"No, sir, we ain't had no words . . . he done all the talking."

Papa was quiet as he gazed out at the greening lawn. "You understand what he was talking 'bout?"

I didn't answer right away. "Well, I think so . . . most

of it. But, Papa, Uncle Hammer, he didn't have to go burn Jeremy's picture thataway. He didn't have to. He didn't understand 'bout Jeremy."

"He understood all right. Jeremy's a white boy. You got no business with his picture."

Papa's voice was harsh. I stared at him, surprised. Usually he understood the things that Uncle Hammer didn't.

"You think I'm being hard 'bout Jeremy?"

I lowered my eyes, not daring to answer.

"Well, I ain't. Jeremy seems to be a right fine boy and maybe he'll grow up to be a right fine man, but you can't never forget that he's white and you're black. You forget it and you likely to find yourself hurt."

He paused.

"You 'member me telling y'all 'bout Grandpa and how he come to leave Georgia and come to Mississippi?"

I remembered very well. Grandpa Logan had been born a slave on a Georgia plantation. He was two years old when freedom came. "Yes, sir. His mama died and he didn't want to stay there no more."

"I ever tell you 'bout his daddy?"

I frowned, trying to remember. "He was the plantation owner."

"Now, what that tell you?"

"Sir?"

"What that tell you 'bout your grandpa's daddy?"

I thought of the large picture of Grandpa which hung over the fireplace. In it the straightness of his hair, the pale coloring of his skin, distinctly showed his mulatto heritage.

"He—he was a white man," I answered.

Papa nodded. "A white man that kept slaves . . . owned them like you own cows or a pig, and the slave women had to do what he said . . . and that's how your grandpa came to be born. Your great-grandmama didn't have no say 'bout it. No say at all. White men been using colored women for centuries—they still doing it—and believe me, it's a mighty hurting thing . . . mighty hurting, and I feel just like your Uncle Hammer do 'bout it. Any time I see a colored woman with a white man, a colored woman who wants to be with that white man, it makes me want to cry, 'cause that woman don't care nothin' 'bout herself or how that white man look down on her and her folks. You understand that?"

"Yes, sir."

Papa breathed in deeply, looked again at the lawn, then back at me. The hardness was gone from his eyes. "Cassie, soon—too soon for your old Papa—boys gonna start wantin' to court you—"

"Ah, Papa," I sighed. I had heard that before from Big Ma, and the thought of it depressed me. Not that I didn't like boys; I liked them just fine. In fact, as friends they had always proven closer friends than any girls I had known. But for that fine relationship, which had taken years to build up, to suddenly be ruined because of a foolish change in the way of things was something to which I was not looking forward.

Papa smiled. "I know what you thinking, sugar, but it's gonna happen, and when it does you'll be happy enough about it." His smile faded. "Trouble is, there's gonna be white boys looking at you too—for no good, but they'll be looking. I don't want you looking back."

I glanced up at Papa, then out to the field again. I wanted to ask him about Cousin Bud and how he had come to marry a white woman, but was unsure whether I should.

Papa was watching me. "You wanna ask me something?"

"Well . . . what 'bout Cousin Bud? I mean, he went and married that white woman."

Papa sighed and rubbed his mustache. "Well, I tell ya

. . . it ain't something I would've ever done, but who knows? Maybe that's the way things'll be naturally one day. I ain't saying I wanna see it, not with how they treat us, but sometimes I get to thinking 'bout your mama's folks and the folks on my side of the family. Your mama's grandmama was full-blooded Indian and here my granddaddy was a white man. I ain't had no say 'bout my white granddaddy and your mama ain't had no say 'bout her Indian grandmother. Ain't none of us got no say-so 'bout our past. They just part of us now, no matter if we like it or not, and that's that.

"I s'pose all folks mixed up some kind of way. White folks and black folks and red folks, and when we dead and gone it don't make a speck of difference to the folks that's dead, only to thems that's left behind. Maybe in fifty or a hundred years, folks won't have to even think 'bout it . . . whether you're black or white. Way it seem now, it ain't likely, but maybe. . . . Right now, though, it does. It makes a whole lot of difference and we can't turn our backs on it. There's colored folks and there's white folks. They don't want nothing to do with us 'ceptin' what we can do for them, and Lord knows I don't want nothin' to do with them. They leave us alone, we leave them alone. And it wouldn't worry me one bit if a whole year'd go by and I wouldn't have to see a one of 'em."

"But, Papa, what 'bout Mr. Jamison?"

Papa considered. "Well . . . Mr. Jamison, he's a rare man and I got a lotta respect for him. Far as I can see, there ain't no better man, black or white, I know 'bout."

"Yes, sir. Papa?"

"Yeah, baby?"

"You think things'll change one day—I mean 'bout how we get treated by the white folks?"

"I sure hope so, Cassie, but white folks ain't just gonna

change out of the goodness of their hearts, I'll tell you that. It's gonna take a whole lot of doing on somebody's part."

I frowned, thinking.

Papa looked at me. "What's the matter?"

"I wonder if they ever think what it'd be like if they was the ones getting treated like us."

"They ever do," Papa said with a sly smile, "I imagine they don't think on it too long."

"You think they'll be changing anyway soon?"

"Don't know 'bout soon, Cassie girl, but I tell you one thing. I'm sure hoping that if I don't live to see the day, you will. I'm praying right hard on that."

Cousin Bud left that evening. It was clear that Mama blamed Uncle Hammer for his going, and she moved moodily around the house not saying much to anyone. Nothing was said about Cousin Bud that night, but the next morning Uncle Hammer talked to Papa about him. The morning had dawned warmer than the day before, and though there was still a chill in the air, it was not too chilly for us to attend to part of our morning toiletries on the back porch, as we did every morning when the weather was warm. While Christopher-John and I brushed our teeth, Papa and Uncle Hammer peered into their small oval mirrors hanging from post nails and shaved.

"Mary still upset with me 'bout Bud?" asked Uncle Hammer, adjusting his mirror.

Papa slid the straight razor down the right side of his face, stripping away the soap lather. "She got a right to be, don't you think?"

Uncle Hammer shrugged and began to lather. "Didn't say nothin' but the truth."

"Thought you wasn't gonna say nothin' at all."

"Wasn't planning to . . . but it's done now." He finished lathering, but hesitated before starting to shave. "What 'bout Mary?"

Papa slid the razor down his face once more. "Now you know Mary feel real special 'bout Bud. He's like a brother to her, and she didn't like the way you talked to him. Yeah, she's plenty mad at you all right. I 'spect you wanna get back on her good side, you'd best go talk to her."

Uncle Hammer glanced over at Papa and nodded. "Yeah, guess I'd better."

By the time the boys and I returned from school, it was obvious that Mama and Uncle Hammer had mended their differences. There was no more talk about Cousin Bud and the house settled back to normal, though thoughts of Mr. Farnsworth still bothered us. With each day we heard more talk around the community about the beating, but no one really knew how badly Mr. Farnsworth had been injured or who had done it. There were some who speculated privately about it, yet as far as we knew no one but the boys and I had actually seen the beating, and even had we recognized the men, we certainly wouldn't have said so. As the week wore on and no one approached us about it, we assumed that no one knew about us and we all began to relax a little.

On Saturday morning we went to the fields. Through the week as the boys and I had reluctantly gone off to school, last year's cotton stalks had been thoroughly broken, the ground tilled, then laid into rows about three feet apart. Now it was time to sow the cotton seeds. As Papa drove Jack over the length of the field pulling the planter—a plowlike implement with a small container attached that cut the earth, then dropped seeds along the opening and covered them—the rest of us came behind covering any seeds left uncovered and packing the dirt snugly over them.

We worked well throughout the morning and were nearly ready to break for dinner at noon when Sheriff Hank Dobbs drove up and stopped on the road. Stepping from his car along with another man, he parted the barbwire and both came onto the field. "How y'all doin'?" he called.

"Sheriff," said Papa, who had by now halted Jack and was waiting for him.

Uncle Hammer, standing in the next row, was leaning on his hoe. The sheriff's eyes shifted to him. "Hammer, didn't know you was back."

Uncle Hammer wisely kept quiet and only nodded.

"Be here long?"

"Ain't decided that yet."

Sheriff Dobbs kept his eyes on Uncle Hammer a moment longer, then gestured to the man beside him. "This here's Mr. Peck. He's gonna be the new county agent. Peck, this here's David, brother Hammer. Wife, Mary, and Mama over yonder."

Mr. Peck was a nervous-looking man with a pale cast about him which made me guess he was new to all this. He nodded cautiously. Papa and Uncle Hammer did the same.

"I s'pose by now you heard 'bout what happened to Mr. Farnsworth," said Sheriff Dobbs. "—'bout him getting beat up and all?"

"Heard some talk," Papa said.

"In all this talk, you heard 'bout who done it?"

Papa shook his head. "Can't say I have."

"Well, I tell ya, David, I know it wasn't none of y'all. Mr. Farnsworth, he says it was white men done it to him. Seems like he felt he had to say that, though he ain't said no more'n that. Won't tell us who it was. But I'm tellin' everybody that Mr. Peck here is under my protection. Mr. Farnsworth, he's gonna be laid up a right long spell and I ain't having none of the kind happening to Mr. Peck. One hair on this man's head gets mussed and I'm personally gonna thrash the living daylights outa whoever mussed it."

This declaration did very little to improve Mr. Peck's nervousness as he looked around uneasily and spotted Mr. Morrison in the distance.

"I figure this kinda stuff's happening 'cause of this union business," Hank Dobbs continued. "These here outside folks comin' down in here stirring things up like we don't have worries enough with the hard times and all. Understand a couple of 'em been goin' 'round to everybody, white and colored, talkin' 'bout this union mess. Mr. Granger don't like it. Mr. Montier, Mr. Harrison, none of 'em. Jus' got everybody riled up, and this beating of Mr. Farnsworth is just the beginning of it. Socialist conspiracy, that's what it is. Socialist conspiracy!"

He looked at Papa as if expecting him to agree that that indeed was what it was. When Papa made no comment, he turned to go, with Mr. Peck close behind. A few steps away he stopped again. "By the way, David, y'all know a fella name of Willis? Jake Willis, I believe his name is. Knifed another colored boy in a card game last night, and I figure I better put him in jail a few days. I ain't gonna have a lotta niggers cutting themselves up 'round here."

Uncle Hammer straightened, pulling away from the hoe. The movement was not lost on the sheriff, who looked over at him. Papa glanced at Uncle Hammer and said flatly, without emotion, "Name ain't familiar."

The moment lingered as the sheriff and Uncle Hammer kept their eyes on each other. Then the sheriff nodded at Papa and without another word went back across the field with Mr. Peck. As the two drove away, Papa said, "What'd you say that fella's name was at church got on your wrong side?"

Uncle Hammer smiled. "Jake Willis."

"That's what I thought. By the way, I been thinkin' 'bout maybe letting Morris Wheeler have his meeting here. What you think?"

Uncle Hammer took a moment, pursed his lips, and said, "You sure you wanna do that?"

"Figure it won't hurt to listen."

"Well, they have to meet someplace. But I was you, I'd choose the folks to come."

Papa nodded and turned back to his planting.

The meeting was held two nights later and the people who came were all people we knew very well—the Laniers, the Averys, the Ellises and Mrs. Lee Annie, and the Shorters. They came all in one wagon or by foot, so that anyone passing by would not be prompted to wonder about several wagons dotting the drive. When they arrived, they slipped quietly in to listen to Morris Wheeler and John Moses, while outside Mr. Morrison stood guard in case someone came along who shouldn't.

As the meeting got underway, the boys and I were sent off to another room, but we soon cracked opened the door to listen, and though both Mama and Papa saw us, they did not make us close it. The union men spoke in more detail about the union they proposed, what they planned to achieve, and how they planned to achieve it. Once they had said all they had come to say and all the questions people were willing to put to them had been asked and answered, they left. But the others stayed awhile longer talking into the night about all that had been said, and from what I could gather, mostly everyone thought the union to be a good thing. The drawback, however, was the risk involved and the fact that no one could bring themselves to trust the white farmers of the area, or even Morris Wheeler. There had been too many years of distrust, too many years of humiliations and beatings and lynchings and inequalities. They would wait, they decided, and see what happened.

A few days before Uncle Hammer was to leave, Papa leaned against a back porch post, his eyes on the newly plowed field. Christopher-John and I, finishing up the supper dishes, watched him standing there, and when Mama came to join him, we grew silent. We knew something had been bothering Papa, and although no one had spoken of it, we all knew what it was.

"You're going back to the railroad, aren't you?" Mama said.

Stacey came in from the dining room and, hearing Mama's question, stopped to listen as well.

Papa turned to her. The answer was on his face.

"I knew it."

"Mary, what you want me to do? I been to every place I can think of and there ain't been no work——"

"They say there'll be work when they start building at the hospital——"

"Baby, we can't count on that. You know we can't take a chance of coming up short come tax time. I got a job I can go to, then I gotta go."

Mama's voice rose. "And what about next year and the year after that? The children are growing fast and they need you here. Look at Stacey, nearly fourteen. He needs you, David. They all need you."

Papa spoke sharply. "And don't you think I know that?

But they need other things too. They need this land. Long as we've got this land, we've got something, something most folks ain't, and we can't risk losing it."

"David, just don't go this year. We'll find another way to get the money."

"Well, you tell me what other way there is."

"Hammer put in twenty dollars—"

"Most likely went without just to give it to us."

"We'll figure it all out again. See if there's something we can't do without . . . sell . . ."

Papa sighed wearily. "We've done that already."

Mama was silent a long time. Then quietly she said, "Maybe you like being a single man on the railroad."

"Mary—"

Mama moved away from Papa and started down the porch. Papa stopped her, turning her to him. "Mary, now you know that ain't so."

"I know," she said, just as quietly as before. There was a pause. "When are you going?"

"Figured to leave Saturday with Hammer."

Mama looked toward the drive. "I think I'll go walk down to the pond."

"I'll go with you."

"No . . . David, I know you're doing what you think's best, but I can't help how I feel. I just can't help it." Her eyes lingered on Papa a moment longer, then she turned and walked along the giant stepping stones leading to the drive.

Stacey turned abruptly and left through the dining room. Big Ma, who had been mixing bread dough at the dining room table, brought the dough into the kitchen and plopped it into a waiting bowl. She covered the bowl with a damp towel, wiped her hands, and went out to the porch.

"Son," she said, touching Papa's arm. "Son, now you

know I ain't never come messin' in nothin' 'tween you and Mary and I ain't wantin' to do it now. But you knows I loves Mary much as I do you, and me bein' a woman, I understands how she feels. You been leaving her a lot these here last few years to bring them children up by herself and take care of this place. I know you ain't wantin' to do it and Mary, she knows it too, but she got a right to 'spect you to be here."

"Now, Mama," Papa said, his voice sounding tired, "don't you start in on me too."

"I ain't gonna start in on ya! All I'm sayin' is you gotta understand how she feel, and maybe you can try and make it up to her some way, like comin' home more times than you done before. That'd make her feel better. Sho' would me. And you jus' 'member how special she is——"

Christopher-John dropped a spoon on the floor and Big Ma looked over her shoulder. Realizing that we were listening to every word, she took Papa's arm and walked with him out into the yard to the old bench under the walnut tree. As they crossed the yard, Christopher-John said, "You s'pose Papa gonna ever be able to stay?"

I shrugged. "Maybe . . . someday."

Christopher-John took a plate from the rinsewater and slowly dried it.

"Cassie . . . know what?"

I looked at him.

"I don't think I can wait that long. . . ."

Saturday was a lonely day. The boys and I stuck close to Papa and Uncle Hammer for most of the morning, but in the afternoon when Papa and Mr. Morrison and the boys went down to see about Dynamite, I stayed behind sitting on the back porch steps, staring out across the pasture, wondering if the time would ever come when Papa would not have to go away.

"Now what you doing sitting out here all by yourself?"

I looked around. Uncle Hammer was standing in the kitchen doorway.

"I—I was just thinking."

He closed the door and crossed the porch to the water pail hanging on a rafter nail. Filling the dipper with water, he drank slowly, then walked over to where I was sitting and leaned against the post.

"I imagine you most likely thinking 'bout your papa leaving—that right?"

"Yes, sir."

He didn't say anything else for several minutes, and I figured that he was lost in his own thoughts, forgetting I was even there. I wanted to move to another place, for I felt uncomfortable with Uncle Hammer standing there. But I couldn't just get up and walk away without saying something, and since I couldn't think of anything to say, I just sat there.

"You know," he said finally, making me start at the sound of his voice, "I recall one time when my papa went off for a spell—not as long as your papa has to go off for—but it was long enough. He was doing some lumbering up near the Natchez Trace, and David and me, we was fit to be tied, we missed him so. Him and our oldest brother, your Uncle Mitchell, was up there trying to get money together to get themselves a horse and pay on this place. Couldn't wait for them to get back here."

He smiled at the remembrance, then stood and waved toward the horseshoe stake out in the yard. "How 'bout a game of horseshoes with me?"

I looked at him, then went to get the horseshoes from

where they were hooked over a spike at the other end of the porch.

"You know, I used to be right good at this," he said, walking to the pitching line. "Your papa and me, we was two of the best shots at Great Faith when we was boys."

We tossed a round and Uncle Hammer won. I started the second round with a shot that nicely zinged around the stake and stayed put. Uncle Hammer held his shoe, but didn't throw it. "Ya know, Cassie, you ain't had much to say to me this time since I been here."

He was sure right about that. I glanced up at Uncle Hammer and, finding his eyes on me, immediately looked away again. I had made it a point not to say much to him. In fact, I had stayed out of his way as much as possible, for I wasn't about to put myself in the path of his anger again. One thing I wasn't was stupid.

"Your papa told me he thought you was kinda upset with me. That right?"

I kept my eyes riveted on the horseshoe I had successfully thrown and didn't answer.

"Cassie?"

I was afraid Uncle Hammer would hear my heart beating. I looked up at him.

"Look here, sugar, don't you know you got no need to ever be scared of me?" He paused, gazing softly down at me. Again, I looked away.

"I know I ain't the easiest person to get along with. Maybe sometimes I speak too rough to y'all. But don't you know I wouldn't never do nothin' to hurt you, and I wouldn't never tell you nothin' I didn't think was right? You know that, don't you?"

He waited patiently, expecting me to answer.

"Y-yes, sir."

Uncle Hammer glanced at his horseshoe and tossed it. It landed squarely on top of mine. He wasn't looking at me when he spoke again. "Ain't got no children of my own. Probably never will have. But even if I did, I couldn't love 'em no more than I love you, Christopher-John, Little Man, and Stacey. Y'all ever need me, y'all know there ain't nothing in this world I wouldn't do for y'all that I thought was right. Nothin'. Y'all . . . y'all like my own children to me. . . ."

Neither of us looked at the other; our eyes were on the stake. I wanted to throw my arms around Uncle Hammer and hug him, but that wasn't the way it was between Uncle Hammer and me. I hugged him when he arrived and hugged him when he left. Hugging him at any other time would have been awkward, even now. Instead, I threw another horseshoe and Uncle Hammer threw his. He said no more about what had happened between us or about his feelings, but he didn't need to. He had said enough.

After dinner Papa and Uncle Hammer prepared to go. Big Ma, who had spent a good part of the morning frying chicken and sweet potato turnovers for them to take, took the lunch boxes to the car and placed them gently on the backseat. By the time she came out, the boys and I were already standing with Uncle Hammer and Mr. Morrison near the barn, the coming loneliness already hanging over us. A few minutes later Papa and Mama came out and the good-byes began. Once Uncle Hammer had shaken Mr. Morrison's hand and hugged the rest of us, he neatly folded his suit jacket across the middle of the front seat and got in the car. Papa, having hugged us all, kissed Mama one last time and followed, but before he closed the door, Little Man, with huge tears swelling in his eyes, tugged at his arm. "P-Papa, do you gotta go?"

Every year the question was the same; every year Papa had to explain once again.

Papa looked softly at Little Man, then, cupping his thin face in his large, rough hands, said: "Now, son, I'm afraid I do or how else we gonna pay these taxes and keep this land? You know I ain't wanting to leave, don't you?" Little Man nodded. "We all got a job to do. My job is to go see 'bout getting back on the railroad and try to get us some cash money. Your job is to grow strong and help your mama and Big Ma and Mr. Morrison here while I'm gone. Now I'm gonna be counting on you to do that . . . you think you can?"

With a sniffle which he tried to conceal, Little Man said he could, then Papa held him close, smiled sadly at the rest of us, and with a wave closed the door.

"Y'all take care of y'allselves now," Big Ma called as the Ford pulled away. "And drive careful!"

Before the car had turned into the road, Little Man fled up the drive to the barn to hide his tears. Mama started to go after him, but Mr. Morrison stopped her. "Let me, Miz Logan," he said. As Mr. Morrison went up the drive, Big Ma followed, the spring suddenly gone out of her steps with both her sons gone. But Mama, Stacey, Christopher-John, and I remained by the road watching the car until we could see it no longer. As the swirls of red dust settled back to the earth, we crossed the lawn and headed for the house, still hearing the hum of the Ford's motor, faint, distant, too far away. Papa and Uncle Hammer were really gone now. It would be too long before they came again.

"I thinks I wants to vote," announced Mrs. Lee Annie one rainy afternoon in mid-April as she sat with Big Ma and me in front of the fire finishing a patchwork quilt started in winter.

Big Ma looked sharply across at her old friend. "Say what?"

"You heard me. Said I was gon' vote."

Big Ma's fingers moved deftly over the patch that had once been a part of Little Man's trousers to make sure it hadn't puckered. "Lord-a-mercy, Lee Annie, you gone foolish in yo' old age?"

"Naw . . . I just wants to vote. Done made up my mind."

"But Miz Lee Annie, you said you didn't wanna vote," I reminded her as I took this opportunity to put aside the quilting which had been forced upon me by Big Ma as one of those things young ladies needed to learn. "You said you just wanted to read that constitution."

"Well, that's the truth all right, sugar. But I jus' been thinking. Now's I'm learning the law, why shouldn't I jus' go on down and vote jus' like them white folks——"

"You done gone foolish——" Big Ma said again.

"Probably knows it better than a lot of them," Mrs. Lee Annie continued, unperturbed. "My papa voted. Said it was a right fine feeling. He voted and he didn't know no law at all 'ceptin' that he was a free man and a free man could vote. And here I jus' been readin' the constitution, and I ain't votin' at all——"

"You been readin' too much, that's what you been doin'," Big Ma retorted.

"Well, I'm gon' do it, Caroline. Gon' vote . . . sho' is. Where that Mary? Ow, you, Mary! Where you at?"

Mama came in from the kitchen and Mrs. Lee Annie told

her what she had told us. Mama glanced from Mrs. Lee Annie to Big Ma.

"Don't look at me," Big Ma said. "I done told her she was crazy. 'Round here talkin' 'bout she free and she gon' vote . . . like she got somebody to vote for."

Mama came back to the circle and took her seat, but she didn't pick up the quilt. Instead, she put her hand on Mrs. Lee Annie's arm. "Now, Mrs. Lee Annie," she said, "why you want to do this thing? You know these people aren't going to let you vote."

"I knows what I gotta do to take that test," Mrs. Lee Annie contended stubbornly, pounding her knee through the heavy quilt for emphasis. "I gots to have my poll taxes paid—and they gonna be, Russell give me the money—and I gotta tell the registrar what them there words in the con-stitution mean—and I gonna be able to do that—then I can vote."

"Mrs. Lee Annie, how many colored folks you know vote?"

"Ne'er a one. But part of that's 'cause these ole white folks think ain't no colored folks gon' come down to their ole voting places to vote. Well, this here ole aunty gon' strut right down there and show them I knows the law. Ole Lee Annie Lees gon' vote jus' like her daddy done."

"Now, Mrs. Lee Annie—"

"Lee Annie Lees, that's 'bout the silliest thing I done heard of!" exclaimed Big Ma in exasperation. "Now jus' who you think you gon' vote for if they lets you vote? Bilbo?"

"Humph!" grumped Mrs. Lee Annie.

"Mrs. Lee Annie," Mama said, "now have you thought about what could happen if you try to register? First of all, they most likely won't even let you, and even if they do, they won't pass you on the test, but they'll remember you tried to vote and they won't think too kindly of you for it either."

"That ain't what I'm living for, for these crackers to think kindly of me!"

Mama smiled and nodded. "But more than that, have you thought of what Harlan Granger might say?"

Mrs. Lee Annie looked surprised. "Harlan Granger? What he got to do with it?"

Mama took Mrs. Lee Annie's hand. "You're living on his land and he expects certain things—"

"And I gives 'em to him, too! Works my land and puts in my crop 'longside Page and Leora every year."

"Yes, ma'am, I know that, but—"

"And he knows it too!"

"Yes, ma'am. But Harlan Granger doesn't expect you to go off trying to vote, and he's not going to like it. Not one little bit."

For the first time Mrs. Lee Annie was silent.

"He's not going to care," Mama continued, "about your papa or your dreams. All he's going to care about is that one of 'his' colored people is trying to do something he figures is white folks' business, and believe me, Mrs. Lee Annie—I know that man—when he doesn't like something, that means there's going to be trouble . . . for you. . . . Things could happen."

Mrs. Lee Annie was thoughtful, one hand fingering the quilt, the other still held by Mama. She remained unspeaking for so long that Mama finally said, "Mrs. Lee Annie?"

Mrs. Lee Annie looked back at Mama. "Mary, child, all my life whenever I wanted to do something and the white folks didn't like it, I didn't do it. All my life, it been that way. But now I's sixty-four years old and I figure I's deserving of doing something *I* wants to do, white folks like it or not. And this old body wants to vote and like I done said, I gots my mind made up. I's gon' vote too."

Mama patted her hand. "Promise me you'll think about what I said."

"I'll think 'bout it all right, but it ain't gonna change my mind none. What I really wants though is for you to help me. You and Cassie. What Cassie and me ain't learned, you can teach us. Will you do that for me, sugar?"

"Mrs. Lee Annie—"

"I said I'd think 'bout it, ain't I? But I still wants your help."

Mama puckered her lips and sighed. "You think about what I said and you think hard now—"

"And you gonna help me?"

"It's against my better judgment . . ."

"But ya will?"

Mama shook her head, allowing a frustrated laugh. "I suppose."

"Good!" said Mrs. Lee Annie, smiling brightly and picking up her quilting.

Mrs. Lee Annie did not change her mind. The most devoted of students, she listened intently to Mama's explanations of the constitution and laboriously attempted to commit them to memory. There were nearly 300 sections of the constitution and Mrs. Lee Annie wanted to know each and every one of them. Already she could quote many of them word for word, but it was the understanding she needed and was determined to have. Her enthusiasm for learning was, in fact, so strong that it proved contagious, affecting Big Ma, Mr. Tom Bee, and even me.

"Ain't gon' vote, but I guess it ain't gonna hurt me none to know some of that stuff," Big Ma had decided as she sat with Mrs. Lee Annie, Mama, and me around the dining room table. "Now, Mary, child, what you say that business 'bout them courts bein' open to everybody was?"

Mr. Tom Bee, who was often at Mrs. Lee Annie's when Mama and I went there, was more indirect about his interest. He sat through a number of the sessions seemingly uninterested, whittling on a piece of wood as Mama explained the sections and Mrs. Lee Annie attempted to understand. None of us thought he had paid any attention to anything that was going on until one afternoon when Mrs. Lee Annie was trying, with difficulty, to explain to Mama what "jurisdic tion" meant, and he suddenly exclaimed: "Naw, naw, Lee Annie! Don't ya 'member? What you talkin' 'bout is a jury. Jurisdiction tells ya' who got the power in a thing."

We all looked at him in amazement.

"You sure you won't join us over here, Brother Bee?" Mama invited.

"Ah, no, ma'am, Miz Logan. I's fine right where I is."

But despite his feigned lack of interest, Mama and I both noted that more and more often he was at Mrs. Lee Annie's when we arrived, and on several occasions even accompanied Mrs. Lee Annie down to our house for the lessons held there.

"That Tom Bee, don't he bother you none sittin' off to hisself whittling when you be teaching?" asked a vexed Big Ma after one of the sessions. "He do me. Pretending he ain't payin' no 'tention, but always ready to correct a body if she ain't said the right answer."

Mama smiled, aware that Mr. Tom Bee's correcting Big Ma three times during the afternoon had not exactly sat well with her. "Not at all. I love it."

As for me, under Mama's instruction I suddenly found the dry words of the constitution beginning to take meaning. Mama explained that a number of the laws were quite good and in theory quite fair. The problem, however, was in the application, and that if the judges and the courts really saw everyone as equal instead of as black or white, life could have been a lot pleasanter. Mama said that maybe one day equal rights would be for everyone, but as far as she could see, that day was still a ways off. I personally hoped that it wasn't as far off as she made it sound. I figured that before I died, I'd like to enjoy a little of that liberty and justice the constitution kept talking about myself. And I didn't intend to be sixty-four when I did either.

By the first week in May the young shoots of cotton were up and we had gone through the backbreaking chore of chopping and our first weeding. More than anything I hated weeding. It was sweaty, tiring work which was unending, for no sooner had we pulled the weeds from the last row of all three fields than we found more had worked their way into the first rows. Each morning before the color of the land had changed from predawn gray to the emerald brilliance of spring, we had already eaten breakfast and were finishing the last of the morning chores. By the time the sun itself peeped over the horizon, we were in the fields bending and pulling.

As May wore toward June and the fieldwork continued, news that work was soon to begin at the hospital building site spread through the community. When the work announcement became official, men, both black and white, gathered at the old Huntington farm where the hospital was to be built, sleeping long nights on the hard ground to be ready as soon as the call to work came.

"You ever think 'bout seeing 'bout working up there yourself?" Stacey asked Little Willie when he learned that Mr. Wiggins had gotten on at the site.

We were sitting on the Wiginses' back porch eating

roasted peanuts. Little Willie popped a peanut into his mouth before answering and shook his head. "Naw. Why would I? All them men up there, what chance I got?" He looked questioningly at Stacey. "What? You thinkin' to get on?"

"He might be thinkin' it," I said, reaching into the pan, "but that don't mean nothin' long as Mama ain't."

Stacey glared at me as if I were the burden of his life, but I paid no attention as I went on eating. "I figure it wouldn't hurt to try," he said.

"S'pose not," agreed Little Willie. He popped another peanut into his mouth. "Ya wanna go over there?"

Stacey stared out at the gloom of the drizzling day and decided that he would, then along with Little Willie tried to persuade the rest of us to stay behind. But since we were having none of that, they finally gave in, and after telling Mrs. Wiggins we were going for a walk, we crossed the north field to the forest beyond. Coming to Soldiers Road, we walked the half mile down to the Huntington place. As we approached it, a newly painted sign with large black lettering, oddly out of place among the ferns and weeds already coiling around its legs, loomed on the left side of the road. On the sign was printed:

PROPOSED SITE OF THE
SPOKANE COUNTY MEMORIAL HOSPITAL.

I looked around. Only the forest was visible. "Well where is it?"

Stacey nodded past the sign. "Must be that road there."

What Stacey had politely called a road was no more than a wagon trail. We went up it, our bare feet caking with the red mud, and soon saw what had once been the Huntingtons' house, a gray clapboard dwelling with a tin roof, now being used as an office for the site. Standing in front of the building in an orderly single file were over a hundred men, all of them white. Little Willie pointed to the side of the house. "Papa say they got the hiring place for colored 'round there."

Following Little Willie's lead, we passed the men and went around to the right side. The line here was just as long with men standing patiently, unable to sit because of the muddy ground. To our surprise, Dubé Cross was in the line.

"Hey, this where you been keeping yourself?" Little Willie asked. "Ain't hardly seen you 'round no place these last few weeks."

Dubé shook his head. "J-jus' come up here yesterday. B-b-been spending t-time with Mr. Wh-Wheeler and Mr. Moses w-with the union."

Stacey's brow furrowed.

Dubé noticed it. "Th-that's right. I ffff-figures that's the only way folks like me g-g-gonna get anywheres."

Stacey chose not to get into a conversation about the union, and instead looked back down the line at all the men gathered. "You figurin' you gonna be able to get on here?"

"G-g-gonna try."

"They hirin' less'n sixteen?"

"D-don't know. You mos' likely g-g-gotta ask Mr. Crawford 'b-bout that."

"Mos' likely you get hired," said Little Willie. "You got the muscles." He looked out at the fields, where groups of black men were working under the direction of white leaders. "You seen my papa anywheres?"

"G-g-got work early on th-this mornin' pullin' stumps."

"Where 'bout we find this Mr. Crawford?" Stacey asked.

Dubé looked around, then pointed to the edge of the yard. "Th-there he go y-y-yonder with Mr. Harrison."

We wished Dubé luck and headed toward the two men, but before we reached the end of the line, Jake Willis stopped us. Smiling broadly, the two gold teeth clearly visible, he said, "Well, looka here! Y'all Logan younguns, ain't ya? I reckon y'all don't 'member me, now do ya? But I 'members y'all all right. 'Members the whole family."

"We remember you," Stacey said without enthusiasm.

Jake Willis laughed. "Well, ain't that something! Yeah . . . What y'all doing out here? Job hunting?"

"Little Willie's father here. He's working up yonder in the field," Stacey said, slyly skirting the truth.

"Ya don't say?" Jake Willis glanced out at the field. "Well, seem everybody get lucky but me and I don't never get lucky. Been out here since six o'clock and ain't got nothing." He turned back to us with a laugh. "Ain't gonna get no Packards that way, now am I?"

Stacey put a hand on my shoulder to urge me on. "We gotta go."

"Well, anyways, it was good to see y'all. I'm just glad y'all ain't out here job hunting too. For a moment there, I was thinkin' I was gonna have to fight for my job 'gainst a Logan. Thought maybe things had gotten so bad for y'all, maybe y'all had been sent out for hire." He laughed then, a raucous, distasteful laugh, and Stacey pushed us on.

"That man, I don't like him much," Christopher-John admitted as we walked away.

"You ain't the only one," I said.

"Look here, Stacey," Little Willie said as we neared Mr. Harrison and Mr. Crawford, "ya wanna do the talking?"

"Don't matter to me."

"Okay, then you go 'head."

When we reached the two men, Mr. Harrison, a white-haired man in his seventies whose plantation bordered our land to the west, took the time to speak to us. Mr. Crawford, however, tall, weathered-looking, and occupied with both rolling a cigarette and hollering orders across the field, didn't even see us. Mr. Harrison asked what we were doing there and Stacey told him.

"Well, I must say, that's right ambitious," he decided, and when Mr. Crawford turned his full attention back to his cigarette, he said, "Sam, these here young fellas come to see you 'bout a job."

Mr. Crawford glanced over, licked the cigarette paper, and gently sealed it to the roll, locking in the tobacco. "How old you be?"

"Fourteen. Both of us," answered Stacey, indicating Little Willie and himself. "We strong and we can do our share."

Mr. Crawford stuck the finished cigarette between his lips and lit it, his eyes on the flame. "What kinda job you want?"

"Anything you got. We're willing to do whatever needs doing."

"This boy Stacey here's a good worker, too, Sam," praised Mr. Harrison with a gentle slap to Stacey's shoulder. "Known him and his daddy both since they was born. Known his granddaddy too. All of 'em good, dependable men and fine workers."

Mr. Crawford looked across the field to the line of men and nodded at them. "You see them men out there?"

We all looked at the line.

"Yes, sir," said Stacey.

"Your daddy in that line?"

"No, sir."

"He been in it?"

"No, sir."

"What's he do?"

"Work on the railroad."

Mr. Crawford nodded. "Then y'all got something. Most of them men there got nothing at all. Mr. Harrison says you a good worker so I believe that to be so, but I can't go hiring no boy of fourteen when there's men out there been waiting months, maybe years to make some money. Now can I?"

Stacey looked directly at Mr. Crawford. I thought he was going to agree with him, but instead he said: "We all trying to keep from losing what we got. Me no less than them others."

Mr. Crawford seemed somewhat surprised by the statement. Glancing at Mr. Harrison, he looked back at Stacey with appreciation. He waved his cigarette hand at him. "I tell you what. This here project's s'pose to keep going the next five years. You come back when you get to be sixteen, and if I'm still here and the money's still comin' in, I'll hire you. That's the best I can do— Farley, didn't I tell you them men was s'pose to be working on the other side?" He turned back to Mr. Harrison. "Look here, Henry, I'd better see to this myself. Don't nobody 'round here seem to know what they doing."

Mr. Harrison watched him hurry off, then turned to Stacey, a look of piercing scrutiny in his eyes. "You serious 'bout working, boy?"

"Why . . . yes, sir."

"Then I got a job, you want it. Whitewashing. 'Bout a week's work, I figure. Pay you five dollars."

Stacey was silenced by the offer.

"Well, you want it?"

"I'll—I'll have to ask Mama."

"All right. I'm on my way home now. I'll drop y'all there and you can ask her."

Mr. Harrison took Little Willie and Maynard as far as the north end of their farm, then continued to our place, where we hurried into the house while he waited in the car. We found Mama in the kitchen battering okra. She looked up smiling as we came in, but as soon as Stacey blurted out Mr. Harrison's job offer, her face grew solemn, and dropping a handful of the okra in the hot oil, she said simply, "No."

"Ma'am?"

"I said no."

"But Mama—"

"Stacey, your papa's not leaving us nine months out of the year, breaking his back on that railroad, so that you can go work on some white man's place. You've got land—four hundred acres out there—of your own to work, and if you want to work somewhere, then you work it."

"But, Mama, we need that money!"

Mr. Harrison's horn blasted outside and Mama looked around.

"That's Mr. Harrison," I explained. "He brung us home."

Mama frowned, then took off her apron and went outside with us following.

At the car, Mr. Harrison said: "That boy of yours there tell you what I proposed to him?"

Mama nodded. "He did and we appreciate your offer, Mr. Harrison. But with David away, I really need Stacey here."

There was a look in Mr. Harrison's eyes that said he recognized in Mama something he understood. "Well, I was afraid of that. May get another boy from my place to do the work needs doing. Or maybe the Wiggins boy. Ain't gonna worry 'bout it though for the next few days, so you find you can spare Stacey at all, you send him on down."

"That's very kind of you, Mr. Harrison, but I don't think I'll be changing my mind."

"Well, you tell your mama I said hello now."

"I'll do that."

Mr. Harrison backed the car into the road and headed

west toward his plantation. Without thinking, I took it upon myself to say, "Well, there go that five dollars."

Mama turned to look at me. "What's that?"

I met Mama's eyes and figured it was better not to repeat it. "Nothin'."

Her eyes burned with displeasure. "And what were you doing riding home with Mr. Harrison? Haven't I told you about riding with white folks? I'd better not catch you doing it again. You hear me?"

Christopher-John, Little Man, and I murmured a distinct "Yes, ma'am," but Stacey turned from her without a word and started across the backyard.

"Stacey," she said, "did you hear me?"

Stacey turned and glared at her. "I heard. I heard everything and I figure you're wrong 'bout that five dollars. We need that money, Mama. Much hard times we been having with the cotton and everything, and then you not teaching and Papa's leg gettin' broke, we can't hardly be talking 'bout not working for the white folks. They the ones got the money, then they the ones we gonna hafta get it from."

I thought Mama was going to walk up the drive and knock Stacey down for his insolence. She didn't. Instead she patiently folded her arms and met his accusing gaze. "That may be, but it'll be quite a few years yet before I have you going out into that white man's world bowing and scraping."

"Papa don't bow and scrape!"

"No. But he has to bend. We all do, and the longer I can keep you from having to, the better I'll feel. The land, Stacey, that's more important than Mr. Harrison's or any other white man's five dollars."

"Well, what you think I want the money for? That five dollars of Mr. Harrison's could've gone toward the land tax. Plenty boys my age work outside their place—"

"Well, plenty of boys don't have land of their own . . . you do."

Stacey shook his head, as if Mama could not possibly understand how it was with him. "I ain't no baby no more, Mama, and you gotta stop treating me like one. We need the money and I figures to get me a job—"

"Oh, no," Mama said as Big Ma crossed the backyard from the garden. "Not as long as I have anything to say about it."

"Then maybe you won't."

Shocked, Christopher-John, Little Man, and I stared in disbelief at Stacey. None of us had ever talked to Mama that way. Looking as though he were as shocked as the rest of us, Stacey glanced our way, then dashed across the yard toward the garden. Mama called after him, but he didn't stop.

"Boy, don't you hear your mama callin' you?" Big Ma demanded as he went past her. But he did not heed her either. "I hear my ears right? That boy sass you?" Big Ma demanded of Mama. "Well, he done got too big for his britches 'round here. Needs a good whippin', that's what he needs."

Mama stared after Stacey in silence. Christopher-John, Little Man, and I kept our eyes on her, wondering what she would do next. "No," she finally said and slowly walked up the stepping stones to the side door. "It's not a whipping he needs. . . ." She took one last glance at Stacey's retreating figure. "It's David," she said, and went into the house.

8

Stacey was changing. In the last year he had grown more than a foot, making him taller than Mama and nearly as tall as Papa. In addition to his new height, his voice had deepened. One morning several months ago he had awakened speaking in somebody else's baritone. I told him to clear his throat, but he insisted that nothing was wrong with his throat and informed me that all boys' voices changed. Although I had been aware of Clarence's and Moe's voices cracking up and down the vocal scale, Stacey had undergone none of that. When I asked him why he hadn't, he answered that he was just lucky, he guessed. I suppose he guessed he was lucky as well to have what he called his "mustache," a simple fuzz line which he cultivated with delicate daily care and about which, upon Mama's advice, I wisely kept quiet.

Had the change in Stacey been only physical, I think I could have handled it better, but unfortunately the change had affected other areas as well. Now fourteen, he was a very private person and much preferred to be off by himself somewhere or with Little Willie, Clarence, or Moe rather than with Christopher-John, Little Man, and me, and I frankly resented it. I had always accepted Stacey's need to have friends his own age, just as the rest of us did, but always before Christopher-John, Little Man, and I had been accepted, no matter how grudgingly, in whatever he was doing, and he had to some extent confided in us. Now too often we were hearing that we were too young to listen to something, or that something or other did not concern us, and the confidences became fewer and farther between.

Sometimes in an attempt to keep things as they had been, I followed Stacey when he went off alone or with one of his friends. Most times he tried to send me back; other times he simply ignored me. I hadn't yet decided which bothered me most. Once when Moe came over and he and Stacey crossed the road to the forest, I sat for some time debating whether or not to follow. Finally deciding that I had just as much right to be in the forest as they did, I wound my way among the trees to the clearing, where I found them sitting on the bank of the pond, their backs to me. Neither noticed me as I approached, and not feeling like arguing with Stacey on this particular day I settled down some feet away without a word to them. With my hands cupping my head and my eyes on the circle of sunlight sifting softly through the magic of forest green above, I lay comfortably upon a cushiony mattress of pine needles enjoying the stillness of the forest and paying little attention to Stacey's and Moe's conversation; after all, I had not come to eavesdrop. But then Stacey said: "You heard any more 'bout Jacey Peters? I mean 'bout her being with Stuart Walker and Joe Billy?"

My ears perked up. Anything to do with Jacey Peters these days caught my attention.

Moe shook his head. "Nothin' 'cept for that time at school . . . and, oh yeah, Little Willie did say somethin' 'bout Clarice and Jacey walking over to Aunt Callie Jackson's and Stuart and them coming along and offering 'em a ride."

"But they didn't get in the car, did they?"

Moe laughed softly. "Little Willie said he didn't know 'bout Jacey's folks, but if Clarice had gotten in that car, by the time Mr. Wiggins had've gotten through with her she wouldn't't've been able to sit for a good week."

"But you ain't heard nothin' else?"

Moe turned curiously toward Stacey and looked at him for a long moment before answering. "Naw, I ain't heard nothin' else." He hesitated, glanced out toward the pond, then back at Stacey. "How come you so interested in Jacey Peters all of a sudden? What? You kinda likin' her or some-thin'?"

Now it was Stacey who was quiet. He threw a pebble into the pond and shrugged. "Oh, I don't know. I mean she's pretty and she's smart and she's got a way about her. . . ."

"But you worried 'bout maybe her messin' 'round with Joe Billy and Stuart?"

Stacey nodded. "She messin' 'round with white boys, I don't wanna waste my time with her."

Again Moe laughed his good-natured laugh. "Stacey, man, you'd probably be wasting your time anyway. That girl's two years older'n you."

Stacey laughed too. "You probably right. But . . . I don't know . . . sometimes I've seen her looking at me like . . . like maybe she wouldn't mind me talking to her."

"Well, you think that, then go on then. Won't hurt nothin'. Like you said, she is awful pretty and she's real nice. Ain't never heard no bad talk 'bout her, so I wouldn't worry none 'bout Stuart or Joe Billy."

"I guess I won't. I was thinking maybe this Sunday at church I'd—"

"Ah, confound it!" I leapt up from my bed, having realized too late that giant red ants had gotten there before me.

"Cassie, what you doing down here?" Stacey demanded to know, as I danced madly about, swatting at the ants.

"The pond, Cassie," Moe suggested. "Get in the pond."

I took his advice and dashed into the water; it rose cool and soothing to my neck.

"You all right?" Moe asked sympathetically.

"Yeah, I guess."

Stacey, however, showed no concern at all for my discomfort. "Cassie, you follow me down here? Didn't you ever think maybe me and Moe had something we wanted to talk 'bout in private?"

"Yeah, something private like Jacey Peters," I retorted, angered by his uncaring attitude.

If looks could kill, I would have been finished right there. But Stacey deigned to say nothing further concerning it, choosing instead to change the subject. "Moe, how's your cotton coming?"

Moe smiled at me before he answered, showing at least he cared about my misfortune. "It's looking good," he said, his voice lifting as it always did whenever he spoke about his cotton. "I think it's gonna work out for us this time."

"You know I hope you're right, Moe. But don't get your

hopes up too high—you know how things turned out last year and—"

Moe dismissed the reminder with a wave of his hand. "I know . . . But this year it'll be different. You'll see."

Stacey looked as if he wanted to say more, but then seemed to reconsider. "I just hope you're right, Moe."

"Stacey! Cassie! Ow, y'all!"

We looked toward the trail leading back to the house and waited for Christopher-John and Little Man to appear. Twice more they yelled before they actually burst into view.

"What's the matter?" Stacey asked.

"Y'all guess what!" cried Christopher-John.

"Y'all ain't never gonna guess!" exclaimed Little Man.

"Well, what?" I said.

"It's Cousin Bud!" Christopher-John blurted out. "He come back."

Stacey's face went cold. "He's here?"

"Yeah, he's here," Christopher-John answered. "He jus' come and y'all ain't never gonna guess——"

"—he brung Suzella—"

"—that's his daughter—"

"—and Mama, she say that makes her our cousin—"

"—so y'all come on! Y'all just gotta see her!"

"Owwwww! She so pretty!"

With that, they turned and without waiting for us to follow ran as quickly as they could back toward the house.

"They sure are excited enough," laughed Moe as I came from the pond. "This cousin of y'all's must be something."

Stacey stood without saying anything and the three of us went back to the house. Expecting to find Cousin Bud and his daughter in Mama and Papa's room, we entered the house through the side door. The room was empty, but with the door opened to the dining room, we could see Cousin

Bud sitting at the table with Big Ma and Mama. Little Man and Christopher-John sat on the side bench, but there was no Suzella.

"Come on in and speak to your Cousin Bud," Mama said. "Cassie, how'd you get so wet?"

"I fell in the pond," I said as we crossed the room.

"How y'all doing?" asked Cousin Bud, smiling.

"Fine," I said; Stacey didn't answer.

Mama cast a stern eye on him. "Stacey."

Stacey glanced at her, then back to Cousin Bud. "We're fine. You gonna be here long?"

Cousin Bud's eyes met Stacey's. I think he must have seen a little of Uncle Hammer there, for he sighed gently and rubbed his chin. "Just a few days. Brung my daughter, Suzella, though. She's gonna stay awhile."

"Where is she?" I asked.

"She's in your room changing," Mama answered. "Why don't you go on in and meet her?"

I nodded and left the kitchen eager to see this Suzella. All the boys went with me as far as Mama and Papa's room, where they settled in chairs around the darkened hearth.

"Bring her on out here, Cassie," Moe softly instructed. "I wanna meet her too."

"Thought you said you couldn't stay long," teased Stacey.

"Did. But there ain't no way I'm going 'fore I see your cousin in there."

I pushed open the door and went in. Standing on the far side of the room, on the other side of the bed, was a tall slender girl, her head bent downward as she pulled a flared A-line skirt over her hips. Her skin had a creamy cast, but was not as pale as I had thought it would be, and her hair, which hung loose and long, enveloping her face so that I could not see it, was auburn with deep silky waves. She zipped the skirt which clung neatly to her womanly figure, and looked up. Her face had the same square-jawed cut of Mama's people and, except for the gray eyes and the creamy skin tone, her resemblance to Mama was striking. A smile spread brightly across her face as she saw me, and she said: "You must be Cassie."

I nodded.

"Well, I'm Suzella, but you can call me Su if you want. That's what my friends at school call me." I started to say that I thought she didn't have any friends, but deciding that would be impolite, I said nothing at all. "Daddy told me about you," she continued.

"Did?"

"Um-hmm. He told me about all of you—Stacey, Christopher-John, and Little Man—I already love Christopher-John and Little Man. They're adorable. Is Stacey here?"

I motioned toward the door behind me. "He's out there."

"Oh, I really want to meet him too. Daddy says we're nearly the same age."

"He ain't but fourteen."

Suzella picked up one of her dresses from the bed and laid it neatly over a chair. "Well, I'm fifteen, so I guess a year's not so much."

"Uh-huh. You gonna be here long?"

"Well, I don't know. Daddy's going back in a day or so, but he wants me to stay awhile."

"He going back to New York?"

Suzella nodded.

"Alone? I mean, he's going to live by himself?"

Suzella had just reached for another dress from her suitcase. She stopped and looked at me. "No . . my mother's there."

"She is? But I thought that she . . ." I stopped short,

realizing that I was about to say too much.

Suzella glanced down at her suitcase, then back at me. "Did Daddy tell you he and Mother were separated? I mean they were, but Mother's home again now. They just had a misunderstanding, that's all."

I stared at her and before I took the time to think, I said, "What's it like?"

"What's what like?"

"Having a white mama."

Now it was she who stared.

"I mean, I wouldn't even know how to act 'round her," I contended, baffled by the very thought of a white person living in the same house, let alone having one as a mother. The whole thing seemed incredible to me. "Don't you feel kinda funny, her being white and you being colored——"

The pleasantness of Suzella's face quickly faded and she said acidly, "I am not colored, Cassie."

"Well, I'd jus' like to know what you think you are then!"

She breathed in deeply, her cheeks reddening, then turned back to unpacking. "I'm mixed blood."

"Same thing."

She was silent, her eyes downcast. Taking out another dress, she held it a moment, then looked back to me. "You say Stacey's out there?" Her voice was soft once more, almost apologetic.

"Uh-huh."

"Then I want to meet him. This can wait."

Making sure that her sleeveless blouse was fully tucked inside her skirt, she rounded the bed and followed me into the other room. As soon as the door opened, Moe and Stacey stood. Little Man and Christopher-John remained seated, but they grinned widely, almost glowing, as they gazed upon Suzella.

Suzella greeted Stacey with adultlike poise and I could see that the resentment which had been in Stacey's face upon greeting Cousin Bud was not there as he met his daughter.

"Yeah, well, it's real good to meet you," Stacey said. "How long you gonna be here?"

"I don't really know. Maybe the summer."

"You ever live in the country before?"

Suzella laughed lightly. "No. I was born in New York and except for sometimes getting to go with Daddy to Jersey, I've never even been in the country."

"Well, I hear living in the city is a whole lot different from living in the country. Sometimes I think maybe I'd like to try living in the city—" He stopped abruptly and glanced over at Moe, who had just nudged him. "Oh, you didn't meet my friend Moe yet, did ya? Well, this here's Moe Turner. Moe, my cousin, Suzella Rankin."

Suzella smiled, displaying even white teeth, and held out her hand to Moe, who took it without speaking. But there was really no need for him to speak; his eyes said it all. I glanced around at each of the boys. From Little Man and Christopher-John to Stacey and Moe, it was evident that each was entranced by Suzella. As for me, I didn't know if I even liked her.

"What're you doing, Cassie?"

I looked around at Suzella. It seemed perfectly obvious to me what I was doing. Sitting on the back porch with one foot in hot water and the other crossed over my leg and a needle plunged in my big toe, what else could I be doing but pulling out jiggers? I wanted to tell her just what I thought about her stupidity, but reminding myself that she was a guest, I kept my remarks to myself. As far as I was concerned, she asked just too many questions anyway, though no one else seemed to think so. They were all too crazy about her.

Since her arrival, she had managed to endear herself to just about everyone. Christopher-John and Little Man couldn't do enough for her and Stacey, who never had time for me anymore, always could find time for Suzella. She was forever in the kitchen laughing and talking with Big Ma, eager to do her bidding and claiming to want to learn all her recipes, and she had even taken to calling her "Big Ma," which didn't sit too well with me. After all, Big Ma was not *her* grandmother. She also spent a good deal of time with Mama, and the two of them laughed and talked like good friends instead of an aunt and a great-niece.

At church she had been met with the same welcome. All the young men of marrying age and boys old enough to be impressed by the female figure turned adoring eyes upon her as soon as she arrived. Moe, dressed in his patched but clean white shirt and string of a tie, had come all the way from Smellings Creek to attend church, a trek he seldom made on a Sunday since there was a perfectly good church only a mile from his home. Joining us, he had stood nervously and silently by as Clarence and Little Willie, among others of Stacey's friends, had sauntered over in feigned nonchalance. Suzella had been cordial to each one, but granted no special attention to any of them. Instead she had stayed close to Mama and Big Ma, and allowed none of the boys a moment alone with her. Nonetheless, everyone adored her, and by the time Cousin Bud left a few days later, she had not only been accepted by the community but was firmly entrenched in the family circle as well. I, however, was not won over. She

was a guest and a cousin, which meant that I had to be nice
to her. It didn't mean I had to like her.

When I didn't answer her question, Christopher-John
spoke up quickly. "She pulling out jiggers. In summertime
you always gotta look out for jiggers 'cause we go barefooted
all the time. Every night 'fore we go to bed, Mama say we
gotta wash our feet and check 'em real good so's to see if
jiggers done got in 'em. But sometimes ya just don't see 'em
till a day or so later and they get to hurtin'."

"And ya don't get 'em, they can make you so sick, 'cause
they get in and they get big," Little Man added. He turned
to Christopher-John. "'Member that time ole Baker Norris
got them jiggers in his foot and didn't get 'em out? That ole
foot got this big." He demonstrated the swelling of Baker
Norris's foot with his hands. "Swolled all up."

Suzella grimaced, then came closer to watch me as I
expertly plunged the needle farther into the tough outer tissue
of my toe to get at the dark mass below. "Does it hurt?" she
asked.

I finished tearing back the skin. "Unh-unh."

"Will too you gotta go any deeper," contradicted Little
Man. "Uh-oh, there it is." He and Christopher-John drew
nearer and all watched in curious silence as I gently sank the
needle once more into the skin and attempted to slip it
beneath the flea. Assured that the needle was in position, I
pulled up slowly to extract the jigger, but as sometimes happened, the mass broke in two at the pressure.

"Ah, shoot!" I cried.

"I better get Big Ma," said Christopher-John, getting up.

"Her and Mama, they's in the field," Little Man said.

"What's the matter?" asked Suzella.

"Well, once they break they gets awful hard to get out,"
explained Christopher-John. "And they gotta come on out

now or they'll work their way back in. Cassie keep picking at it, she gonna have her foot so sore she won't be able to walk on it."

"I ain't gonna get it sore," I retorted, wiping the blood from the needle before plunging it in once more. But the skin did feel tender, and despite willing myself not to I flinched noticeably.

"Here, let me try," said Suzella.

I looked up at her as if she were crazy, then back at my toe. I wasn't about to let her near my foot. I started to work again, but Suzella softly touched my hand, stopping my attempt. "Cassie, I'm good at this sort of thing. Really. I won't hurt you."

"Yeah, I know you won't 'cause I'm gonna do it myself."

"Please, Cassie. People say I have a gentle touch. If you feel any pain at all then I'll stop."

"Ah, Cassie, let her try," said Christopher-John.

I eyed Suzella doubtfully as she smiled and took the needle. She sat down beside me and cradled my foot in her lap, then as I tensed waiting for the pain and kicking myself for the fool that I was to let some girl who didn't even know what a jigger was put a needle in my foot, she put the tip of the needle against my skin, but not where I had already opened it.

"Girl, what you doing?" I cried.

"You've already got it sore there, Cassie," she said without looking up. "It's better I try to get it from this way."

Deftly, she picked open the skin and, probing gently, worked the needle below the black mass. Although at one point I did feel a twinge of pain, I didn't tell her, for the jigger was deep and there were times when even Big Ma could not extract the creatures without some pain.

"There it is! You got 'im!" cried Little Man as Suzella brought out part of the mass.

She smiled, then wordlessly went after the rest. When it too was out, she sat back, a look of satisfaction on her face. "Did it hurt, Cassie?" she asked.

I took my foot from her lap and inspected it. "Just one time, but that's okay."

"Wait a minute before you walk on it," she said standing. "I've got some alcohol my mother packed. We should put some on your toe so it won't get infected."

"It ain't gonna get infected," I said.

"Well, this way we'll make sure it won't."

As soon as the kitchen door closed behind her, Christopher-John admonished, "Owww, Cassie, you didn't even say 'Thank you.' "

I looked at him, then back at my foot. "I'll thank her . . ." I said, "if the alcohol don't burn."

In the afternoon, Little Man and Christopher-John entered the house, fishing poles in hand, and announced: "We goin' fishin'. Suzella, ya wanna come?" Although neither Stacey or I had been invited, we grabbed poles from the barn as well and went along. This was Suzella's first trip into the forest, and she seemed enthralled by the pines and the oaks and the sweet gums surrounding us. But as we went deeper into the forest and the trees began to thin, exposing stumps and the fallen trees, she wanted to know what had happened. I told her nothing, since I figured that she had found out quite enough about us and our land, but Stacey told her about the lumbermen and how they had destroyed so much of the forest until Mama had sent him to Louisiana to get Papa, who had stopped them. Suzella seemed saddened by the account, and as we walked on, she said nothing further until we came to the pond.

"This here's the Caroline," Christopher-John informed her. "Big Ma say Grandpa called it that after her."

"It's lovely." Suzella took a long look around and after nodding her approval said, "All right, now what's the first thing we do about fishing?"

The boys showed her, doing practically everything from digging the worms out of the soft ground of the bank to baiting the hooks. Had she wanted them to, they would probably have held the pole, and as it was about the only thing they didn't do was put a fish on the end of it. Sickened by the whole thing, I left my pole where it was and went looking for a sweet gum tree. When I found one with its bark cracked and oozing out its chewy goodness for anyone who cared to take it, I went back to Stacey and asked him for his penknife.

Already settled on the bank with his fishing pole in hand, he looked up irritably. "What for?"

"Jus' wanna borrow it, that's all!"

"I said what for?"

"If you jus' gotta know, I wanna get me some gum. Now let me have it."

Stacey glanced over at Suzella. "You want some gum?"

"Lord," I murmured.

Suzella said she did, and for her Stacey got up and went over to my sweet gum. Curious, Suzella jumped up and followed him with me tagging along behind.

"What're you doing?" Suzella asked as Stacey scraped a glob of gum from the tree.

"You said you wanted some gum. We get it from swee' gum trees like this here."

"But, I thought . . ." She looked at the gum on the knife and laughed. "I've never seen natural gum before."

"Well, you want it or not?" I asked crossly.

"Of course." She peeled off the gum and stuck it into her mouth. She grinned at the taste.

"Like it?" said Stacey.

"It's lovely."

"Let me have the knife," I said, putting out my hand to take it.

But Stacey wouldn't give it to me. "I'll get the gum for you." He hollered to Christopher-John and Little Man to see if they wanted any and the two of them came running.

"Boy, I don't see how come you won't let me use your ole knife. I ain't gonna hurt it none."

Stacey slit off another glob of gum. "Here."

"Ah, chew it yourself. One of these days I'm gonna get me my own knife and I won't have to be askin' you for yours, you so particular 'bout who using it." With that, I went back to the pond and took up my pole.

Later, when each of us had several fish to our credit and Suzella had calmed down after her excitement of actually catching a fish, she started asking questions again, this time about Mr. Morrison. "I was just wondering why he didn't stop the men from cutting the trees."

"Wasn't here," said Stacey. "He come a few months after that. Papa brung him."

Suzella nodded thoughtfully. "I just can't get over how big he is. In fact, he's so big, he frightens me just a little."

"He wouldn't never hurt you none," reassured Christopher-John gently. "You're family."

"But folks make him mad 'nough though, he sure 'nough can hurt 'em bad all right," bragged Little Man. "He stronger than anybody. I betcha he the strongest man in the world. We seen him lift a car one time, and last year he broke a man's back—"

"Man," said Stacey quietly. Little Man glanced over at Stacey, knowing he should say no more, and grew quiet.

Suzella looked from Little Man to Stacey. "What is it?"

Stacey was silent a moment before he answered. "Nothing. It's just something we don't talk 'bout much."

"How come?"

Stacey studied Suzella as if considering whether or not he should tell her. He decided against it. "'Cause we just don't, that's all."

But I said: "'Cause the man's back he broke was white."

"Cassie!" Stacey cried, reproval etching his face.

"Well, if she's family, I don't see how come she shouldn't know. White folks are always doing something or other and you know Papa say you can't much trust none of 'em."

"Hush up, Cassie."

I turned on Stacey. "What you telling me to hush up for? It's the truth!"

Stacey's eyes met mine and he said harshly, "You know you talking 'bout things ain't s'pose to be talked about."

Christopher-John and Little Man looked at me sympathetically, but they knew what Stacey said was true. I knew it too. There were some things that were not to be discussed with anyone outside of our own family circle; this was one of them.

I got up. "I'm going back to the house."

"I'll go back with you, Cassie," said Suzella, jumping up after me.

I glanced back at her. "You ain't gotta go 'cause of me."

"No, I want to."

"Suit yourself," I said as the boys too got up.

When we emerged from the forest, Stacey pulled me aside. "You just better be glad Suzella didn't take offense to what you said. You know good and well you ain't s'pose to offend company and she's company, so you just better learn to keep a lid on that mouth of yours 'round here."

I didn't say anything, just cut my eyes at him, but as he walked away, I couldn't help but resent Suzella. Stacey had been hard enough to live with these past few months. I certainly didn't need the additional frustration of having him defend Suzella against me. I wanted things to be as they had been, but Suzella was just making things worse, and I looked forward to the day when she was packed and gone.

Crossing the backyard, I went through the garden to Mr. Morrison's cabin. Other than me, he seemed to be the only one not affected by Suzella, or at least he didn't seem to favor her above everybody else, and I wanted to talk to him about her. "Mr. Morrison, you in there?" I called, knocking on the door.

There was no answer.

Feeling dejected, I sat on the plank step and looked out at the house. I could see Christopher-John and Little Man playing in the yard and Big Ma making a momentary appearance on the back porch. For several minutes I sat there waiting; then, deciding it was Mama I should talk to, I got up and went back to the house.

"Where's Mama?" I asked Big Ma as I entered the kitchen.

Big Ma turned from her pot of black-eyed peas and glanced at me. "She back in the house there," she said, then frowned down at the pot and, dipping a spoon into the liquid, tasted it. As I left, she was reaching for the salt.

Entering Mama's room, I found no one there, but I heard

Mama's and Suzella's voices coming from my room. I sighed and went over to the doorway.

". . . now just what would I look like with a city lady's clothes on way out here in the country?" Mama asked Suzella as I entered. Dressed in a pale-blue dress of Suzella's, Mama was standing in front of the mirror scrutinizing the fit. The dress was wrap-around in style with padded shoulders, and it looked elegant on Mama. Standing side by side, both of them slender and tall, Mama and Suzella looked like sisters.

"But Aunt Mary, you're so slender you can wear this simple cut and look absolutely grand. I copied this from a magazine I got at the library."

Mama smiled, and after brushing back a strand of her long coarse hair, which had slipped from the chignon knotted against the back of her neck, she put her hands on her hips, threw back her head and struck a model's pose. "I do look rather good, don't I?" She laughed.

Suzella struck a similar pose. "But, of course. We both do. We look so good we could be models for *Vogue.*"

"*Vogue?*" Mama said, still holding her position.

"That's a very stylish New York magazine of high fashion. I love looking through it."

Mama inspected herself closely in the mirror. "I wouldn't imagine there are any colored models in that very stylish magazine."

Suzella glanced over at her. "No. . . ."

"They probably think we're not much interested in any kind of clothes." Mama walked her model's walk, then laughing turned and hugged Suzella, who laughed too. As she released Suzella, she saw me. "Cassie, how do you like Suzella's dress on me?"

"You look pretty."

"I'm trying to get Aunt Mary to let me redo a couple of

her dresses in this style. I've gotten pretty good at ripping apart old dresses and making new ones from them. Come on, Aunt Mary, let me do it."

"Well . . ."

I turned to go.

"Cassie, did you want something, honey?"

"No, ma'am. I was just looking."

Going back into the kitchen, I leaned against the cabinet, silently watching Big Ma as she carved strips of bacon from a side of meat.

"You find your mama?" she asked.

"Yes'm. . . . Big Ma, how long that Suzella gonna be here?"

"Oh, I don't rightly know. Till her papa come get her, I reckon."

"I wish he'd come on tomorrow."

Big Ma stopped her cutting and stared down at me. "Now how come you wanna say a thing like that?"

I shrugged. "That Suzella, she jus' get on my nerves."

"Now what she do to ya?"

"She jus' always in the way, that's all. Me and Christopher-John and Little Man and Stacey, we don't never get to be alone no more."

"Seem to me you jus' got a bad case of the jealous. Jus' 'cause you ain't the only girl in this family no more ain't no reason to go dislikin' that child."

"Well, that ain't all. She look near white."

"Now what she look like ain't got nothin' to do with it! Your grandpa was mulatto and looked it and it didn't make no difference to me. That child ain't had nothin' to do with her mama bein' a white woman and we ain't got nothin' to do with it neither."

Big Ma resumed her slicing, but kept her eyes sternly

fixed on me. "Now I 'spects you to be nice to Suzella. That girl's your company. What's more, she's your blood, so you just best get your head straightened out right now 'bout treating her right, 'cause we ain't gonna have none of that jealous business in this house. You hear me, girl?"

"Yes'm," I murmured and went out onto the porch. For a moment I just stood there, then seeing the speck that was Lady galloping across the pasture, I went to join her. At least Lady was not crazy about Suzella; Suzella was afraid of horses.

The law said: "The marriage of a white person with a Negro or mulatto, or person who shall have one-eighth or more of Negro blood, shall be unlawful and void."

I looked up at Mrs. Lee Annie and thumped the page of the constitution I had just read. "Now that one I understand," I said. "Mama told me 'bout that word 'void' meaning something can't be used."

Mrs. Lee Annie laughed delightedly. "Better be one we all understands or we sho' 'nough would be trouble. Now which one of them articles that one?"

"Fourteen," I said. "Section two sixty-three."

"Fourteen, section two sixty-three. All right, I gots that. Now how it goes again?"

When Mrs. Lee Annie and I finished our reading, I crossed the yard and headed down the woodland trail toward the stream where Christopher-John and Little Man had gone with Don Lee. As I approached the stream, music mixed with the quiet of the forest, and drifted southward through the trees. Intrigued by the sound, I left the path in search of its source. Going inward some five hundred feet from the trail, I came to a high perch overlooking the stream. Wordell was haunched there, his harmonica to his lips, his eyes on the stream below. Squirrels which had settled in the pines nearby scurried away and blackbirds which had strutted over the forest ground pecking for their afternoon meal fluttered to escape as I emerged. As they did, Wordell stopped playing and looked at me.

"Don't stop," I said. "I . . . I just heard the music and wanted to get closer. I sure like your music."

Wordell stared at me, then, looking back at the stream, slipped the harmonica into his pocket. When he made no move to leave, I hesitated, then haunched beside him. Below us wading in the stream and shrieking with laughter were Christopher-John, Little Man, and Don Lee. Suzella, who had also come along, sat on a log nearby encouraging them in their play. Christopher-John yelled for her to join them, but Suzella refused, saying that her dress would get wet.

"Well, I got a pin!" cried Don Lee, as captivated as the rest of the boys. "You can pin it. That's what my sisters do."

Suzella, with the dress pulled up and between her long legs and secured by the pin, tossed off her sandals and laughing dashed into the water, where she immediately became "it" in a game of water tag. Before Suzella had come I had always joined in the water play. But now that Suzella was here, I wasn't even missed.

"Yeah," I mumbled, "take over that too."

Wordell looked at me and, surprised at myself for having spoken, I glanced over at him, then back to the stream and shrugged. I thought he would look away, but when he didn't, I turned back to him.

"Well, that ole Suzella jus' done 'bout got on my last nerve!" I exploded, tired of trying to keep my feelings to myself. "I guess she nice enough, but ever since she come, things been all different. She jus' all the time 'round talking to Big Ma and Mama like they her grandmama and mama, and Christopher-John and Little Man, they just wanting her to do everything with them. What's worse, Stacey, he always call himself so busy—can't go nowhere with me—but soon's Suzella asks him to do anything, he's right there. Big Ma, she say I'm jealous, but that ain't it. Least that ain't all of it. I just want things back the way they was before. Before she come. If she was gonna stay a week or two more, it wouldn't be so bad, but now she talkin' 'bout stayin' till September sometime, and that's jus' too long. I just want her to get on a train and get on back home!"

Wordell's eyes had not strayed from me as I vented my rage against Suzella. Now he turned and looked again at the stream.

Feeling somewhat awkward about my outburst and not knowing what Wordell was thinking, I said nothing further as I too watched the play. After several minutes I stood. "I—I gotta go."

Wordell did not turn to look at me; his gaze remained on the stream. I started down the trail.

"Cassie."

I stopped and turned. Wordell was looking at me.

"Ya wrong and ya know it," he said. Then, standing, he pulled the harmonica from his pocket and put it to his lips again. Turning his back to me, he walked deeper into the forest, leaving his music to trail him. I waited until the music was so faint that I could no longer distinguish between it and the sounds of the forest, then continued down the trail.

I felt miserable.

"I don't think she's so pretty," said Mary Lou Wellever after Sunday school. "Oh, I know she's your cousin, Cassie, and she looks all right, but she ain't looking all *that* good."

Ignoring Mary Lou, who had just come up with Gracey Pearson and Alma Scott as I sat on the steps of the lower-grades class building, I continued searching the yard for Wordell. Although he seldom came into church for Sunday school or the sermon, he was usually around the fringes of the church with Joe. But today I had not seen him and I needed to see him, for I knew that I had said more than I should have about Suzella, and I was afraid Wordell thought less of me because of it. I was unsure what I would say to him once I did see him, or if he would even be interested enough to listen to me, but I had to try.

"I betcha one thing though." Gracey giggled. "I betcha you think she's prettier than Jacey Peters."

Mary Lou frowned. "Ah, I don't think that Jacey's pretty at all."

"I guess you don't," laughed Alma. "Seeing that Stacey's always talking to her. There they go now."

Stacey and Jacey were crossing the school yard alone, having just left a group of older boys and girls at the end of the field. Stacey was doing all the talking, but Jacey was nodding, her eyes on him as if greatly interested in what he was saying.

"Well, I just think he's so cute," said Mary Lou, "and I just don't see what he sees in that ole Jacey."

"I betcha he see somethin' in her you wish he'd see in you," teased Alma.

"Ah, hush up!" cried Mary Lou.

I got up.

"Where you going, Cassie?" Mary Lou asked.

I stared at her. All of a sudden her interest in me had risen markedly. I glanced out at Stacey, knowing that he was not yet that hard up. "I ain't going over to where Stacey is if that's what you're wondering."

"No, I—"

I walked away, tired of their chatter. As I crossed the yard, I noticed Jake Willis standing alone by the lower-grades building, his eyes on a circle of young women near the church. I studied the group, knowing even before I looked that Suzella was in it. As much as I disliked Suzella, it bothered me that Jake Willis had taken to her. He was as old as Papa, maybe older, but since Suzella had arrived, he had watched her with the same intensity as the boys and young men. But his look was different. There was something distasteful about it.

I saw Joe and asked him about Wordell. He told me he hadn't seen him since before Sunday school. Despondent, I joined Son-Boy and Maynard, who were standing with Little Willie, Moe, Clarence, and two ninth-grade boys, Ron and Don Shorter. "She smiled at me, man!" claimed Don as I walked up. "Jus' parted them pretty lips, showed them pearlies, and smiled."

"Ah, man, she was looking at all of us," argued Little Willie. "But did ya hear her? She called me by my name. She know who I am."

"Man, she oughta know more'n that!" cried Ron, Don's twin brother. "If me and Stacey was as tight as you two're s'pose to be, I'd have his cousin all to myself."

I looked around feeling just a bit crushed. Despite myself, I had begun to look at Ron Shorter in a new light lately, and his continued attention to Suzella bothered me, even though I knew he would never even look at me. I was too young.

"What 'bout you, Moe?" Ron said. "How you doin'?"

"What?"

"You and Suzella, man," Ron repeated, laughing. "How you gettin' 'long with Suzella?"

Moe seemed distracted. "Oh . . . fine."

"Sure," said Ron derisively.

"Ah, face it," said Clarence. "Suzella ain't hardly thinkin' 'bout none of us. She probably got some high-toned boyfriend up in New York."

"Well, boyfriend or not, me and Suzella gonna get together," claimed Little Willie.

The Shorters laughed. "How?"

"Well, I tell ya——"

The bell began to ring, and by the time it had stopped, Little Willie had reconsidered sharing his thought and walked off with Clarence; Don and Ron followed with good-natured teasing. Moe, his head down and his hands in his pockets, went along behind them. I touched his arm. "Anything the matter, Moe?"

He shook his head.

"But you so quiet."

"Well, it's jus' that . . ." He looked out across the yard. "Our cow died last night and Papa's real broken up 'bout it. Seem like it's jus' one thing after another."

"Ah, Moe, I'm sorry."

He shrugged. "Crop be good, maybe we can get another cow."

I knew that was a hopeless dream, but I didn't say it. "What 'bout till then?"

He smiled crookedly. "Till then we drink water," he said and walked on alone.

"What's the matter with him?" Son-Boy asked, coming along with Maynard. "He feeling down and out 'bout Suzella like the rest of these fellas?"

I turned on him. "Now how come everything gotta be 'bout Suzella? Jus' 'cause she's here don't mean folks ain't got other things to be thinking 'bout."

"Maybe not," said Maynard, grinning, "but she what a lotta folks wanna be thinkin' 'bout."

"Well, me for one, I'm jus' 'bout tired of hearing 'bout her every time I turn around."

Son-Boy laughed. "Ah, Cassie, you jus' jealous 'cause she's so pretty. Uh-oh! There's ole Deacon Backwater with that switch of his. We'd better get on inside."

After church I stood in front of the mirror, my church dress still on, and harshly examined myself. I was long-legged and growing. The dress, which Uncle Hammer had given me last Christmas, was already too short. But other than height, nothing else seemed to have changed. I turned sideways and stuck out my chest. Flat. There was no hint of a womanly figure anywhere. I sighed, then objectively tried to assess my good points. Though my facial features favored Papa, my skin coloring was a yellowish brown like Mama's and my body build was slender—at least that was good. My hair was done up in my favorite hairdo, one long braid on the side and another at back center, with each coiled in a small bun and pinned against my head. It had always been an outstanding feature because of its length and thickness, but I had never managed to do anything with it. To get it to look like anything at all, Mama or Big Ma had to comb it; otherwise it was disastrous.

For several minutes I stood in front of the mirror wondering how long it would be before anybody thought I was pretty like Suzella, or if Ron Shorter ever would. I wondered if boys would ever look at me the way they looked at Suzella, then wondered why I cared. Suddenly, without thinking, I pulled the pins from my fine hairdo, unbraided my hair, and ran the comb through it. Parting it on the side, I tried to get it to hang like Suzella's, but it bushed out full and thick like a huge black halo around my head.

"Why don't you let me comb it for you?"

I wheeled around. I hadn't heard Suzella come in. "I can comb it myself," I told her angrily and turned back to the mirror. With the comb in hand, I attempted to restyle it as it had been.

Suzella moved across to a chair and sat down to watch me. "You know, Cassie, you've got such pretty hair. But if you want it to hang like mine, you'll have to straighten it—"

I turned on her. "Who said I wanted it to hang like yours?"

"Well, I—"

"You think you such a big deal that everybody's 'round here tryin' to look like you or something?"

"I never said—"

"I like my hair jus' fine like it is. Ain't tryin' to change it neither . . . like yours or nobody else's."

"I didn't say you were, Cassie."

"Mama says there's all sorts of ways I can wear my hair when I get a bit older. Says she learned 'em when she was in school in Jackson and says she's gonna show me."

When Suzella didn't reply to that, I went back to work on my hair. I managed to get a braid in the front and one in the back, but the hair all around the braids was puckered and the part separating the braids crooked. If Suzella had not been in the room and I had not been so angry at her for interfering, or at myself for taking down my hair in the first place, I would have laughed. As it was, I simply coiled the braids in a circle and pinned them down. Having done the best I could, I changed into a school dress and turned to leave.

"Cassie, why don't you like me?"

I stopped and stared at Suzella. I had never expected that she would put the question to me point-blank.

"I like you all right."

"No . . . I don't think so. Ever since I came there's been something about me that you don't care for. Have I done something to you?"

I looked out the window. "You ain't done nothin'."

"Then is it because . . . is it because, Cassie, my mother's white?"

I looked at her, but didn't say anything.

"Cassie, you can't just not like me because my mother's a white woman. My mother's simply my mother and my father my father, and I love them both just like you love yours. Don't blame me for something I can't help . . . Cassie?"

"Big Ma said she need me to help her in the kitchen," I said, opening the door.

"All right," Suzella said softly as the door closed between us.

At dinner Stacey told the rest of the family about the Turners' cow dying. Big Ma frowned at the news and after a moment's thought turned to Mama. "Mary, it be all right with you, sugar, tomorrow first thing I'm gonna take that four-year-old milker of ours over there. Orris Turner with all them young children be needing that milk and here we gotta be throwin' it away, folks don't come get it. Hurts me to my heart." Mama agreed, and early the next morning before the full heat of the day descended, Big Ma, with the boys and me, started out for Smellings Creek leading the cow, Nadine.

It was a fine summer's day. Overhead the sky was the

deepest of blues; beneath our feet the road was warm but not burning, and the world was awash with the dazzling brilliance of growing things. Filled with the joy of it, for a while Little Man, Christopher-John, and I ran games of chase along the road, then fell in stride with Big Ma and Stacey. As we walked, Big Ma told us stories of when she and Grandpa had first come to the land, of how things had been then. She told us stories of all her sons: of Uncle Mitchell, who had been killed in the World War; of Uncle Kevin, who had drowned; of Papa and Uncle Hammer. Most of her stories were funny, and we laughed a lot as we passed vast cotton fields where dark figures, as much a part of the earth as the cotton itself, waved a spirited greeting. Several times we stopped to talk with the people in the fields, stretching a two-hour trip into three, and consequently, by the time we reached the Turner farm, the sun was riding high in the eastern sky.

"Well, looka here!" exclaimed Mr. Turner, wiping his hands on his overalls as he, Moe, and Elroy, Moe's twelve-year-old brother, came from the fields to greet us. "What brings y'all all the way over here, Miz Caroline?"

"Come to bring y'all this here cow. Heard y'all lost y'all's, and you know we got more cows'n we can use the milk from. I figures y'all needin' a cow, y'all can jus' take this one off our hands awhile and put her to good use. Jus' lending her to y'all till y'all get on your feet and can get ya one."

Mr. Turner looked gratefully at Big Ma, but shook his head. "I sho' 'nough 'preciate this, Miz Caroline, but I jus' can't go take y'all's cow knowin' I can't pay for her."

But Mr. Turner was no match for Big Ma. "Now, Orris Turner, I done come all the way over here to bring this cow and I ain't takin' her back."

"But Miz Caroline——"

"Ya got seven younguns here and they needs milk, 'specially them babies there," Big Ma contended, her eyes resting on the younger children who had gathered 'round. "Christine—that fine woman—would jus' turn over in her grave she knowed ya was refusin' milk for them babies. Ya feels ya gotta pay, then send Moe and Elroy over when they get some free time and let 'em chop wood a day or two."

Mr. Turner gave in. "Well, we sho' do thank ya, Miz Caroline. You's a fine woman."

"Ah, go on with ya, Brother Turner," Big Ma said, turning away embarrassed. "Y'all helping us out to take that cow." And before Mr. Turner could say anything more, she changed the subject. "See y'all keeping Christine's flower garden lookin' right nice."

Mr. Turner glanced over at the neat bed of flowers encircling the one-room shack, and tenderness softened the deep lines of his face. "We don't tend to nothin' else like we oughta, we makes sure we tends to them flowers. Christine, she was always sho' proud of 'em. . . ."

"Yes, she sho' was. . . ."

"Well, look here, Miz Caroline, y'all come on in and let me get some coffee for ya."

"No thank ya, Brother Turner. We ain't come to visit and we ain't wantin' to keep ya from your field." Her eyes surveyed the cotton field, which extended almost to the Turners' front door. "I tells ya, it's lookin' mighty good all right."

Mr. Turner nodded. "So far, it's comin' 'long right nice. Look to me, it be the best crop we done had in a spell."

"I figure the way it's lookin' got a whole lot to do with that fertilizer we used this time, don't you, Papa?" said Moe, his eyes gleaming as he looked out at the cotton. "Hey, Stacey, ain't I told ya it was looking good?"

Stacey smiled, pleased for his friend. "Yeah, ya did."

"Yeah, it's gonna be something. Really something!"

Mr. Turner laughed and motioned proudly toward Moe. "That boy, he got plenty of big plans for this crop here. Wasn't for him with all his questioning that Mr. Farnsworth 'bout fertilizers and seeds and such and all his hard work, I don't much 'spect that cotton'd be lookin' good like it is."

"Well, I jus' hopes y'all can get a good price on it come the sellin'," said Big Ma. "Hopes we all can."

"Yes, ma'am, that's what we hopin' too."

Big Ma looked up at the sun. "Brother Turner, we'd thank y'all for some nice cold water from your well there, then we gonna hafta be gettin' on back home 'fore that ole sun yonder gets to burnin' down too hot."

Mr. Turner tried to get Big Ma to sit and rest awhile, but when she refused, he sent Moe into the house for cups and went to the well to draw some fresh water. As Moe came back, a car drove up the road and turned into the yard. Mr. Peck and Deputy Haynes stepped out.

"Papa, what you think they want?" Moe said, fear leaping into his voice as it did with many of us when white people arrived unexpectedly.

"Orris!" called Deputy Haynes. "Got business with ya! Come on over!"

Mr. Turner, still holding the rope to the water bucket, looked out blankly, then nodded and handed the rope to Moe before walking over to the men.

"Hello there, Orris," the deputy said. "Ya knows Mr. Peck here. Taking Mr. Farnsworth's place as county agent?"

Mr. Turner looked at Mr. Peck and back to the deputy. "Yes, suh."

"Well, he come with some news for ya."

Once again Mr. Turner looked at Mr. Peck. "Yes, suh?"

"Well, Orris . . ." Mr. Peck started, then pulled at his

ear and looked away from him to the fields. "Ya know in thirty-three we asked farmers to plow up part of their cotton, and then last year and this year we asked farmers to plant less than what they was used to planting . . ." He paused as if waiting for Mr. Turner to say something. When Mr. Turner did not, he glanced back at him. Mr. Turner nodded slowly and Mr. Peck looked back to the fields. "Well . . . uh . . ."

Without a sound Moe hung the water bucket onto the hook and waited for Mr. Peck's next words.

". . . uh . . . we're finding that there's been a miscalculation. The AAA committees made a mistake in figuring the likely production of certain acreage, and based on the figures they turned in to the state board, Mr. Farnsworth allowed too much cotton to be planted. Well, uh, now that the committees discovered their mistake, we're gonna have to correct it. . . . You understand what I'm saying, Orris?"

Mr. Turner looked suspiciously at Mr. Peck. "I understands what Mr. Farnsworth told me. Early on this spring he told me how much cotton I s'pose to plant."

"Well . . . uh . . . yes, that's so. But we got a problem here, ya see. These mistakes—"

"Look here, Mr. Peck," Deputy Haynes interrupted. impatiently, "all these here explanations ain't necessary. Don't ya see the nigger don't understand nothin' you saying? Let's jus' do what we come to do and get on with it."

Mr. Peck nodded meekly, glanced at Mr. Turner, then away again, as if he could not face him. Taking out a pad and pencil from his breast pocket, he walked past Mr. Turner and the deputy to the end of the field. There he stopped and looked over the field, then with his head bent to the pad scribbled madly for some time while we waited, wondering what it all meant. Finally, he put the pencil in his pocket and stood for several moments staring at the pad. Then, as if he did not want to come back, he walked slowly up the field in measured steps. He stopped and pointed down the row.

"Now . . . uh . . . Orris . . . ya gonna have to plow up everything from the road to—"

"Noooooo!" cried Moe, his voice rending the morning like the crack of summer thunder. He dashed from the well and grabbed frantically at Mr. Peck. "Ya can't make us plow it up! That's our cotton out there! We done worked hard and ya can't jus' go make us plow it up! No way ya can!"

Mr. Turner rushed over and pulled Moe away from Mr. Peck before Deputy Haynes could get him. "It's all right!" Mr. Peck cried to the deputy as he turned to take Moe from Mr. Turner. "It's all right, Mr. Haynes."

The deputy looked at Mr. Peck and after a long, tense moment stood aside.

"Papa, we can't let 'em do it! We done put too much into it!"

"Hush, boy!"

"Maybe you gonna let 'em, but I ain't!" Moe jerked from his father's grasp and headed for the house. "I'll stop 'em!"

Mr. Turner caught Moe again and this time he hit him, so hard that Moe fell backward onto the ground.

I let out a gasp; Big Ma told me to keep quiet.

Mr. Turner helped Moe up and held onto him. Mr. Peck, a sorrowful look in his eyes, wiped the perspiration from his face. "I know how y'all feel and I don't like this no more'n y'all do. But it's gotta be done. Ain't nothin' 'gainst y'all. This here's happening to colored and white alike, and plenty of other folks gonna come under the same hardship. I'm the first one recognize all the work you folks done put in your crop. It's a mighty fine-looking crop. But we gonna hafta correct the figures." He sighed hard and looked at Moe. "I don't fault you, boy. I'd hate to lose this crop my own self." He stared out at the field in silence, then stuck the stick he carried into the soil. "I jus' hope y'all can understand this in time, Orris."

Mr. Turner didn't say anything.

Mr. Peck sighed once more and turned to face Mr. Turner, but it took him so long to speak, I wondered what he was waiting for. "You gonna have to do it now, Orris. I gotta see you plow it up."

Mr. Turner stared blankly at the agent.

"Get a move on ya, Orris," Deputy Haynes ordered impatiently.

As if in a stupor, Mr. Turner glanced at the deputy, then walked behind the barn and brought back his mule. Asking none of his children to help him, he went into the barn, returned with his plow, and hitched the mule to it. He led the mule to the marked row and, stopping, gazed out at his fields. Taking off his hat, he wiped his head with a red bandana, replaced the hat, and looking straight ahead yelled, "Ged on up, mule!"

As the plow cut through the earth, uprooting the plants to lie withering in the summer sun, Moe slowly followed his father out across the fields. Midway down the first plowed row he stopped and picked up one of the uprooted plants. For some time he stood unmoving, staring down at it. Then he bent his head to it; his shoulders shook and he cried.

I felt like crying too.

9

Mr. Peck had been right. The Turners weren't the only ones to have their cotton plowed up. The Shorters and the Laniers lost an acre each, the Averys a quarter, the Ellises and Mrs. Lee Annie a third, as all through the community fields blooming with large cream-colored blossoms and plants hanging heavy with bolls beginning to fill with soft puffs of cotton were being turned back to the earth as they had been two years ago. But our fields were not touched; neither were the Wigginses'. Only plantation fields were being plowed up, including those of white farmers. As the hot days of summer moved into July and the plow-ups continued, dissatisfaction grew more intense and the grumblings louder.

"Shuckies, man," said Ron Shorter as a group of us crossed the school lawn after a morning of Bible classes which were offered each summer, "I thought my papa was gonna bus' somebody sure when that Mr. Peck and that little Deputy Haynes come tellin' us we had to plow up that field. Lord have mercy! What they 'spect us to do?"

"S'pose to get a higher price," Clarence reminded him. "Guaranteed."

"Shoot!" Ron exclaimed. "Ya oughta know as well as me ain't none of us sharecroppin' gonna see no money, higher sellin' price or not. It's always the same. After the deducts, we got nothin'. I tell y'all, this kinda stuff keep up, me and Don thinkin' bout goin' into the CCC or maybe goin' up to Jackson looking for work, 'cause we don't much see how we gonna hold out this year we don't get none of that government money Mr. Granger holding on to."

Don nodded, affirming his brother's statement.

I sighed, hoping they were both just talking.

"Well, shoot, man," said Little Willie, "ain't hardly no jobs no place 'ceptin' at that hospital building site, and they ain't even hiring now. Way I figure, you ain't got a job, you most likely ain't gonna get one."

"What 'bout the cane fields?"

Little Willie stared apprehensively at Moe. "The cane fields?"

"In Louisiana."

Stacey studied Moe. "You thinkin' 'bout going?"

I looked at Moe, still feeling his pain at the loss of so much of his cotton.

"No reason much to stay here now. Be better I could get me work where I can get me some money."

As we reached the road, Dubé Cross came running up and

the subject changed from cane fields to union. "Y-y-y'all hear 'bout the m-meeting? Wh-wh-white and colored. F-f-first time. Night after n-next."

"Night!" exclaimed Little Willie. "Man, ain't nobody in they right mind 'round here gonna be meeting with no white folks at night!"

"S-s-seven o'clock. Still be light. Over at M-Mr. Tate S-Sutton's."

"What's it gonna be 'bout?" questioned Stacey. "The plow-ups?"

"A-A-Ain't y'all heard?" he cried. "M-Mr. Wheeler back from W-W-Washington and say he know'd how c-c-come all this plowin' up b-been goin' on. W-W-Wasn't ordered by Washington. Them folks on the AAA committees—M-Mr. Granger and Mr. Montier and th-th-them—th-they's the ones at f-f-fault. SSS-Seems they figured a way to plant more cotton than they was s'pose to, and Mr. F-F-Farnsworth, he gone along with it, th-that's what Mr. Wheeler f-figure. Th-Them ole landlords come tellin' Mr. Peck th-they jus' done made a mistake. Shoot! Th-They made a mistake all r-right. Th-they was plantin' a whole bbb-buncha acres they wasn't s'pose to be plantin' and bbbb-buyin' up other folk's bale tags too so's th-they wouldn't hafta pay that fifty percent t-t-tax."

Dubé stopped and looked at our stunned faces, then nodded firmly in confirmation of his own words.

"Th-That's right! Th-They was gettin' government money for th-them acres and then figures to g-get money from the cotton they grow'd on th-them same acres. G-G-Gettin' money on 'em twice was what they was d-doin'. M-Mr. Wheeler, he say the Washington AAA folks was 'b-bout to come down here and dddd-do some checkin' and these here ole landlords heard 'b-b-bout it and set everybody to plowin' to g-g-get they figures straight 'fore th-they checked. A-A-Ain't that somethin'!"

"Lord!" said Moe. The word was no more than a whisper.

"Y-y'all tell y'all's folks 'bout the m-meetin', h-hear? I-I still g-g-gotta tell everybody up and d-down the road 'long th-this way, so I-I-I'm gonna hafta g-go." He took off, running toward the Ellises', then yelled back. "Stacey! S-see y'all later when I-I-I come up that way."

For a while the older boys continued standing in the road talking of this new revelation and what could happen at the meeting, but Christopher-John, Little Man, and I, growing restless, started slowly down the road; Suzella went with us. By the time we reached the crossroads, Moe and Stacey still hadn't caught up and we stopped to wait.

"Wish they'd come on," I said.

"They be 'long directla," said Christopher-John, then cocked his head. "Car comin'."

We waited a moment. Stuart Walker's Hudson appeared on the rise. As soon as I saw it, I sighed and turned back toward the school. Christopher-John and Little Man, understanding, followed my lead, but Suzella wanted to know why we were turning back. "Them boys always up to no good," I explained as she unwillingly came behind us. "Better we meet up with Stacey and Moe." We managed to get only a short distance down the road before the car rolled along beside us. "Keep on walking," I ordered, not even looking around.

But then Stuart said, "Excuse me, ma'am."

I turned, wondering who he was talking to.

"Would you mind stopping for a minute?"

Against my advice, Suzella stopped, so that we had to do

the same. Stuart, at the wheel, braked and, stepping out, took off his hat. He smiled somewhat sheepishly at Suzella and said, "Ma'am, excuse me, but by chance you Mr. Henry Harrison's niece visiting from Shreveport?"

Suzella looked at him blankly.

"Not to be forward, ma'am, but we hear tell she's here and we seen ya here with these younguns, and knowing they live next to Mr. Harrison's place, we thought maybe they was escorting you someplace. Figured you might be her."

I spoke up hastily, afraid where this was heading. "This here, she ain't Mr. Harrison's niece, this here's——"

"My name's Suzella," she said, cutting me off. "Suzella Rankin."

I stared at her, and shook my head at her stupidity.

"Where you from?"

"New York."

"Ah, I see. You gonna be here long?"

"A few weeks."

Stuart fumbled somewhat awkwardly with his hat; I had never seen him act like this before. "Well, Miss Suzella, my name's Stuart Walker. My family owns a plantation on the other side of Strawberry." He motioned toward the car. "That there's Joe Billy Montier in the front seat . . ." Joe Billy immediately jumped out, swept off his hat, and nodded to Suzella. "And Pierceson Wells there in back."

Pierceson respectfully touched his hat. "Ma'am."

Stuart waited a moment for Suzella to speak. I waited too, afraid for her to say anything, afraid to say anything myself. Stuart had made an embarrassing mistake and I knew it wasn't going to be very pleasant when he realized what he had done. "Who you visiting, if not Mr. Harrison?"

Suzella crimsoned. She kept her eyes on Stuart, away

from us. "It was nice to have met all of you, but I really have to be going on now."

She started to turn away but Stuart stopped her. "Forgive me, Miss Suzella, but you being new to these parts, I'd be most happy to show you around."

I shot a quick glance at Christopher-John and Little Man and their eyes said what I already knew; we had to put a stop to this. I braced myself. "Suzella, come on."

Stuart's eyes left Suzella and fell on me. "You best watch your manners, gal."

"I—"

"Please don't talk to her that way," Suzella said.

Stuart's voice ran smooth again. "You being from the North, Miss Suzella, you most likely don't know that down here we demands respect from our nigras. We let something like this slide by, they'll go walking all over us."

My anger rose, fiery and hot, but I now knew better than to say what I felt.

Suzella moved away from Stuart. "We really have to be going. It was very nice to have met you."

"My pleasure. One thing 'fore you go. I'd like to come calling on you, you don't mind."

For the first time Suzella appeared nervous. "No . . . that wouldn't be possible."

"I'm really quite a reputable person. I'm persistent too." He smiled charmingly. "Maybe I could see you at church."

I started down the road, about to explode. Little Man came with me. Christopher-John, torn, looked around indecisively and waited for Suzella.

"I . . . I really have to go," she repeated and started walking.

"Can we give you a lift?"

"No . . . no, thank you."

"Well, I'll be seeing you again, though, Miss Suzella. I'll make sure of that!"

The car door slammed, then the car passed us with a honk, moving slowly to avoid raising the dust. When the car was gone, Suzella ran to catch up with Little Man and me. "Cassie—"

I was burnt and let her know it too. "Don't you talk to me, girl! Don't you say one devilish word!"

"But, I—"

"Can't stand you no way!"

She pulled back, her face growing pale at my attack. Then Christopher-John quietly reprimanded her. "Suzella, you was wrong to do what you done. Uncle Hammer, he say that kinda thing get you in trouble."

"'Round here acting like you white," grumbled a disenchanted Little Man with an angry, disappointed glance back at her.

On the way home, none of us said anything further about the meeting, and Stacey with his mind on other things seemed not to notice how quiet we all were. I certainly didn't feel like talking, but I was surprised when neither Christopher-John or Little Man said anything either. I supposed they were feeling let down that Suzella had acted as she had; another idol had fallen. As for Suzella, I didn't know what she was thinking and, frankly, I didn't much care. I was tired of her.

When we reached the house, Russell Thomas was there sitting on the back porch with Mama and Big Ma. It was a surprise to see him, and the boys and I brightened noticeably. "How long you gonna be with us this time?" Stacey asked, pumping his hand.

"Got myself a whole week." Russell stepped back to look Stacey over. "Man, how you get to be tall as me?"

Stacey laughed. "I jus' keep growing."

"Miz Mary, you don't watch out, you gonna soon have yourself a full-grown man 'round here."

"Sometimes I feel I already have one. By the way, Russell, I don't think you've met my niece, Suzella."

"No, ma'am, ain't met her but I gotta admit, done heard 'bout her." He extended his hand. "Russell Thomas. Miz Lee Annie's grandson."

"She's spoken of you. I'm sure she's pleased that you're home," Suzella said graciously. Then, excusing herself, she went into the house.

Russell stared after her. "Well, like everybody say, she's mighty pretty all right." He sat back down. "Kinda short on her words though."

"That's her way," said Big Ma.

"Humph!" I grumped, but no one but Christopher-John, who shot a disapproving glance my way, heard.

"Mama, we run into Dubé," said Stacey, "and he told us Mr. Wheeler come back and said how come all this plowing up been going on."

"He did? What'd he say?"

Stacey repeated what Dubé had told us.

"Well, I declare."

A discussion of the plow-ups followed as Russell asked about what had been happening in the community. In the midst of the conversation, Big Ma turned to Stacey and told him to get the watermelon that was cooling in the well. I went with him and together we tugged at the heaviest of the three ropes hanging from the scaffolding and brought up the melon, a large, round, dark-green one, the kind Big Ma preferred above any other. Later, when all of us but Suzella, who had decided to keep herself in the house, were finishing up our second slices of watermelon, Dubé arrived. Immediately, he started in about the union, his voice rising in angry indignation as he quoted Mr. Wheeler about the reasons for the plow-ups, then about the conditions of sharecroppers and day laborers across the South.

"I understand you been doin' quite a bit of work with them union leaders," Russell said.

"W-work with 'em when I-I can. Th-th-this here union c-could mean a whole lot, w-we stand together."

"And at this here meeting folks gonna be deciding what to do 'bout the plow-ups and the checks, I take it."

Dubé nodded. "Th-th-that's right. Mr. Wheeler, he s-s-say too the union g-g-gonna demand buck s-seventy-five a day for field wages too. That there, it'll help f-f-folks like me a whole lot. Mr. Wheeler, he s-s-say we stick together, everybody be living a whole lot b-better. He say——"

Russell smiled at Dubé. "You kinda think a lot of this Mr. Wheeler, don't ya?"

Dubé looked a little shamefaced and lowered his head. "I-I guess I-I does." Then quickly he looked Russell in the eye. "But I-I-I ain't T-Tomming none."

"Wasn't thinking that."

Dubé looked relieved, for he, like most of the boys and young men in the community, admired Russell and wanted his approval. "J-jus' that what he s-s-say make sense and he be d-doing somethin' 'bout it."

"From what I been hearing, it makes sense to me too. What else ya know 'bout it?"

Obviously pleased by Russell's interest, Dubé talked a good half hour more about the union and Morris Wheeler, John Moses, and other union leaders; about how the union was started and what its goals were; about the importance of the union and his role in it, his excitement growing as he talked and his stuttering lessening. "R-Russell, you j-jus' oughta meet Mr. Wheeler and them your own s-s-self and talk to 'em. Th-th-they's good folks and they can 'splain everything b-better'n me." His eyes brightened. "F-fact to business, why don't ya c-come on with me now? I-I-I be going there soon's I-I make these last few stops."

Russell thought a moment. "Where they live?"

"O-over by Mr. J-J-John Bass's place."

"I understand they stay there together—colored and the white union men."

"Y-Y-Y-Yeah, they do."

Again Russell was thoughtful. Finally, he said, "Tell ya what. Can't go today, and tomorrow I gotta make a run into Strawberry with Cousin Page. What 'bout late tomorrow afternoon sometime? You think you might be going that way?"

"G-g-go if ya wanna."

"All right then, why don't you stop by Mama Lee's on the way over 'round four. Should be back from town then."

After Russell and Dubé left, I walked out to the pasture to figure out what I should do about Suzella; then, deciding to talk to Stacey about her, I came back and crossed the yard to the barn where he was working. "I wanna talk to you," I said as soon as I cleared the door. "You know what that Suzella done today?"

Stacey turned to look at me. "This here's 'bout Suzella I don't wanna hear it."

"Whaddaya mean ya don't wanna hear it?" I demanded, just about sick of him too. "You don't even know what she done!"

"And I don't wanna know. All you do is complain 'bout that girl."

"But she—"

Mr. Morrison came up the drive in the wagon loaded with

hay and Stacey went to meet him. Little Man and Christopher-John sat upon the stacks, and as Mr. Morrison turned the wagon around to back into the barn, they yelled directions to him. "Ya all right now, Mr. Morrison! Jus' a bit farther now!"

When the wagon came to a halt and Jack had been unhitched, Stacey hopped up on the stacks to push them into position for unloading. I hopped up as well, and once the stacks at the edge of the wagon had been taken off, I struggled to pull a stack out by myself.

As he worked, Mr. Morrison spoke about other hay crops he had gathered through the years, some in Mississippi, some in states like Kansas, Missouri, and Texas. He had traveled a lot, and it seemed to me, who had gotten no farther than Strawberry, that he had been just about everywhere.

"Mr. Morrison, you wouldn't ever think 'bout leaving us, wouldja?" Stacey asked, pulling a bale close to the wagon's edge.

I looked up from my struggle, wanting to hear his answer.

"Don't 'spect I would," he said. "Y'all's my family now."

Assured that he wasn't going anywhere, I went back to tugging at the bale. Mr. Morrison saw me and let out a bemused laugh. "You figure you got enough muscle on you, girl, to be doing that?"

"Ah, Mr. Morrison, I got plenty of muscle."

Mr. Morrison grunted. "Well, I 'spect it wouldn't hurt none if them muscles of yours had a little bit of help now, do you?" He glanced over to Christopher-John and Little Man and told them to help me.

Christopher-John and Little Man stepped in beside me, and Little Man said, "Move, gal. Let some real muscles in."

Mr. Morrison stopped and looked back at him. "What's that you said?"

Little Man looked up, his face showing his surprise. "Sir?"

"You used the word 'gal.' Ain't that right?"

"Y-yes, sir."

"You ever hear your papa or your Uncle Hammer or anybody in this house talking to womenfolks with that word?"

"No, sir."

"Then don't you use it. It's common. White folks use that word to talk down to colored women, and too many colored folks done gone and picked it up. White folks don't respect our female folks, so that give us all the more reason to respect 'em and don't be speaking to 'em the way the white folks do. That make sense to ya?"

"Yes, sir."

"Good. Then get on back to work."

Once the bales were stacked, I tried to continue my talk with Stacey, but he abruptly cut me off, refusing to listen. "I done told you once, Cassie, I don't have time to hear 'bout it," he said and walked off.

"You just wait!" I cried after him. "You just wait till you need somebody to talk to! Need to talk to me!"

That little outburst did not even make him miss a step, and both discouraged and angry, I went across to the yard where Mama was taking down the wash. I grabbed one of Stacey's shirts and slapped at it furiously before folding it.

"Now what's the matter with you?" Mama asked from the next row.

"Ah, that Stacey, he just make me so mad. I told that boy I wanted to talk to him, but he say he didn't have the time."

"Here, help me with this sheet." I stepped back and took down one end of the sheet as Mama took down the other, and we folded it in half. "You know, Stacey has a bit of a problem of his own and I don't think things are going that well for him."

"What kinda problem he got?"

Mama shook the sheet to straighten it. "Liking someone that's special to him and having trouble with it."

"You mean Jacey? Ah, that ain't nothin'."

"When you care for someone, it's something."

"Well, I'm sorry 'bout all that," I said, though I couldn't dredge up too much sympathy about it, "but he didn't have to be so mean to me just 'cause he's feeling bad."

"He probably didn't intend to be."

We finished the sheet and started another. "Mama, Stacey and me, we used to be such good friends. Now he don't even hardly say 'boo' to me."

Mama smiled. "Ah, don't you worry," she said. "Stacey's at an age where he's looking for room. He's changing and he's looking for his life to change too, and he really doesn't have much patience with folks he's been around all his life. But that'll all pass. I remember when your Cousin Bud went through the same thing and I was one upset little girl, because I just loved Bud so and we'd always been close. I just didn't understand why he had to change, and if we both eventually had to change, why it couldn't be at the same time." She laughed. "It didn't make any sense to me that just because there were three years between us it should make any difference. But it all worked out all right. We went through a few years there when we were always at odds with each other, but when we both got a bit older we became friends again . . . closer than ever. It'll be the same with you and Stacey."

"You really think so, Mama?"

"Most certainly do."

Assured of the prospects for improved relations with Stacey looming in the future, my thoughts turned once more to Suzella. I asked Mama if she thought Suzella was pretty.

"Very," she said.

"Well, I don't see how come everybody get so excited 'bout the way she look. Jacey and Clarice jus' as pretty."

Mama agreed. "Yes, they are."

"Well, how come everybody make such a fuss 'bout Suzella then?"

"Well . . . Suzella's pretty in a different way. When I was in school in Jackson, there was an Italian family lived near the school and there were three daughters in the family. Very pretty. Suzella reminds me of them. She's got an Italian look about her. Also, you have to remember that some people are taken with her just because she does look white."

"Why?"

"It makes her special."

"But why?"

"Oh, it goes back a long way. We've been taught so long to think we're less than anybody else, many of us have grown to believe it, in some ways if not others. And a lot of us figure the lighter we are, the better we are . . . like white people."

"But it ain't so."

"No, it's not. But that's how some people figure."

"Well, she may look to suit some folks, but Big Ma always says pretty is as pretty does."

"Now just why do you bring that up?"

"'Cause if you ask me, Suzella don't always do so pretty, and besides, she makes me so doggone mad—"

"I've told you I want you to be nice to her."

"I been being nice as I can be, but when she was standing up there today talking to Stuart—"

"Stuart?" Mama stopped folding the sheet and looked sharply at me. "Not Stuart Walker?"

"Yes'm."

"What were you doing talking with Stuart Walker?" she demanded.

"Wasn't me. It was Suzella. I told her to come on."

"What were they talking about?"

I knew it was not out of idle curiosity that Mama was asking. I also knew she should be told, though I wondered if I wanted her to know mainly so that Suzella could fall from her grace as she had from Christopher-John's and Little Man's.

"Well?"

I decided to ponder the ethics of the situation later and told her. Mama was silent when I finished, the expression on her face not quite readable. She helped me finish the sheets, then went into the house. I gave her a moment and followed, trailing her through the house to my bedroom. "I understand you ran into Stuart Walker today," Mama was saying as I came in.

Suzella was sitting in a cushioned chair by the front window with an open book on her lap. She looked up hesitantly. "Yes . . . I did."

"I understand, also, you led those boys to believe you're white."

Suzella bowed her head, allowing her hair to fall, half covering her face.

"Is that so?"

"I didn't tell them I was white."

"You didn't tell them you were colored either."

Suzella looked up, her face defiant. "Why should I? I've got as much white blood as colored."

Mama eyed her sharply. "Get this through your head, Suzella. If you've got *any* colored in you, that makes you colored."

"My mother says I'm not. She says I'm not colored."

"That's her problem," Mama snapped. "My problem is seeing to it that you recognize what you are, at least as long as you're down here."

"Stuart didn't question what color I am—"

"He didn't think to question it. But let me tell you something. Once he finds out—and he will—he won't be so polite anymore. And one other thing. He's not going to like being fooled that way."

"I didn't fool him!"

"I'm not going to stand here and argue with you about it. But I am going to tell you this: You leave these white boys around here alone and don't you let them think you're white when you're not."

"Aunt Mary, I'd like to get to know Stuart—he seems nice." Mama folded her arms and looked at the floor; even from where I stood I could feel her rising anger. "I made up my mind a long time ago that I won't marry a colored man . . . I won't live like my mother."

Mama kept looking at the floor for a long time. When she did look up again, it was evident she had not managed to suppress her anger. "If your Uncle David were here, he'd probably pack you up and send you back to New York right now. Me, I'm going to give you a choice: You can do what I say and stay, or if you don't like being with us—"

"Aunt Mary, I never meant—"

"—and you can't follow the rules we have in this house, then you can go back to New York. Today. We'll all miss you, but I'm not going to have trouble about this, not if I can help it. Now you think on it and let me know." Turning from her, Mama walked brusquely from the room, passing me without ordering me back to the clothesline.

For a moment I stayed in the doorway watching Suzella, who turned to the window. I started to leave her to her misery; then thoughts of how she had acted with Stuart came rushing back and I went in. I sat on the bed across from her. "Well, you going?"

She turned. "What?"

"You going? Mama said she's leaving it up to you."

Her eyes stayed on me. "Be honest, Cassie. You'd like for me to leave, wouldn't you?"

I shrugged. "Wouldn't cry none."

"I asked you once why you didn't like me and you wouldn't tell me. Maybe you can tell me now."

"Well, long as you the one brought it up . . . How you 'spect somebody to be liking you when you going 'round here thinking you better'n they are?"

"Cassie, I don't think that."

"Well, I'd like to know what you call it then! 'Round here talking 'bout you ain't colored. Ain't nothing wrong with being colored!"

"I never said there was." But she looked away as she said so.

"And another thing," I said, deciding to lay it all out for her as long as I was letting her have it, "I ain't one to be appreciating somebody going 'round here always being nice and grinning in folks' face, when they don't think no better of 'em than not to even mention they kin to 'em."

"I . . . I'm sorry about that, Cassie."

"All you had to do was open your mouth and say, 'These here are my cousins and I'm staying with them.' That's all."

"I said I was sorry."

"Uh-huh. Well, sorry don't make it right."

She looked at me and shook her head. "You don't understand."

"I understand all right," I coldly assured her.

"No, you don't." She got up and looked out the window. "If you heard what Aunt Mary said to me, then you heard what I said to her. I meant what I said about not marrying a colored man. My mother did and it's just brought her a lot of misery."

"I guess so, she white," I replied unsympathetically.

"That was her choice . . . then. But she's told me over and over, 'Suzella, you can pass. Do it.' " She turned suddenly to look at me. "Do you know what it's like when people think you're white? You can do just about anything, Cassie. Sometimes Mother and I go to some of the better beaches, just the two of us, and the boys are so nice to me—"

"White boys?"

"There are no colored boys at those beaches," she answered pointedly.

"What 'bout your father? Don't he ever go with y'all?"

She looked back out the window. "We don't go many places together, the three of us. People stare and both my parents feel uncomfortable about it."

"What about you?"

She didn't answer. "Usually I go places with my mother. Where we live are all colored people, but when we just get on a bus and go to another part of town, there's not any staring . . . and we're accepted."

"Well, you like being white so much, I guess you'll be glad to get on back to New York then."

She sat again and, kicking off her shoes, tucked her legs under her. She was very quiet. I got up. "Cassie, you're very lucky. You know that?"

"What?"

"I mean . . . you've got family. And friends. At home, people don't come visiting like they do here. My mother's a saleswoman at a five and ten and she has friends there, but she never invites them home. She doesn't accept their invitations to visit either. Daddy's friends, they're all colored, and every now and then they come by, but they always feel uncomfortable with Mother there . . . so there's just the three of us most times. It's different here."

I studied her. "What 'bout your friends?"

She was silent a long minute. "All my friends are at school. . . . I go to a Catholic school outside the neighborhood. Mother says that schooling is my way out."

"How come your folks still together, your mother hate it so much?"

Suzella looked at me as if the answer was obvious. "They love each other."

"Oh," I said, though it didn't seem much like love to me.

She sat awhile longer, then got up and put her shoes back on. "I guess I'd better find Aunt Mary."

"To tell her you going?"

"No . . . my father wants me to stay longer. Maybe even start school here."

"What!"

"I want to stay myself if I can get lessons sent from my school in New York."

"Lord," I sighed, afraid we would never be rid of her now. "I don't see why."

Her eyes met mine before she turned away. "I know," she said.

The next morning at Bible class, Moe said, "Joe Billy Montier come by the house last night asking 'bout Suzella."

"What!" cried Little Willie, who had practically appointed himself Suzella's personal bodyguard.

Stacey's brow furrowed. "What he say?"

Moe glanced across the field, where Suzella was talking to several girls her own age. "He made like he was comin' 'bout farm business, but it was her he really wanted to find out about. Pierceson was with him. Said he'd seen her on the road and wanted to know 'bout her. Said she was with Cassie and them and he was wondering if I knew who she was staying with."

"And what'd you tell him?" said Stacey.

"Nothin' 'ceptin' she was your cousin and—"

"You told him that!" I cried.

"Yeah . . ."

"Oh, Lord."

Moe looked puzzled, as he had a right to be. "Joe Billy, he looked real funny about it too. Then Pierceson laughed and said something 'bout 'Wait till Stuart get a-hold of this!' "

Stacey, looking uneasy, glanced over at me. He knew what Suzella had done now. Everybody at the house knew. "Don't be looking at me," I told him, still vexed with him for not listening to me in the first place. "She your cousin."

"What's the matter?" asked Moe.

Stacey shook his head. "Misunderstanding, that's all."

"My foot," I mumbled.

"Lord," said Little Willie, "them scounds take a liking to Suzella, I'm gonna have to bust some heads 'round here! Stacey, you better tell your cousin not to be messin' with them. Don't want her in the same kinda mess Jacey in. Them scounds—"

Moe cut a disapproving glance at Little Willie, who faltered and grew quiet. An awkward silence followed. Stacey glanced from one to the other. "What kinda mess?"

"Ah, man—" started Little Willie.

"I said what kinda mess!"

Little Willie looked at Moe.

"Come on! Tell me!"

"Man," said Little Willie, "ain't you seen her?"

"She been sick the last few weeks—you know that. Went up to her house a couple of times, but her mama say she can't see nobody. She up and around now?"

"Yeah . . . seen her yesterday."

Stacey looked anxiously out around the schoolyard. "You seen her this morning? She here?"

"Wouldn't hardly think so. That girl—"

"Stacey, you better come on with us," Moe said quietly. "There's somethin' you gonna have to know anyway." His eyes were on me as he spoke.

"Well, what is it?" I demanded.

Both Little Willie and Moe ignored my question as they walked away with Stacey between them. I started after them, but Moe said, "Cassie, we gotta talk to Stacey alone, okay?"

It wasn't okay, but since I didn't have much choice, I stopped. I watched them cross the playing field to the edge of the forest on the other side. For several moments they stood there. Then Stacey waved his hand in an angry gesture and started away. Little Willie and Moe grabbed him and talked some more, but he pulled away again and stalked into the forest. Little Willie started after him, but Moe stopped him, and after another glance at the forest the two came back across the field as the bell for Bible classes began to ring.

"You going in?"

I looked around. Alma Scott, who could be quite civil when Mary Lou Wellever wasn't around, was standing beside me.

"Yeah . . . I guess." Absently, I walked over to the church with her.

"What's the matter?" she said.

I turned to her. "You seen Jacey Peters lately?"

"Yeah, couple of days ago."

"There anything the matter with her?"

Alma looked surprised. "Jacey Peters? You kiddin'?"

I stared at her blankly.

"Cassie, don't ya know? Jacey Peters 'bout to have a baby. Folks say it could be any of them white boys and Jacey herself say it's Stuart's. She's this big already." Alma held out her hands to indicate how advanced Jacey was.

We walked on, Alma continuing to talk, but I wasn't listening. I felt bad for Jacey. That she was pregnant was bad enough; that the father was Stuart Walker, a white boy, was total disaster. Had the father been black, Mr. Peters could have seen to it that the boy married Jacey and Jacey's future could have been saved, but with a white boy there was no recourse. All the shotguns in the world gave Mr. Peters no power where a white boy was concerned.

Stacey stayed in the forest until the bell rang dismissing the classes, and as he walked home in an angry silence, I said nothing to him about Jacey. But after supper when I found him standing alone on the back porch, I told him that I knew. He said nothing, just stood there, rage lining his face, his eyes on the horizon.

"Heard Stuart's the father."

Still he said nothing.

I reached out to comfort him. "I'm jus' real sorry. I know how much you call yourself likin' her."

"Like to kill him."

"What?"

"Like to jus' snap his neck with my bare hands. Him and every other cracker 'round here."

"Boy, you know you can't——"

He stepped from the porch and quickly crossed the yard to the garden gate and headed toward the pasture. I stepped down to follow, but the kitchen door opened and Mama said, "Let him go, Cassie."

I looked back at her. "You know?"

She nodded.

"He talk to you about it?"

She didn't answer right away. "No. This is something he'd talk to your father about . . . if he were here."

"Well, how'd you find out then?"

"News like this always travels fast, Cassie. You'll find out as you grow older that people like to pass bad news."

"Mama, what's gonna happen to Jacey?"

Mama stepped out farther onto the porch and leaned against a post. "I can't really say. Maybe she'll meet a nice young man who'll love her and won't care about a white man's child. Maybe she'll have to struggle through life alone. One thing though. It's gonna be hard on that child being part of two worlds, maybe wanting to belong to the white one and having to belong to this one."

"It's like that for Suzella too, ain't it?"

"Well, it's not easy for her. It's not easy for anybody being both black and white. You and I, we have only one world and we know which one it is. The world's a tough place for mostly everybody, but for colored people it's even tougher. People caught in the middle like Suzella, who could most likely pass, sometimes decide to do just that. And I can't really say I can blame them."

"Mama, if you looked white, would you pass?"

Mama puckered her lips, thinking; finally she shook her head. "No, my sweet child, I wouldn't. I love the people in this black world I'm in too much." She waited a moment. "What about you?"

I too thought on it. "No, ma'am, I don't 'spect so. But I tell ya one thing. Them white folks give us the same things they got, seem to me folks wouldn't even hafta be wondering 'bout passing at all."

Mama's eyes settled on me and she smiled. "Did I ever tell you what a smart young person you are?" I smiled back, pleased, then we both looked out to the pasture. My thoughts were on Jacey and her baby. They were on Suzella too. I still didn't like her and didn't intend to like her, but somehow Jacey's having this baby made me feel just a little bit for her somehow. Not much, but a little.

It was late when the dogs started barking and Dubé and Russell came hammering at the door waking us up. They sat before the fireplace, Dubé saying nothing, Russell telling us that they had just seen the house where the union men stayed set afire. "You know I was going over there with Dubé," Russell said. "Well, when me and Dubé got over there late this afternoon, Mr. Wheeler and Mr. Moses and another colored fella and two more white union men was there. Dubé, he told 'em I was interested in the union and they seemed real pleased to talk to me 'bout it. Offered us coffee and we sat on into the night talkin'. Then 'bout nine o'clock, me and Dubé, we decided we better get on home and we left, but 'fore we got to the road we seen headlights coming down the road real fast. We didn't like the look of it, so we jumped off in the bushes."

"Was—was they night men?" I asked.

Mama looked back at me, but didn't say anything. Russell shook his head. "Don't know 'xactly who they was. They wasn't masked or nothin'. Jus' got outa them cars and set that place afire . . . burned it down."

"Lord, no," moaned Big Ma.

"What 'bout the union men?" said Mr. Morrison, who had come up as soon as the dogs had started barking. "Wheeler and Moses and the rest? They get out?"

"Believe they did, 'cause I heard one of them burners yell something 'bout folks slipping out the back door and a bunch of 'em took off after 'em hollering 'bout there wasn't gonna be no socialist union down in here. That's when Dubé and me decided we better slip off, but we couldn't much risk the road 'cause they had a car goin' 'long it slow, seeing if anybody was on it. We stayed 'long the creek till we couldn't hear 'em no more, then after that we waited a long time 'fore comin' out, 'fraid they was playin' possum. Finally, we slipped out, coming 'long the edge of the woods. We was gonna try and make it home, but we seen lights again and we decided we best get inside somewheres. Y'all's place was the closest we could think of. Y'all don't mind, we figure to stay here a while 'fore going on."

Mama decided that it was too late for them to think about going anywhere farther tonight, and she and Stacey set about making pallets for them on the floor in the boys' room. Meanwhile Big Ma fussed over Russell, whose arm had been badly scratched during his flight. Russell assured her that he could hardly feel it, but Big Ma insisted that she put some antiseptic on it. "Now you just take that ripped shirt on off. I'll sew it up first thing in the morning."

"Ah, Miz Caroline, you ain't gotta—"

"I know I ain't! But I wants to, so you jus' go on and get outa it and give it to Suzella there and let me get to that arm."

Russell looked back over his shoulder. "Suzella . . . I didn't see you there. Sorry to be waking you up." When she didn't speak, he grinned good-naturedly and took off his shirt, exposing his bare chest, and handed it to her. Wordlessly she looked at him, then took the shirt and returned to the bedroom.

After I had said good night to both Dubé and Russell, I followed her in and as soon as the door was closed, let her have it. "You could've at least said good night to Russell. It wouldn't've hurt you none."

She jumped, startled by my entrance. She had been staring at the shirt, holding it close to her. Now she laid it carefully over a chair and slipped into bed while I got down on my pallet, where I had been sleeping since she had come. Along with everything else, I greatly resented the fact that she had taken over my side of the bed, and when I had fussed about it, Big Ma had said that I could still sleep in the bed if I wanted to—in the middle. But seeing no reason why I should be sleeping in the middle when it was Suzella who was the intruder, I had chosen the pallet. "Russell's my friend," I continued to grump. "Everybody like him."

"Cassie . . ."

"What?"

"Let's not talk about it."

I started to say, "Yeah, let's talk about it," but realized before I said it that I didn't really want to talk about it either. I supposed I simply wanted to talk, to keep men who carried fire and wandered the roads in cars with headlights that shone like cat eyes in the night from crawling into my sleep. They had done it before; no doubt they would do it again. I sighed helplessly and turned my back to Suzella. There was no keeping them out.

Talk of the burning spread as quickly through the community as if it had been the fire itself, and people got the message. Without Morris Wheeler and John Moses and the other union members, courage fizzled, and the integrated meeting which was to have taken place did not. It was uncertain what had become of the union men, but everyone knew that they had been run out, though no one seemed to know where they were now.

Then John Moses's body was found in a creek bed near Smellings Creek.

"Th-they th-think they's g-g-gonna b-bus' up the union by k-killin' Mr. Moses," said Dubé, who took the death hard, "b-but they a-ain't. C-can't nothin b-bus' up the union now. Th-they'll ssss-see. . . ."

Life settled down again. The days passed, dry and hot, good growing weather for the cotton after the heavy spring rains. Papa wrote often. His letters sounded cheery, but we could read the loneliness in them. He said he was looking forward to coming home for revival Sunday in August. He said, too, that work on the railroad had not been going well. He was no longer working a full six-day week, but only two or three days or whenever there was work. Still, three days' pay was better than no pay at all and he stayed on.

Each time Papa wrote he asked about the cotton. Mama wrote back that the cotton looked good. And it did. Yet despite how good it was looking, Mama, Big Ma, and Mr. Morrison seemed worried. Stacey was worried too. One burning hot afternoon, when every person with good sense should have been sitting under a shade tree somewhere, I saw him walking the rows, his head bent to the cotton. I followed behind him. "What you studyin' on so hard?" I asked.

He didn't answer right away. I waited. He peered at one of the plants, then sitting on his haunches broke off a boll and opened it up. The cotton had begun to form. He held it over for me to see. "See that, Cassie?"

"What?"

"Them fibers. They're gonna be long-staple, white."

"Well, that's good," I said.

"Yeah, it's mighty good. Might be one of the best crops we done had."

"Then how come you look so worried?"

"'Cause as good as it is, we ain't gonna get near 'bout what it's worth. And what we do get, it ain't gonna be enough." Stacey looked across the fields to the acres planted in alfalfa that should have been planted in cotton. "We'd've been able to plant them other acres there, things wouldn't't've been so bad . . . or we'd've had a contract and they'd've paid us for them acres we ain't usin'."

I followed his gaze. "We made out last year," I reminded him, "and we lost part of them acres anyway 'cause of the fire and we ain't had Papa's railroad money or Mama's scrip most of the year."

"But Uncle Hammer was able to help then. Now he gotta repay that money he borrowed to buy the land clear from the bank, so he ain't got much to give this year. Not only that, but 'cause of the way things been, we had to buy on credit from that store in Vicksburg, and ya know that's something Mama and Papa and Big Ma always tried to keep from doing. But we ain't had no choice. A good part of the crop gonna hafta go to paying the store debt . . . and Cassie, there's always them taxes on the land. . . ."

That scared me. We grew quiet, and in our silence all the sounds of the day seemed louder. A bee zoomed past trumpeting its presence, and a dragonfly spun in rapid delight above our heads, then flew on in happy celebration. I shaded my eyes with my hand and looked out over the land. The forest, deep greens and shades of brown, the fields looking like a patchwork quilt of growing things, the house, the orchard, the meadowland, were as much a part of me as my arms, my legs, my head. There couldn't be life without them. The look on Stacey's face told me he felt the same.

"Been thinking," he said. "Been thinkin' . . . maybe I can get me a job——"

"Like the last time?" I said dryly. "Boy, you and Mama done been through that business before."

"Ain't gonna ask Mama. She still think of me too much like a baby. Papa most likely be home come revival Sunday and that ain't so far off now. I'm gonna talk to him 'bout it then. He'll understand."

I thought on that and agreed. "He say you can get a job, where'bouts you gonna find one?"

"Somewhere 'round here. 'Member Mr. Harrison, he jus' up and offered me one."

"Boy, that job been gone."

"Most likely. But I figure to find something. Gotta."

"Stacey! Cassie! Mama, she say y'all come here!" Little Man hollered from the back porch.

Stacey stood and wiped his hands together to remove the dust. "Cassie, do me a favor, huh?"

"What's that?"

"Don't say nothin' to Mama or nobody 'bout me thinkin' 'bout a job, huh? She jus' be getting all upset, and I'd jus' rather talk to Papa 'bout it first. All right?"

I looked up at him, wondering if he realized how good I felt to have him confiding in me again. "All right," I said.

When we reached the front yard, we found Christopher-John sitting under the chinaberry tree, his knees pulled to his chest and his head buried against them. "What's the matter with you?" I said. He looked up. He had been crying.

"What's the matter?" Stacey repeated.

"Mr. Morrison brung a letter from Papa."

"Did?" cried Stacey. "Jus' now?"

Christopher-John nodded.

"Then what you cryin' 'bout?" I questioned.

"Papa . . . Papa say he ain't comin' home for revival."

An awful feeling shot through me and my stomach sank. Without looking at me, Stacey started toward the house. I followed. Inside, Mama read Papa's letter to us without emotion, then she put it away and did not speak of it again. All of us understood why Papa thought it better that he stay where he was to earn as much money as he could, whenever he could work. But understanding did not take away the loneliness; we missed him so. Stacey wandered off alone after he heard the letter. I watched him, wondering what he was going to do about that job of his now.

August came and all of us, including Suzella, went to the fields dragging the cotton bags at our sides. Through the long days from sunup to sundown we worked, bending and picking and stuffing the cotton into our bags. Soon the days of August passed into September and Mr. Morrison made an overnight trip up to Vicksburg to sell our first load of cotton; he took Stacey with him. When they got back late the next day, they reported that cotton prices were the same in Vicksburg as they were in Strawberry.

Mama sat silently, thinking. "And they're not any higher than they were in August?"

Mr. Morrison shook his head. "They steady, but you know you can't never tell. They could rise . . . or fall. . . ."

Mama pursed her lips and looked at Big Ma. "I think we ought to wait until near the end of the month before selling any more of the cotton, and see how prices are then." Both Big Ma and Mr. Morrison nodded, confirming their agreement. Mama looked at Stacey. "What do you think, Stacey?"

If Stacey was surprised that Mama had asked his opinion, he didn't show it. "I think that's the best thing, too," he said.

Mama kept her eyes on him a moment, then nodded. "All right then. Come the end of the month, we'll take the cotton into Strawberry."

On the last Friday in September when we came from the fields, Mr. Morrison and Stacey put the side boards on the wagon. The side boards were regular plank boards which fitted neatly on top of all four wagon sides, making the wagon's interior deeper, and allowing it to hold some 1500 pounds of cotton. We loaded the cotton, packing it tightly until the wagon was filled, then covered the top with the tarpaulin and fastened it down.

The next morning Mr. Morrison hitched up both Lady and Jack. Then he and Mama climbed onto the wagon seat and Stacey and I climbed on top of the cotton bed. Frankly, I was surprised that I was going. I had pointed out to Mama several times that Stacey had been allowed not only to observe business since he had been ten, but to take care of some of it as well. I supposed I had finally convinced her that my education in practical matters was just as important as his. After all, she had had to run the farm and sell the crops; perhaps I would too someday.

It was still early when we reached the Granger-Walker mill to have the cotton ginned, not yet six o'clock. Already wagons had begun to gather and more than fifteen were ahead of us, their occupants taking the time before the mill opened at seven thirty to catch naps on top of the cotton or stretch their legs in the dawning light. Here there were no segregated lines. There was only one large, barn-door-like gate opening to the mill and one road leading into it; it was simply a matter of first come, first served.

At seven-thirty exactly the huge doors swung open and Stuart Walker, his father Hamden, and Pierceson Wells stepped out. At the sight of Stuart, anger snapped alive in Stacey's eyes. I saw it; so did Mama. "Not a word, do you hear?" she quietly told him. "Not one word." Stacey sucked in his breath and looked away.

The ginning of cotton was a slow process, and it was after twelve o'clock when we reached the entrance. "How do there, Mary?" Stuart said as we pulled up.

I saw Mama bite her lower lip before she spoke. I bit my lip as well, remembering that Mama had told me to keep my mouth shut. But it was hard. Mama was a good fourteen years older than Stuart, and for her to have to show him respect when he did not do the same for her was galling.

There was a strange smirk on Stuart's face as Mama answered. I was afraid he was going to say something about Suzella, but he didn't. He waved us into the mill. There pipes were placed inside the uncovered wagon and the cotton was sucked into a machine which cleaned the cotton, then removed the seeds from it. Afterward the cotton was cleaned once more and funneled into a ginning press, which compressed it into five-hundred-pound bales. Our cotton came to one bale, a neat rectangular package, covered on two sides with burlap and held together by iron bands. Mama paid the ginning charge; then the seeds from the cotton, and the bale of cotton were loaded onto the wagon and we headed to the warehouse, where the cotton buyers were located. As we pulled into place at the end of a long line, we spied Moe Turner standing some ways off staring at the buyers in the open field surrounding the warehouse.

"Hey, Moe!" Stacey called. "Moe! What ya doing here?"

Moe looked up, somewhat surprised. We all knew that he

wasn't in town to sell cotton. Sharecroppers like the Turners were not allowed to sell their own cotton. At the end of each day they took their cotton to the plantation center and turned it over to Mr. Montier, who saw to its ginning and sold it as well. Whatever money, if any, Mr. Montier felt was due the sharecroppers was then given to them after all the deducts had been figured.

Moe came over to the wagon and greeted us. "Papa had some errands to run in town, so me and Elroy come 'long with him. Y'all gettin' ready to sell y'all's cotton, huh?"

"That's right," Mama said.

"Top price goin' at eleven cents a pound."

Mama nodded. "That's what we heard."

"Ain't enough," said Moe.

"It's more'n it was two years ago, son," said Mr. Morrison.

"Yes, sir. . . . Say, Stacey, could ya come here a minute? I got somethin' to show ya."

Stacey jumped off the wagon. As I jumped off after him Mama warned us not to go far. At the end of the field which circled the warehouse, Moe stopped. "Look here, Stacey, I done made up my mind—" He looked at me, then pulled Stacey away. "Come with me a minute, will ya?"

The way Moe had looked at me I knew I wasn't wanted, so I let them go without protest and returned to the wagon. As I neared it, I saw that Mr. Granger had come up and taken it upon himself to pull a handful of cotton from our bales to inspect it. Mama stood beside him.

"It looks good, Mary," he said after a moment. "Long-staple. Clean. Strong. Mighty good."

"Thank you, Mr. Granger."

"Y'all'll get top price for it."

"We're hoping so."

"Course eleven cents a pound don't hardly compare to the thirty-five cents a pound we got in 1919. Surely don't. Still, it's better'n we have had."

"That's very true, Mr. Granger."

Mr. Granger let his cotton sample drop to the ground. I heaved an angry sigh, but of course I could say nothing; neither could Mama.

"Now even though prices are some better, Mary, you and me both know they ain't enough to keep y'all goin'. I know the kinda bills y'all got. My offer to buy y'all's place still stands, same as last year."

"Well, we appreciate your concern, Mr. Granger, but we still aren't thinking of selling."

Mr. Granger shrugged. "Well, it's up to y'all," he said, then glanced up at Mr. Morrison, whose eyes had never left him, and walked back toward the warehouse.

"Get in the wagon, Cassie," Mama said. A pent-up rage was in her voice.

I knew now was not the time to express my comments on Mr. Granger. I climbed onto the wagon without another word and waited.

When the cotton had been sold and we headed down the main street of Strawberry in the empty wagon, we met the Turners on their way out. Glad to have the company on the long journey home, we trailed the Turners as far as the Wallace store. There, as the Turners continued west toward Smellings Creek, Moe called to Stacey, "See ya tomorrow?"

"You coming to church at Great Faith, Moe?" Mama asked.

"I'll be down that way, yes, ma'am," Moe said after a moment's hesitation. "Bright and early."

"See ya tomorrow then, Moe!" I cried as our wagon turned south and headed for home.

The sounds of late summer were in the air. We sat for a while on the front porch enjoying the last taste of the long day, and finally, as the moon rose full and yellow overhead, Mr. Morrison stood and said good night. Stacey jumped up and walked out into the yard with him and the rest of us went into the house. While Suzella dallied with Mama and Big Ma in the other room, I made up my pallet, then returned to Mama's room, where Big Ma sat doing some late-evening darning and Mama and Suzella were writing letters. As I entered, Stacey came through the side door and for a moment he just stood there. Then he did a strange thing. He walked over to Mama sitting at the desk and kissed her, then did the same with Big Ma.

"Good night," he said.

Mama looked up from her letter. "Good night, honey. See you in the morning."

Stacey crossed to his room, looked back once more, and softly closed the door.

"Lord, I don't 'member the last time that child kissed us good night," said Big Ma, smiling, obviously pleased.

"That was sweet, wasn't it? And now, Miss Cassie, don't you think it's time you were saying good night too?"

"What 'bout Suzella?"

"Good night, Cassie," Mama answered with a lilt to her voice.

I said good night and went back to my room. I changed into my nightgown, then turned the lamp low and headed for the pallet. But just as I slipped under the covers Stacey called to me from the porch. Grumbling because he had waited until I was already lying down, I got up and crossed to the door and pulled the latch. Stacey stood there, his penknife in hand.

"Boy, I thought you went to bed!"

"I'm goin' in a minute. I jus' wanted to give you this," he said, and extended the knife toward me.

I studied him suspiciously. "What make ya wanna give it to me?"

"Jus' do, that's all. Well, you said you wanted it. You still do?"

"Yeah, I want it."

"Well, take it then."

I took the knife and held it gingerly, not quite believing it was mine. "Stacey——"

"You best not let Mama see you with it. You know how she feel 'bout knives."

I nodded. As I did, Stacey bent and kissed my forehead. "Boy, you all right? You feeling feverish or somethin'?"

Stacey walked back to his room and turned at the door. "I'm fine, Cassie. Now you jus' be careful with that knife, you hear?"

I nodded again.

"Now go on back in and pull the latch."

"You sure you all right?"

"I'm sure. Go on now," he said and watched me until I closed the door.

I slipped the latch, then heard Stacey's door close. Clutching the penknife in my hand, I went back to the pallet, where I had a few minutes to examine the knife before I heard Big Ma coming and had to put it under my pillow. I just couldn't get over the fact that Stacey had actually given the knife to me. I tossed and turned for a while, wondering why he had, and finally decided that if this was a new kind of phase Stacey was going through, I hoped it would last for a while.

In the morning we found the note. Written in Stacey's sprawling, awkward hand, it said:

Dear Mama
I know yall aint gonna understand this but I gotta go. I found me a job pay $8 a week. Problem is I gotta leave here to get it. Mr Morrison I know he take good care of things. Dont nobody worry about me now. Ill be just fine.

Your Son
Stacey

I love all of yall.

10

The words, the note, were like a shotgun blast. Silence settled over the dimly lit kitchen and a terrible fear welled within me as we stood in our nightgowns, Mama, Big Ma, Suzella, and I, staring with disbelief at the piece of paper Mama held as if we could change what it said. It was the kind of nauseous, terrifying fear which had come when Papa had been shot and the men had come to lynch T.J. Now here it was again, coming without warning, enveloping my whole being and shattering the peace of the Sunday morning.

"Mama, most likely he just outside somewheres."

"Mos' likely," Big Ma agreed, not willing to believe it either. "That child, he can't be gone."

Her face looking drained under the light of the lamp, Mama glanced from Big Ma to me, and I could see she did not believe either of us. "Cassie, do you know anything?" Her voice was an urgent demand. "Did Stacey say anything at all to you about leaving?"

I shook my head and looked away; I did not want her to see my fear.

"What about you, Suzella? Anything?"

Suzella tried desperately to think of something, but finally she too said there was nothing.

The door to the boys' room opened and Christopher-John and Little Man stepped out, blinking into the light. "Mornin'," they said. Mama spoke to them, then quietly told them about Stacey.

"Gone?" questioned Christopher-John, not understanding. "Where? Out to the pasture with the cows?"

"No. He's gone to find work. He's left home, and we don't know where he is."

"Don't know!" exclaimed Little Man. "Whaddaya mean ya don't know?"

Christopher-John's eyes were round with fear, but he tried to comfort Mama. "Ah, Mama, we find him. Stacey, he be 'round this place somewheres. Don't ya worry now."

Mama's eyes were soft on him and for a moment I thought she was going to cry. But then, as if she were afraid to let her feelings out, her face grew suddenly stern and the look of tears disappeared. "Cassie, go get Mr. Morrison. Quick now! The rest of us better get dressed. We've got a lot of looking to do."

I dashed out into the gray dawn, across the lawn, and through the garden. "Mr. Morrison!" I yelled as I ran. "Mr. Morrison!"

Mr. Morrison's door opened and he stepped out, already dressed.

"Mr. Morrison!"

"What is it, Cassie?"

I reached the porch and flung my arms around him. "It's Stacey, Mr. Morrison! He's gone!"

Mama decided that the first person to whom she wanted to talk was Moe Turner. If anyone knew anything about Stacey's leaving, he would. Having begged to go with her, Christopher-John, Little Man, and I climbed into the wagon and the four of us headed toward Smellings Creek, while Mr. Morrison, riding Lady, went up the road toward Great Faith to see if families along the way knew anything that might help us. Big Ma and Suzella stayed behind to attend to the morning chores; then they would go on to the church to wait for the rest of us.

At the Turners', Moe's father shook his head despondently. "I was jus' 'bout to come see you, Miz Logan. I been searchin' 'round here all mornin' . . . Moe, he gone off too."

Mama's lips parted slightly and for a moment she seemed unable to speak. "Then they're together."

"Mos' likely so." Mr. Turner glanced around at his other children, bewilderment and fear on their faces. "That boy, he always talkin' 'bout leavin' . . . makin' money. Always dreamin' . . . I 'spect I got to the place I jus' ain't paid much 'tention. Seems it was all I could do jus' to get them crops in and feed these here younguns." He wiped at his eyes beginning to tear, and swallowed. "'Spect I shoulda listened more. Sho' shoulda."

"Brother Turner, do you have any idea where Moe could've gone?"

Mr. Turner bowed his head, then looked back sorrowfully at Mama. "No, ma'am, Miz Logan. Ain't got no idea. No idea at all."

Mr. Turner said that he would start checking around the Smellings Creek area for word about Stacey and Moe, and we climbed back into the wagon and headed for Soldiers Road. Passing the Granger Road, we crossed to the Hopkins place, where Mama questioned Clarence. But Clarence knew nothing. From Clarence's we went directly to Great Faith, where a crowd was waiting as we pulled onto the grounds. The services forgotten, everyone gathered around the wagon in frenzied excitement, offering advice and consolation as Mama and Mr. Morrison tried to decide what to do next.

"You talk to Little Willie?" Mama asked Mr. Morrison. "He could know something."

"Yes'm, he sho' did," Little Willie spoke up, pushing his way to the front of the crowd. "But Miz Logan, Moe and Stacey, they ain't said a thing to me 'bout this."

"You're sure? I mean, maybe there's something they said a while back about going? Anything, Little Willie."

Little Willie thought a moment and, after a glance at the Shorters, shook his head. "Miz Logan, tell you the truth, we all talked sometimes 'bout goin' away gettin' a job. Once Moe said something or 'nother 'bout the cane fields, but that's 'bout all."

"I say what we oughta do here," put in Mr. Lanier, "is get ourselves out to everyplace 'round here—white folks' places too—and get to asking 'bout them boys. See if anybody done seen 'em."

"Can't believe them younguns done gone off alone," Mrs. Lanier lamented. "Nothin' but babies."

Mr. Wiggins looked over at Mr. Lanier. "We better split up then, 'cause we go all through here, that's a lotta folks to cover. Me and my family, we'll take the Harrison plantation, then head on down toward Smellings Creek."

"Good idea," said Reverend Gabson. "Better take more'n your family with ya, though. Get another group and we go on up the road toward Strawberry. Another one go on back over to the Montier place and help out the Turners."

"Don't you worry now, sugar," Mrs. Wiggins said to Mama. "We gonna have them boys back here 'fore nightfall."

Mama acknowledged her with a grateful smile. "Well, if you all will check around here, then Mr. Morrison and I'll check in Strawberry."

"Strawberry!" exclaimed Mrs. Lee Annie. "Lord, child, you ain't thinkin' them younguns done gone that far!"

"I think," Mama softly said, "that maybe they could've gone even farther than that."

More plans for the search were made, then before everyone departed all heads bowed in prayer and Reverend Gabson, for once keeping it short, beseeched God to lead us to Stacey and Moe. Everyone said, "Amen," and the search began.

Dusk settled and still Stacey had not come home. People returned from their appointed search routes, read the emptiness of the faces around them, and stayed, crowding the rooms and talking in low voices, waiting for the good news which could send them home. The Turners arrived, but they had no news either, and by the time the wagon rolled into the yard with only Mama and Mr. Morrison in it, we all recognized that there was to be no good news. Not this night.

"Mary, child, y'all ain't found out nothin'?" Big Ma said.

"Nothin' at all?" questioned Mr. Turner.

Weary and discouraged, Mama looked out at all the people waiting to hear. She put an arm around Little Man. "There were men recruiting for the cane fields yesterday in Strawberry. Truck left out of there first thing this morning. . . . We think maybe Stacey and Moe were on it."

"Lordy!" cried Mr. Tom Bee. "Them younguns gone to the cane fields, then they be lucky to get back here at all."

"Hush your mouth, Tom Bee!" ordered Mrs. Lee Annie. "You wanna upset these younguns more'n they already is?"

I felt the day's fear slipping into a new terror. "Mama, what we gonna do now?"

She turned to look at me. "I sent a telegram to your papa," she said. "When he gets here, we'll know."

In the middle of the night I heard Little Man and Christopher-John sobbing loudly and Mama trying to comfort them. I lay very still on my pallet, my eyes dry. I refused to cry. Crying would be like admitting Stacey was really gone, and he couldn't be gone . . . not far, not long. He just couldn't.

When Papa came, he held Mama to him, then the rest of us, before shaking Mr. Morrison's hand and greeting Suzella. Looking tired from his long journey, he settled down to read the note and listen to all that we knew about Stacey's leaving.

"Most likely, if he working cane," said Mr. Morrison, "he in Louisiana somewheres."

Papa nodded. "But the thing is, we can't be sure. They got cane here, some of these other states too."

"But Louisiana, they the ones got them big cane plantations," Mr. Morrison contended. "That's where they be needing the most choppers."

"You say nobody could tell you where that truck was headed?"

"From what we could gather," Mama said, looking

exhausted from so little sleep, "the cane people never really said. Just said the pay was eight dollars a week and for anyone who wanted the work to be in front of the Mercantile on Sunday morning or at the Wallace store. Evidently the truck came right down through here."

Papa ran the flat of his hand over his head and was very quiet. When he spoke again, he said, "I called Hammer. Soon's he get here, we'll go looking. Take the main road outa here and ask 'long the way if folks know anything 'bout transport trucks to the cane plantations."

"Ya know," Mr. Morrison said, "I shoulda seen it comin'. Him so worried 'bout the crops and all."

"Don't go blamin' yourself now. It surely ain't your fault."

Mr. Morrison nodded. "That boy . . . ya know he mean an awful lot to me too."

"I know," Papa said.

"You gonna bring Stacey on back, ain'tcha, Papa?" said a confident Christopher-John. "Ain'tcha?"

"I'm gonna try, son. I'm gonna try."

Uncle Hammer arrived that same evening, and without taking time to rest he and Papa climbed into the Ford and left again. We watched as the car sped away, the autumn sunset casting a pale glow upon it. We watched and waited.

"Cassie . . . where you going?"

I didn't answer Christopher-John as I plunged into the forest.

"Wait up, Cassie!" he hollered, following with Little Man.

I ran faster, past the gray-bark sweet gums and the wintery-smelling pines, past the stately black oaks and the nut-laden hickories. Near the pond, I stopped and flung my arms around a massive pine, needing its comfort. I felt the rough of its bark against my skin and I wanted to wail out my sorrow to it, but hearing Christopher-John and Little Man, I tore away from the tree, and ran on. By the time Christopher-John and Little Man reached me, I was sitting on the bank of the pond. They looked at me in silence and collapsed beside me.

For a while we all were quiet, then Little Man said, "Why'd he go, huh? That's what I wanna know." He took a pebble and threw it angrily into the pond. "How come Stacey jus' gone off like he done and ain't even said goodbye or nothin'? He got tired being with us or what? Huh? Don't he care?"

I felt the same anger, but feeling it my duty as the eldest now to try and comfort him, I said, "He cares. He jus' thought he was doing what he had to do . . . I guess."

"Sure he did," confirmed Christopher-John. "Stacey, he probably figured he had to go. That it was the best thing."

"Well, why didn't he take us with him then?"

"Boy, he probably had a hard enough time jus' to get outa here himself," I explained irritably. "How you 'spect him to be worrying 'bout you too?"

Little Man looked away, hurt. "I wouldn't've been no trouble."

I felt his pain. "I know."

We heard someone coming from the east and looked out over the pond, waiting. After several moments, Jeremy Simms appeared. He waved and when he reached the pond, settled beside us. He had heard about Stacey.

"He'll be back, ya know. He'll be all right too." He caught the misgivings in our eyes and chastised us gently for our poor faith. "Y'all ain't give up, have ya? Why, Stacey, he gone all the way to Louisiana by hisself over two years ago now and he was a lot younger then. Y'all forgotten that?"

It took us a moment, but we finally said we hadn't.

"Then don't," he ordered, leaning back on his elbows. "Stacey, he can take care of hisself all right."

With Jeremy we did not have to talk when we had no more words to say, and now as he grew quiet, we grew quiet as well. Around us the world of green trees reaching toward blue skies sang a sad song in the soft breeze, sharing our loneliness. Forgotten for the moment was the work waiting for us, as tree boughs fanned above us and birds, silhouetted like dark messengers against the sky, called out to invite us to go with them. I thought of the everyday times Stacey had sat here with us watching the same trees and the same sky, and as the birds flew away taking their messages with them, I wondered if he ever would again.

A week after Stacey left school started, and for the first time we walked the red road without him. Suzella had received a letter from Cousin Bud saying that she would have to stay awhile longer, and she enrolled the first day at Great Faith as a tenth grader. But by the end of the day it had become painfully clear to her teacher that Suzella's educational level was much too advanced for the class, and she was skipped to the eleventh-twelfth-grade class under the instruction of Mr. Wellever himself. In addition to her promotion Suzella had her New York lessons to keep up with, and she juggled her study time between lessons from Great Faith and lessons sent from St. Anne's, which Mama helped her with.

Being in the sixth grade this year, I found myself in Mrs. Mabel Thompson's class. Mrs. Thompson seemed satisfactory enough; I felt nothing for her one way or the other.

Little Man was fortunate enough to have Miss Rosella Sayers, a young teacher from Jackson, but poor Christopher-John, now in the fourth grade, had fallen into the hands of Miss Daisy Crocker. I greatly sympathized with him, but as in everything else, Christopher-John tried to see the bright side in having to face such a shrew each morning. "Maybe she done changed," he said hopefully on the first day of school. However, when classes were over he was noticeably quiet.

"Well?" I asked him.

He shrugged dejectedly and admitted, "She still the same."

No doubt she was. Certainly little else seemed to be. Without Stacey, nothing much was the same.

The days passed, with each day growing longer than the day before. Every day Little Man and Christopher-John stared out the window watching the road, waiting for Stacey, who never came. Every day on the way to school, we listened anxiously for any sound on the road—a car, a wagon, footsteps—that might bring news of him. In the mornings I awoke with the dread of Stacey's absence hanging in the air, and throughout each day I was consumed with the hope of seeing him walking in that loping gait of his past the old oak and the cotton fields, and up the drive. But then each night I went to bed feeling helpless once again, and angry. Angry at the cane people for coming to Strawberry waving their eight-dollar offer under the noses of needy boys, and angry at Stacey for leaving us. Through one week we waited, then two. In the middle of the third week, Papa and Uncle Hammer returned.

Stacey wasn't with them.

"How many places you go to?" Mama questioned as we sat at the kitchen table. "Wasn't there anyone who could tell you something?"

Papa put down his coffee. Unshaven, eyes bloodshot, both he and Uncle Hammer looked exhausted. "Seems there's men that just make a business of getting workers for the cane fields. They ain't hired by the plantation owners. They just get the workers, bring 'em to the plantations, get their money, and go on. Usually most of 'em don't take boys young as Stacey and Moe."

"Well, you talked to some of them, didn't you?"

There was an unexpected harshness to Mama's voice, and Papa noticed it as we all did. "Some . . . but ones we did talk to claimed they wouldn't've known if they'd carried Stacey or not, since they don't keep any lists. Then, too, they said that jus' 'bout anybody with a truck for hire could take up the business of trucking people to the fields. It'd be near to impossible finding them all."

"'Sides that," added Uncle Hammer, "sometimes they keep the workers moving, taking them from plantation to plantation, chopping cane."

Mama accepted this in silence. She closed her eyes and took a deep breath. Then she looked at Papa. "When are you going out again?"

Uncle Hammer glanced over at Papa. Papa met the glance, then put his hand over Mama's. "Honey, you got any idea how many people grow cane?"

"You saying it matters how many?"

"It's gonna have to matter—"

"Well, I don't care how many there are. I want Stacey back in this house."

"Mary—"

"When, David?"

"Right now, I don't see much point—"

"Much point? Your son is out there somewhere—"

"Don't you think I know that? But we don't know where to look. I figure we may do better just to wait for some word from Stacey. Leastways, we'll know by the postmark 'bout where he is."

Mama pulled away from him. "You don't want to go looking for him, I will."

"Mary, use some sense—"

"He's been gone too long, David, and I'm not going to rest till he's back in this house." A look of accusation was in Mama's eyes. Saying nothing else, she rose abruptly and left the room.

Big Ma patted Papa's arm. "You gonna have to be patient with her, son. It's hard on her."

"She think it ain't hard on me?"

"She be all right. I'll go talk to her." Then Big Ma, too, got up.

Papa watched her leave, shook his head, and sighed.

It was late when I heard their voices. Unable to sleep, I had left my pallet and sat in a chair by the open window. As I stared out into the blackness listening to the sounds of the crickets and the katydids, I heard the door to Mama and Papa's room open and close and, shortly afterward, the opening and closing of the door to the boys' room.

"Thought I heard you out here," Uncle Hammer said in a low voice.

"Couldn't sleep."

"Me either."

There was silence, then Uncle Hammer said, "David, I'm gonna leave my car here."

"What?"

"Gonna leave my car. That way, you find out anything, you can go see 'bout it."

"Man, what I'm gonna hear? I tell you, Hammer, I don't know how much to fault myself and how much to fault Stacey and how much to fault the times. But I'll tell ya something else. Much as I love Stacey and want him home, I can't help feeling sometimes like he was old enough to go off by himself, he's old enough to get back here by himself."

"Maybe that's just how it'll have to be."

"He oughta know we was gonna worry. When I think . . . I get real angry sometimes at that boy, and I know I oughtn't—"

"And why oughtn't you? He went off. Ain't told you where. Ain't sent no word—"

"Now that's what's really got me worried. Maybe he *can't* send no word. . . ." Papa's voice trailed off and in its place came a sound I had not expected to hear. It was a strange, muffled sound, one I knew but had never heard from Papa. I trembled, frightened; for Papa, who was always so strong, was crying. Suddenly the crickets and the katydids seemed louder and the pounding of my heart louder than both.

Uncle Hammer said nothing.

Finally Papa cleared his throat and was silent. After a long while he spoke once more. "Lord, Hammer, I wish I knew where he was."

"I can stay and we can go searching again."

"What 'bout your job?"

"It don't matter."

"Naw . . . naw, I still feel the same way. It's better to wait and try to get some information first 'fore I start running 'round out there again, not knowing where I'm going. I figure to ask some questions, find out more 'bout them plantations." There was a break in his words, and when he spoke again, I could hardly hear him. "I tell myself he's near fifteen and that a lotta boys have to make it on their own time they're his age. Then I think 'bout all he don't know yet and I get scared . . . real scared."

"David, I 'spect you got a right to be scared, but you gotta remember you and Mary, y'all taught Stacey good. He's smart and he's got good sense. I figure he'll be all right. 'Sides, maybe he just had to learn on his own what this life business is all about."

"Had hoped he wouldn't have to this soon."

"Well, that was his choice."

"Perhaps . . . but maybe he wouldn't've made it, I'd've been here for him to talk to. Mary blames me, you know, 'bout him leaving, and I can't blame her either. She told me over and over not to go 'way."

"Mary's upset."

"I know, but if I'd've stayed—"

"Look here, David, don't go faulting yourself and don't let Mary wear at you. You two, y'all got something special here, and Stacey going ought not spoil that. There's still Cassie, Christopher-John, and Little Man to think 'bout. Now I ain't much good in talking 'bout stuff like this, seeing I ain't never even had a wife, but I know y'all got too much to go laying blame. What I heard Mary say this afternoon wasn't coming from Mary. That was coming from a woman all torn apart with worry and fear. You listen to me, David, and get this here thing straightened out between y'all. You hear me now?"

"I hear."

"And David, you need me to come go looking again, you just call. Remember that."

". . . I'll remember."

At breakfast the next morning Papa looked tired, as if he

had not slept at all. He and Mama said nothing to each other during the entire meal. When breakfast was over and I had finished the dishes, I sat absently swinging on the front porch thinking of the silence between them. As I stared out at the field, soggy with the day's continuing drizzle, Christopher-John and Little Man rounded the house from the drive and joined me.

"What you doing?" Little Man asked, disrupting the rhythm of the swing as he and Christopher-John sat down.

"What it look like I'm doing?"

Little Man chose not to comment on this. "Papa and Mama, they was fighting in the barn."

"They wasn't either fighting," objected Christopher-John. "They was just discussing."

"Well, seem like fighting to me."

I looked at Little Man. "What they fighting 'bout?"

"Well, me and Christopher-John was down by the smokehouse and we heard 'em. Mama, she said if Papa didn't go back to look for Stacey, then she was gonna go her own self. But Papa, he said that was crazy. Wasn't no way she gonna find Stacey less'n she went to near every cane field in the South. Then Mama, she said if Papa hadn't've gone back to the railroad, Stacey, he wouldn't've left looking for no job."

"She said that?"

"She didn't mean it though," contended Christopher-John. "She jus' upset, that's all. When she seen us and seen we'd heard, she looked real sorry."

"What'd she say?"

"Told us to come back to the house."

I sighed and looked out at the forest.

"I don't like it when Mama and Papa fight that way," said Little Man.

Christopher-John turned on him irritably. "How many times I gotta tell you they wasn't fighting?"

Little Man allowed the question to hang a moment in the misty air before repeating, "Well, sho' seemed like fighting to me."

"Ah, there y'all are!" Papa came across the stepping stones from the drive and climbed the steps. "I was wondering where y'all'd gotten off to." He leaned against a post and immediately Christopher-John hopped up.

"Papa, you wanna sit down?"

"No, thank you, son. This here post's fine enough." As if to show it was fine enough for him too, Christopher-John took up a similar position at the post opposite Papa.

"Papa," I said, "you really ain't goin' back to look for Stacey?"

"Baby, if I had any idea where Stacey was, I'd go get him . . . this very minute. But I ain't. I got no idea at all 'cepting he's working the cane fields somewhere. Now much as I hate it, we may just have to wait till we hear from him, and seems to me, him knowing we'll be worried, he oughta be writing soon."

None of us spoke and he said, "You think I don't know how y'all feel?"

We looked at him without answering.

"Got a great big empty spot that aches all the time and can't nothing fill it 'cept for Stacey to come home? Well, I know it 'cause I got it myself. We all got it. We all part of one body in this family, and with Stacey gone, we just ain't whole. I know that. But till he do come back, we just gonna have to keep on being strong and we gonna have to support each other and stick together in this thing, 'cause we all going through the same hurt and worry."

"But, Papa," I said, "what if we don't hear from Stacey?"

Papa hesitated, as if he did not want to answer my question. "Just gonna have to have faith, Cassie . . . that's all I can say. Faith Stacey's all right and faith he's gonna come home. Lord willing, that's the way it'll be. Now it's gonna be hard livin' without him till he do come back, but we just gonna have to try. Gonna have to try hard."

I had never heard Papa sound so tired. "Papa, don't you think you oughta get some sleep? You said you didn't sleep so good last night."

"I will, Cassie girl, I will." But he didn't move from the porch. He stood there for some time sharing the aching pain of loneliness with us, and when he finally did go, it was not into the house, but across the lawn to the road, where he went into the forest alone.

That night, I cried.

11

"Maybe he's dead," said Mary Lou Wellever. "Maybe they're both dead."

I laid into Mary Lou with all I had, hitting her so ferociously that she fell whimpering upon the ground, her thin arms over her face to protect herself from my fury. Son-Boy and Maynard tried to pull me off.

"Cassie, ya gonna hurt her bad, ya keep it up!" hollered Maynard as I beat at her cowering form.

"He ain't dead, ya hear me? He ain't! So you keep your filthy mouth to yourself!"

"Let her go, Cassie!" Son-Boy yelled, taking hold of my arm. "Cassie!"

Maynard grabbed my other arm, and together he and Son-Boy pulled me away. Mary Lou continued to cringe on the ground, too paralyzed with fear to move. As tears slipped down my cheeks, I shrieked wildly at her, trying to get at her again, but Maynard and Son-Boy's hold was too strong.

"Cassie Logan!"

I looked up just as Miss Daisy Crocker stepped from the crowd and grabbed my arm. Son-Boy and Maynard released me with a helpless shrug, then looked on sympathetically as Miss Crocker led me away. I hollered back at Mary Lou one last time. Miss Crocker gave me a jerk. "Now, that's enough of that," she said.

She led me to her empty classroom, ordered me to sit, and left. I waited for her return trembling with anger and fear, a fear not of Miss Crocker or anything she could do, but of Mary Lou's words. It was mid-November and Stacey had been gone nearly eight weeks now. In all that time, there had been no word of him, no word from him or Moe, and inside me I was scared all the time as the knot of fear swelled with the passing days, eating at my ebbing faith that he was all right.

A few minutes later when Miss Crocker returned, Suzella was with her. "Now I know that life is not easy for you right now, Cassie," said Miss Crocker in her familiar, brusque way, "but even when times are hard, we cannot go around taking out our frustrations on others. That's just not the Christian way. Suzella, now I want you to talk to her, and afterward I'll take her to see Mr. Wellever. Sorrow or not, we just cannot tolerate fighting here at Great Faith."

Suzella agreed wholeheartedly with Miss Crocker, and then said if Miss Crocker didn't mind, she would like to talk to me alone. Miss Crocker looked somewhat askance at both of us, as if we were taking advantage of her sympathetic gesture, and agreed. "But only a few minutes. Class will be starting promptly at one, and I want Mr. Wellever to see her before then."

After she had gone, Suzella sat sideways at the desk in front of me, her eyes on me, but for a while saying nothing. Finally she spoke. "Well, what were you fighting about?"

"Didn't she tell ya?" I asked, still angry.

"She said she thought it was something about Stacey. Was it?"

"That devilish Mary Lou! Said he was dead!"

Suzella was silent a long time. Then she stood. "Come on."

"Where?"

"Outside. I want to go for a walk."

"But Miz Crocker told you—"

"I'll worry about Miss Crocker."

"Mr. Wellever too?"

"Him too. Come on." She walked out, not waiting to see if I would follow. I waited several moments, thinking on it, and went after her. Suzella was headed for the trail leading into the forest. "You know, Cassie," she said when I had caught up, "I know you might not think so, but there are some ways we're alike."

I stared at her. "What's that?"

"What we love, we love very deeply. I understand why you jumped on Mary Lou."

"Would you have?"

She looked back at me and was honest. "I don't think so. Maybe I would've liked to, but I don't think I would've. It's just not me." We walked in silence until she spoke again. "I've wished a lot of times, though, I were more . . . more hot-tempered and could just say what I think."

"You'd just be getting yourself into trouble. You jus' keep

staying near to perfect like you are and you'll do better," I advised.

Suzella stopped and laughed. "Near to perfect?"

"That's what you try to be, ain't it?"

"Not really."

"Seem that way."

"Well, maybe I do . . . sometimes."

"That's what I thought."

She looked away, then back at me. "Maybe I should try being more like you," she teased.

"Maybe," I said and the two of us walked on.

We came to the fallen tree where I had played my last game of marbles. It seemed so long ago. We sat down and talked, mostly about Stacey.

"I swear to God, Suzella, he ever come back, I won't ever do anything to make him mad again. He wanna go off by himself, I'll let him be. He wanna keep changing, he can do that too. I won't say nothin'. He wanna— What you laughing 'bout?"

"Because you couldn't do it, Cassie."

"Yes, I could."

She shook her head. "It wouldn't be like you. Besides, as much as you might get on his nerves sometimes, Stacey would want you to be you." Her eyes twinkled. "He wouldn't know you otherwise."

When the bell rang, we did not go back. There was no rush, Suzella said.

"You gonna get in trouble."

"You want to go back then?"

"No," I decided. "'Sides, I think trouble'll look good on you for a change."

She laughed. "Not too good, I hope."

After school Christopher-John, Little Man, and I sat with

Little Willie and a group of other friends by the well waiting for Suzella, who was still inside explaining to both Mr. Wellever and Miss Crocker why she had been late for her class. I had already gotten a stern lecture from Mr. Wellever for fighting with Mary Lou and had been dismissed. But they had kept Suzella.

"Ain't heard nothin'? Not a word?" questioned Little Willie, as he did practically every day even though he knew we would have told him if we had.

"I still can't get over them leavin' in the first place," said Clarence.

Don Shorter leaned against the well. "Wish they'd've let me in on it. I'd've gone with 'em."

Clarence looked over at him. "Wouldja?"

"Sure. Me and Ron."

"Well, when they get back," said Little Willie, "I'm gonna sho' get on them. Not even sayin' nothin' to me 'bout this thing."

"Umph!" Ron said. "They must be havin' some kinda good time."

Little Willie looked at him as if he were crazy. "Working the cane fields?"

"Naw, that ain't what I meant. Meant off seeing the country. Taking care of themselves."

"Oh." Little Willie did not sound convinced. There was silence around the well. Then, with a shake of his head, he mumbled, "Shoot! Wish they'd come on back. I miss them scounds!"

"Well, least one thing," said Don.

"What's that?"

"They ain't gotta be bothered with no Stuart Walker where they are." He nodded toward a car coming onto the school grounds. "Look there."

The black Hudson pulled in front of the well and Stuart stepped out. He looked out over the car's hood at us, taking his time before speaking. He knew he already had our attention. Finally, he said, "Y'all younguns know a nigger by the name of Dubé Cross?"

Dubé, who had been sitting quietly on the ground with his back against the well, looked up in surprise. Fear welled in his eyes and he said nothing. But our eyes had automatically shifted to him when his name was mentioned, and now Stuart looked at him too.

"You, boy, what's your name?"

"M-me, suh?"

Stuart waited, saying nothing else.

Dubé leapt to his feet. "D-D-Dubé, M-Mr. W-W-Walker, sir. Dubé C-Cross."

Stuart studied him. "Heard you was helping them union men when they was here."

Dubé trembled. He kept his eyes on the ground and did not look at Stuart.

"Heard now that Morris Wheeler been seen near this way over by Pine Wood Ridge. You seen him?"

Dubé glanced up, his eyes pleading with Stuart. He tried to speak, but he was so terrified by Stuart's presence that he was unable to make anything but a sputtering sound that did not turn into words.

"He don't speak so good," I said, not liking to see him like this. "He can't answer you."

Stuart's glance slid my way. "Well, you seem to do all right. Got plenty of mouth on you." He grinned; I didn't like the feel of it. Christopher-John and Little Man moved in front of me and Stuart laughed. His eyes lingered a moment longer, then he turned his attention back to Dubé. "Well, boy, I'm waitin' here."

Dubé kept trying, but it was no use. He couldn't speak. Finally, in desperation, he shook his head.

"You tellin' me the truth, boy?"

Dubé nodded.

Stuart stared at Dubé; Dubé stared at the ground. "You hear from him or any other of them union men, I wanna know 'bout it. You hear me, boy?"

Dubé nodded, not looking up.

"That go the same for all of y'all. There ain't gonna be no union down in here, so y'all tell that to your folks. No union!"

His eyes circled the group and he started to get into the car. Then he saw Suzella. She was coming out of her class building with Miss Crocker and Mr. Wellever; all three were smiling. Stuart waited for her to leave them and head our way, and when she finally saw him, he smiled icily, tipped his hat, and then left. Suzella stared after him, then hurried over. "What did he want?" she asked.

"Nothin' 'bout you," I said and turned quickly to Dubé, who had fallen to his knees, trembling with his fear. "Dubé, you all right?"

Dubé took several deep breaths and nodded.

"Man, you seen them union fellas?" asked Little Willie.

Dubé shook his head and after one more deep breath said, "B-b-but I-I-I do, I-I ain't t-t-tellin' him nothin'. N-not one dddd-devilish thing."

At supper, Papa mentioned that hiring had begun again at the hospital. "Maybe I'll go over and see if I can't get on," he said, trying to bring conversation back to our daily meals.

"It's a little late for that, don't you think? When you should have been working here, you weren't."

"Mary, don't start in on me now."

"It's just the truth."

Papa ate his food in silence and before he was finished left the table. Mr. Morrison went after him.

"You can't keep blaming him, Mary," Big Ma chided when they both were gone. "You know he's blaming himself. This thing, it's eating him up inside."

"It's eating me up inside too," Mama said and began to clear the table.

My eyes met Christopher-John's and Little Man's, confirming what we all felt. Nothing was the same anymore. Since Stacey had left, there was no more laughter in the house, and the warmth between Mama and Papa which we had always taken for granted seemed to have gone with Stacey. Breakfast and supper passed with little talk, evenings were strained, and although both Mama and Papa attempted to soothe our fears and keep life without Stacey as normal as possible, the tension between them bothered us almost as much as Stacey's absence.

After supper, Little Man and Christopher-John went off to find Papa; I started the dishes. "Mama," I said as she scraped the leftovers from our plates into one dish for the hogs, "don't you love him anymore?"

Mama stopped and stared at me, a frown lining her brow. "What?"

"Papa. Don't you love him anymore?"

"Of course . . . what makes you ask a thing like that?"

"The way you are with him. . . . Mama, it ain't Papa's fault 'bout Stacey. It's Stacey's own doing."

Mama turned away and began to scrape again.

"Mama, you can't blame him."

"Cassie, what's between your papa and me is something we'll have to work out, and it's something I don't wish to discuss with you."

"But, Mama——"

"Just wash the dishes, Cassie," she said and left.

Christopher-John and Little Man returned a few minutes later. "Papa, he said for us to come on back," Little Man explained. "He with Mr. Morrison in the cabin."

Through the evening, we kept waiting for Papa and Mr. Morrison to return to the house. As our bedtime neared and passed and they did not come back, Mama ordered us to bed. We protested, but Mama was firm and would not even let us go across the garden to say good night. Once I was in bed, I tried to stay awake, listening for Papa, but I fell asleep without hearing him come in.

"Hey, Son-Boy! You seen Wordell?" I hollered as I dashed off Mrs. Lee Annie's front porch after a Saturday-morning reading session. Son-Boy sat on his own porch with his legs astraddle the rail and his head forward resting against a post. Without looking up, he shrugged. I went over. "What's the matter with you?"

This time Son-Boy pulled back from the post and looked at me. "Feel a bit sick on the stomach, that's all."

"I'm sorry. You tell your mama?"

Son-Boy frowned. "And have her give me some of that ole bad-tasting castor oil of hers and put me to bed? No, thank ya, ma'am!"

I shrugged. "All right then. What you say 'bout Wordell?"

"I ain't seen him, Cassie. Mos' likely he in the woods somewheres," he said, putting his head back to the post.

I patted his shoulder sympathetically. "I hope you feel better. . . . You sure you don't wanna tell your mama?"

Son-Boy shook his head.

"Well, then, I'll see you later," I said. I headed down the

path leading to the stream and saw Little Man and Christopher-John running wildly about on the bank in a game of chase with Don Lee. As I reached them, Mrs. Ellis called down the trail, summoning Don Lee.

"Ah, shoot!" he said. "Y'all wait. I'll be back in a minute."

We waited several minutes, but when Don Lee did not return, we started toward home. Christopher-John and Little Man said that they had seen Wordell earlier walking south along the Little RosaLee, so we walked that way as well, hoping to see him.

Since Stacey had gone, we had spent a great deal of time with Wordell. Often as we walked to or from school, he would suddenly emerge from the forest and with a wave of his arm beckon us to follow him. Leaving the road, we would do just that, letting him lead us along the hidden forest paths. The forest was Wordell's home and he knew it well. Without a word he would point out to us the tracks of the forest animals. Sometimes he even led us directly to some occupied animal's lair, where he would sit on his haunches gazing at the animals until they left or we reminded him that we had to get on to school or to home.

A few days ago he had taken us to an old pine tree where a bird sat grounded on a lower branch, its broken wing tied securely to a stick. Gently Wordell had lifted it from its perch and showed it to us. The bird had acknowledged us with a cheerful chirp and Wordell had set him back again. Following the flow of the Little RosaLee, we headed for that same tree and, as we had guessed, found Wordell there.

"Hey, Wordell!" we called.

He didn't answer.

Then we saw the dead cat at his feet. Then the dead bird in his hands.

"What happened?"

His eyes on the bird, Wordell said simply, "That there cat killed the bird. I done killed it." Then he laid the bird at the foot of the tree and began clawing at the hard ground, scooping out a grave. He put the bird in the hole, covered it up with dirt and leaves, and without another word to us walked off.

"How could he do it?" questioned Christopher-John, staring down at the cat. "Jus' kill it like that?"

Little Man stooped to inspect the cat more closely. "Neck's broke," he observed.

Christopher-John shook his head. "Jus' don't understand how he could do it."

I didn't say anything, but I thought I did. I remembered what Mrs. Lee Annie had once said, that when Wordell loved anything, he wouldn't let anyone or anything hurt it if he could help it.

Christopher-John insisted that we bury the cat as well, and once we had, we waited awhile at the tree hoping Wordell would return. Finally, realizing he would not, we continued on to the road and headed for home.

As we neared the house, we saw Mr. Jamison's car in the driveway and began to run, hoping that Mr. Jamison had brought some news of Stacey. Twice Mr. Jamison had been to the house since Stacey had gone. With him Mama, Papa, Big Ma, and Mr. Morrison had drawn up a list of likely areas for which men and boys were recruited to work the cane fields. The list was a long one and Mama had spent most of her time since writing letters to each town sheriff in the designated areas asking for any information they might have about Stacey and Moe. Mr. Jamison had provided the stationery, his own letterhead, and the letters had been written in his name as well. The reason was a practical one: A sheriff would pay more attention to a business letter from an attorney-at-law than to a letter from a black family pleading for news of their child. But so far the letters had brought no news of Stacey.

"Mr. Jamison here was jus' tellin' us 'bout a place he jus' heard 'bout down in the bayou country that had trucks up in here recruitin' for the cane fields," Papa told us when we arrived. He paused. "I figure to go down and see."

"And then you be bringin' Stacey on back?" asked Little Man hopefully.

"Well, son, don't get your hopes up, but if he's down there, I'll be bringin' him."

"How long you gonna be gone, Papa?" Christopher-John wanted to know.

"Week. Maybe two, dependin'. I'm gonna have to trace the route of that truck, see where all it stopped. That could take some time."

Big Ma shook her head mournfully. "I jus' can't believe that child ain't wrote."

"Maybe he just can't, Miz Caroline," said Mr. Jamison. "The cane fields aren't known for making things easy on a person. Most likely he just hasn't been able to get a letter out yet."

"I jus' prays to the Lord that's all it is."

Mr. Morrison turned to Papa. "When you planning on leaving?"

Papa looked Mama's way; her eyes didn't meet his. "Soon as I can. Right after I get some things together."

"Well, I sure wish you well, David," Mr. Jamison said. "I think you know that."

"I do . . . we all do."

While Papa packed, with Christopher-John and Little Man helping him, Big Ma, Suzella, and I fixed some food for him to take. Mama, however, left the house and walked across the pasture. When she returned, Papa was on the back porch taking down his shaving mirror. He waited for her as she crossed the yard; I watched them both from the kitchen window.

"You all right?" he said as she stopped at the steps.

She nodded.

He waited as if expecting Mama to say something, and when she didn't, turned and started down the porch.

"David."

Papa stopped and looked back at her.

"Do you know what Cassie asked me the other day?" She didn't wait for him to answer. "She asked me if I still loved you."

There was a moment when neither spoke. Finally Papa said, "What did you tell her?"

"Don't you know?"

Papa answered with a dry smile. "Well, it's hard to tell . . . these days."

Mama stepped onto the porch, hesitated only a moment, and then went into his arms. "David," she said as he held her to him, "just bring Stacey back. Please, honey . . . bring him back."

It was hot in the kitchen, miserably so. All Saturday huge kettles, two filled with sliced apples brought from the orchard, two others with hulls and cores for jelly, had been cooking on the stove as Big Ma went about her annual canning. I sat at the kitchen table with Mama, Big Ma, and Suzella peeling more apples, but the heat coming from the stove was getting so intense that my stomach churned with nausea and my head ached. I looked down at the bushels of apples, pears, and peaches still waiting to be pared and felt suddenly tired. Getting up, I went over to the water bucket, and finding it empty, checked the bucket hanging from the porch rafter. But there was no water there either. I thought of going to the well to get some more, but right now, as tired as I was, it seemed too much to tackle. Grumbling, I returned to the table and sat down again.

"Now, jus' what's the matter with you?" Big Ma demanded.

"I don't see how come we sittin' 'round here peeling apples and pears and peaches and such and making preserves and jelly like everything's all right and Stacey ain't gone nowheres."

"You don't?" Mama said without looking at me, as she continued to pare. "Cassie, life goes on no matter what, and if we don't keep on doing the everyday kind of things, it means we've given up. That's what you want? To give up and not believe that Stacey's coming back?"

It was one of those questions Mama had a habit of asking that made me think and feel guilty at the same time. I picked up my pan again without answering. "It sure is hot in here."

This time Mama looked at me. "It's not that hot."

"Well, it sure is hot to me."

Mama reached over and, taking my head between her hands, turned my face to hers. Her touch felt cool and soothing. She frowned. "Cassie, how long you been feeling hot like this?"

"All afternoon."

"Anything hurt you?"

"Jus' this heat got me feeling sick on the stomach and my throat's sore."

With her hands still on my face, Mama called to Big Ma, who had gone back to the stove. "Feel this child's face."

Big Ma's rough hands took the place of Mama's. They too felt cool.

"She says she's been feeling like this all afternoon. Nauseous and she has a sore throat."

At that, Big Ma frowned and straightened. "Well, we better get her to bed."

Under normal circumstances I would have vigorously protested being put to bed, but at this particular moment bed seemed a very good place to be. Mama and Big Ma worried about me through the long afternoon, and late that night when a red rash appeared on my neck, they looked frightened. I heard them say it was scarlet fever. I didn't know what scarlet fever was and I was too weak to ask. I just knew by their whispered, anxious tones that it was something to be feared.

Before the dawn, Mr. Morrison wrapped me in a blanket and carried me to his cabin. He said that he and Big Ma would take care of me there so that Christopher-John, Little Man, Suzella, and Mama would not get the fever. I nodded, trying to understand. After that everything was hazy. Once I opened my eyes and found Christopher-John and Little Man staring down at me from the window, and Little Man cried, "Cassie, don't ya die, ya hear! Don't ya die!"

"She ain't," Christopher-John assured him, his voice cracking strangely.

Then I felt Big Ma hovering over me. I closed my eyes for a moment, and when I opened them again, it was dark and Little Man and Christopher-John were gone.

Day faded into night and darkness into dreams, and I couldn't separate them from each other. I drifted in and out of sleep, in and out of dreams that were real and terrifying. Stacey was in them, one minute alive, the next cold and dead in the cane fields. Each time I saw him lying there I ran away, fleeing the sight of him, and then he would come alive again, running and playing with Christopher-John, Little Man, and me. Lazily, he lay on the bank of the pond with us, staring up at the trees; ran games of chase with us on Lady and Jack across the pasture; and walked beside us on the red road to school. I would feel relief then. But only for a little while, for the dreams kept repeating themselves. No matter how hard I struggled to keep Stacey alive, always, just before I awoke, he was lying in the cane fields, unmoving and cold once more.

Somewhere I thought I heard someone say Don Lee was dead. I thought I heard that, but I wasn't sure. I wasn't sure of anything anymore. Maybe Stacey was really home after all. Maybe the whole business about his going was just a dream, and when I finally awakened he would be there by the bed waiting, grinning down at me. Maybe that was the way it would be.

When the fever broke Big Ma told me I had been sick for almost a week and that Papa had come home. I asked about Stacey. There was no news of him.

"Owwww, Cassie, we sho' was scared," said Little Man as he sat on the edge of the bed. Christopher-John sat on the other side, and Suzella stood at the foot leaning against the bedpost. I was finally back in my own bed again, and this was the first day I had felt well enough to sit up.

"Sure was," agreed Christopher-John. "'Specially after . . . after ole Don Lee died. . . ." Tears welled in his eyes as his voice trailed off. Turning toward the window, he wiped the tears away.

"Y'all went to the funeral?"

"Jus' Mama and Mr. Morrison," Little Man replied. "Too many folks carrying the fever and Mama ain't wanted us 'round it. They buried him the day Papa come." He waited a moment, then added in a small voice, "Other folks, they died too."

I had heard enough to know that the fever had swept the entire area, attacking both black and white. I looked up. "Who?"

Both Christopher-John and Little Man looked away.

Suzella took my hand. "The Wellevers' baby boy. Also a little girl from over near Smellings Creek . . . it's been so sad, Cassie."

I nodded, wondering why I felt no loss about Don Lee, or any of them. "How's Son-Boy?"

"He's feeling better," said Suzella, "but he's still weak like you, and they say he's taking Don Lee's death pretty hard."

Again I nodded, feeling numb.

"Wonder what it's like," said Little Man.

"What's that?" I asked.

"Death."

"Oh."

"Jus' lying' there all still all the time." He got down on the deerskin rug and lay down. With hands at his sides, he stiffened, closed his eyes, and just lay there.

Christopher-John studied him. "How you feel?"

Little Man didn't answer right away, but finally when he chose to arise from the dead, he opened his eyes and hopped up. "Must be awful," he concluded, "not being able to move. Get stiff."

"Boy," I said, "when you're dead, it don't much matter You can't feel anything no way."

Little Man was thoughtful. "I s'pose the worms get at you. . . ." He looked over at the rest of us, as if hoping we would deny this. When none of of us did, he said, "Don't think I'd like that. Worms running all through my body."

"What you care?" questioned Christopher-John. "You be gone."

"No, I wouldn't. I'd be in the box."

Christopher-John shook his head. "I asked Mama 'bout it and she said when you die, that part that's you just ups and leaves the body part. She say it's just like when a butterfly leaves its caterpillar skin. Jus' ups and flies away. Says it be free then." He thought on it and decided, "It ain't so bad."

Little Man thought on it too, but did not change his mind. "Yes, it is too. I like my body jus' the way it is and I don't much care for worms to be running all through it, I'm in it or not." Then his eyes took on a faraway look and his words were softer. "Guess they told you, Papa ain't found Stacey."

"Yeah . . . they did."

Christopher-John took it upon himself to change the subject. "Ya know, Cassie, there ain't been no school this past week and last."

"Ain't?"

"They say they was trying to keep the sickness from spreading."

"And I had to go be one of the sick," I complained, upset at the thought of missing the unexpected vacation.

"Say, Cassie, how you like them flowers?" I followed Christopher-John's glance to the vase filled with late-blooming asters. "Cut 'em myself. Thought I'd bring a little of the outdoors inside for ya."

"You did?" I said, thinking how nice it was to have them around me again. "They're real nice."

"Yeah, and when they don't look good no more, I'll bring you some more and—" He broke off abruptly and cocked his head, then, jumping off the bed, ran to the window. "There he is again!"

"Who?"

"Wordell. He been coming every day since ya been down sick. Jus' come and sit by the road and play that harmonica of his."

"He has?" I said in total surprise. I pushed the covers back. "I wanna see."

"Girl, ya better stay where you are," Little Man advised. "Big Ma, she say you can't be getting up yet."

Suzella readjusted the covers around me. "That's right, Cassie. You've got to get your strength back."

Still feeling weak, I complied. "He ever say anything?"

"Jus' play," said Christopher-John.

Little Man jumped from the bed. "I'm gonna go ask him to come in."

"He won't," I told him.

"Well, we can ask him anyways," Christopher-John insisted. "We do every day. Big Ma say that just manners." With that bit of explanation, he and Little Man dashed out the front door.

Suzella shook her head. "I don't understand it . . . I mean why he just comes and plays."

I smiled knowingly. "Don't worry 'bout it. Not understanding him, I mean. Ain't too many people that do." When Christopher-John and Little Man returned, I said, "Well?"

"Wouldn't come," said Little Man.

I nodded, disappointed, even though I had known he wouldn't.

Big Ma came in, waving her hands in the air. "All right now, I'm gonna have to shoo y'all younguns on outa here so's Cassie can get some rest. She mos' likely gettin' tired out 'bout now."

"No, ma'am, Big Ma, I ain't—"

"Yes, you is. Now all y'all jus' go on now. You can visit with her again this afternoon sometime."

After Suzella and the boys left, I fell off to sleep. When I awoke, Papa was sitting in the rocker next to the bed reading the Bible. As I turned, he looked up and smiled.

"Well, you looking better each time I see you, sugar. How you feel?"

I smiled back. "I feel fine, Papa. Fact to business, I don't see how come I gotta stay in bed all the time."

"You just ain't well enough to go getting up quite yet. You do like Big Ma says and you'll be just fine in a little of no time."

"Yes, sir. . . . Papa?"

"Yes, baby?"

"Papa, what we gonna do? There's all them bills to pay . . . and the taxes . . . and you having to leave the railroad to go look for Stacey, well . . . Papa, what we gonna do? You said one time we'd never lose the land."

"And we won't."

"Yes, sir," I said, still worried.

"What is it, sugar?"

"Suzella said Mama sent a whole lotta telegrams to places so's to be sure to reach you 'bout me . . . that cost quite a little bit of money, didn't it?"

"Right nice sum all right."

"I—I'm sorry 'bout that, Papa. That money, I know we need it for a whole lotta things more important than telegrams. . . ."

Papa leaned back in his chair and smiled. "You know,

Cassie, while you was sleeping so peaceful there, I was thinking 'bout when you was born."

"You was?"

He nodded. "I was twenty-four years old then and was working down at that old sawmill near Smellings Creek. It was run by an ole cracker by the name of Joe Morgan, and most of the colored folks that worked for him had a really hard time with him, but for some reason or other he hadn't never bothered me. I s'pose that's 'cause I didn't never have nothing to do with him or say to him outside of what had to do with the business of that sawmill, while some others would drink with him and so forth. And I ain't never approved of that, getting too familiar with these crackers.

"Anyways, on that particular day, the day you was born, ole Joe Morgan had drunk more'n he should've for lunch and he called me from my work and asked me 'bout drinking with him. I told him 'no thank ya' and went on back to work. Well, I s'pose that really made him angry, me not drinking with him after he'd invited me and all, and he stayed up there in that office of his a good part of the afternoon and from the look of him when he come out, he'd been stewing and drinking most of that time.

"He come down to the mill where I was and began talking loud and saying things like I wasn't half doing my work and that I was sneaking off 'fore quitting time and such. Well, I knew he was drunk and I didn't say nothing to him, just kept on working. But that just made him madder, and he said I better answer him when he talked to me. I told him I didn't know I was s'pose to answer him, and Lord, if he wasn't mad already, he sure was mad then. He said I was just too uppity for my own good and he better just chop me down to size. Then he come grabbing an axe."

"And he was gonna use it on you?" I asked breathlessly.

Papa smiled slyly. "I believe that was what he was planning on doing."

"Papa, what'd you do?"

"Nothin' . . . just stood there . . . and told him he planned on using that thing on me, he better plan on killing me."

"That's all?"

"That's all."

"And what'd he do?"

"He stood there a moment all red in the face, then turned and went back to his office."

'And what'd you do?"

"I got my stuff and came on home without my pay, not knowing what that old white man was gonna try and do to me once he got sober. But guess what?"

"Sir?"

"When I got home, I forgot all about Joe Morgan."

"You did?"

Papa nodded.

"How come?"

"'Cause you was here. Born that same afternoon."

I smiled.

"There you was, the prettiest, baldest baby I'd ever seen in my life."

I laughed.

"And I said to myself: 'What I gotta worry 'bout these white folks for? Or a job? Or money I ain't got? This little girl right here, she's what's important. Ain't never gonna be nothing more important than this little girl.' "

I felt a lump growing in my throat. "Papa," I said, "I love you."

Papa smiled and took my hand, enveloping it in his own. "I love you too, Cassie girl. I love you too."

Finally, on the day Papa was to return to his search, I was given permission not only to get out of bed for a few hours but to put on my pants and shirt. I felt a little wobbly at first, but as soon as I was dressed I hurried out the front door and down the softness of the lawn to the road, where Wordell had already taken up his morning vigil. When he saw me coming, he took the harmonica from his lips and smiled. I grinned back and sat beside him. The question was on his face, so I answered it.

"I'm fine."

To my surprise, he said: "I'm glad."

"I—I really like your music. Thank ya for coming and playing it for me every day. It was so pretty."

Wordell looked down at his harmonica.

"It sure helped a lot, that music. That business of staying in bed all day ain't no fun at all when ya gotta do it day in and day out. And being hot all the time and coughing and feeling sore, that wasn't no fun either. I ain't never really been sick before, but I tell you one thing, I ain't never wanting to be sick again. I guess I was sorta lucky though, 'cause my fever was so high and I don't 'member most of it 'cept . . ."

I stopped. The dreams had lingered with me, like a ghostly foreboding about which I had been unable to speak. I could feel Wordell's eyes on me, but I didn't turn to look at him. "'Cept the dreams. I 'member the dreams. . . . They was so real and . . . and Stacey, he was in 'em and he . . . sometimes he was . . . dead."

Frightened by my own words, I turned frantically to Wordell. "What that mean, Wordell? Me dreaming something like that? That ain't no vision, is it? It can't be no vision! I couldn' stand it if Stacey was dead! Couldn't stand it if any of 'em was dead."

"Cassie!" Big Ma summoned from the house.

"Anything happen to 'em, I'd die my own self. I wouldn't wanna live they wasn't here!"

"Cassie, where you at, girl?"

Wordell stood up. Frightened, I searched his face looking for comfort. He looked down at me, the gentleness in his eyes reminding me of Papa, and placed a hand on my shoulder. "Everybody gotta die, Cassie."

"But Stacey—"

"And he die, you'd live . . . 'cause that's how come the sun shines."

Gently, he pressed my shoulder, then, turning, put the harmonica to his lips and walked down the road, the music trailing him. He did not come to play for me again.

12

When Uncle Hammer arrived a few days before Christmas, he cupped my face in his hands and asked me how I was. Once assured that I was fine, he looked around the house and said: "Where Christmas done got to? Ain't seen a sign of it nowheres. No pine and holly over the fireplace. No good cooking smelling through the house. Y'all hiding it from me?"

Big Ma smiled weakly at his teasing. "Tell you the truth, son, we gettin' us a slow start 'round here. Jus' got them hogs slaughtered a few days ago and David not home, we ain't fooled with that souse 'ceptin' to cook the head. Ain't even got the coon yet. Got my nuts cracked for my pecan pie and brought in my sweet potatoes, but ain't none of us much in the Christmas spirit."

Uncle Hammer took this in silence, then looked at Mama. "When's David coming back?"

"He said by Christmas . . . it depends. . . ."

Uncle Hammer nodded and rose from his chair. "Well, seem to me we got a lot to do 'round here, and the first thing we gonna do is take care of that souse. Can't have New Year's without no hoghead souse!"

"But Papa, he always make the souse," Little Man reminded him, for it was a job Papa took special pride in doing each Christmas season.

Uncle Hammer looked his way. "Don't you figure I can handle it?"

"Yes, sir," said Little Man, not concealing the doubt in his voice.

Uncle Hammer laughed. "Well, nephews and little niece, y'all come on and give me a hand and let's see how we do."

We went with Uncle Hammer to the kitchen, where he took off his suit jacket, rolled up his shirt sleeves, and after washing his hands tackled the hoghead. He delegated the job of picking the meat off the head to Christopher-John, Little Man, and me, while he chopped the sausage. Once the meats were ready, he ground them together, then added salt, red and black pepper, sage, and vinegar. He mixed everything well and tasted it. He frowned, added a bit more vinegar for a tangier flavor, and after a final taste exclaimed, "Now, that's some good souse!" He passed around the bowl and the rest of us agreed. He winked at us. "Bet y'all thought your papa was the only one could make souse like that 'round here."

Uncle Hammer molded the souse, wrapped it in a cloth, and put it in a bucket with a brick on top to squeeze out any excess oil. Then Christopher-John, Little Man, and I went with him to the well, where he tied the bucket to a rope and lowered it to above the well's water line to season until New Year's Day. With that done, he clapped his hands together and said, "Now let's go get us that Christmas tree!"

The four of us walked deep into the forest, Uncle Hammer carrying an axe, Christopher-John, Little Man, and I bushel baskets for the holly branches and mistletoe. East of the pond we found a nice-sized cedar tree, and not far from it holly intertwined with forest vines. We set to work. Uncle Hammer chopped the tree while Christopher-John, Little Man, and I cut the holly. After a while Uncle Hammer glanced our way. "How y'all doing?" he asked. "How y'all making it without your brother?"

We were silent in answer.

He swung the axe again. "He'll be back, ya know."

Christopher-John, with strings of ivy vines swinging from his neck like a long green scarf, went over to him. "Uncle Hammer, what's the cane fields like?"

"Ain't y'all asked your papa?"

"Asked Mr. Morrison. He said it's terrible hard work."

"Backbreaking work is what it is."

"But he said cane-field work be ended come December sometime."

Uncle Hammer nodded.

"Then maybe," said Little Man hopefully, "maybe Stacey, he'll be home for Christmas?"

I turned quickly back to the holly bush, but not before Uncle Hammer had seen the doubt in my eyes. "I wouldn't count on it, son. I wouldn't count on it for Christmas. But one of these days I got a feeling the best present y'all ever had'll come walking in the house there, and it won't even be Christmas Day."

That evening, with the Christmas tree sitting near the window and holly interwoven with mistletoe and pine branches on the mantel, Uncle Hammer and Mr. Morrison talked of hunting a coon as if it were any other Christmas. They filled the evening with stories about coon hunting which made us laugh and, for a little while, took our thoughts off Stacey. Finally, when the evening came to an end and everyone stood to go to bed, Mama unexpectedly went over to Uncle Hammer and hugged him softly. "Thank you, Hammer," she said.

Christmas Eve Papa came home, once again alone. Even though both Papa and Uncle Hammer had warned us not to get our hopes up about Stacey's return, none of us, including Mama and Big Ma, had totally dispelled the hope that if Stacey was ever coming home again, it would be for Christmas; and we listened for him in every footstep coming up the steps, every knock on the door. Now Papa's return without him punctured our Christmas hope, and the emptiness without Stacey settled once more.

"Papa," Christopher-John said, "Stacey, he don't come for Christmas, he gonna be awful lonesome by hisself."

Papa, looking tired from the long days of search, reminded him that most likely he wasn't alone. "Remember, he's got Moe."

Christopher-John nodded and looked away.

"But when he gonna come home?" said a mournful Little Man. "We been waitin' so long."

A tear slid down his cheek and Papa brought him close. "One day, son," he said. "I'm praying one day soon now."

We arose in the early-morning darkness, greeting each other with merry Christmas wishes, but the words were hollow, without feeling, and before we tended to anything else, we gathered before the fire in a circle as we did each Christmas morning and sang "Will the Circle Be Unbroken?" It was a song of family, of love, of loss; we all felt it deeply. Then we fell to our knees, hands still clasped, and prayed, each of us in our turn, for Stacey and Moe's safe return. Big Ma broke down and cried afterward, but Mama, Papa, Uncle Hammer, and Mr. Morrison tried to be cheerful. "All right," Papa said when the prayers were finished, "let's see what Santa Claus done brought!"

After breakfast we dressed and went to church. As we drove up, bells were pealing joyfully, ringing longer and louder than usual on this Christmas Day—Joe was having a marvelous time—and church members were clustered around the entrance giving each other season's greetings, while boys and girls lucky enough to have gotten some new bit of clothing strutted proudly around the churchyard. Leaving the car, we were heading toward the entrance to join the other churchgoers when Uncle Hammer turned sharply and said, "It's Russell Thomas, ain't it?"

Russell, his back to us, turned from a group of young men and grinned. "Why, Mr. Hammer! How you doing?" The two shook hands, then Russell greeted the rest of us, his eyes resting last on Suzella. He smiled warmly. "I'm glad to see you're still here."

"Thank you" was all she said.

"I heard you'd joined the Army," said Uncle Hammer, "but each time you come home, I never quite made it home the same time, so I kept missing you. Glad it worked out this time. Get a chance to talk."

"Yes, sir, I'm looking forward to that. I've got me two weeks this time and—"

"Hammer Logan, you ole good-lookin' thing you!"

"Miz Lee Annie!" Uncle Hammer exclaimed as Mrs. Lee Annie hurried over. "It sure is good to see ya."

"Good to see you too," she said after she had gotten her hug. "Thought maybe you'd try slippin' outa here without seein' me like ya done that one other time."

"Ah, Miz Lee Annie, ain't you gonna never let me forget that?"

"Naw, I ain't," she admitted with a laugh. She looked around, her attention seemingly distracted. "Well, I don't see her."

"See who?"

"Your wife."

"Miz Lee Annie, you know I ain't married."

"Well, that's jus' the point. When you gonna get married, boy? Big ole handsome thing like you runnin' 'round here single. It's a cryin' shame."

"Now, Miz Lee Annie, you know good and well I been in love with you since I was a wee bitty boy and jus' wouldn't nobody else ever do."

Mrs. Lee Annie laughed and hit him fondly. "Ah, you get on 'way from here, Hammer Logan!"

The bell stopped ringing for a few minutes, then started up again, signaling that service was about to begin. As we entered the church, I saw Son-Boy sitting with Henry and Maynard near the front, and throughout Reverend Gabson's service I found myself glancing over at him. Without Don Lee, Son-Boy looked so alone. When I had first learned of Don Lee's death, it had affected me very little; the news that he was dead had been only words to me. It wasn't until my first Sunday back at church, when I felt his absence from the Sunday school pew and waited for his husky laughter when class was over, that it hit me that I would never see him again. I cried then, not for Don Lee, but for myself. I missed him and I ached and I hurt, knowing all the while that Don Lee, lying cold in the church cemetery, no longer had use for such feelings. What was worse was that I felt selfish and sinful, for even as I attempted to console Son-Boy I was thankful that if anyone had had to die, it had been someone else's brother and not mine.

After his usual lengthy stay in the pulpit, Reverend Gabson ended the service with a powerful prayer asking God to bless all those families who had suffered the sorrow of losing a loved one during the year and then asked a special blessing for Stacey and Moe that they might return to us, well and unharmed. After a round of "Go Tell It on the Mountain," followed by the benediction, the congregation left to go to their own or neighbors' houses for Christmas dinner.

The Averys came home with us, and in the afternoon Mr. Tom Bee, the Laniers, the Ellises, and Mrs. Lee Annie with Russell crowded into the house to share the day. Sitting before the fire, the adults told their stories as they always did. They laughed. They joked. But underlying it all was the absence of both Stacey and Moe, and every now and then spoken words of them would surface and the mood of those gathered would change.

"Anybody know how y'all feel, ya know we do," said Mr. Avery. "It's a sorrowful thing to lose a child. Sho' is. . . ."

"We don't figure we've lost Stacey yet," Mama said.

Mr. Avery glanced at her. "No, I wouldn't reckon so— y'all still got reason to hope."

Mama nodded sympathetically. Everyone was silent.

Mrs. Avery pinned her eyes on the fire and began to rock in a slow, nervous motion. Claude, sitting with Christopher-John, Little Man, and me on the other side of the room, was quiet as he always was now. He stared blankly at his mother. Christopher-John put an arm around his friend's shoulders, but Claude didn't even look around.

"Well, I tells ya," said Big Ma, "what with all these younguns gone one way or the other, it makes it hard to keep on goin' sometimes."

"That's sho' the truth," Mrs. Ellis agreed, dabbing at her eyes.

"But the Lord, He understands why they gone," Big Ma said faithfully, "even if we don't."

"Ya think He does?" Mrs. Avery questioned, speaking for the first time.

"Course He do, Fannie."

Mrs. Avery turned back to the fire and continued to rock. Mr. Avery watched her and shook his head. "Yes, suh, it's a sorrowful thing to lose a child . . . sho' is. . . ."

There was an affirmation of silence. Then Mrs. Lee Annie slapped her hands to her knees and everyone looked at her. "Got me some news," she announced.

Mama smiled at her. "What's that, Mrs. Lee Annie?"

"Got me a birthday comin' up here January two. Be sixty-five years old!"

"Well, happy birthday to you, Miz Lee Annie!" said Uncle Hammer in congratulations.

"Thank you, Hammer. Yes, sir, sixty-five, and I done decided to give myself a birthday present." She looked around at our waiting faces. "Gonna go register to vote."

For a long moment, there was only a shocked silence. Then Mr. Page Ellis cried, "You gonna what!"

"Gonna go to register. I figures I'm ready. I knows all that's in that book and I'm ready to answer them registrar's questions." She looked at Mama. "Don't you think I'm ready, Mary?"

Mama seemed not to know how to answer as she glanced

at the faces of both Mr. and Mrs. Ellis, their fear unconcealed. "There's no denying you know it," she said reluctantly, "but don't you think it's too soon? I mean I was thinking you had in mind another year or two."

Mrs. Lee Annie shook her head. "No, ma'am. May not even be 'round come no 'nother year or two. I knows it now and I'm gonna do it now."

"It's crazy!" Mr. Ellis yelled at his aunt. "Always done thought it was foolishness. Thought you'd work yourself outa it! Why, even if they was to let you take that test—which ain't likely—they ain't gonna pass you—"

"It's the principle of the thing—"

"The principle gonna get you dead then. Now, Aunt Lee Annie, you listen to me! You can't do this thing!" Desperately, he turned to Russell. "Ain't you got nothin' to say 'bout all this?"

Russell glanced at his grandmother. "Rather she wouldn't, but she do it, I'm gonna have to support her."

"Then you crazy too!"

Mrs. Ellis leaned past her husband to touch Mrs. Lee Annie. "He's right, Aunt Lee Annie. Ya jus' can't do this. It's too dangerous—and there's Mr. Granger to think 'bout."

Mrs. Lee Annie listened in silence, then quietly said, "I'm gonna do this thing. I know don't none of y'all like the idea, but that's too bad. Now, I knows what could happen, but I jus' gotta do it. Gotta stand up once in this life, and that's jus' what I'm gonna do." She paused, looking around at us. Then her eyes settled on Mama. "Mary, I'd be obliged you go with me. But ya feel like ya can't, then I understands. I understands if can't nobody go with me, and I won't hold it hard. But even if I has to go walkin' to Strawberry by myself, come January two, that's what I'm gonna do."

Mr. Ellis leapt from his chair. "You watch, old woman! You gonna be the ruination of us all. You jus' watch!" Then turning angrily, he left the house. Mrs. Ellis, looking a bit like a nervous, frightened bird, glanced around the room, then went after him.

A long silence filled the room. Finally Mama said, "Mrs. Lee Annie, won't you change your mind?"

"No, ma'am."

"But what about Page and Leora?"

Mrs. Lee Annie looked troubled. "Nobody got cause to be puttin' blame on them." Then, as if to make herself believe that, she nodded firmly and added, "Mr. Granger won't do nothin' to 'em."

"And what about you?"

Mrs. Lee Annie thrust back her shoulders. "Me . . . I'll be all right . . . soon's I goes to register. . . ."

Mr. Tom Bee shook his head. "Foolishness. Plumb foolishness. Why I recalls the time colored folks gone to take that there test and the ole registrar, he puts out a jar of jelly beans and says for 'em to tell him how many there is in the jar, and that there was yo' test. Plumb foolishness!"

"Wasn't so long ago neither," said Mr. Morrison. "I seen that same thing jus' a while back . . . man got lynched for his trouble."

"Foolish old woman," Mr. Tom Bee muttered. "Foolish!"

Everyone tried to talk Mrs. Lee Annie out of going to register. They told stories of humiliations and loss, of tragedies and death, but Mrs. Lee Annie would not be dissuaded. Her mind, as she had said many times before, was made up, and as the day darkened toward evening and people began to head for home, they could only shake their heads at her hardheadedness and wish her well.

Then Jake Willis came.

"Well, merry Christmas to you all!" he said loudly, stepping inside.

"Merry Christmas," Papa said and invited him to sit down.

"No, sir, I don't think I will." He smiled widely, exposing the gold teeth. "This here place jus' 'bout too fine for a nigger like me." Laughing, he nodded at Uncle Hammer. "Mr. Hammer Logan, how you doin', sir?"

Uncle Hammer, his eyes and his voice displaying no warmth, said: "I'm just fine, Mr. Willis. Yourself?"

"Glad to hear it. I'm right fine." He then looked at Mama. "Any word 'bout your boy, Miz Logan?"

"No, not yet."

He shook his head. "Sad thing. Sad. Particularly on this glorious day not to have your boy home, not to know if he's alive or dead. Sorrowful!"

"You sure you won't have a seat, Mr. Willis?" Mama said, her manner indicating that she had been unmoved by his words.

"No, ma'am, I thank ya, but I jus' come by 'cause I got a little present for Miss Suzella there." He grinned, his eyes caressing Suzella across the crowded room. I saw Russell glance from Jake Willis to Suzella and take note. "Ain't nothin' much. Jus' some candies—some chocolates I seen wrapped real pretty up in Strawberry, no doubt waiting for some white man to buy it for his lady—and I figured I'd get it for Miss Suzella here." He held out the store-wrapped package to Suzella, who made no move to take it.

Papa glanced over at Suzella, who was flushed with embarrassment, and spoke to Jake Willis. "We thank you for the thought, Mr. Willis, but our niece ain't of courtin' age yet and it wouldn't be fit for her to accept presents from gentlemen."

For a fleeting second the grin left Jake Willis's face and the eyes went mean. Just as quickly the smile returned, but the change had not been lost on Uncle Hammer, who got up from his chair and leaned against the fireplace. "She look of courtin' age to me," Jake Willis said.

"No sir, she ain't but fifteen," Papa said cordially. "Perhaps because you're new to this area you don't know, but girls 'round here don't start courtin' till they sixteen and of marrying age."

Jake Willis wet his lips, the grin still there. "Well, I paid quite a bit for this here candy. I can at least give 'em to her, can't I?"

Papa met his eyes. "I just explained to you, Mr. Willis, that it ain't fit for girls not of courtin' age to accept gifts from gentlemen."

"Truth is, even if she was, you wouldn't let me court her, would ya now? Truth is, y'all think that white-looking niece of y'all's is too good for a black nigger like me. That's the truth of the matter, ain't it?"

Papa, who never allowed himself to be rushed into anger, breathed in deeply, waited a moment, and said calmly: "The truth of the matter, Mr. Willis, is that Suzella's not of courtin' age and if she was, I don't believe it would be proper for you to court her anyways, seeing that you must be some twenty years her senior."

"Well, why don't you leave that to her?"

"Long as she's in my care, I'll do what I think's best for her, and I say she ain't of courtin' age. Now there ain't nothing gonna change my mind 'bout that."

With those words I knew that the conversation was closed; Papa would discuss it no further.

Jake Willis grew quiet, then the grin widened and he

shrugged. "Well, can't blame a fella for tryin', now can ya? She one of the prettiest things in these parts, black or white, and looking white like she do with that silky hair—no doubt like her white mama—makes her something special. . . . Well . . . no matter. There's other girls who'll be glad to get these chocolates from Jake Willis. Yes, sir! Well, no hard feelings." He opened the door. "Merry Christmas . . and happy New Year to y'all too!"

The door closed and Mrs. Lee Annie shuddered. "Don't like that man," she said. "Lord, help me, but I sho' don't."

Uncle Hammer sat back down. "That no-count nigger, one of these days he's gonna get his head cracked open."

"Forget it, Hammer," Papa said, coming back to the fire. "Don't let him spoil Christmas. He ain't worth it."

Mrs. Lee Annie looked over at Papa, shuddered once again, and pulled her shawl closer to her.

When everyone had gone and Christmas Day came to a close, Little Man, Christopher-John, and I were sent off to bed. Suzella came to bed too and fell right to sleep after the long day, but I lay restless on my pallet, unable to sleep. As always, Stacey was on my mind; but finding it too painful to think of him, I forced my thoughts from him and thought of Mrs. Lee Annie instead.

If she had her way, she was going to try to register, and I hoped she would. I felt right proud of her. I had heard enough to know that it would be tough, even dangerous, for her to attempt it, and I trembled at all I had heard. But then I thought about all those afternoons Mrs. Lee Annie and I had spent reading together, studying the constitution. I thought of what she had said about her father voting and how he had been beaten because of it. I thought about what

Mr. Jamison had said about jurors being selected from the list of people who could vote. I thought about T.J.

I made up my mind.

Leaving the pallet, I crossed over to the door and went into Mama and Papa's room, where the adults still sat before the low-burning fire. They looked up at my entrance and Mama said, "Cassie, what're you doing up?"

"I been thinkin'—"

"Oh?"

"Been thinkin' 'bout Miz Lee Annie and her goin' to register. . . . I wanna go with her."

Mama glanced at Papa, then back at me. "Why, Cassie?"

I frowned, trying to think of the best way to say what I was feeling. "Well, I figure me and Miz Lee Annie, we been in this constitution-reading business together since she got them books of hers. And she done told me 'bout her papa and all and how powerful much she wanna vote . . . well, I jus' figure I oughta be goin' with her." I hesitated, then added, "'Sides, I'm kinda interested in the law and all."

Big Ma muttered something I could not hear and shook her head. Everyone else was silent, looking at me. Finally Papa said, "Cassie, sugar, that's right admirable, your way of thinkin', but what Miz Lee Annie's 'bout to do is a dangerous thing. Your mama and me, we don't even know if we goin' yet."

"Well, Papa, you decide on goin', can I go?"

Papa rubbed his hand over his head, taking several moments before he answered. "That's gonna call for some serious thinking, Cassie."

"Yes, sir."

"Best now you be gettin' on back to bed."

I said good night again and went into my room. But I didn't go to my pallet. Instead I curled up in the rocker in front of the bedroom fireplace and listened to the talk on the other side of the wall.

"Y'all ain't gonna give no thought to this, are ya?" Uncle Hammer said before I was even settled. "It'd be crazy for any of us to go and pure foolishness to take Cassie."

"Lord, jus' the thought of what could happen," Big Ma said. "Gives me pure fright . . ."

"I know," said Mama softly. "Still—"

"Still what?" questioned Uncle Hammer. "You jus' heard Mr. Morrison here tellin' us 'bout that lynching up 'round Tupelo jus' a year 'fore he come here, and that was 'bout some Negro trying to vote. This whole idea is crazy and it'll jus' end in trouble."

"Maybe. But you know how smart Cassie is. This thing she's wanting to do, it could be something she *needs* to see."

"Mary!" Big Ma exclaimed. "You ain't thinkin'—"

"I don't know, Mama. David . . . I've just got a feeling. I'm just as scared as anybody about walking up to that registrar's office talking about voting. But I've got this feeling. Cassie's seen so much . . . learned so much about what it means to be black in these past few years. She's nearly witnessed a lynching. She's seen a boy sentenced to death. . . . This thing Mrs. Lee Annie wants to do, it's foolish perhaps, but it's something to be proud of too. If Cassie witnessed it, it could just mean a lot to her one day."

"Lord . . ." Big Ma mumbled.

"David, what you got to say 'bout all this?" Uncle Hammer demanded.

Papa let out a troubled sigh, but didn't answer right away. When he did speak, I leaned forward, anxiously waiting to hear. "'Bout Miz Lee Annie goin' to register, there ain't nothin' I can do 'bout that. 'Bout any of us goin', I'm gonna have to think it through—"

"And 'bout Cassie?"

There was a long silence.

"I don't know yet, Hammer," Papa said at last. "Right now I jus' don't know. . . ."

On the third day after Christmas a car pulled into the driveway, and unexpectedly Cousin Bud stepped out. Led by Mama, we rushed outside to greet him, and a few minutes later he was seated in front of the fire with Suzella across from him. Suzella seemed glad enough to see her father, but she was very quiet, watching him, waiting, as if she knew why he had come.

"David home?" Cousin Bud asked, turning to Mama. "Mr. Morrison?"

"They went over to Smellings Creek on some business. Hammer's with them. They should be back shortly."

Cousin Bud looked uneasy. "You say Hammer's here? Well, then, I won't be staying. Ya know, him and me, we don't much see eye to eye."

"Don't worry about Hammer," Mama said.

Cousin Bud smiled, somewhat embarrassed, then we started talking of all that had happened in our lives. He shook his head sadly as we talked about Stacey, and looked at me in genuine concern as he learned more about my illness. For more than an hour he sat by the fire with us. Then suddenly he stood, saying he wanted to stretch his legs after the long drive, and asked Mama to go walking with him. Mama looked a bit puzzled when he did not extend the invitation to Suzella; after all, Cousin Bud had not seen his daughter in more than six months.

"All right, Bud," she said, and the two of them went out.

When Mama returned alone, Suzella seemed not at all surprised to learn that Cousin Bud was waiting to talk to her down by the pond. She simply nodded, put on her coat, and went out. Then Mama told us why Cousin Bud had come. He and Suzella's mother were getting a divorce and Cousin Bud was here to take Suzella home.

Christopher-John, Little Man, and I stared at Mama and said nothing. Suzella had come to mean a lot to Christopher-John and Little Man, and at that moment I realized she had come to mean a lot to me too. Since Stacey had gone, I hadn't even thought about her leaving.

"When they goin'?" Big Ma quietly asked.

"Bud wanted to leave tonight because of Hammer being here, but I talked him into staying until tomorrow. I figure Suzella'll need at least that much time to pack and say good-bye to folks."

Outside we heard a car pull into the drive and Christopher-John said, "Papa and them's back."

Big Ma got up and walked slowly across the room. "'Spect I'd best get them dresses Suzella done washed and iron 'em up for her 'fore I start supper." She stopped at the dining room door and looked around. "Lord, I'm gonna sho' miss that child . . . sho is. . . ." Then she turned and went into the kitchen.

A short while later, Suzella was packing. "You know, I don't really want to go," she said as she pulled her dresses from the chiffonier. "This seems more like home now than New York." She looked around the room and was thoughtful.

I folded a sweater for her and carefully placed it in the suitcase. "I'm sorry 'bout your folks. 'Bout them gettin' a divorce and all."

Suzella shook her head. "I'm not, not really. I knew it was coming."

"Which one you gonna stay with?"

She didn't look at me. "My mother."

I didn't say anything.

She glanced at me, her look somewhat guilty, and continued to pack. "It'll be easier for me, Cassie, if I stay with my mother."

"I guess." I shrugged. "You wantin' to be white so bad."

"Cassie . . . please don't start that."

I sighed. "I wish you could stay."

"Thought you couldn't wait for me to leave," she laughed.

"Well . . . you kinda grew on me."

"You kind of grew on me too. All of you. I only wish . . ." She didn't finish.

"What?"

Noisily she wrapped a shoe in newspaper to cover the cracking of her voice. "That Stacey had gotten back before I left." She stopped and met my eyes. "When he comes back again, give him a big hug for me and tell him . . . tell him I really missed him."

I handed her the other shoe. "I promise," I said, looking away. Then, feeling a new loneliness at the thought of her leaving too, I went around the bed and hugged her tightly, something I had thought I would never do. When everything was packed, we joined Christopher-John and Little Man sitting on the front porch.

"Suzella, ain't there no way you can stay?" said Christopher-John.

"You heard Mama," I said sullenly. "She can't stay."

"I know," he admitted.

"But I wish I could."

Little Man looked around at her. "We gonna miss you, Suzella," he said and quickly looked away again.

Suzella bit her lower lip and wiped at her eyes. Then she

stooped down between them and put an arm around each one. "I'll be back though," she promised. "Stacey and I, we'll both be back."

Christopher-John rubbed the back of his hand across his nose and nodded to the road. "Truck coming," he announced in a husky voice.

A few moments later a truck turned into the driveway. Mr. Tate Sutton and Charlie Simms got out. Jeremy was with them. Christopher-John hopped up immediately and ran inside. "Papa, there's some white men out here," he said. By the time Mr. Sutton, Mr. Simms, and Jeremy got to the steps, Papa and Uncle Hammer were on the porch; Christopher-John slipped back out behind them. Jeremy nodded at us, and Mr. Sutton said, "David. Hammer."

Papa and Uncle Hammer nodded their greeting; an awkward silence followed. Then Mr. Sutton, who obviously had been elected to do the talking, spoke up. "I s'pose y'all done heard the union's getting started up again."

"Union?" Papa said, as if he had never heard the word.

Mr. Sutton nodded. "That's right. One Morris Wheeler got started."

Papa was silent, feigning ignorance. Uncle Hammer stood several feet behind him, leaning against the house, allowing Papa to do the talking.

"One got ended when Morris Wheeler got burnt out. . . . They say he's back, by the way. You had heard that, hadn't you?"

"I can't say that I have."

"You jus' don't know nothin', now, do you?" said Mr. Simms, a sour look on his face.

Jeremy shot his father a disapproving glance. Mr. Sutton rushed on, not giving Papa time to answer. "Well, we come now 'cause we know things only gonna get worse. Can't figure on nothin' much gettin' better after what happened over at the Walker place yesterday——"

"Maybe he don't know 'bout that neither," interrupted Mr. Simms with a sarcastic snarl.

Mr. Sutton looked irritably over his shoulder at Mr. Simms, then returned his attention to Papa. "The Walkers putting twelve of their families off the land—white and colored."

"Mostly white——"

"Say they can't make no money with a quarter of the land fallow. Say the families have to go 'fore the week's out. We figure the Walkers can do that, then so can Mr. Granger, Mr. Montier, Mr. Harrison, anybody. So some of us been talkin' and we figure it's time to get the union back on its feet." He paused, looking embarrassed. "Come too 'cause we figure maybe Mr. Wheeler was right 'bout colored farmers . . . 'bout colored farmers being a part of it."

"I see," Papa said.

"Hope you do," said Mr. Sutton. "You get the colored in this thing and we can get to moving with it. Do some standing up for ourselves. Keep this kinda thing from happening to the rest of us."

Papa stood in silence; Mr. Sutton and Mr. Simms and Jeremy waited. Then Papa said, "I 'spect y'all wanna get the union goin', then you best talk to the folks sharecropping on plantation land."

"We figures to do that," said Mr. Sutton. "But we also figured Mr. Wheeler mos' likely started with you, best we do the same."

Papa did not confirm having ever spoken to Mr. Wheeler and Mr. Sutton did not press him about it, but he did try to get Papa to commit himself to talking to other black farmers in the community. Papa, however, committed himself to nothing, including ever having even heard of the union. Finally Mr. Sutton gave up and started away. "We gonna have us a meeting come another week," he said in a parting attempt to gain Papa's alliance. "You remember that."

"Come on, Tate," Mr. Simms ordered brusquely. "I never did like the idea of beggin' no nigger—"

Mr. Sutton shook his head and walked back to the car, with Mr. Simms following. Jeremy turned to go with them, then stopped and looked back at us. "Any word?" he asked.

I shook my head. "No word."

Jeremy's lips parted as if he wanted to say more, but he left without speaking again, probably not even realizing his eyes had said it all.

Uncle Hammer and Papa watched the truck pull away, then went back into the house. A few minutes later Cousin Bud came out and said that if Suzella still wanted to say good-bye to Mrs. Lee Annie, we had better get started. Christopher-John, Little Man, and I decided to go with them.

At Mrs. Lee Annie's, Russell said, "You know, I was kinda planning on trying to get you to talk to me a little bit." H- ° sed a smile from Suzella. "'Fraid I don't have no chocolates though."

"You don't need any."

"You encouraging me then?"

Suzella seemed embarrassed. "Where's Wordell? I was hoping I'd get a chance to see him."

"No telling. But I'll tell him you said good-bye."

"I didn't really get to know him."

"Few people do."

"But I like him."

"I'm glad."

"By the way, Cassie," Russell said, turning my way, "tell your folks that if they decide to go on into Strawberry with Mama Lee next week, then we'd be obliged to go with them. Cousin Page won't let us take the wagon. Cousin Leora say she'll be going and I'll be going. Y'all don't go, then tell your papa I'll be speaking to him 'bout borrowing the wagon."

"All right," I said.

"Well, here we is," announced Mrs. Lee Annie proudly as she stepped back from her cabinets, where she had been searching the last several minutes. She had a jar in each hand. "Got some pickled beets for ya and some crackling. Wants ya to have some of these here pickled cucumbers, onions, and tomato preserves too, ya liked 'em so much."

Suzella smiled and shook her head, speechless. Russell nudged her. "Ain't she something?"

"Oh, yes," Suzella agreed, looking into his eyes. "Something mighty fine."

For a moment their eyes were fixed on each other. Then Russell said: "You wanna see Wordell 'fore you go, I got an idea where he went off to. You want, we can go check."

Suzella glanced over at Cousin Bud, engaged in hearty conversation with Mrs. Lee Annie, and got up. Half an hour later when Cousin Bud decided it was time to go and Suzella and Russell hadn't come back, I was sent to get them. As I ran outside I saw them coming up the trail from the Little RosaLee. I was about to call out to them when to my surprise Russell turned Suzella to him and kissed her. Suzella allowed the kiss, then looking confused pulled from him and ran back to the house.

"Cousin Bud said he's ready to go," I told her as she hurried past me. Hardly looking at me, she nodded and went inside.

A few minutes later when we were in the car and going down the trail, I whispered, "I seen Russell kiss you."

Suzella glanced at me, a bit embarrassed. "It didn't mean anything."

I stared at her.

"Really," she protested.

"You say so," I said, letting her have her way about it.

As we pulled into the road, we saw Dubé Cross up ahead and Cousin Bud offered him a ride. Dubé hopped gratefully into the backseat with Suzella and me; he was headed over to the Harrison plantation. I told him about the visit from Mr. Sutton and Mr. Simms and what they had said about Mr. Wheeler's being back. Dubé, however, claimed he didn't know anything about Morris Wheeler. "I-I-I ain't seen him," he said earnestly enough, though I had my doubts about the truthfulness of his statement. "Th-th-they here, they must bbbb-be hidin'."

"You sure you ain't seen him?" I questioned. "Thought y'all was so close."

"I-I-I jus' helped 'em out s-s-sometime. I-I—" He stopped and stared out the side window. "Uh-oh! Th-there that Stuart."

Coming toward the crossroads from the north was Joe Billy Montier's car. We could see two other men in the car and figured they were Stuart Walker and Pierceson Wells.

Cousin Bud slowed, then turned onto the Granger Road. I kept my eyes on Joe Billy's car as it picked up speed; I didn't like the feel of it.

Joe Billy honked at us and Cousin Bud slowed down.

"Don't," I said. "Don't stop."

Cousin Bud looked in the rear view mirror at the car. "Ain't gonna stop. Think they just wanna pass."

Joe Billy's car was now at our tail. Cousin Bud pulled

over to let them pass. They pulled along beside us. "Say, boy!" Stuart hollered from the front passenger seat. "Pull over a second! We wanna talk to ya!"

"Please, Cousin Bud, don't," I said. "I got me a feeling. Them boys, they up to no good. Dubé, you tell him."

"C-C-Cassie, she most likely r-r-right. B-b-better speed on up."

Cousin Bud glanced over at Stuart. "It's probably nothing, I don't make it anything. I'd better stop."

He slowed to a stop and a nagging remembrance told me he was wrong. Dreadfully wrong.

Joe Billy stopped as well, and Stuart and Pierceson Wells got out. Pierceson walked around to the other side of the car and put his foot on the front bumper. Stuart came over to Cousin Bud's window and peeped inside; his eyes rested on Suzella. "Say, Suzella," he said, "I hear your father's here. This him?"

Suzella blanched and nodded.

Stuart stepped back from the car. "Well, well. So this is the boy who sired a pretty thing like you."

Cousin Bud gripped the wheel and stared straight ahead.

"He don't look quite light enough to me." Stuart looked over at Joe Billy, then Pierceson. "What 'bout y'all?"

"Not that I can see," Pierceson replied. Joe Billy did not answer.

Stuart laughed. "Ya know, this gal of yours, she pulled a pretty good one on me a while back. Had me thinking she was white. Had me bowing and scraping to her like she was a lady. . . . Yeah . . . I won't be forgetting that." His eyes settled on Suzella, lingering too long. She crimsoned as he stared, but did not look away. Finally Stuart stepped back and motioned Cousin Bud out of the car. "Get on out and let's take a look at you."

Joe Billy stepped from his car and came closer. Cousin Bud, his hands still gripping the wheel, looked over his shoulder at Suzella.

"Move, boy!" snapped Pierceson.

Cousin Bud released the wheel and got out. Dubé opened his door to get out as well, but Pierceson stopped him. "You, boy, you stay put now."

Stuart circled Cousin Bud to inspect him. "Don't look no lighter out here to me than he did inside," he decided.

"Maybe it's the sun got him so dark," suggested Pierceson. "Probably he real light-skinned under that fine suit he got on. Maybe he need to just take that off."

"Maybe so," Stuart agreed.

"Please . . ." said Cousin Bud. "My daughter——"

"Now that's just what we trying to find out . . . 'bout your daughter. Why she look so much like she white. Can you tell us why?"

Cousin Bud, as chilly as it was, began to sweat.

"Well, what you say, boy?"

"Her mother . . . she—she's real light-skinned——"

"Yeah, now that's just what we heard. Heard in fact she's so light, she's white. Now what you say 'bout that? You been bedding a white woman?"

"No, sir, I . . . it's a colored girl's Suzella's mother."

"Way I hear it," Stuart continued, "up in New York they 'lows most anything. Even niggers wedding white women. You hear that too, Pierce?"

Pierceson nodded. "Yep, heard that too."

Stuart turned back to Cousin Bud. "You hear that, boy?"

Cousin Bud swallowed hard, his eyes cast to the ground.

"Tell me, you ever sleep with a white woman?" Stuart taunted. "Ever want to? Huh? Bet you did. Don't be scared. You can tell me."

"You white trash. Leave him alone."

There was a moment when nothing moved and nothing was said. Then slowly Stuart turned and stared in silence at Suzella. I waited, unable to breathe. Finally, very quietly, Stuart said: "You might look like you white, gal, but you best remember you ain't. You vex me today and I'm gonna take you outa that car too."

Suzella met his gaze and did not look away. "Don't you hurt him. I mean that . . . don't you hurt him." Her voice was calm, yet threatening, and Stuart seemed not to know how to react to it. He started toward her.

Joe Billy moved forward quickly and grabbed his arm. "Ah, come on now, Stuart, this done gone far enough now——"

"I say what we oughta do is make the nigger strip," said Pierceson.

Suzella leaned forward to protest, but Cousin Bud hissed sharply, "Hush, Suzella! Hush!"

Stuart took a deep breath and pulled his arm from Joe Billy's grasp. He kept his eyes on Suzella a moment longer, then turned to Cousin Bud. "That's an idea, Pierceson. We'll see jus' how light the nigger is. . . . All right, nigger, go 'head. Get them clothes off."

Cousin Bud looked stunned. "Please, sirs, don't make me do that. My daughter, the children——"

"But look here, can't you see it's for your own good? You light as you claim you are under all that clothing, we'll have to believe what you say 'bout that gal's mama. Go on now. Do like you told——"

"Stuart, for God's sake!" objected Joe Billy. "He'll catch his death of cold out here!"

Stuart turned on him angrily. "You jus' shut your mouth, Joe Billy. You ain't got the stomach for this, then get back in the car. As for me, I'm gonna find out 'bout this nigger—you heard me, boy. Get them clothes off!"

Cousin Bud's whole body trembled. "Please," he pleaded. "Not in front of my daughter—"

Stuart's hand lashed out and struck Cousin Bud across the face.

"Oh, God!" Suzella cried and opened the car door. Before she could get out, Joe Billy slammed it shut. "Stay there," he ordered.

Dubé leapt from the other side of the car. "P-p-please, Mr. Stuart—" He didn't finish; Pierceson punched him hard in the stomach and Dubé fell to his knees.

"Dubé!" we cried from the car. Stunned, we gazed on as Pierceson grabbed Dubé and, pulling him up, slung him hard against the hood and twisted his left arm back to hold him. Blood spurted from Dubé's nose and I felt the knot of fear tighten within me.

"All right," Stuart said to Cousin Bud, "I'm waiting. Get them clothes off."

Trembling, Cousin Bud took off his tie.

"Bet you strip a whole lot faster'n that when you got some gal waiting for you." He laughed obscenely.

Cousin Bud glanced around at Suzella, then took off his coat, then his shirt.

"Get that undershirt off."

Cousin Bud complied.

Stuart again walked around him as if examining a prime steer. "What you think, Pierce?"

Pierceson shrugged. "Still can't tell. I think we'd better see his legs."

Stuart nodded. "You heard him, boy. Take off them pants."

"Please, just let me go down in the woods there—"

"Get 'em off!"

Cousin Bud did as he was told. He stood there, his back to us, his body shaking with only his shorts left to cover him. I looked away, feeling his humiliation.

"What you say now, nigger?" taunted Stuart. "You ever sleep with a white woman in New York? You know what we do down here to a nigger tries that, don't you?" Cousin Bud lowered his head and stared at the ground. Stuart grabbed his chin and jerked it upward. "Wants the truth now! This gal's mama white?"

Suddenly, before I could stop him, Little Man flung open the door and leapt from the car. Skirting Pierceson, he dashed madly up the road toward a wagon which had just appeared on the rise. Mr. Morrison was driving it.

Joe Billy stared at the wagon and turned back to his car. "We'd better go."

Stuart laughed. "Just 'cause of some nigger in a wagon?"

"If I ain't mistaken, that ain't no ordinary nigra. That's the one folks say broke Dewberry Wallace's back and put Thurston's arm in a sling."

The wagon drew closer. Mr. Morrison, his eyes sure and steady, took in the scene. A few feet from us he stopped and pulled Little Man up beside him. Then he nodded toward Pierceson. "Be obliged you let go of that boy."

Pierceson looked uncertain.

"Or you want, I'll get down and you can try holdin' my arm."

Pierceson glanced over for Stuart's approval, and getting no reaction released Dubé

"Uncle," Stuart said, "you messing in something don't concern you and I ain't gonna hold for it, not from no—"

"Mr. Rankin, get your clothes on."

"Nigger, look here now—"

"That y'all's car there, then it be best y'all get in it and get on home and let us do the same." Mr. Morrison's voice was soft and quiet, as always, but the unspoken threat hung over the still forest.

Joe Billy got in. "Come on, Stuart," he said.

Stuart stood in a rage, not moving, as he glared up at Mr. Morrison.

"I said come on!"

Stuart turned, then looked back again and pointed a finger at Mr. Morrison. "I ain't gonna forget this!"

"I ain't either," said Mr. Morrison.

There seemed nothing else to say. Stuart got in the car; Pierceson followed him, slamming the back door angrily. Joe Billy turned the car around and drove off. Mr. Morrison waited until they could no longer be seen and spoke once again to Cousin Bud. "Mr. Rankin, put your clothes on and we'll get on home."

Cousin Bud nodded and reached for his clothes, but broken with fear, he retched upon them. Mr. Morrison got down from the wagon and, picking up the clothing, led Cousin Bud into the woods. Not knowing what to say, we said nothing while they were gone. In a few minutes they came back.

"Daddy, you all right?" asked Suzella, her face pale, her eyes filled with pain.

"Yeah, baby, I'm fine," Cousin Bud replied, getting into the car, but his hands shook violently as he reached for the ignition.

"M-M-Mr. Rankin, I-I-I can drive, ya want me t-t-to," said Dubé, holding the bottom of his shirt to his nose. "He ain't hurt me n-n-none."

Without looking at him, Cousin Bud scooted over.

Mr. Morrison, with Little Man beside him, turned the

wagon around and headed home. Silently we followed. Before the car rolled to a stop in the driveway, Cousin Bud got out and went to the outhouse, and when he finally came to the house, he would not look directly at anyone. That evening, before dusk, he and Suzella left for New York.

13

Little Man pressed his face against the front window, staring out at the misty rain which covered the land, and waited for New Year's Day to pass. Several times Mama called him from the window and obediently he left it, but after a while he would return to it to stare out once again.

So far the new year had been uneventful. Mr. Wiggins, along with Little Willie and Maynard, had stopped by in the morning, and Big Ma had walked up to the Averys' to visit, but now we sat, just the family, in front of the fire, not much wanting to leave it and not much wanting company either. Then as the afternoon darkened toward evening and Little Man still stood at the window, he turned suddenly, his eyes bright, and announced that Mr. Jamison was coming.

"I don't want to get your hopes up," Mr. Jamison said, sitting in the chair Uncle Hammer had vacated for him, "but I just heard from the sheriff of a town in Louisiana who had some information about some boys from Mississippi who'd worked a plantation near Baton Rouge." His eyes swept our anxious faces. "He said there was a possibility one of those boys could have been Stacey."

The room went silent, our eyes glued to Mr. Jamison.

"Where?" Mama asked breathlessly. "What's the name of the town?"

"Buford. But I don't really know that much yet. Mrs. Jamison and I've been out of town this whole Christmas week and just got back late last evening. This afternoon I checked my messages and mail at the office, and found a note from my secretary saying that a Sheriff Conroy had called a few days back about the letter we sent."

Papa leaned forward. "You get a chance to talk to him?"

"I tried calling, but it being New Year's, I couldn't raise anybody at the jail. Operator said the sheriff would be in tomorrow. Thought, though, that you'd like to know about this as soon as possible."

"How far is Buford into Louisiana?"

"I'm not sure, but I think it's north of Baton Rouge."

Mama leaned toward Papa. "We could leave now and be in Buford by tomorrow, couldn't we?"

Before Papa could answer, Mr. Jamison said, "I wouldn't do that, Mrs. Logan—go there, I mean. Not yet. I think it'd be better if I got a chance to talk to this Sheriff Conroy on the phone and see if those boys are actually there." He took a moment to clear his throat. "One other thing. I checked with my secretary about the call . . . she said Sheriff Conroy mentioned something about some of the boys who worked at that plantation being in jail in another county."

"Jail!"

"Don't alarm yourselves yet. We don't even know if Stacey was at that particular plantation. I imagine a good number of Mississippi workers go into Louisiana to chop cane."

"You say you'll call tomorrow?"

"First thing."

"Can't you give him a call at home?" questioned Uncle Hammer.

"Hammer, it's New Year's," Big Ma reminded him.

"Mama, what I care what day it is? Stacey in a jail somewheres, I wanna know 'bout it now."

"Tried his house," Mr. Jamison said. "No one at home."

Uncle Hammer sighed impatiently.

Papa glanced at him, then back to Mr. Jamison. "What time you planning on calling in the morning?"

"Beginning of business hours. Eight o'clock. You want, after I find out something, I can come back out—"

"No. We'll be in."

Mr. Jamison's eyes met Papa's. "All right." Then he stood. "I guess I'd better be getting on back to town. I don't like neglecting Mrs. Jamison on a holiday." At the door he looked back at us. "Please don't get your hopes up. It might not even be him."

When he was gone, Papa, Uncle Hammer, and Mr. Morrison drove over to Smellings Creek to tell Mr. Turner about the call, and upon their return little was said. Mr. Morrison excused himself early. Uncle Hammer and Papa exchanged a few words, then they too grew quiet. Even Christopher-John and Little Man made no speculations about the possibility that Stacey was perhaps only a phone call away. It was as if after all this time of hoping, thoughts of Stacey were now too fragile to be spoken aloud, and we each kept our own thoughts, afraid of speaking them, afraid of somehow dashing this new hope.

I couldn't sleep. The night was too long, the thoughts racing through my head too labored. As I waited for the crowing of the roosters, which seemed as if it would never come, I kept trying to picture what it would be like to see Stacey again. I had to remind myself that we didn't know much of anything, not really, and that thought made me want to rush the coming of morning even more, so that we would know something.

Several times I got up, crossed to the window, and looked up at the sky trying to see if the moon had gotten stuck up there, making it impossible for the sun to rise. On my fifth trip to the window Big Ma said, "Child, you jus' wearin' out that floor. It be mornin' in the Lord's own good time." She sounded wide awake; she hadn't been able to sleep either. "Come on back to bed and rest yo'self."

"I ain't gonna sleep."

"Mos' likely you ain't, but rest yo'self anyways. It's gonna be a big day tomorrow."

Long before dawn I heard Mr. Morrison in the barn hitching Jack to the wagon. He was getting an early start into Strawberry. Then I heard Papa and Uncle Hammer join him. The three talked for several minutes, and when Mr. Morrison had gone, Papa and Uncle Hammer reentered the house and went into the kitchen. A few minutes later Mama and Big Ma got up and went there too. With so much activity going on, I wasn't surprised when Christopher-John and Little Man pushed open the door and padded in, whispering, "Cassie, you sleep?"

I sat up. "No."

They came over and sat on the bed.

"You think it's him?" asked Little Man, his voice a mere whisper.

"I dunno."

"If it is," Christopher-John said, "what he doing in jail?"

"It's jus' gotta be him is all I gotta say," Little Man decided. "High time he come on home."

I heard one sniffle and then no more. They lay back on the bed, saying nothing else, and together we watched the moon sliding too slowly westward. Finally I fell asleep.

"Cassie . . . Cassie, wake up."

I opened my eyes. Mama was sitting beside me on the bed. Little Man and Christopher-John lay crossways on the bed covered by a blanket, still sleeping. Mama talked softly, not to waken them.

"Cassie, your papa and I've decided to go with Mrs. Lee Annie this morning, and we've decided you can go too."

I sat up immediately. "I can?"

Mama glanced over at Christopher-John and Little Man to see if I had awakened them. They were still asleep. "Mr. Morrison left early to get Russell, since there's not enough room for everybody in the car. Mrs. Ellis and Mrs. Lee Annie'll be going with us."

I nodded, excited not only about going with Mrs. Lee Annie, but that I would be in Strawberry when Mr. Jamison made the call about Stacey.

"Now, Cassie," Mama said, her voice low, strained, "we've talked about this before. How dangerous this thing can be." She took my hand. "We decided you should go because it's important that you see this. But, Cassie, I expect you to keep that mouth of yours shut. I don't want to hear one word out of you all the while we're in that office, do you hear me? I'll do the talking."

"Yes'm," I promised.

An hour later I was sitting in the car with Mama, Papa, and Uncle Hammer. Little Man and Christopher-John stood beside the car bemoaning the fact that they couldn't go. "Sho' wish we could go," each of them managed to slip in at least twice. And Big Ma said: "Mary, hug Lee Annie for me and wish her well."

"Yes, ma'am, I will."

"And y'all bring back some good news this time 'bout that boy. Good news, ya hear?" She dabbed at her eyes, then waved us on. "Y'all go on now. And be careful. . . ."

We said good-bye and headed down the drive with Big Ma, Christopher-John, and Little Man waving after us. At the rise where the oak stood, I looked back once more. They were still standing there.

It was a little after eight o'clock when we reached Strawberry. Mr. Morrison and Russell, dressed in civilian clothes, were waiting for us in front of Mr. Jamison's office across from the courthouse square. To our surprise Mr. Tom Bee and Wordell were with them.

"I told that old woman she was crazy," Mr. Tom Bee explained as we got out of the car, "but she crazy 'nough to come try'n' register, I guess I'm crazy 'nough to come in with her."

The door to Mr. Jamison's office opened and Mr. Jamison came out looking tired, as if he had gotten as little sleep as we, and not for the first time I wondered why he cared so much. "I just called Buford," he said after greeting us, "but I wasn't able to get anyone. I guess they're a little late getting in this morning."

Mama glanced away to hide her disappointment, but Papa said, "How long 'fore you planning on trying again?"

"Another half hour the operator's supposed to try again. You want to, you can come in and wait."

"We've got a bit of business to take care of first, but I'll be back 'fore you call again."

"All right, I'll see you then." He gave us a nod and returned to his office.

"Ya know, Mary," said Mrs. Lee Annie, "you and Cassie here, y'all ain't gotta go in with me. This here 'bout that child is what y'all need to be tending to. I can make out with jus' Leora."

Mama refused to hear of Mrs. Lee Annie's going without her. "We've got half an hour yet before we hear anything, so let's just put that time to good use and get you registered."

"Well, Miz Lee Annie," Papa said, "you ladies going to the courthouse, I imagine we best get started. We'll walk y'all over."

Mrs. Lee Annie made a quick but useless adjustment to her hat and the bow-tied ribbon of her best dress, then ran her hand over the front of her coat. "All right. Let's go."

It had been decided earlier that only Mama, Mrs. Ellis, and I would go into the courthouse with Mrs. Lee Annie and that none of the men would go; their presence could prove too threatening. Mr. Tom Bee stayed in the wagon, Mr. Morrison beside it. The rest of us—including Wordell, who jumped from the wagon to follow at the last minute—crossed the street to McGiver.

"Wordell," I said as we crossed the street, "you think it's him?"

Wordell looked at me, not even needing me to explain my words; he knew my thoughts. "Ya think it is?"

At that exact moment, I decided I did. "Yeah . . . I do."

"Then mos' likely it's him then."

At the courthouse steps, Mama said, "David, you hear anything, anything at all, you let me know."

"Don't worry, sugar." He kissed her lightly, then looked at me. "I'm right proud of you. I want you to know that."

"Yes, sir."

Mrs. Lee Annie started up the steps and Mrs. Ellis, Mama, and I followed her. At the top we took a moment to look back, then stepped inside the courthouse.

The registrar's office was on the first floor. We stood silently before the door leading to it, reading the lettering and giving ourselves another moment to gather our courage. Mama looked around at each of us. "Ready?" she said. We nodded, and she opened the door.

A woman sitting at a typewriter, her fingers busy at the keys, glanced up as we entered, then back at the sheaf of papers from which she was typing. We stood before her, waiting. She finished a page, pulled it from the typewriter, and took the time to separate the carbons from the original before finally looking at us again. At last she deigned to speak. "What y'all want?" she asked.

Mrs. Lee Annie told her.

The woman looked as if she had just gone hard of hearing. "What?"

"Come to register so's I can vote," Mrs. Lee Annie repeated.

The woman stared at us. "All of y'all coming for that?"

"No, ma'am," Mrs. Lee Annie spoke up again. "Jus' me."

The woman rose from her chair, her eyes on us as if we

were some strange alien creatures who had wandered in, then crossed the room to another office in the back. The door was open and we could see her talking to a man there. He looked up surprised, much as the woman had done, and when she pointed to Mrs. Lee Annie, he stood and walked out with a scowl on his face. The woman followed.

"Whose nigger are you?" the man demanded.

Mrs. Lee Annie, the dignity of her being lining her face, replied, "I works Mr. Granger's land."

The man eyed her a moment and turned to the woman. "Doreen, Mr. Granger in town?"

"Seen him upstairs in the hall just a little bit ago, Mr. Boudein."

"Then go get him and tell him we need him here," ordered Mr. Boudein, and returned to his office.

Within minutes Doreen was back with Mr. Granger. He cast us a disapproving glance as he entered, but waited for Mr. Boudein to hurry from his office before speaking. "Now what's going on here, Sam?" he demanded, his voice soft but annoyed.

Mr. Boudein flashed a vexed look at Doreen that said she was supposed to have told him, but Doreen was already busying herself at the typewriter once more, removing herself from the explosion that was sure to come. "This ole aunty, she says she one of your niggers and she wants to register," Mr. Boudein explained.

Mr. Granger's silence filled the room. "Lee Annie," he said at last, "what kinda nonsense is this?"

Mrs. Lee Annie took a deep breath before answering. "Wants to register so's I can vote."

"Vote?"

"Yes, suh."

Looking around at Mr. Boudein, Mr. Granger allowed a lopsided grin. Mr. Boudein, seemingly relieved, shrugged his own disbelief. "Now, Lee Annie," said Mr. Granger, "you old enough to know that voting is white folks' business. Now what make you think to be butting in it?"

"I . . ." Mrs. Lee Annie's words failed her.

Mama spoke up for her. "Her father voted. She wants to do the same."

Mr. Granger ignored Mama as he spoke again to Mrs. Lee Annie. "You gonna make a fool of yourself. You know that, don't you?"

"I hopes not, suh."

Mr. Granger pursed his lips at her reply, then fixed his gaze on Mama. "This here your doing, Mary? Putting this old woman up to trying to vote. Thought I'd stopped you from messing in what you got no business."

"You stopped me from teaching at Great Faith."

"Look like I ain't stopped nothing else."

Mama did not reply, but animosity sparked her eyes. Her lips trembled, then her eyes shifted, not to the floor as Mr. Granger would have expected, but to Doreen, Mr. Boudein, and back again to him. Mr. Granger noted this in silence and turned to Mrs. Ellis, who was nervously twisting a handkerchief in her thin hands.

"Leora, what you and Page doin' supportin' this old woman in this?"

Mrs. Ellis looked confused.

"Maybe y'all rather be living someplace else."

"Oh, no, suh!"

"Ain't I been good to y'all? Letting y'all work that land even when y'all's crops don't hardly bring in enough money to pay for your seed and your clothing and such I given y'all credit for? Ain't y'all come to me during these hard times and asked me for more credit and I done give it to ya? Ain't that so?"

Mrs. Ellis was trembling. "Yes, suh." Her words were barely a mumble, a wordless shaking fear.

"Even forgiven y'all for supportin' that wagoning business up to Vicksburg a while back," he noted, continuing to laud his goodness, "and this here's how y'all pays me for my trouble. Y'all trying to do something y'all know good and well I don't approve of. 'Round here messin' in something you got no business!"

"We tried to talk her outa it, Mr. Granger," Mrs. Ellis managed to say, "but her mind was set to it. Ain't none of us meant no harm. Truly we ain't."

Mr. Granger eyed her in true disappointment; then, seemingly almost ready to forgive the behavior of the morning, turned and said, "That how you feel, Lee Annie?"

"Yes, suh."

"Then you gonna give up this foolishness?"

A pause from Mrs. Lee Annie. "No, suh."

Mr. Granger sucked in his breath, his patience gone. He was about to speak again when the door was flung open and Stuart Walker rushed in, his face white and anxious. "Mr. Granger, thank the Lord you here!" he said. "Something awful's 'bout to happen! My daddy sent me—"

"Stuart, calm yourself," said Mr. Granger. Stuart took a deep breath. "Now what is it?"

Stuart glanced over at us. "Maybe we oughta talk in the hall."

Mr. Granger followed Stuart's gaze and pursed his lips, and the two of them went out. The rest of us waited, including Mr. Boudein, who seemed unwilling to move from behind the counter until Mr. Granger had decided how to handle this. I wondered what the awful thing was that Stuart was talking about, and whispered to Mama about it. Ole Doreen looked up angrily. "Y'all gonna be talking in here," she said, "y'all can just go on outside."

I cut my eyes at her, but now remembering Mama's warning grew silent.

Several minutes passed, and when the door opened, Mr. Granger came in alone. Mr. Boudein waited for him to speak. "Sam, I'm gonna leave this to you," he said to Mr. Boudein's surprise. "Give her the test."

"But . . . Mr. Granger . . . I ain't never registered no nigra!"

"Giving her the test and registering her are two different things," Mr. Granger concluded. "She got her poll taxes paid?"

"Why . . . I don't know——"

"They is," said Mrs. Lee Annie.

"I'd have to check," Mr. Boudein finished, speaking still to Mr. Granger.

"Then you do that. Everything in order, you let her take that test, she got her mind set on it so bad." He put his hand on the door knob.

"But Mr. Granger . . . a nigra!"

Mr. Granger's gaze went cold. "You the registrar, ain't you?"

"Well, yes sir, but——"

"Then do your job." His eyes swept once more around the room, and he went out.

Mr. Boudein stared at the closed door; Doreen's typewriter clattered noisily. "All right," said Mr. Boudein tightly, "what's your full name here?"

As he checked the poll tax records, Mrs. Ellis, her voice

a raspy whisper, urged Mrs. Lee Annie to give it up. "Aunt Lee Annie, ya can't go doin' this now. Not after what Mr. Granger said."

"Yes'm, I can."

"Please, Aunt Lee Annie!"

"Leora, thought I done explained this to you. Now either you stay or you go, but hush, 'cause I'm gonna do this thing."

Defeat swept over Mrs. Ellis's face and she said no more.

Mr. Boudein's brow went up quizzically after several long minutes, then he slammed the poll ledger shut, took out a book, a sheet of paper, and a pencil, and handed them to Mrs. Lee Annie. "Section two forty-three. Explain the meaning of it on this here paper."

Mrs. Lee Annie looked pleased. "Section two forty-three, ya say?" He only looked at her and she took it as his affirmation. "Yes, suh."

"This here's plumb foolishness," he admonished as she went over to the table. "Can't no darky understand the complexities of the constitution. Ain't got the sense for it."

Mrs. Lee Annie turned. "Mr. Boudein, suh," she said. He kept his eyes on her, but didn't acknowledge her address. "Mr. Boudein," she repeated, her voice low and dignified. "I done studied. Done studied near a year now and I knows the constitution. Can't nobody tell me I don't. Knows sections one through two hundred eighty-five. Knows articles one through fifteen. Knows 'bout the judiciary and the legislature. Knows 'bout the executive too. I knows all that stuff and I wants you to know I knows it. And even if I don't pass this here test, I knows it and can't nobody take way nothin' I know. Nobody."

Then, her shoulders back, she sat down to the stares of both Mr. Boudein and Doreen. "I swear to God," Mr. Samuel Boudein said, shaking his head and going back into his office, "the older they get, the more childlike they become. . . ."

Mrs. Lee Annie had been taking the test only a few minutes when the registrar's door opened and Russell motioned for Mama. Doreen looked up irritably at yet another intrusion into her sanctum, but did not say anything as Mama, Mrs. Ellis, and I quietly slipped into the hall.

"Russell, what've you heard?" Mama immediately asked.

"Mr. Jamison raised the sheriff over at Buford. Got him on the phone now."

"Do they know about Stacey yet?"

Russell shook his head. "Sorry, but he ain't said. All I know is Mr. David said come get y'all."

"All right." Mama looked at the door. "What about Mrs. Lee Annie?"

"I'll go in and wait for her," said Russell.

Mama hesitated. "No, I don't think you should. A young man in there . . . well, it'll just make for trouble." She turned to Mrs. Ellis. "Leora, do you think you can wait for her alone?"

Mrs. Ellis looked frightened and uncertain.

"I'll be right outside the building, you need me," Russell assured her.

Mrs. Ellis nervously bit her lip and finally said she would stay.

Mama watched her a moment longer, as if uncertain whether Mrs. Ellis should be left alone. "Just don't say anything more than necessary," she instructed, "and things should be all right. But keep a close watch. Mr. Granger gave in too easily about that test and I don't like it."

Mrs. Ellis nodded weakly and watched us as we hurried out the door. Leaving Russell at the steps, Mama and I practically raced across the lawn and were almost at the street when someone called to us. Jake Willis came running up. His eyes were bloodshot; he was unshaven, and his clothes were wrinkled, as if he had slept in them.

"Lord, Miz Logan, am I glad to see y'all!" he laughed. "Come in town New Year's Eve and got stuck here. My ride went off and just left me. Like to go back with y'all."

"It might be a while yet."

"Don't matter." Once again, he laughed that laugh of his. "Got caught up in a card game that took every penny I had, so's I can't hardly go being choosy 'bout waiting . . . now can I?"

"We're parked over there," Mama said, starting off again with me at her side. Jake Willis caught her arm. Mama turned, her gaze a chilling one. He let her go.

"'Scuse me, Miz Logan, but ain't that Russell standing there yonder in front of the courthouse? He with y'all?"

"He is and we're in quite a hurry, Mr. Willis."

"Ya don't say? Well, 'scuse me again. Guess I'll jus' go on and wait with Russell then."

"Suit yourself," Mama said, and we walked on.

When we reached the wagon, Mama told me to stay with Mr. Morrison.

"But, Mama—"

"Mind me now!" she ordered, without giving me a chance to protest, and rushed inside. I watched the door close behind her, then, feeling scared and alone, sat on the car's running board, my eyes fixed on the office door. After a few moments Mr. Morrison quietly said, "Jus' a while longer now, Cassie. Jus' a while longer."

"Yes, sir." I sighed and looked around. "Mr. Morrison, where Wordell?"

Mr. Morrison, too, looked around. His brow furrowed. "Ain't he over on the other side of the car there?"

"Was a minute ago," put in Mr. Tom Bee. "Said somethin' 'bout Lee Annie likin' flowers and jus' went off."

Mr. Morrison stepped back from the wagon. "I 'spect then I best go look for—"

"Lord-a-mercy! What's this here?"

I stood up to see what Mr. Tom Bee was shouting about. Coming from the north, down the main street of Strawberry, was a wagon drawn by two plodding mules and loaded some six feet high with shabby furniture and household goods while poor-looking people sat atop it all staring out blankly at the street ahead. Behind it came another wagon looking very much like the first, followed by another, then another. It was a procession. Cars and trucks were a part of it, loaded down like the wagons and coming just as slowly. Most of the people who sat atop the wagons and in the cars and the trucks were white, but there were some black faces too. All were the same, grim and humorless, reflecting the despair of the dispossessed.

As the procession grew, rolling forward as if it were one continuous body, townspeople came from offices and shops to stare silently. The people in the procession were just as silent, and for a while the only sound which could be heard was the crunching of wheels against the pavement and the whir of poorly kept motors in poorly kept vehicles. Then the lead wagon swung onto the courthouse lawn. Those following did the same and a townsman cried: "What the devil!" And another: "Somebody, get the sheriff!"

We stood, as curious as the townspeople, not knowing any

more than they, though I couldn't help but wonder if this was the awful thing Stuart had been talking about.

"Cassie, what ya doin' here?"

I looked across the street and saw Jeremy Simms running our way.

"Y'all see what's happening?" he asked.

"See a whole lotta folks," I said.

"Some of 'ems from the Walker plantation," Jeremy explained. "They's the ones Mr. Walker put off. Bunch of them others are day laborers and folks got put off their places a while back and been livin' down 'long the river north of here."

"Oh."

"Friend of ours come up late last night and said they was gonna do this. Ain't it somethin'?"

"Yeah . . . it's somethin' all right."

"What bring y'all into town? Y'all know 'bout this?"

"We come 'bout Stacey," I said, deciding it was better not to mention anything about Mrs. Lee Annie's attempting to register.

Jeremy's eyes brightened. "Y'all done got some news?"

"Mr. Jamison says he might be 'round Baton Rouge. He checking now."

Jeremy started to ask another question, but seeing his father across the street, he said hastily, "I'm gonna hafta go, Cassie, but I'll be a-hopin' it's him. I jus' betcha it is! I'll talk to ya later, hear?"

"Okay," I said. As Jeremy left to join his father, I heard Mr. Jamison's door open and ran to meet Papa, Mama, and Uncle Hammer. "Is it him?" I cried. "Is it?"

Papa put his hand on my shoulder to calm me down. "We still don't know," he said. He looked out at the wagons and cars continuing to come, then back at me as Uncle Hammer walked over to Mr. Morrison to find out what was going on. "What we know is this: The sheriff there said he'd heard 'bout five boys running away from a plantation some ways south of Baton Rouge during the week of December eighth—"

"But that was over three weeks ago!"

"I know, sugar. But seems that what happened was some money was stolen and the law went looking for the boys done it. They caught up with two of the boys in a place called Shokesville. They caught two others quite a ways from there headed west."

He was silent; I was silent.

"But you said there was five," I said. "What happened to the fifth one?"

Mama touched Papa's arm.

"The fifth one . . . he got killed."

I bit deep into my lower lip, my mind blanking out, unaware of all that was bubbling around me.

"But we don't know who the boy was. Or even if Stacey and Moe are among the five. One other thing. Seems one of the boys they caught headed west had the stolen money. The others ain't had nothing to do with it. . . . We know, too, Stacey and Moe, they wouldn't't've been going west."

Mama came closer. "What we're waiting for now is to speak to the sheriff in Shokesville. He'll have the names of the boys that are there. The sheriff in Buford didn't."

I didn't say anything.

"David," said Uncle Hammer, coming back with Mr. Morrison, "I don't much like the looks of this. It could get ugly."

"What's going on?"

Mr. Morrison explained it.

Papa looked out at the courthouse, the lawn and McGiver Street no longer visible as the farm families claimed space for their wagons and trucks; the procession was still coming. "Ain't it 'bout time Miz Lee Annie was finished?"

"Should be by now," Mama said. "The section she had to explain dealt with the poll tax. She knows it well."

Papa's brow furrowed. He listened to the crowd, no longer silent—not noisy either, but producing sounds that massed into an indistinguishable murmur. "Hammer, I think you and me better go get her and Leora. They ain't gonna make it through there alone."

Mama reminded them that Russell was waiting outside the courthouse.

"Think we still oughta go," said Uncle Hammer.

"Why don't I go?" suggested Mr. Morrison. "That way y'all can be here come the call."

Papa shook his head. "You don't mind, I'd rather you stay here and see to things if the crowd move back this way."

Mr. Morrison nodded, understanding.

"David. Hammer," Mama called as they started off. "Please . . . be careful."

"There they are!" I cried. "There Miz Lee Annie and Miz Ellis!" I was standing with Mr. Tom Bee in the wagon to better see over the crowd; Mama and Mr. Morrison remained on the sidewalk.

Mr. Tom Bee stared out, searching. "Where, child?"

"Up there at the top of them steps, standing 'longside Mr. Granger and the sheriff."

"What're they doin' there?" he questioned. "Why don't they come on down?"

"They wouldn't be standing there unless they had to." Mama shook her head. "I don't like this . . . not at all."

Mr. Morrison frowned. "Seem peculiar all right. Russell's there too, a few steps down, next to Jake Willis."

"Lord," mumbled Mr. Tom Bee, "why don't they come on back?"

Sheriff Hank Dobbs climbed onto the courthouse ledge so that everyone could see him. "You folks know this here's an unlawful assembly!" he cried. "Y'all's on government property and y'all's breaking the law! Now I want y'all to get on back in y'alls wagons or y'alls cars or y'alls trucks and get on home!"

"Home, where?" someone cried from the congestion. "You tell us where!"

Another voice rose angry and piercing. "Had a home, but Hamden Walker put us off it! Now where we s'pose to go? Huh? Where we s'pose to take our families?"

"Hamden Walker say the government tell him he can't plant all his land," someone else shouted. "And he say that's why he put us off it. Well, that the case, we figure maybe it's the government owe us! Figure to stay here till we gets heard."

A mighty clamoring rose from the crowd. The sheriff held up his hands signaling for quiet, but several minutes passed before he could be heard again.

"Now y'all wanna speak y'all's piece, y'all jus' gonna hafta go through the proper channels. Y'all present y'all's complaints in a civilized manner in the proper way and at the proper time—"

"Right now's the proper way and the proper time!"

"Yeah! You got a roof over your head, ain't ya, Hank?"

"Y'all shut us up before, y'all ain't shuttin' us up no more! Ain't got nothin' else left to lose!"

"Should've stood up for the union before! Maybe we'd have something now."

Stuart Walker leapt to the ledge to stand beside the sheriff. "It's that damn Communist union got y'all not listening to reason! Morris Wheeler's behind this here—I know it! Where is he? Where is that Communist agitator? You out there, stand up and show yourself, Morris Wheeler!"

"He ain't gotta show hisself!" a voice cried out. "He been right all along. It's you and your damn daddy and these here other landlords doin' all the devilment!"

"Now y'all listen to me—"

"We'll listen! We'll listen a-plenty, when y'all give us our farms back!"

"And us day laborers get a dollar fifty a day!"

With these words, the noise grew so tumultuous that Stuart's words were lost, dead, unheard as the crowd shut him out, refusing to listen. The roar continued for several minutes; then someone started shouting, "Dollar fifty a day! Don't take our farms away!" The chant caught on, and the disorganized onslaught of noise took on one voice and there was nothing Stuart could do against it. He stepped down.

At that moment, Mr. Jamison's secretary opened the door and called Mama inside; Mr. Jamison had Shokesville on the line. "Go on, Miz Logan," Mr. Morrison said when Mama hesitated. "Ain't nothin' you can do 'bout up there, and I'll be here." Mama looked gratefully up at him and followed the secretary inside.

The noise ran unabated for several minutes as Stuart conferred with Mr. Granger and Sheriff Dobbs. Then Harlan Granger himself, looking as confident as ever, stepped out on the ledge. The crowd saw him and the chanting weakened. But someone heated up enough to take on even Harlan Granger started the chant up once more and the crowd grew boisterous again. Harlan Granger, however, was a formidable adversary; he outwaited them.

When silence reigned, and not before, Harlan Granger spoke: "I take it y'alls for the union!" he said glibly.

A mighty cheer went up.

"I take it," he said when there was quiet again, "y'all's for a dollar fifty cents a day and keeping your farms!"

Another cheer rose to the heavens.

"I take it," he said in the same calm, steady voice, "y'all's for schooling with nigras, socializing with nigras . . . marrying with nigras!"

An uneasy murmur waved over the square and a man spoke up. "Now, Mr. Granger, don't go mixin' up what's for the union with that other stuff."

"Well, y'all got a mixed organization here, ain't ya? Y'all white and colored working together in this thing, ain't ya, for this dollar and a half a day business and this farm-keeping business? I see quite a number of black faces out there 'mongst y'all."

The people looked around; Harlan Granger knew where to strike, and he had struck very well.

"Seem to me," he said, "y'all got y'allselves the beginning of a lot of trouble here. Don't y'all know by now, once a worm gets in an apple, the apple's ruined? You wanna save the barrel, you best rid yourself of the worms."

Nothing now was said.

Then someone spoke up, defying him. "Don't y'all see what he's doing? He's playing on your racial feelings to tear down the union, to keep us from being strong together!"

All eyes shifted to a wagon near the statue of Jefferson Davis. Standing in the wagon with several other men was Morris Wheeler, and Dubé Cross was with him.

"Why, what's ole Dubé doing up there?" I wanted to know. My question went unanswered.

"Now nobody's talking about schooling together, socializing together, and certainly not marrying together. What we're talking about here in this union is a decent living for everybody, both white and colored, and we all know we can't have that less'n we stick together in this thing!"

Harlan Granger waited a moment, as if pleased at having flushed out his prey. "Y'all think I don't want y'all to have more money and a roof over your heads for yourselves and your families? I want that my own self. But I say you can get it without this here Communist union. This here Communist union that mixes the races, colored with the white. Y'all mark my words, this here union mixing is only the beginning of what's to come! Of nigras totally misguided by white people like Morris Wheeler there! Of nigras who get to feeling like they done mixed with white folks a little bit, they got the right to take over white folks' things——"

"Harlan Granger!" cried Morris Wheeler. "You're deliberately exaggerating extremes here! This is *not* a Communist union! The union wants only——"

"I'm exaggerating, am I? Well, just take a look over here on these steps. At that ole aunty right there——y'all other folks step back out the way now so the folks out there can see Aunt Lee Annie Lees. Hank, move 'em back."

The sheriff did as he was told; the white people fell back, leaving Mrs. Lee Annie, Mrs. Ellis, Russell and Jake Willis exposed, an island of dark faces on the steps. Jake Willis attempted to move away, but Deputy Haynes pushed him back with the others.

"There now, y'all see her? That old aunty right there. Been living on my place for going on near forty years, off and on. Ain't much had no trouble from her . . . till now. Till this union business put ideas in her head!" He looked over the faces of the poor white farmers staring up at him with little more to hold onto than the belief that they were better than black people, and continued to chisel at them. "After all them years, y'all know what she done this day?" Again his eyes skimmed the faces waiting anxiously to hear. "'Gainst my advisement, she gone in and tried to register to vote!"

The murmurings swelled, crescendoed in disbelief, then fell mute in stunned dismay.

"No education! No understanding of the constitution of this great state! No natural mental ability to understand, and she goes and does a thing like that! I tell you this now as I been telling you all along: There's no place for unions or mixing in the state of Mississippi! You thought of what'll happen to our great state if people like this try to perform tasks that they ain't even got the God-given makeup for?" He turned an accusing gaze upon Mrs. Lee Annie, pointing his finger at her. "You deny that's what you done, Lee Annie?"

Mrs. Lee Annie bowed her head and didn't answer.

"You hear me talking to you, Lee Annie?" He waited for her to speak. We all waited.

"Well, Lee Annie!"

Suddenly, Russell spoke up, his voice distinct and clear as it carried across the square. "Mr. Granger's asking if my grandmama went to try to register. Well, the answer is she did!" He rushed on, hushing the crowd. "But that's got nothing to do with the union! What Mr. Wheeler said 'bout a decent living, that's what the union's about. That's why colored people are standing up for the union—a decent living's what we all want!"

"That's right!" added Mr. Wheeler. "Don't get caught up in Harlan Granger's trap! He's got other reasons than the ones he's giving you for not wanting this union. He's getting plenty of money from the government with their crop-reduction plan. Money that's s'pose to be yours—"

"I say Mr. Granger's right!" someone shouted. "What we wanna be a part of a nigger organization for? Niggers get to tryin' to boss white folks 'round pretty soon. Y'all jus' heard that nigger talkin' up there, oratin' like a white man!"

"But what he was a-saying is the truth!" another declared. "I don't care what that old woman done! Can't destroy the union 'cause of it!"

"Maybe you don't, but I do. Me for one, I ain't gonna have no nigger talkin' down to me and mine! Ain't gonna have no niggers votin' neither! I say any niggers gettin' beyond themselves oughta be taken care of, and we can begin right now with that ole woman up there!"

Someone laughed. "Wouldn't take much to give her a whippin'! Course, she might fall dead, ya do.."

Mrs. Lee Annie looked up; Russell stepped in front of her. "Union or no union," he cried, "nobody touches a hair on her head! She ain't done nothing ain't her legal right! She got much right as anybody—"

"Right?" questioned Harlan Granger. "Right?"

Russell looked around the square and didn't answer. I knew that he had said too much. Everyone knew. An awful silence settled over the day, and the tension swelled like hot air in a balloon. Everyone was silent, waiting. Then someone shouted something vile, and from the steps of the Jefferson Davis statue a man threw a bottle aimed at Russell. It hit, shattering against Russell's head. Jake Willis grabbed at his left eye as if he too had been hit, and both men went down.

Several shots rang out. Then everything happened at once. Papa and Uncle Hammer leapt up the steps and, grabbing

Jake Willis and Russell, pushed them and the women back into the courthouse. The crowd stirred, alarmed by the sound of gunfire. Near the Jefferson Davis statue a fight broke out. Horses and mules neighed nervously, and engines roared to life. On the street people were trying to move themselves and their possessions out of the congestion, but there seemed nowhere to go.

"Cassie! Get off that wagon and get inside!" yelled Mr. Morrison.

Mr. Tom Bee hurried off the wagon and I turned to follow. But then I saw Wordell, coming from nowhere, his lithe body slitting razorlike through the congested street. He wove madly toward the square, headed not for Russell but the man at the statue.

Suddenly I panicked, remembering the dead bird and the cat Wordell had killed because of it; and without thinking further, I jumped over the side of the wagon into the street to try and reach him.

"Cassie!"

I heard Mr. Morrison calling me, but I couldn't answer. The congestion in the street was even worse than it had looked from the wagon. A man stepped heavily upon my foot and a large woman pressed me against the wagon as she squeezed by, making it hard for me to breathe. What was even worse was that I couldn't see beyond the press of people around me. I tried to push through, but found it useless; I felt as if I were drowning.

Then powerful hands lifted me straight upward and I found myself in the wagon again. Mr. Morrison held my face in his hand and Mama said, "Cassie, you all right?"

I tried to catch my breath, glad she had come back out. "Yes'm, but Wordell—"

"Wordell?" questioned Mr. Morrison.

I nodded, then turned to look out over the crowd. I spotted Wordell, slowed like everyone else. I pointed to him. "He's heading for that fella threw the bottle."

Mr. Morrison glanced out over the square, then immediately jumped off the wagon and began bulldozing his way through the crowd toward Wordell.

Another shot cracked the morning and the sheriff yelled across the square: "I want everybody to move on out! Everybody! That go for you too, Stanley Crawes! Get a move on! D. T. Cranston, help direct that traffic outa here! Wade Jamison over there! Give us a hand at that end!"

"Where we s'pose to go?" someone remembered to ask again.

"All I can tell ya is outa here! I have to shoot off this gun one more time, I'm gonna call the governor and get the national guard! Now move!"

I wanted to stay in the wagon, but Mama hurried me off and into Mr. Jamison's office. There we waited huddled with Mr. Tom Bee for the others to come back.

Mama told me there was still no word about Stacey.

A good while passed before we saw Mr. Morrison again. Wordell was with him, stone faced, his eyes staring straight ahead. When they reached the wagon, Wordell climbed wordlessly onto the back and sat haunched there staring out across the square. Mama slipped outside to talk to Mr. Morrison, then came back in.

"Mama?" I questioned.

"Mr. Morrison stopped him."

I looked at Wordell so still, so quiet, and I wondered.

As the farmers moved out and the crowd began to thin, Mrs. Lee Annie, Russell, and Mrs. Ellis wove their way across the square. Russell's head was bandaged with what looked to be part of a cotton slip, the eyelets giving it a decorative effect. When they neared the wagon, all of us but Wordell rushed out to meet them. Wordell watched, but did not move from where he was.

"Don't worry now," Russell said, stepping wearily onto the sidewalk. "We're okay and I ain't bad hurt."

Wordell scrutinized his cousin sharply, then settled back, his eyes still on him.

"The doctor look at you?" Mama demanded.

"No . . . Mama Lee fixed me up. When that bottle hit, it knocked me down, didn't knock me out though."

Mrs. Lee Annie fingered the bandage in concern. "Cut wasn't so mighty deep, but my mind'll rest more easy once that doctor do take a look or Caroline one."

"Lordy," said Mr. Tom Bee. "What I wanna know is how y'all got stuck up there like ya done. Just what the devil was goin' on?"

Mrs. Ellis shook her head, tears streaming down her face, her eyes already swollen from crying. "We never shoulda come. None of us, we never shoulda come. . . ."

"Just what happened?" Mama asked again. "Where's David and Hammer?"

Mrs. Lee Annie sat down wearily on the raised wooden sidewalk. "Well, child, we come outa that registrar's office —ain't passed the test—and Mr. Granger was waiting for us. Tried getting out that side door there, but it was locked and Mr. Granger, he said come on, go through the front. Got outside and Russell and Jake Willis was there. Ole sheriff wouldn't let us leave. Then there was all that ruckus and that fool threw that bottle. Hit Russell and broke, and that glass went flying everywhere. Caught Jake Willis in the eye. . . . David and Hammer, they pushed through when that bottle hit and got us all back inside. Them two, they took

Jake Willis over to the doctor." She paused, then let out a tired sigh. "I 'spect he gonna lose that eye. . . ."

"Never shoulda come," Mrs. Ellis lamented once more. She bowed her head into her hand. "The whole thing, crazy foolishness . . . whole thing. . . ."

Suddenly a lone voice rose above the din of moving things and we looked back toward the courthouse. Standing defiantly alone on the steps of the Jefferson Davis statue, Dubé was shouting, "D-d-dollar fifty a d-d-day! Don't t-take our farms away!" He was the last defender of the chant; no one joined him.

"Haynes! Get that nigger off that statue!" the sheriff yelled to the deputy. "And do like I told ya and get them other union leaders done caused all this ruckus!"

Dutifully, Deputy Haynes led Dubé from the statue, and a few minutes later we saw him and two other townsmen bringing Dubé, Morris Wheeler, and Mr. Tate Sutton back toward the jail, their hands cuffed behind them. The people in the wagons and the cars and the trucks paid little attention, moving out of Strawberry as silently as they had come.

The union, for the time being anyway, was broken once again.

The street was nearly back to normal. A few wagons still passed by on their way out of town to who knows where, and townspeople could still be seen on the sidewalks talking in small groups, but soon they too drifted away. Mr. Jamison came back from directing traffic and went into his office to try to call Shokesville again. We remained where we were to wait for Papa and Uncle Hammer. It was almost an hour later when they finally returned. They confirmed that Jake Willis had indeed lost his eye.

"It ain't a pretty sight," Papa said, "and he ain't taking it well. Not well at all."

"Well, anyone lose an eye . . ." Mama sympathized.

Uncle Hammer looked over at Russell. "Think you oughta know, he's blaming you."

Russell looked up, incredulous. "Me? Why I got hit my own self!"

"Blaming you jus' the same. For speaking up."

Mrs. Lee Annie shuddered. "He'll most likely get over it . . . when his pain passes."

"If I'd've thought that, I'd've never even mentioned it. But I've seen men like Jake Willis before. He's mean and he won't let it pass. Russell, you watch out for him."

Russell bowed his head and sighed wearily. Papa turned to Mama. "Mary, what 'bout Mr. Jamison? He get that call through?"

"We got a clerk, that's all, and she wouldn't tell us anything. Said we'd have to speak directly to the sheriff, but he's still not there. Mr. Jamison's been trying the last hour."

Restlessly, Papa paced the sidewalk, then leaned against a post. But when a few minutes more had passed, he pulled from the post and headed for Mr. Jamison's office. "It's taking too long. I ain't waiting no longer."

Mama caught his arm. "What're you going to do?"

"Going down there."

"Then I'm going too."

Without his saying anything I knew that Uncle Hammer, already at Papa's side, would be going as well. I wanted desperately to go with them, and even though I feared the answer would be no, as Papa opened the door to Mr. Jamison's office, I blurted out, "Papa, let me go with y'all."

Papa's glance fell on me. "It's a long ride."

"I don't care. I can stand it. Please, Papa. . . ."

Mama gave her approval and he said, "You been waiting

long as we have . . . 'spect you have a right to go."

Papa went into the office with Mama and Uncle Hammer. Several minutes later they came out with Mr. Jamison. "I didn't have to go up to Vicksburg tonight for that trial starting in the morning, I'd go with you," he said. He looked at us with some concern, as if he were letting us down. "Can't get out of it. It's a murder trial. . . . I'll keep trying to get the Shokesville sheriff. You all need me down there, here's my number in Vicksburg, and remember, you want me to, I can be down there first thing Saturday morning."

Papa thanked him and turned to Mr. Morrison. "You'll see everybody get back?"

Mr. Morrison nodded. "Don't worry now 'bout us. Jus' bring the boy back with ya. Jus' bring the boy on home. . . ."

As we got into the car to leave, Mr. Granger's silver Packard turned onto Main and stopped in the middle of the street across from us. Mrs. Ellis, who had been sobbing off and on since she had returned, was dabbing at her eyes now. Mrs. Lee Annie, not a tear in her eyes, said, "Wipe them eyes, Leora. Don't you let Harlan Granger see you cryin'."

"Lee Annie! Leora!"

The two women met his gaze.

"'Fore the sun rise in the morning," he said, his words a long, slow drawl, "I want y'all and everything's y'all's off my land."

"Lordy, no, Mr. Granger!" Mrs. Ellis cried, running into the street to plead with him. "Mr. Granger, no!" Mr. Granger saw her coming, but disdainfully he gassed the Packard and sped away, leaving Mrs. Ellis desperately yelling after him. And I knew even as she stood there crying out for mercy, Harlan Granger would not change his mind. He had gotten what he wanted.

14

We sped through the darkness, the car's headlights the only light anywhere. Stones hit noisily against the car's underbelly and dust swirled around us as the lights cast an eerie glow, making the trees and bushes along the road loom larger than they were. A little past midnight we reached Shokesville. The town was almost as dark as the countryside, and had we not seen a sign hanging from a post which read, "Shokesville Farming Supplies," we would not have known it was even there.

We passed through looking for the sheriff's office, but were unable to find it in the dark. Knowing that it would be closed by now anyway, Mama, Papa, and Uncle Hammer decided there was nothing to do but wait until morning, and we drove on. About a mile outside the town, Uncle Hammer pulled onto a side road and stopped out of view of the main road. "Let's just hope," he said as he turned off the engine, "we ain't sitting in some cracker's driveway. Too blasted black out there to see."

He switched off the lights, then he and Papa got out to stretch. Mama stayed with me urging me to sleep and when she thought I had drifted off, she joined Papa and Uncle Hammer. For a long time I lay very still concentrating hard on Stacey, willing him to be one of the boys in the jail, then tried to sleep so that morning would arrive quicker. But sleep wouldn't come and after a while I too got out of the car.

"Cassie, girl, ain't you tired?" Papa asked. His voice was soft and low.

"Yes, sir, but I'd rather be out here with y'all."

"Come on then," he said, extending his hand to me. "Button up your coat and we'll keep watch for the sunrise together."

When the dawn came, we freshened up as best we could, waited anxiously for eight o'clock, then said a prayer and went back into Shokesville. We easily found the sheriff's office, but when Uncle Hammer had parked the car, we sat unmoving, staring at the building. Finally Papa took a deep breath and opened his door. Mama and Uncle Hammer followed him out. I remained behind, thinking Papa would not let me go inside.

"Ain't you coming?" Papa said, holding the door open.

I looked at him eagerly. "Can I?"

"You done come this far. Might as well."

Inside, the sheriff of Shokesville listened quietly to Papa as he told him why we had come; then, unexpectedly, stood and pulled some keys from his desk and tossed them to another man tending to paperwork. "J.C., go bring the boy that's feeling some better on up." The deputy took up the keys and went through the ring to find the right one before standing. Our eyes followed him anxiously down a dark corridor to a stairway leading to the basement.

"Been expecting y'all," the sheriff said as we waited for the deputy to reappear. "Got a call at home early this morning from outa Vicksburg from a lawyer fella—a Mr. Jamison, I believe—said y'all was on y'all's way. Like I told him, there ain't no charges 'gainst these here boys. What happened was we'd gotten notice here 'bout some boys stealing money from the owner of a cane plantation farther south, and when we found these boys a couple weeks ago and one of 'em was carrying papers come from that plantation, we figured we had the ones done the stealing. One look at them hands and we knew they'd been cuttin' cane."

He rolled himself a cigarette as he talked. "Ain't found no money on any of 'em, but we figured maybe they'd hid it and would've sent them on back south if they hadn't've been so sick—they's doing pretty good now," he took the time to assure us. "Old colored woman been in seein' 'bout 'em every day. Aunt Mattie Jones. She good as any doctor I ever seen." He shook his head as a compliment to Aunt Mattie, and lit his cigarette. "Myself, I was gone most of Christmas week and I come back yesterday to find that they had done caught the boy done the stealing clear over to the Texas border. Money still on him."

"The boys you got here in the jail," Papa said, "their names Stacey Logan and Moe Turner?"

The sheriff waved a languid hand toward the doorway. "Ya'll can see for ya'selves."

We heard the echo of footsteps on the stairs. Our eyes focused on the corridor. I could hardly breathe.

"Now, technically, I'm s'pose to send these here boys back 'cause they run off and ain't finished their contracts—"

The deputy appeared at the end of the corridor. Someone was with him; it was too dark to see his face.

"But me, I ain't never cared much for the way them kinda plantations are run and I got no sympathy for the most of these owners when their workers run off—"

The boy came slowly down the corridor beside the deputy. Light filtered in from the doorway, allowing us to see his form. He looked too tall for Stacey, too gaunt, and he was limping.

"So I ain't gonna send 'em back. Them boys yours, ya can take 'em on home."

Halfway up the corridor the boy stopped, the darkness still keeping him from us. My heart raced ahead of itself, pounding like a hammer.

"Come on," ordered the deputy with a tug to his arm, and he came forward. Near the doorway he stopped once more, and the deputy allowed him to take the last steps alone.

One step. Then two.

He reached the doorway, hesitated, and stepped silently into the room. The light played across his face as he stared out, his eyes blinking as they adjusted to the light. There was no movement from any of us.

Then he smiled.

"Mama . . . Papa," he said weakly, and Stacey fell into our arms.

There was a round of hugging and crying and kissing like I had never seen before: Mama crying and holding Stacey to her, not wanting to let him go; Papa holding them both; and Uncle Hammer standing silently by grinning, just grinning. As for me, I was jumping all over the place, laughing, crying, going crazy as I hung on to Stacey and followed his every move. I had never been so happy.

Stacey grinned down at me. "Lord, Cassie, you've grown!"

"So've you! Even got your little mustache growing."

He laughed a lovely, deep laugh. His eyes went over us all. "Lord, it's so good to see all of y'all! What 'bout Big Ma and Christopher-John and Man and Mr. Morrison? How they doing?"

"Oh, they're just fine!" Mama said. "And just wait until they see you!" She squeezed his arm joyously.

"And Uncle Hammer! Lord, it's good to see you!"

Uncle Hammer's voice went husky. "Seem you done had yourself quite a time."

Stacey managed a dry laugh. "Yes, sir . . . that's a fact." Uncle Hammer looked closely at him, then nodded, as if understanding a meaning deeper than the words.

There were so many questions to ask, so many to be answered, but first there was Moe to think about. Stacey said that Moe was too weak to make it up alone, so while Stacey stayed with Mama and me, Papa and Uncle Hammer followed the deputy back to the cellar. As we waited, sitting on a bench by the window where the light fell full upon Stacey, I realized just how thin he had become. Both the confinement and the illness had worn at him, making his eyes look large in his face and giving his skin a dull cast. As I stared at him a jab of pain went through me at what he and Moe must have suffered.

He felt my eyes on him and looked around. "Guess I must look and smell something terrible, huh?" He ran his hand over his uncombed hair, then lowered his voice so that the sheriff, writing at his desk, couldn't hear. "'Fraid we couldn't much keep clean down there. Miz Mattie—she the one nursed us, fed us—she brought us some soap and water when she come, but still it was hard . . . living down in that filth."

"I don't know 'bout all that," I said, "but you sure look good to me."

And again he laughed that laugh that was so good to hear again.

A few minutes later, Papa and Uncle Hammer returned, supporting Moe between them. Even thinner than Stacey, Moe blinked into the unaccustomed light as Stacey had done, then smiled in that gentle way of his, and a new round of hugging began. Shortly afterward we left the jail, and as soon as we stepped outside, Stacey stopped and took in a deep breath. It had been three weeks since either he or Moe had breathed the air of the outdoors or felt the sun warm upon their faces, and as Stacey took in the day, clear blue and fresh with just a touch of winter frost, he seemed amazed by the beauty of it all, even in this squalid town.

"Never knew before," he said, "how T.J. had to feel, locked up like that."

"Lord, me neither," said Moe, leaning on Uncle Hammer. "And for a while there I thought for sure we was gonna end up like him."

"Well, I 'spect," said Papa, "you've both learned a lot. Maybe learned it ain't so easy out here in this world."

"Yes, sir, that's a fact," Stacey admitted. He shifted his eyes from Papa's, seemingly unable to meet them at first, then looked straight at him. "Papa, you and Mama, y'all upset with me, I reckon."

"You done wrong, son, going off like you done. Had your mama, me, everybody worried to death 'bout you." Papa's voice was unexpectedly harsh.

"I know. I never meant for y'all to worry though. I never

meant that. . . ." Moe looked at Stacey, then lowered his head. A look of shared guilt was on both their faces.

Mama saw the look and her glance at Papa said she did not wish this to be pursued now. "There'll be plenty of time for talking about all this later," she said.

Stacey waited for Papa to speak again. Papa gazed at him in momentary silence, then put his arm around him. "I gotta admit, son, that for a while there I had in mind to give you a hug first when you come home then wear you out with one good whippin'. Truth is though, I forgot all 'bout that whippin' a long time ago."

"Lord, sure am glad!" Stacey admitted with a spirited laugh, and we all laughed with him.

As soon as we were in the car we went searching for Mrs. Mattie Jones and soon found her in a house at the edge of town. An elderly woman, small, wiry, and weathered looking, Mrs. Mattie Jones was overjoyed to see Stacey and Moe. It took her awhile to get over the fact that they were really out of jail, but once she had, she said, "Now I knows y'all's anxious to get on home with these here younguns, but y'all owes me to stay jus' a while longer and sit here 'round my table. All my younguns gone, husband gone. Them two boys there, they feels jus' a bit like mine."

Mama and Papa tried to thank her for all she had done, but Mrs. Mattie Jones dismissed her deeds with a happy grin. "Ah, jus' done the Lord's work. Jus' the Lord's work, sho' did . . . Wish I coulda gotten word to y'all though. Them boys, they asked me 'bout writin' y'all, but like I told 'em, ain't no colored folks 'round here can halfway read or write. School's clear way over to the next town. Got paper to the younguns there one time, but that ole deputy took the letter from me, wouldn't let me send it. And that ole sheriff told me not to be sneakin' nothin' else in or outa there. Told me not to mess in it." She shook her head peevishly at the order. "Well, wasn't no white folks I coulda asked 'bout phonin' or writin' the sheriff wouldn't'a knew 'bout, so's I was thinkin' to get me a ride up to Baton Rouge to send y'all some word." Once again, she shook her head. "Yes, indeed, sho' wish I coulda gotten some word to y'all."

"Believe me," Mama said, "you did more than enough and we'll never forget you for it. Never."

Mrs. Mattie Jones let out another happy laugh, then set about fixing breakfast. Mama helped her, while outside Papa and Uncle Hammer began chopping a fallen yard tree to replenish Mrs. Jones's dwindling firewood supply. Moe, feeling cold and weak, remained inside by the fire, but Stacey preferred to be outdoors where he washed his face in the bright sunlight, then cleaned his teeth with a sweet gum stick.

I stayed with him, not wanting to leave him for even a minute. I wanted to help him if he needed me but at the same time I felt somewhat shy of him. I couldn't get over how adultlike he had become, and that bothered me. It bothered me as well that there was a large chunk in his life now that I could never share. But I guessed there was nothing I could do about that, that it was all a part of that thing called change.

"Cassie, how come you so quiet?" he said as he wiped his face. "You ain't gone and changed on me, have ya?"

"I don't 'spect so."

He looked at me. "Or maybe you thinking . . . I'm the one changed. That's what you thinking?"

"Ain't you?" I accused.

He pursed his lips and was thoughtful "Guess I have . . . but that ain't necessarily bad."

I looked at him warily.

"It ain't, Cassie. Really. Why, if we don't change, things don't change, we might as well stay babies all the time. 'Cause when we grow, we bound to change. You eleven now, you oughta understand that."

"And I s'pose you do, huh?" I questioned, growing just a bit tired of his attitude of adult superiority. "You ain't grown yet, ya know."

He grinned at me. "Now you sounding more like Cassie."

I grinned too, then laughed, as I remembered what Mama had said before Stacey had even gone away, that one day we would be better friends than we had ever been before. I could feel the truth in that now.

Stacey finished washing his hair and I passed him a comb, all the while continuing to study him, how thin he had become and how scarred his hands were. Finally, I said what had been on my mind for so long. "What was it like, Stacey? The cane fields?"

A pained look came into his eyes and he stopped combing.

"Stacey, what happened out there?"

"It was awful, Cassie. It was jus' so awful. . . ."

"They brung us down from Mississippi, crowding us into that truck like cows," Stacey said when we all sat before Mrs. Mattie's fire. "Picked up workers all 'long the way, and when we got deep into Louisiana the truck started stopping at farms and plantations letting off workers. Me and Moe, we got taken all the way to the Troussant plantation 'long with a whole lotta others."

"That plantation was some kinda big," put in Moe. "Must've been larger than Mr. Granger's even. Mostly planted in cane."

Stacey emphasized Moe's statement with a nod and went on. "We stayed in a shack. Dirt floor . . . holes in the roof

. . . rats all over. We were crowded in there too, each of us with just a little spot to sleep. Weren't no beds. No chairs. Nothin' 'cepting some kinda shelves 'long the walls. And they didn't give us anything. They said we wanted blankets, we could sign for 'em up at the plantation store and they'd be charged to our pay. Said we could charge other things too. Clothes and such. Then they told us we had to have a machete and said we could charge it like everything else."

He bowed his head and looked at his hands, then spread them open so that we could see the palms, scarred deep with dark welts. Mama took one of his hands and held it between her own.

"Never knew chopping cane could be so hard. Sunup to sundown. And them cane leaves, they cut up our hands something terrible. Some of the workers, they got gloves from the store, but it didn't do much good. Still cut through."

Moe shook his head, remembering.

"Worked six days in the fields," Stacey said, "raining or shining, we worked till we was bone tired. Then come one full week of work and we didn't get paid. We was kinda upset 'bout that, but then we figured we was to get paid every two weeks. But then that next week we still didn't get paid, so all of us there talked it over and finally got up the nerve to ask the boss man 'bout our pay. Well, he told us that we was under contract to work till the cane was all cut. Said if we was paid every week, we'd run off after we got a little money, and the plantation, it just couldn't function that way they had to go out and get new workers every week. Said we'd get paid when all the cane was chopped, not before. Well, we didn't much like it, not getting paid till then, but what he said made some sense 'cause there were some men talking 'bout quitting, and couldn't nobody fault 'em, the way we had to work. So, anyway, we went on back to work, figuring to get our money come December." He looked at Papa. "Me, I figured to bring back enough money for taxes. Figured to bring back over a hundred dollars and I didn't care how hard I had to work to get it. Thought of that money was what kept me going."

"Me, too," Moe laughed curtly. "Kept thinking how that money was gonna help get us off Mr. Montier's place. Figured to have plenty of money 'cause all me and Stacey charged up at that store was for a blanket and a knife, and some writing paper and stamps. Come every Sunday, we wrote letters to y'all and come every Monday, we mailed 'em up at that store, thinking y'all was gettin' 'em. Wasn't 'spectin' none back 'cause we ain't put no addresses on 'em. 'Fraid y'all'd come get us."

"Guess them plantation folks, they was 'fraid of the same thing," said Stacey, "'cause they musta not sent 'em."

Moe shook his head wearily. "Lord, my poor papa . . ."

Stacey glanced at Moe and went on. "Come December and some of us got fever. The boss man, he said he was gonna get us a doctor but in the meantime, he 'spected anybody who could walk to work. Well, me and Moe, we were feeling sick, but we went on out working anyway. Second day we worked that way we was loading cane onto a wagon and the cane got loose and rolled off on my foot.

"Moe, he went for the boss man. Said we had to have a doctor for my foot, but the boss man, he just said for Moe to get back to work and that he'd come see 'bout it. Well, I waited, all that evening and that night, and I was paining something awful. Next morning the overseer he come and he called himself checking my foot. Said it was just sprained, but I figured there was bones broke in it and I got scared . . . scared I could lose my foot if it didn't get treated.

"So I told Moe I was gonna go. I couldn't work no way with my foot broke and I figured they was bound to give me my money, me being sick and all. I figured to get my pay, get a bus and come on home. Moe, he said, if I was going, he was going too. There was another boy name of Charlie Davies said the same thing, so we went to talk to the boss man. Mr. Troussant, the owner of that place, he was there in the office, and when we told 'em we were sick and we wanted to get our pay and leave, they said we couldn't leave. Said we owed them money 'cause of all the cost of transporting us down, and food and housing and everything we charged at the store. Said we had to work out our time till all them charges was paid, and what was left, they'd pay it to us come the last of the cane.

"We'd been working nearly ten weeks and they tell us that! Ten weeks! But we knew there wasn't nothin' we could do about it." His voice went low. "Nothin'." He paused and I saw both hurt and anger in his eyes. "Told the others what they'd said and some of 'em wouldn't believe us, said the boss was just joking us. But there was two other boys, name of Ben and Jimmie B., believed us, and 'long with Charlie and Moe and me they decided they was gonna get outa there that same day.

"That night when we were ready to slip out, Charlie, he said he had something to tend to first and for us to go on and he'd catch up. Well, we did, we went on. Ben and Jimmie B., they weren't sick, and they helped Moe and me along and come nighttime we stopped. Charlie, like he said he would, he caught up with us and told us why he had took so long. Told us **he** gone back to the office looking for money and found it. Said it was money owed us and he was gonna divide it with us. 'Minded me of T.J., Charlie did. . . .

"Jimmie B., Moe, and me, we didn't want no part of it. But Ben, he went 'long with Charlie 'bout the money. So we told 'em we didn't want them traveling with us. They got caught with that money, we didn't want nothing to do with it. When we left outa there, Charlie and Ben headed on west and we went north. Got rides some of the way with colored farmers, but mostly, we stayed to the woods, 'fraid to come out on the road. Made pretty good time. But then just west of Shokesville, Moe and me, we both give out and Jimmie B., he went looking for some colored folks to help us, maybe put us up a few days."

As Stacey had talked, his voice had become so low that I had to lean forward to hear him. Now his words were a mere whisper. "They shot Jimmie B. . . . We heard them. Some white men out hunting seen Jimmie B. and when Jimmie B. got scared and ran, they shot him . . . killed him, 'cause he ran." He cleared his throat and spoke up. "Moe and me, we didn't know what to do, but we knew we couldn't run. We was too sick to run. We hid . . . but they got us and took us up to the jail."

Stacey fixed his eyes on the fire and stared blankly into it. A long time passed and he didn't speak. Moe said nothing. We waited.

"Heard they'd 'spected us of stealing that money." Stacey's words were drawn, paced, quiet. "Heard they'd caught Charlie and Ben. Then heard they was gonna send us back. For three weeks, we heard all that. Then the deputy this morning, he come and didn't say a word, just grabbed me up and I thought for sure, thought . . ." Smiling weakly, he shook his head and sniffed back his tears. "Lord . . . who'd've ever thought," he said, "who'd've thought . . ." Then, unable to say anything more, he broke down and cried.

When breakfast was over, we waved good-bye to Mrs. Mattie Jones and started home. Stacey sat in back between Mama and me, Moe up front with Papa and Uncle Hammer. They were still weak and despite their attempts to keep awake, they kept drifting off to sleep. Papa, Mama, and Uncle Hammer managed to stay awake, talking softly, watching over us, but I too drifted off, awakening several times with a start to gaze once again at Stacey, not quite believing yet that he was really there beside me. Then I would nudge him just a bit so that he would move in some way and, once I knew that he was all right, would go off to sleep again.

Past midnight we reached Strawberry, and following Soldiers Road to Smellings Creek, we took Moe home and witnessed the Turners' joyful reunion before swinging east again. Stacey, wide awake now, leaned forward to peer out into the darkness that cloaked the woods and the fields that were so familiar to him. We sped over the bridge once more, past the Wallace store, and Jefferson Davis, down to the first crossroads, past the Simmses' place to the second crossroads, then west toward home. The old oak, veiled in gray by the moonlight, became visible, then the meadow and the field, and finally the house, dark, asleep like the land, and as much a part of it as the trees, black against the midnight sky on the other side of the road.

As we pulled into the drive, the dogs started barking. Almost immediately a dim light appeared in the house, and from across the garden a round light came moving slowly toward us. The side door swung open and Christopher-John and Little Man were standing there in their nightgowns with Big Ma behind them, a kerosene lamp in her hand which she held out into the night.

"David . . . Mary . . . Hammer, that y'all?" she called.

Papa turned and smiled at Stacey. "You answer her, son."

Stacey grinned and, unexpectedly, squeezed my hand. "Look at 'em, Cassie," he said. "Look at ole Man and Christopher-John."

"David, y'all bring that boy?"

For a moment Stacey was too choked to answer. Then he cleared his throat and followed Mama out of the car. "Yes, ma'am, Big Ma. They sure did."

Stunned, the three of them did not move from the doorway. The light in the garden went out. Then, all together, Big Ma, Christopher-John and Little Man let out a tremendous whoop and came tearing down the steps. Mr. Morrison came running across the yard. "Lord, the boy done come home!" he cried. "He done come home!"

"Yes, sir," Stacey said, limping to meet them. "I done come home . . . and it's the very best place to be."

I agreed.